THE WIND OF WALKERS AND BLADES

KELLY FARINA

ISBN:979-8-9944175-2-2

Contents

To you, for entering this dream with me.

PROLOGUE

"I won't do it, Father. I won't."

Kurt Bruckton, the heir to House Bruckton, paced back and forth across the large bedroom. It was the picture of frivolous abundance—fine wood accented the walls, and large windows were adorned with velvet drapes of deep forest green. Lush bouquets of springtime blooms burst from the vases that had been arranged around the room in an attempt to liven their dour situation. Kurt's father, addled with disease, wasted away under his ivory sheets.

"There isn't much time," Lord Bruckton wheezed, eyes bloodshot and swollen. His russet beard paled under a ray of dawning sun creeping through the window. "I'll be damned if our house falls because my son is a coward."

Kurt stopped in his tracks, hurt. "Isn't there another way? There has to be..." The stale stench of long-held power enveloped him, inescapable.

"This has been the reality in Friese for thousands of years," Lord Bruckton whispered through his chapped lips. "If you don't do this, we will fall. Our house will crumble and be absorbed by the likes of the Exleys." His final word was punctuated with a ragged cough, spraying flecks of blood over the bed.

Kurt ran a shaking hand through his rust-colored hair and imagined the power that would come to him if he complied. He'd be admitted into the elite circle of nobles in Friese who held the wrath of the wind in their hands. The *Skylords*. The notion nearly made him smile in excitement, despite the morbid atmosphere in the room. Steeling himself, Kurt walked over to his father's bed on unsteady legs.

"Do it now. If you wait any longer, our windblade will go to the atmosphere. We can't afford... to lose it." Lord Bruckton's voice cracked from the effort.

Kurt leaned over his father's head and kissed his thin, withering hair. "I'm sorry it has to be this way, Father." He barely managed to speak as rough sobs threatened to overtake him.

"Now." The old man was urgent—the light was leaving his pale eyes.

Kurt locked his jaw and squeezed his eyes shut. Hot tears ran down his cheeks, splattering onto the blankets. He thought of all of his allies who were Skylords—were they all such monsters? Surely there must be redemption for such a grisly deed?

Kurt drew a dagger from his belt with weak, clammy hands. He gripped the handle and tried to forcefully ease the tightness that had woven its way around his chest. "Goodbye," he whispered as he drew back and plunged it into his father's heart.

CHAPTER ONE
THE ORPHAN

I wish you were here to help me. Nobody told me
how difficult caring for a baby is.
-Unsent Letter from Elie Roale

G radient shades of blue and purple stretched over the dawning sky as I made my way out of the abandoned bell tower I lived in. It was a ramshackle old place whose convenient location and unoccupied status redeemed its innumerable deteriorations. Despite the seclusion and ostensible loneliness of such a living arrangement, through the years, I'd found it to be the ideal place to find some peace.

Birds sang their dawn songs as I began my daily walk from the edge of the Exley property and into the port slums of Friese. Our kingdom had a vibrant trade market and had shipments of industrial and agricultural goods constantly coming in and out. Friese's major sectors of industry were controlled by the Skylords—the nobility who wielded windblades. Despite the undeniable raw power granted to the ruling class by their windblades, they exploited more conventional means to control the populace. Their unopposed monopolies of trade and industry had nurtured their greed for generations, fostering an ever-increasing disparity between commoners and the Friesian elite. As it stood, there was very little middle ground between the nobles and the slum-dwellers.

Despite the port of Friese being highly utilized, its economic success did nothing for the average citizen. Many of the dock workers worked for fourteen hours straight, and came home to run-down houses and dirty streets. In the slums, the air smelled of dead fish, diseases spread like wildfire, and food was scarce. The discontentment among the population was a bitter, but ultimately impotent, thing. The idea of demanding change by threat of force was nothing but a daydream to the overworked, exhausted, and sick. Even if they tried, no number of angry men could stand against united Skylords. They would be torn to shreds.

Though my position at the bottom of the social and economic hierarchy afforded me very few reasons to appreciate my kingdom, I resolved myself to one day be an instrument of positive change. Not only for myself, but for everyone wasting away in the slums.

I gleaned much of my inspiration from the two women who saved my life. Francie Hanover and her aunt, Crysta, ran the only inn in the slums that would feed the hungry when they had no other options. They were the closest thing to a true family that I could ask for; always making sure I was healthy and fed.

Since I'd been able, I'd done my best to repay their kindness by running errands, collecting donations, and removing the occasional hostile patron. Their generosity to desperate families rendered them unable to support me as an employee, but they fed and cared for me, which was more than I could ask for.

Crysta Hanover, the owner and manager of the inn, had treated me like a son since I was just ten years old. She'd patched up my various injuries, given me shelter in the many Friesian storms, and shared her sage wisdom when I felt lost in the tides of life.

Then there was Crysta's niece, Francesca—or Francie—Hanover. Though she was only two years older than me, there were many childhood years I'd assumed she knew everything. However, as we'd grown together through the tumultuous stages of late childhood, our friendship dynamic had shifted in a way. Not in the way I'd desired, but I kept that to myself.

As I neared the center of the slums, a warm breeze brought the scent of dead fish and low tide wafting through my senses, ruffling my brown hair. Even with all of its faults, our kingdom held an understated charm. It was nestled along the bay like a glistening sapphire—water lapping up around it like a dear friend, desperate to nurture it. Only during our strongest summer storms did the sea attempt to claim Friese to its depths like a jealous lover.

From the west, forested hills gave way to breathtaking views of that glistening, fickle Broad Sea, best viewed from the sea cliffs in the north. The mild seasons made winters comfortably livable and summers beautiful and pleasant. As the summer settled over Friese, the warm, salty winds blew in and refreshed the weary slum-dwellers.

I turned down a cobbled lane and the sounds of the docks grew louder. I slowed down and closed my eyes for a moment, letting my senses overtake me. Seagulls called back and forth to each other as they circled overhead, desperate to spot any abandoned fish laying amongst the emptied nets. Flags whipped and rippled atop thick wooden masts. Workers shouted back and forth, coordinating the various tasks of loading and unloading from the massive trade ships. I began quietly humming a familiar Friesian pub song as I soaked up the feeling of the sun on my face.

"Lev!"

A feminine voice interrupted my thoughts.

"Levick, hey!"

A small smile formed on my face. "Good morning, Francie."

As I opened my eyes, I saw a beautiful woman jogging up to me. Her flaxen hair fluttered in the sea breeze, and her eyes reflected the perfect blue of the sky. Her pert nose came to a slight point at the end and sat above a set of pink, heart-shaped lips. Slightly taller than most women, Francie was naturally athletic and moved almost with a dancer's grace, unknowingly attracting stares wherever she went.

"I was on my way, you know. You didn't have to chase me down," I said, with only a hint of smugness.

She grinned back at me, her cheeks pink with vitality. "It's not my fault you move so slow. What's gotten into you this morning? You're half an hour late."

"That's one of the few perks of being an unpaid employee. I never worry about getting laid off," I replied with a sidelong grin as we began walking together. An uncomfortably extended silence was the only response I got, which was unusual for Francie. Her demeanor was usually one of lighthearted questions and quips.

"Everything okay?" I asked, glancing her way as we walked.

She shook her head and let out a small sound of frustration. "Our supply is low today. I'm not sure we'll have enough food to be giving any away at dinner. I'm going hunting again soon, but I doubt I'll bring in enough for our usual crowd." Her voice got quiet as she stared down the road. She brushed away a strand of flaxen hair that had fallen over her face.

Francie held dear the inn's ability to provide food to people who'd fallen upon difficult times. We often received donations from generous local farms and shops, but sometimes it wasn't enough—especially with the increased accidents at the port rendering more men unemployable. Friese's imports had shot up dramatically over the last decade, putting more strain on the dockworkers and making their jobs more dangerous than it already was. Most of those the inn fed for free were women and children whose fathers or husbands had been killed or maimed working the docks and shipyards. In recent years, Francie had made a habit of hunting small game in the neighboring forests. There was nothing she hated more than sending hungry families away with nothing.

I bit at my lip as we walked. I knew she was only confiding in me, but I immediately began racking my brain for ways to help. There was only one solution that could work by dinnertime. A pit formed in my stomach as I realized what I would have to do. "I'm sure something will turn up, Francie. Maybe I'll ask Arturian," I began casually. "Maybe he'll finally get his father to care about people like us." I tried to keep my expression neutral; Francie always had a way of knowing when I was planning something. Thankfully, her situation kept her from noticing.

She nearly rolled her large, expressive eyes. "You know how stingy Augustus is, and Arturian can't ask him without giving away that he has slum-dwelling friends." She fidgeted with her hair as we approached the old doors of the inn. She placed her hand on the dark wood, but paused. "I just hate letting them down. They need us." She looked at her feet and sighed deeply, eyes darting back and forth as she searched her mind for an answer.

"Something will turn up. I know it," I said with a soft smile as I reached past her to open the door. She looked up at me and returned the smile, but it didn't reach her eyes.

Francie walked through the doors, taking a deep breath. "Yeah, you're right. We'll make something work." When she noticed I hadn't followed her inside, she turned and gave me a questioning look.

"I have some stuff I have to get done. I'll come check in later."

She raised an eyebrow at me. "Lev—"

"It's not a big deal—don't worry about it. I'll be back later!" I called back, letting the door close before she could question me.

After a cautionary glance over my shoulder to ensure I was out of sight, I pulled my tan neck scarf up and over my mouth. I ducked down a nearby alley, leapt up onto an old barrel, and boosted myself up and onto a roof. That familiar salty breeze tousled my hair as I stood up straight.

After a couple of quick stretches, I took in a deep breath and burst into a run. The sloped clay tiles were slick under my feet, but I didn't trip. Unbridled euphoria coursed through my veins as I approached the first ledge, and without hesitation, I *leapt* into the open air.

I began losing altitude. It was too far.

But I didn't worry. A powerful gust of wind pushed from below, keeping me aloft as I shot through the sky. My feet struck the tiles of the neighboring building, and I kept running.

It wasn't long after I became an orphan that I noticed my unusual ability. I possessed a talent for surviving leaps from trees, buildings, and other high surfaces that would surely kill most people. But no matter the situation, I always landed gently on my feet.

At first, I had speculated that I must've inherited some kind of relative to the windblade—but far less potent in its capability. But over the years, I heard tales of old Friesian generals who could manipulate large gusts of wind—*windwalkers*. When I was young and still discovering my abilities, I asked Crysta about the windwalkers, and if any still existed.

"There hasn't been one in centuries. Not since the days of the windwalker generals—the *Caelators*," she'd replied over her shoulder while scrubbing a dirty pot. "The Skylords' windblade is all that remains now, and it holds absolute supremacy."

She sat down with me and explained that the windwalkers were extinct, and even if they returned, the Skylords would hunt them down. Shaking her head, she quoted the High Skylords' Quorum decree, saying, "only our oldest families can be trusted with Echna's blessing."

She told me a story of a young boy who'd walked away unscathed from a ten-foot fall from a roof. Witnesses had called him lucky, but the Quorum of the High Skylords decided that no natural person was *that* lucky. He disappeared three days after the accident, never to be heard from again. "The Skylords don't relish sharing their control of the wind," Crysta finished, returning to her work. That story was incentive enough for me to keep my mouth shut about it, and only use my gift subtly.

The world flew around me in a blur as I ran, jumped and floated across the rooftops. Guilt tugged at me as my thoughts turned to my friends, and how much I wished I could tell them about my gift.

You can't. It's too risky.

Knowledge of any kind of wind control outside of the noble circles could be deadly.

The Skylords would hunt me down, along with anyone who knew about me. It's not like it's a very exciting gift, anyway. It's of no use to anyone but myself.

At my speed, it didn't take me long to reach the edge of town and spot the familiar forest trail that led to the Exley family's property. I leapt from the last roof—cushioning my fall with an updraft—and began down the trail.

Chapter Two
Clay Tiles

"Remind me what you do all day other than gallivant across glistening fields on prize race horses?" I called from the entrance of the stable.

"Hilarious, Levick," a voice echoed from one of the stalls. "If you're going to loiter on my property, at least help me out and pick up a shovel." A tall, distinguished-looking young man with long, dark hair unlatched the stall across from me and walked out. He was wearing fine riding gear emblazoned with the red Exley house crest—a shield with an ornate "E" centered inside, surrounded by vines of thorns.

"Don't pretend like you've ever shoveled shit, lordling," I said as he approached. Arturian chuckled as we clasped forearms in greeting.

"How's my bell tower holding up?" Arturian asked in his lilting high-society accent as we both began walking out of the barn and toward the woods. The grass still had dew on it, crunching under our feet and wetting the hems of our trousers.

"Falling apart a little, but just as cozy as always." My home, a derelict bell tower, was situated at the northernmost part of the Exley estate. I'd lived there for years with no one noticing—except Arturian. "I finished that book you lent me. I'll have to get it back to you soon."

"What did you think?" Arturian asked, glancing over with curious dark blue eyes.

I shrugged. "It was a lot of poetry, and not much action," I said, strategically avoiding having to admit that it bored me to sleep. "Your taste in literature is admirable, but hard to imitate."

"I suppose it is," Arturian replied, a smile playing at the corner of his mouth.

"How was your trip up north?" I asked as I stepped around a formidable looking ant mound.

"You know how my father is. It wasn't fun, but it could've been worse." He ran his hand through his long black hair as he walked. "Trenica is beautiful, though," he finished as he stepped over a log.

I simply nodded in reply. I knew better than to linger on the subject. We walked in comfortable silence for a while until we reached our usual meeting spot. Arturian's father, Augustus, was the Skylord of House Exley. He wielded the Exley heritage windblade, Asgora, and rumors claimed he was unparalleled in its use. He also had a reputation for being as cold-hearted as he was wealthy. Unfortunately, Arturian's mother had died when he was only three years old, so his father was the only family he had left.

As the forest grew denser, we found a slight break in a thick copse of trees and crept through it. We emerged into a small cleared area right on the fence line, complete with tree stumps for chairs, and a fire pit in the center. A large oak tree grew from the other side of the fence, extending thick branches out and over us. Arturian settled into his usual spot—on the ground, with his back against a carved-out stump. I took some time to strike up the fire, then settled against my own stump.

"I might need some help with something," I said as I stared into the small flames, preparing myself for the inevitable tension.

Arturian looked up at me, his dark hair hanging by his eyes. "It's about Francie, isn't it?"

I sat in silence. While I knew Francie had to be mentioned, she'd recently become a delicate subject between us.

Arturian looked into the fire, a knowing smile on the corner of his lips. "You'd never ask if it was only for you."

I took a deep breath, knowing my friend saw right through me. "It's the inn. They don't have enough for dinner tonight..." I leaned forward, bracing myself on my knees. "You know I wouldn't have come to you, but there are a lot of families that will go hungry if we don't find something soon."

A long silence sat between us like a brick wall. Arturian and I had been dancing around the subject for months... maybe years.

"Levick... I understand where you're coming from. It means a lot to Francie, and you don't want to let her down. But you *know* why I don't contribute there. Why I can't," Arturian said slowly, and I didn't miss the guilt flash across his features. I knew that was going to be his answer, but my conscience demanded I tried asking Arturian first, in case there had been some miraculous change.

"Those people will be okay for one night. Francie won't think any less of you if there's nothing you can do." Arturian paused for a while, measuring his words carefully. He continued, "I know she's special to you; she's special to me, too. If I knew of any way to help without exposing our friendship to my father, I would do it."

I chewed on the edge of my tongue. I wasn't dense—I'd noticed how Arturian behaved around Francie. I'd seen how he looked at her—it was the same way I looked at her. The only difference was that one of us was the heir to the most powerful house in Friese—barring the queen's own—and the other was a penniless orphan who lived in an abandoned bell tower. However, Arturian had no control over who he married. Someday, Augustus would name the woman and the date, and Arturian would be there. In a moment of sympathy, I wondered how Arturian Exley, heir to the distinguished Exley estate and the windblade *Asgora*, had less control and agency over his life than an orphan did.

I looked through the flames at my best friend. "I guess it was worth a shot. I'll need to be looking elsewhere, though." I stood, brushed my clothes off, and turned to leave. "I'll see you around, Arturian," I said before I finally crept out of the trees and back toward the city.

Over a bridge.

Up onto a roof.

From ledge to ledge, I ran and jumped. I had resolved myself on my mission, no matter how much it tore at my conscience.

I will not *let her down.*

I made my way into the market district, where throngs of people weaved around vendors selling food items. It was a buzz of life—a vibrant tapestry of sounds, colors, tastes, and smells. Merchants shouted and children laughed. The smell of freshly baked bread wafted over me, making my stomach growl. Eventually, I landed in an alley across from a busy vegetable stand.

There were small crowds of customers standing under the midsummer sun, waiting to browse the selections—a perfect place to blend in. I casually fell in with them, feigning interest in varied shop wares until approaching a vegetable stand. I began picking up some small potatoes, squeezing them and pretending to check for freshness. In a blur of quick hands, I'd stashed five of them in my shirt before someone noticed.

"Hey, this guy is stealing!" Someone shouted from a few feet away.

Dammit. Not as sneaky as I thought I was...

The crowd quickly turned on me as I darted into the cobbled street, adrenaline pumping through my veins.

"Where are the Crownies?" a woman called out for the police.

As I bustled through the crowds, I bumped against a cart of blooming roses, nearly upending it and earning a curse from the elderly woman attending it. "Sorry!" I called backwards, but the weathered woman simply shook her head.

"Someone arrest him!" Someone else called out as I sprinted down the street, heading south.

Whistles started blaring, causing even more commotion. I scrambled up the side of a Temple of Echna, gripping the stones as I climbed past the blue and green stained-glass windows. Faint sounds of worship came from inside; praises sung to the Friesian Goddess of the Wind. The eerie song rang through my ears as I grabbed onto a window overhang. I dared a backwards glance and saw three Crown Police officers racing toward me, their glinting steel short swords at the ready. Thankfully, disappearing into the city was one of my talents.

With the wind on my side, I pulled myself onto the temple's roof and ran toward the edge. Noises of footsteps against clay roof tiles echoed behind me—the Crownies had followed me up. Glancing over my shoulder, I saw a tall, muscled officer racing at me at an alarming pace. His officer's insignia glinted in the sunlight as I moved, legs pounding against the roof.

He's about to close the gap.

I leapt onto the neighboring roof, but the officer followed, still hot on my heels. The roof tiles clicked under my feet as I ran for my life—every step forcing my heart to beat faster. I could barely hear the shouting and whistling above the pounding in my ears.

This guy can really move. I can't outrun him.

An idea hit me, making me wheel around. I scanned the rooftops, looking for the largest gap between the roofs. It was a risky prospect, but I had very few options, and getting arrested certainly wasn't one of them.

My eyes landed on a distant roof—nearly five horse-lengths of open air between them.

There.

I swerved, my legs aching as my feet pounded against the rooftop, and leapt off the edge. I closed my eyes in mid-air, feeling the wind swirl around my face and through my hair. Warm, salty air rushed into my lungs while my clothes billowed around me. Five *long* horse-lengths of open sky later, my feet made contact with the next roof. I rolled to my feet and swiveled around, breathing a sigh of relief when I noticed the officer hesitate on the ledge. We locked eyes; a gulf yawned between us. If looks could kill, I would have died many times over.

I never relished being on the wrong side of the law. As much as I hated the Crownies and their increasingly selective prosecution, breaking the law was not a habit I was eager to fall into. Impoverished young men with no connections rarely got a fair shake in Friese's sham of a justice system. After confirming I hadn't been followed, I went down to the streets and headed back to the inn. I felt guilty, but relief overshadowed it. I would be able to help Francie. To do *something*.

"Lev? Where have you been?" A mature woman's voice greeted me as I entered the front door.

"Crysta!" I choked out as the tall woman squeezed me tight.

"I've found things that might help this evening."

While reaching into my shirt for the potatoes, Francie entered from the hallway and gazed at me with narrowed eyes filled with curiosity.

"Here. It's not a large amount, but it should be enough for one or two people..." I said, trailing off upon realizing that five potatoes were inadequate for the usual crowd.

"Oh dear, any amount is helpful! Thank you so much," Crysta said as she carried the potatoes off to the kitchen, leaving me and Francie alone in the dining area. She shifted from foot to foot anxiously, fumbling with her beige apron.

Just before I could approach her, the bell chimed, signaling the arrival of two men through the front entrance. Francie and Crysta seldom expected visitors so early in the evening. One man was tan and weathered—his face cut deep with wrinkles, and his hair was gray and thinning. The other man stood straighter and bore a youthful countenance.

"Hello, afternoon," the younger man said in the thick coastal accent some people had in Friese. "I figured you wouldn't be serving dinner just yet, but we decided to come and check... just in case."

"It'll be potato soup, but we won't have much. I'd try to get here early if I were you," Francie said politely.

The older man had been watching her intently since he came in. He began muttering and taking small steps towards her, prompting me to edge closer to her.

"You, I know you..." he said.

"Father—you don't know this girl. Come, let's go," the younger man said, looking embarrassed as he attempted to turn his father toward the exit.

"You worked in the country house! I knew you! Must've been twenty years ago," the old man called out as his son dragged him away.

"Sir, I'm sorry, but you must've mistaken me for someone else. I'm only eighteen years old! I hope to see you again at dinner though," Francie said, her voice soft and a warm smile gracing her pink lips. The old man mumbled incoherently, and let his son pull him away.

"I'm so sorry, you have a pleasant afternoon!" the son said, looking embarrassed before closing the door behind them, leaving us alone once again.

Mental illness was commonplace in the slums, so the encounter rolled off Francie like water off a duck's back. Throughout the unusual exchange, she'd been staring at me with poorly disguised suspicion, not saying a word. She furrowed her light brows together as she stared holes through my head.

I stared back. "Everything alright?"

"I think I know how you got those potatoes." She cut me off as I tried to cut in. "Don't deny it. I'm going to let this go today, because it's too late now. But Levick... I swear. If I ever suspect this of happening again, I'll tell Crysta." Her voice shook a bit. "We need you here, and you know what they do to thieves in Friese."

Everyone knew. The fingers that committed the crime paid the price. Friese boasted its fair share of fingerless beggars.

"I know... it was a mistake." I walked over to the window, looking out into the street. I couldn't bear her disappointed stare any longer. "My presence is rarely useful, and I wanted to change that. I'm sorry."

"You *know* that's not true." I felt a hand on my shoulder. "I know you wanted to help. While I really appreciate that, it wasn't worth you risking your life," she said in a softer tone. "I'm going back out to hunt in the morning, so don't worry. We'll scrape by today, and we'll have more for dinner tomorrow." She was so close; speaking right over my shoulder.

I turned to look at her, half expecting her to back away. But to my surprise, she stood firm and met my gaze, causing me to turn away to hide my embarrassment. My heart raced, and blood rushed to my cheeks.

Get it together.

"It won't happen again." I'd disappeared through the front door before Francie could respond.

CHAPTER THREE
THE GIRL WITH BURLAP HAIR

I ran through my usual checklist of hunting gear as I walked out of Friese's port slums and toward the woods. My game hunting provided for much of the meat the inn served when donations ran low, so three or four times a week, I ventured out into the woods to bring back some protein. That night's dinner would be whatever edible game animal I saw first.

Filled with purpose, I walked through the stench-filled streets. Smells of rotten fish and old garbage wafted through the air, driving my desire to escape the cramped alleyways for the serenity of the forest. I fielded cat-calls, rabid dogs, and small flocks of escaped chickens before I made it out of the city. As soon as the fresh forest air hit my lungs, I drew in a deep breath.

Finally, back again.

It was a salve on my wearied soul to be outside and weaving through the trees. The pressures of operating and maintaining the inn had gotten the best of me; not to mention the risks Levick had been taking. I worried that one day he wouldn't be fast enough to escape the consequences of his actions.

Towering trees of dark wood and bright green moss-draped leaves lined the worn, familiar trail. Dense underbrush grew between the tree trunks, limiting my visibility except for the cleared path I walked on. My black boots padded on the dirt of the trail as I walked in a crouch, head on a swivel as I waited for signs of life in the forest. Soon, I would climb a tree and wait for any unfortunate wildlife to walk beneath me. In a moment of light panic, I felt around my pockets and the pack I carried. Relief washed over me when I felt the rectangular shape of my book in my pack. I'd forgotten to bring a book on a hunt once, and I'd thought I might die of boredom; sitting in a tree for hours, nothing to do except wait. Rustling leaves drew my mind away, and my trained eyes scanned the trees for the source of the disturbance. Branches cracked as a scrawny brown squirrel leapt from the dirt and into a tree. I sighed.

Too bony. Nothing to eat.

I let the hungry squirrel continue on his journey and resumed my pace through the brush. A spring breeze rustled through the leaves of the large trees, and I turned my head up. Closing my eyes, I breathed deeply and calmed my mind. As the wind died down, I heard a crack from the shrubs. Then another.

Swish, thump.

Swish, thump.

A rabbit. Crouching and passing my bow to my left hand, I scanned the brush for my target. I stood stone-still, hoping my deep green dress camouflaged me, and waited patiently for movement.

A soft brown head emerged from behind the underbrush. The rabbit's ears were long and pointed, confirming that he was full grown and ready to eat.

There you are.

In a swift, directed movement, I flung my right hand forward, as if I was throwing a knife. A slice of wind as sharp and deadly as a razorblade raced through the air, silent as death. A squelching noise emanated from the brush, signaling that I hit my mark. I paused for a moment, relieved at the instant kill. My aim hadn't always been so accurate, and there were many occasions where an unlucky animal lost a limb or two before its misery ended. Shaking my braid over my shoulder, I stood from my crouch and made sure to bloody one of my arrows before re-sheathing it. The rabbit's fur was warm and soft against my fingers as I lifted it up and secured it to my vest.

For most of my life, I'd considered my windblade a curse. The Skylords would execute me if they discovered it, so I'd been determined never to use it. It took years of hunger, and witnessing others suffer, to decide to hunt with it. It was very useful in keeping the inn stocked with protein for malnourished families, though I hated keeping it a secret from Levick.

He risked his life and stole for you, and you won't tell him about your windblade? How can you call yourself a friend?

Distracted by my guilty thoughts, I wandered further into the forest. It wasn't long before I encountered a very familiar oak tree rooted across an intricate iron fence. The tree's trunk was thick and old, and its branches were strong. One of those sturdy branches jutted out over the fence, hanging over the neighboring property. Smiling to myself, I climbed the tree with pure muscle memory, and stood upright on that thick, jutting branch. Then I began walking until I was nearly over the fence. However, someone interrupted my mission before I could finish it.

"Trespassing is illegal, you know." A level voice spoke through the thicket on the other side of the fence. Arturian Exley stepped out from behind a tree and approached me. His long, dark hair and tailored black attire accentuated his sharp jawline and high cheekbones, making him the subject of admiration among Friesian women since adulthood.

I resumed my walk along the branch until I was on the other side of the fence and sat down to hang my legs off of the overhanging limb. "Technically, I'm not on your property. This tree's trunk is on the other side of the fence," I smiled, kicking my legs in taunt as I played with my long, dark blonde braid hanging over my shoulder. "If you think you can reach me, I'd like to see you try. You might get your shiny boots dirty, though."

Arturian walked closer to the fence and stopped under my feet as they dangled above him. "If I were only a bit taller, I could just pull you down." His voice was smooth as velvet as he reached one hand up to try to touch my boot. "But I suppose if you fell, neither of us would walk away unscathed..."

He began pacing back and forth beneath me, scratching his chin and feigning deep thought. "I could toss a rope around you and pull you down, but I'd have to walk back to the stable to find one, and you'd have run off by then. Difficult, difficult..."

My grin grew wider as he put on his little performance for me. He looked markedly out of place in a forest—his clothing was immaculate and his hair well-kept. His confidence and magnetism were undeniable, even to a girl who'd known him since childhood. I suppressed my distracting thoughts before they ran away with me. He was from a completely different world.

Finally, he stopped pacing and looked up at me. "Why don't you save me from sullying my boots in my attempts to pull you from that tree? Jump down, I'll catch you." He looked up at me, a smile on the edge of his mouth. "I have tea at the stable."

I sighed—tea sounded *very* relaxing. "I wish I could, but I should get back to hunting. Levick was able to help a little yesterday, but we're still running low at the inn," I said, noticing a flash of disappointment on his face before his composed Exley visage took over once again.

A strained silence sat between us. I knew Arturian wanted to help me with our problems at the inn, but he couldn't risk his father finding out. The Exleys dealt only through a line of credit, so his father could easily trace and discover anything he bought. If he did, it would end our friendships and could put us in danger. Augustus Exley didn't tolerate any level of mingling amongst the classes, and I was as far from nobility as a Friesian citizen could get. The risk of exposure was too great, so I understood why he couldn't contribute.

Once, years ago, Arturian snuck a bushel of apples out of the mansion's pantry and gave it to the inn. Its absence was noticed, resulting in a kitchen staff member being accused of theft and disciplined. After that, he'd sworn to never do it again. I suspected he still felt guilt over it.

I finally broke the silence.

"Arturian, you don't need to feel guilty. I know you'd help if you could, but there's nothing you can do," I said as I leaned over the side of the branch.

More silence ensued as Arturian continued to stare at the blooming trees across the fence. I wished I knew what he was thinking. Eventually, he looked up at me, his mouth twitching at the corner. "Thanks for saying that, Francie. I don't think Levick believes it, though."

Brows furrowed, I cocked my head. I'd assumed they were always on good terms—they saw each other more often than they saw me. "He thinks of you as a brother, Arturian... I'm sure he understands. He goes to you for advice *far* more often than he comes to me."

I was uncomfortable with the idea of any division between them. Levick was the constant in our friendship. He was like the *glue* that kept us all together.

Arturian's eyes shot to mine, as if my statement surprised him. However, he straightened his jacket and gave me a small, knowing smile. "I doubt that. But thank you, Francie." He turned as if to walk back home, but stopped short. He pivoted back, stormy blue eyes locking on mine. "I'll see you next week, for my birthday?" he asked.

For a few years in a row, Levick and I had taken Arturian out to a port-side pub for his birthday. It was risky, and he had to disguise himself, but it was worth it.

He tilted his head as he waited for my answer. I couldn't stop the heat from rising in my cheeks as he looked at me.

Has he always looked at me like that?

After composing myself, I stood up on the branch, prompting Arturian to visibly cringe in concern.

"I wouldn't miss it."

With that, I began walking back over the fence, my dress brushing around my calves. "Goodbye," I called out behind me.

I barely heard his response. "Until then."

"I'm back!" I called as I walked through the old wooden door to the inn. It creaked with effort as I stepped over the threshold, brushing my boots against the doormat on the floor. Receiving only silence for an answer, I assumed Crysta and Levick were out.

With no customers yet, the morning provided a tranquil work setting. I brought my three rabbits through the hallway and into the inn's large kitchen and placed them in a deep basin. A small window illuminated the room, walled with dark wooden boards and bare of decoration. A small bunch of blue wildflowers sat in a glass of water on the kitchen windowsill, bringing a smile to my face. I always loved when Levick put flowers in the kitchen. Faint footsteps could be heard coming from upstairs as a guest paced back and forth. I found solace in the familiar kitchen tasks—it was a place to quiet my mind and focus on the work before me.

Using a knife, I skinned the rabbits, then put the blade down. I glanced over my shoulder, making sure no curious eyes watched me. Once I was sure I was alone, I used my windblade to make rough cuts to prep the rabbits for cooking. I severed their legs from their bodies, attempting to cut along the joints as closely as possible. I usually avoided using my windblade indoors, but I found that the practice had helped hone my skills and control. It was difficult to control the velocity of a windblade—it always seemed to want to *shoot* through the air at impossible speeds. I'd been challenging myself to slow down and attempt to *wield* it rather than throw it. It was difficult, but I was making progress.

I was removing the rabbits' entrails when Levick walked in. I waved at him with a fist full of intestines, unintentionally sending drops of blood flying.

He laughed through a comically disgusted expression, his freckled cheeks pulling up to expose a handsome, dimpled smile. "Successful hunt?" he asked as he walked over to see my work.

"Not bad at all." I gestured to the various cuts of meat in the basin. "Three—and they're pretty fat, too. Looks delicious, right?" I pinched one of the rabbit's legs between my bloodied fingers and brought it up to eye level. I teased him by inching the raw meat closer to Levick's face, but he stood completely still, wearing his best cool expression.

"You're pretty confident today, Lev." I brought it closer until it was mere inches from his face.

He didn't even flinch—a daring look danced in his eyes. "You wouldn't." His voice was firm with confidence.

I raised my eyebrows in challenge. I was about to test his resolve when he said, "There's no way you'd risk dropping that perfectly good meat by smashing it into my face."

We stood and stared for a few long moments, searching for weakness in each other's eyes. A gloating smile tugged at the corner of Levick's mouth as he watched me weigh the risks. His dark green eyes shone with self-assurance.

He's right. This is *a great leg.*

I groaned in mock frustration. "I know when I'm beaten. You know me too well, Levick." I returned to dressing the rabbits.

He scooted closer as he leaned against the counter. "It's funny you should say that, Francie, because lately I feel like I don't know you well enough."

I froze, my heart in my throat.

What was that tone?

Did he see me use the blade?

"What do you mean?" I asked casually, despite my racing heart.

He leaned in over my shoulder. "Well, according to a very reliable-seeming older fellow, you worked at some nobleman's country estate twenty years ago. Living a double life, are we?"

I glanced up at him, and to my infinite relief, he was smiling mockingly at me.

Oh, thank Echna. He doesn't know.

I breathed a subtle sigh of relief and laughed. "You caught me! Yes, I remember working there before I was born." An awkward laugh escaped my lips.

He sighed, watching me finish my work in the basin and wash my hands. I could tell he was observing me... studying me.

Drying my hands off, I addressed him directly and hoped I wouldn't regret it. "What's wrong, Lev? I can tell something is bothering you."

He stood for a moment, thoughtfully looking at his shoes. Finally, he met my eyes. "We should go see Arturian soon. He seemed a little down the last time I saw him."

I had a feeling that wasn't what he had just been thinking about, but I let it go.

"I saw him today while I was hunting and he seemed alright. Although, I suppose he was in want of company." I settled against the counter next to Levick.

"What makes you think that?" he asked, stiffening a bit.

"He invited me to tea in the stables," I replied, only just noticing the peculiarity of the invitation. It was rare for Arturian and me to spend time together without Levick. He was always there. I never thought too much of it, but it was consistent enough that it became normal for us.

"Did he?" Levick began grabbing blades of grass from his pocket and pulling them apart. His messy brown hair hung by his sun-kissed face, partially obscuring his eyes.

He was retreating into himself. "It's his birthday next week. We'll see him then. Arturian's birthday is *always* a riot."

Levick looked up at me, an excited smile forming on his face. It was true. Arturian's birthday was consistently the most fun of all of ours. "Yeah, that's true."

I patted his arm. "Come on, let's get to work. I have three rooms I need to clean out, and I could use some help," I said as I slipped off my apron.

"Whatever you desire, Queen of the Inn," Levick joked from behind me as we made our way to the rooms. I smiled to myself, and counted myself lucky to have friends like mine.

CHAPTER FOUR
SEASHELLS

Arturian's birthday came in the early summer, and I had been feeling cooped up. My work at the inn kept me busy, and Arturian had been taking on more duties of his house, so I'd not seen him as much as I used to. He'd seemed... *off* when I saw him in the forest the previous week. I hoped some birthday revelry would bring him out of it.

I was stretching sheets over one of the inn's beds when Levick peeked his head in the bedroom door. "It's the Weigh Anchor, tonight," he said as he ran a hand through his mousy brown hair.

We'd gone to that pub last year for Arturian's birthday, and it took us all at least two days to fully recover. Something about Arturian's birthday got us up to no good every year. Maybe it was because he was the oldest, and we felt as if he was leading us into a new era, in a way.

"Don't let me do what I did last year, Lev," I folded the flat sheet and ran my fingers over the crease, making sure it was straight.

Levick laughed at the memory. "In your defense, those shells really looked like hair combs."

I cringed. We'd gone down to the shore on the northern side of the port and collected shells from the beach. I had drunk so much salt rum that I'd been convinced the shells looked like the perfect hair accessories and arranged some of them in my hair. I woke up the next day with five salty shells shoved in the tangled mess, and looked like I'd just emerged from the depths of the Broad Sea like some kind of aquatic monster.

"It's okay, Lev. We both know they didn't," I finished the blankets, wearing a smile that was equal parts grimace. "When will he be there?" I asked as we made our way down the hallway.

"Soon. If your work is done for the day, we should get ready and leave. I've just finished mine." Levick glanced over at me. He'd gained some new freckles over the summer, and his handsome face glowed with life.

"I wonder which caricature of a commoner he'll dress as this year," I chuckled as we walked down the stairs. Last year, it was a dockworker with horribly oversized clothes and a cap pulled halfway over his face.

As heir to one of the wealthiest and most prolific houses in Friese, he and his father were known faces amongst common folk—especially considering how much business they did through the port. In the rare instances that he ventured into a pub, he disguised himself to prevent anyone from finding out he was there; his father, most of all. Augustus wouldn't look kindly on Arturian visiting the less reputable sectors of Friese.

Levick shook his head, smiling at the memory. "Whatever it is, I hope it's better than last year," he said as he took a seat in the dining area. "I'll wait here and we'll walk together?" he asked. I nodded, thanked him, and made my way back up the stairs to my room.

My room was small, drafty, and the floorboards creaked, but it was mine. I had more privacy than many people did in the Friesian slums. Determined to find something nice to wear, I started searching through my wardrobe. Running my fingers over the various fabrics, I landed on a calf-length dress of deep red hanging in the back. The dress was made of some of the softest material I had ever felt, and it was of higher quality than anything else I'd ever owned. I'd avoided wearing it because of how nice it was—convinced I'd ruin it somehow. However, I felt Arturian's birthday was the best time to debut it, as he'd gifted it to me last winter for the Turning of the Season.

I didn't know how he'd gotten away with keeping it secret from his father and staff, but the risk he'd undertaken with the purchase meant more to me than the dress itself. I slipped it on over my black shift dress and pulled the sleeves over my shoulders. The dress hugged my waist snugly, had a moderately low neckline, and flowing layered skirts. It wasn't anything like the tattered, faded work dresses I usually wore, and I felt *beautiful.*

I need to thank him again tonight.

After tying the top section of my hair with a long black ribbon, I took one last critical glance at myself in the mirror.

My dirty blonde hair, lightened by the summer sun, fell in loose waves almost to my waist.

After smoothing invisible wrinkles out of my dress, I emerged from my room and made my way downstairs, where Levick was reading a book at a table. He wore a dark green shirt that complimented his eyes, and had brushed his hair to the side. Upon hearing my steps, he looked up at me, his mouth ajar.

"Too much?" I asked, suddenly hesitating on the staircase.

"No, no!" Levick stood from his chair. "It's great..." he trailed off as I descended the last few stairs. "I've just never seen it before."

I resisted the urge to lie, and answered quietly, "Arturian gave it to me last year. For the Turning."

The subtle crestfallen look on Levick's face made me wish I'd lied. As we'd all grown older, I could tell the wealth disparity between us and Arturian bothered Levick more than it used to.

Nevertheless, he held his arm out for me and smiled. "Let's get going."

We went out the door and began making our way through the dark streets to the port.

Despite the late hour, the port's pub district was buzzing with activity. Friese had a thriving trade industry, which meant numerous transient sailors looking for women and drink to hold them over until the next time they made port. The summer breeze was humid but cool as it wafted over the bay, tousling my hair and refreshing my lungs. It smelled of salt and dead fish, but that never bothered me. I was just happy to be out in the breeze.

Levick and I walked down the main road along the docks, heading north. "Hey, baby!" a slurred voice called out from behind us, followed by an obnoxious whistle. "I'm free tonight, and you look like you'd scratch my itch."

Levick's pace broke, as if he was going to stop.

"Ignore it, Lev," I said, my voice low with warning. It wasn't the first time I'd been catcalled in the pub district, and Levick had received *and given* a few black eyes because of it. "Keep walking. He won't follow us."

Thankfully, I was right. Levick's jaw was clenched as we reached the Weigh Anchor, but he didn't say anything. He opened the door for me, and the smell of rum and pub food wafted over us. The Weigh Anchor was one of the nicer pubs along the port, but that wasn't saying much. A group of old men picked away at fiddles in the corner, stomping along and singing famous Friesian tunes.

We approached the bar, and a haggard-looking old man stared at us apathetically, as if he couldn't care less whether he got our business. "Two salt rums, dark," Levick called over the noise. Without any response, the old man turned and poured our glasses. I began scanning the room for a suitable spot for us and noticed an empty table in the back corner. I tugged on Levick's sleeve and gestured over there. He nodded as he paid the bartender and collected our drinks, and followed me past groups of sweaty men and sticky surfaces. I settled into a chair and took my glass from Levick.

"This is perfect," Levick said from across the table. I nodded in agreement; the further Arturian was from the crowds, the better.

"I just wish the music was better," I said with an amused grin. Friesian pub songs were notoriously vulgar—I'd often find myself laughing or wincing at nearly every verse.

Levick scoffed at me. "Are you kidding? This is as good as it gets!" Just as he said it, one of the fiddle-players sang out,

*"She holds onto me tight, lovin' rough as she can
Then the door swings wide, and there stands her
man"*

My eyebrows shot up at Levick as he burst into laughter. "Very mature, Lev," I scolded, but made a hypocrite of myself when I couldn't restrain my own laughter.

"I see you two started having fun without me," an even voice sounded from behind me. I turned to see Arturian, a hood pulled low over his face. His black hair hung over his shoulders, brushing against his chiseled jaw. He looked me over, and a slow smile spread over his mouth.

"You look beautiful, Francie," he said, as cool and relaxed as ever.

A blush made its way up my cheeks, but I smiled, regardless. I was suddenly thankful for the dim lighting. "Thank you again for the dress."

"No need to thank me. It was a good investment," he said with a playful glance as he took the seat next to mine, facing away from the rest of the pub.

"Happy nineteenth birthday," Levick said with a smile. "I'll grab you a drink. What do you want?"

Arturian mulled it over for a moment. "Could you see if they have any Corlaean vintage?" he asked, earning incredulous laughter from Levick and I.

"Just get him dark rum. Make it a double," I said to Levick, who nodded in approval before making his way over to the bar.

Arturian turned to me and pushed his hood back slightly. "Are you trying to get me drunk, Francie?" he said with a mischievous smile. His midnight black hair fell past his shoulders in wavy strands, framing his angular face.

"Let's just say that after the embarrassing display I put on last year, it better be *you* waking up with seashells in your beautiful hair, Arturian," I said, taking a very conservative sip from my salt rum.

Arturian chuckled, a growing smile on his face. "They really looked like hair combs, though."

"They didn't!" I laughed, amused at how Levick and Arturian both tried to lessen my embarrassment. "I was washing sand out of my hair for weeks."

We sat in a comfortable silence for a moment, reliving the wild memories. The musicians had transitioned to an instrumental number, granting a momentary reprieve from their customary debauchery. The music slowed, filling the pub with their comforting melody. I closed my eyes and focused on it—I'd always loved music, even the tunes played in disreputable, dirty pubs.

I opened my eyes and noticed Arturian was staring at me, his eyes full of unveiled intrigue. Swallowing my feelings of self-consciousness, I gave him a cheeky smile. "That fishmonger's hood suits you."

Arturian's mouth twitched at the corners. "And red suits you," he whispered, his curious eyes roaming over my dress. Neither of us looked away, and my heart began pounding in my chest. Suddenly, my mind was blank, and no intelligent thoughts would come to me.

A glass of rum clinked down on the table. "Drink up, old man," Levick said, sitting back down across from us. I grabbed my own glass and took a long swig.

Arturian winced as he picked up his glass and rubbed his shoulder.

"Still sore?" Levick asked.

He nodded as he tipped the glass back, draining half of it in one swig. I raised my eyebrows.

"That course is going to kill you," I muttered. Arturian had an elaborate obstacle course set up behind the mansion, almost in the forest. I'd only been up close to it a couple of times, but from what I'd seen, it seemed like a death trap. Arturian loved it, of course.

"I'd like to think it keeps me alive," Arturian said, earning a sound of enthusiasm from Levick. He'd run it a few times, but it was risky for Levick to get so close to the Exley mansion, so he didn't get the chance very often. "Most Skylords have gotten comfortable and lazy. I refuse to be one of those when my time comes," Arturian said, swirling his glass.

I bit the inside of my cheek and tried not to think about the secret I held from my closest friends. Whenever Arturian spoke of one day inheriting his father's windblade, I couldn't help but feel the tingling of power running through my fingers, reminding me of my own windblade. Reminding me of what I was.

Skylady.

I shook the thought from my mind and tried to focus on being present with my friends. There was no reason to dwell on it, and doing so would only ruin my night.

"What's new with you two?" Arturian asked us as he leaned back in his chair, crossing his arms over his chest.

"I found the lizard that was living at the top of the tower," Levick said with a satisfied smile.

"Oh no," I started, my hands going up to my chest in alarm, "did you…"

"I didn't kill him, relax."

Arturian cocked his head at me. "Funny, aren't you the leading cause of death for the poor animals living on my lands?"

"It's different," I said, splaying my hands. "Lizards can't feed anyone, so there's no need to kill them."

Arturian simply smiled at me. "So, what's new with you?"

I racked my brain, trying to think of anything more interesting than the usual guest drama at the inn. "I finished the book of Friesian Folktales you lent me."

"Which was your favorite?" he asked as he leaned forward to prop his elbow on the arm of his chair. His eyes were focused in interest as he awaited my answer.

I didn't even have to think about it. "The King and the Wildcard," I said, and a smile crept onto Arturian's face.

"What's it about?" Levick asked.

I cleared my throat and began summarizing the tale. "It's the story of an ancient Friesian king whose wife, Paressa, was kidnapped by the king of Trenica. He took her to their capital city, Grevalst, and threatened to kill her if the Friesians attempted a rescue mission. However, rather than attempt to escape or fight the Trenican king, Paressa thanked him for saving her from her 'evil,' and 'wicked' husband in Friese. The Trenican king rejoiced, relieved that the woman he expected to be a prisoner was happy to be taken. Over months, she showed him affection and kindness, and was always present when he needed support. She became the image of a dutiful, dedicated woman, and was given the freedoms of such. The king of Trenica was so smitten that he proposed to her. He opened his heart, his bed, and his secrets to her. He had no idea that she was planning her method of escape.

"The day before their wedding, Paressa retrieved a knife from her bedside table and killed the king of Trenica in his sleep. When she left, she simply walked out of the palace. She'd become such a beloved and trusted person in Trenica that no one thought to stop her. By the time they began sending search parties for her, she'd already begun the trek to Port Harrow, where she'd eventually board a ship bound for Friese.

"Upon her return, she relayed months' worth of vital Trenican information to Friesian officials. As the story goes, the information she gathered spared Friese from an attack that would have destroyed the port and crippled the nation for decades, if not centuries.

"However, the king of Friese was far from 'evil' or 'wicked,' and mourned every second of his wife's absence. Even after she'd returned, the knowledge of what she endured in order to escape burdened his heart. Even years later, he'd told his wife that it wasn't worth the price. He'd rather the Friesian docks be destroyed a hundred times over than for her to have gone through what she did."

By the time I finished speaking, a lump was forming in my throat at the tragedy of it.

"It's a good story," Arturian replied, but pursed his lips for a moment. "Although I can't imagine the guilt he felt... to be helpless while the woman he loved was in the clutches of his enemy." He picked up his glass. "It would be the cruelest form of torture," he said before tipping back his glass and emptying it.

"Now that we're all sad..." Levick began, "let's get another round."

Three glasses of salt rum later, and I'd dragged Levick to the small open area beside the musicians for an energetic dance. I wasn't sure if he'd have agreed to it if not for the same amount of salt rum in his system, but he seemed to be having a good time. Arturian laughed at us from the corner of the room, but kept his hood down.

"You're too slow, Lev!" I teased as we spun around the room. While Arturian had taught us ballroom dancing when we were children, *this* dancing was something else entirely. We swung around in skips and turns, and it wasn't long before we both had sweat beading on our foreheads.

Levick spun me on my heel and dipped me low, earning a yelp of surprise. "Don't you dare drop me again!" I hissed through an exuberant smile as I clung to his arms. His green eyes narrowed in mock offense.

He laughed and shook his head as he pulled me back up, continuing the dance. "It was *one time*, years ago!"

"And I'll never forget," I teased as I gave his shoulder a squeeze.

Suddenly, I felt a hard swat against my backside. I flinched and lunged closer to Levick, who put his arms around me protectively. Turning my head, I saw a grizzled sailor, well into his forties, leering at me.

"How about you share some of the fun?" he asked Levick, showcasing a smile of very few teeth.

Levick stepped in front of me. "Who the hell do you think you are?" he growled, leaning closer. Levick had gotten taller, and stared down at the sailor with utter disgust in his eyes. "The lady didn't ask to be touched."

I briefly noticed Arturian had risen from his chair and was watching us, eyes dark and ominous. His rigid posture spoke volumes, even from a distance.

"Any woman who moves her hips like that *wants* to be touched." The sailor leaned over, dragging his ogling stare over me. My lip turned up in distaste.

Levick took a confident step closer to the man, staring daggers at him. "*Get out*," he said through gritted teeth.

Arturian had taken a few steps closer and was nearly a horse-length from us. He was silent, and I hadn't even seen him move.

The sailor smiled, not budging. "You're just worried she'll moan louder for me than she does for you."

Oh, boy.

Although I couldn't see Levick's reaction from behind him, I saw Arturian's. The color drained from his face, and his jaw tensed. Stealthy as a cat, he crouched on his heel, preparing to spring.

Levick beat him to it, and leveled a powerful punch to the sailor's jaw, sending a couple of his remaining teeth tumbling across the floor. However, the man had clearly been in his fair share of pub brawls, and immediately straightened up and threw a fist back into Levick's face.

Shit.

I caught Levick's elbow and had to stop myself from aiming my windblade at the lecherous sailor. "Let's get out of here," I said, urgency thick in my voice.

"Stay back, Francie," Levick said over his shoulder as blood dripped down his mouth.

Out of the corner of my eye, I noticed a dark figure move behind my laughing assaulter. Arturian's arm snaked around the man's throat, and I could barely make out a glint of steel carving a thin line of blood into the man's shoulder. Arturian's face was pure *fury*. His jaw was set in a snarl as he squeezed the man tighter and tighter. He wailed and squirmed against him, but it was useless. Arturian was taller, larger, and clearly trained in combat.

"The lady didn't ask to be touched," he growled before kicking the man's legs out from under him. He sprawled on the floor, staring up at Arturian with wide eyes. "You're lucky to keep your hand, worthless bastard."

"Get out!" the old bartender called over. "Don't make me find the Crownies!"

That's our cue.

Arturian put an arm around my waist and led me through the crowd, Levick trailing us. The rest of the patrons stared at us, eyes wide as we rushed out the doors.

The three of us laughed hysterically as we raced down the port road.

"I can't believe you pulled a knife on someone!" Levick called up to Arturian, who was gaining on me.

"You punched him first," Arturian said through an incredulous chuckle.

"The night isn't over yet!" I yelled, lungs heaving as I ran. I wouldn't let Arturian's birthday celebration end in a brawl. Besides, I knew of a great beach that had shells the shape of hair combs.

Maybe four glasses of salt rum *wasn't* a great idea.

"You sure you're okay?" Arturian asked as he caught up to me. His hood had flown back, and the faint moonlight shone upon his face. The alcohol flushed his face, but he seemed in good spirits despite the confrontation.

"I'm more worried about Levick. He's the one with a split lip," I said, just as he caught up with us.

"It's not the first, and it won't be the last," he laughed as he wiped the last bit of blood off onto his sleeve.

"Where are we going?" Arturian asked.

"Where do you think?"

"Yes!" Levick yelled with a laugh.

Arturian smiled at me as we ran under the moonlight. I soaked up every moment, feeling the sea spray against my neck as we got closer to the northern shore.

As we approached the empty beach, I kicked off my shoes and embraced the feeling of the sand between my toes. I ran until the waves lapped against the sand and walked until it reached my ankles. The water was invitingly warm, typical of Friese's bay in the summer. I breathed in a deep gulp of salty air and closed my eyes, thanking Echna for my friends.

Water sprayed over me, and my eyes shot open to see Levick, clad in only his breeches, sprinting into the bay. "Come on, Francie!" he called over his shoulder before diving into a crashing wave.

I felt a dark presence beside me before I looked. "Unless you'd rather find some more seashells..." Arturian looked over at me expectantly. The salt rum weakened my self-control, and I held his stare for longer than I meant to. His handsome mouth pulled up in a smile, and I could've *sworn* a knowing look flashed in his eyes.

As if I hadn't been blushing enough, Arturian shrugged off his jacket, reached back over his head and pulled his shirt off, tossing it on the ground.

Dear Echna. Why?

All the time he spent exercising on his obstacle course had paid dividends. My mind told me not to stare, but the rum told me to take advantage of the moment. My actions landed somewhere in-between.

Arturian's smile turned smug as he backed closer to the water, beckoning me to follow. His eyes were full of a dark, glimmering playfulness that I wasn't sure I could handle.

"You were too scared last year!" Levick yelled, his head bobbing in the water. "Come on, be brave!"

I took one step closer to Arturian, who stood in the water up to his knees. He held a hand out for me.

I can't ruin this dress... damn it.

"Turn around," I said, loud enough for both of them to hear. Arturian caught on and spun around to face the bay.

Levick, however, looked puzzled. "Why?" he asked.

"Come on, Lev," Arturian said in an unmistakably exasperated tone.

"Oh! Sorry!" Levick said, turning around as well.

I took a deep breath and slid my dress down my shoulders. My black shift, while technically an undergarment, wasn't horribly immodest, making me feel better. I gingerly folded my dress and set it on a nearby rock.

Arturian, ever the gentleman, still faced away. But he had one hand open behind him, waiting for me. I inhaled deeply, then approached from behind and grasped his hand. I tried desperately to ignore the warmth that spread up my arm.

He turned his head ever-so-slightly, so I could see an eyebrow arched in intrigue.

"Hey!" I said, pinching his back with my free hand.

"Okay, okay," he laughed, looking ahead again.

"Let's do this before I change my mind," I said, shaking despite the warm air and water.

Arturian walked on, and I followed him into the bay. Chills ran over me as the water covered my knees, hips, and finally my chest.

"Can I turn around now?" Levick said as we approached him.

Before I could answer, Arturian turned around to face me, a sly grin on his face.

"I didn't say yes," I said, eyebrows raised in feigned offense.

"Would you like me to wait until the water covers your head, too?" he asked as he ran a wet hand through his hair.

Don't look at his arms, Francie. Think of the questionable aquatic life that might brush against your leg at any minute.

Levick turned around and smiled at us. "Now that we're all here..." he trailed off, and before I could react to his sinister eyes, he'd splashed Arturian and I directly in the face.

I made to splash him back, but Arturian had already leapt forward and dunked Levick's head under the water.

While the boys proceeded to try to drown each other in the bay, I took advantage of their distraction and laid back to float in the water. I relished the feeling of weightlessness as moonlight bathed over me in a cool embrace. A pair of sleepless gulls flew overhead past the sea-cliffs, which towered in the sky like a pair of ominous hooded giants just north of the beach. Constellations shone their faint light down on the water, and I began trying to identify each one.

My peace was interrupted when something brushed against my foot, and I shot upright with a yelp. Immediately, something was unnervingly apparent to me. Arturian and Levick were nowhere to be found.

They better not be...

Water filled my mouth as a pair of strong hands yanked me under. I fought against the water as someone pinched me, starting at my side, then my arms, and finally, my feet. Unable to contain my laughter, I gasped for air as my friends playfully attacked me. When I finally broke through the surface again, Levick was treading water in front of me, grinning from ear to ear.

"I thought a fish was dragging me down to become its dinner!" I splashed him right in his smiling face. Arturian rose from the water beside Levick, wearing a more subtle smile.

Nope. Can't let it stand.

I lunged for them, targeting Levick first. I pressed down on his head to dunk him, but unfortunately he was quite tall, and was standing on the sandy floor. He took the opportunity I unintentionally gave him and grabbed my waist, launching me into the air.

"Levick!" I hissed as I plunged back into the bay. I could hear his smug laughter from underwater.

An idea came to me, slinking and enticing. Instead of resurfacing, I began swimming toward their voices, never getting too close to the surface. I was half a horse-length from one of them—I couldn't tell which one—when I noticed the panic in their voices. It had been over a minute, and they'd forgotten how long I could hold my breath. Just as one of them began lunging forward to search for me, I brought my hands up to scare him, and met with planes of hard muscle.

Oh, shit. What was I thinking?

I winced at the contact, knowing it was Arturian. Instead of jumping in surprise, as I'd hoped his reaction would be, he reached down and seized my waist, heaving me from the water. As I broke through the surface, I was immediately met with eyes of deeper blue than the ocean, focused in concern. His stare ran over me for a long moment before heaving a sigh of relief. However, he still held onto me under the water.

"I was trying to scare you," I said, a sheepish look on my wet face. Feeling his hands on my waist was only making me blush even harder.

"Mission accomplished," Levick said from behind me, his voice no longer smug. "We thought you drowned."

"Yeah," Arturian said quietly, "you scared me." His expression softened, and he gave me a small smile.

I wasn't sure if it was the four glasses of rum or the adrenaline, but I felt his thumbs brush a couple of small circles over my waist as he held me. It was an intimate gesture—one I'd never received from *anyone*, let alone Arturian. Hot waves ran through my body, and a small, nearly imperceptible gasp escaped my mouth. He held my gaze for only a moment before releasing me and backing away.

"Let's go wrestle, Arturian," Levick said as he began paddling back to shore, unaware of what had passed between his friends. "You still haven't found any of those seashells, Francie. Your hair is looking plain," he joked.

Arturian spared me one last look—one that seemed dangerously close to regret—before following Levick back to shore. I laid back in the water again and took a deep breath of humid air. Denial possessed me. I didn't want my friendships to change. However, when I looked at him... I knew they would. And things would never be the same.

Why is everything so complicated? Why can't things stay simple forever... me, Arturian, and Levick.

A warm gust ran over the surface of the water, brushing over my exposed skin. It might've been a summer breeze, but it felt like the winds of change.

CHAPTER FIVE
THE BELL TOWER

We miss you. I wish you could see how extraordinary our son is. He finally took his first steps last week. He has so much grace already. As he walks, he almost seems to float.
- Unsent Letter from Elie Roale

Seven Years Ago

At only ten years old, I wandered through the port slums on a rainy morning. I had no destination in mind, no plans except to get away. The small dockside room I'd shared with my mother forever stood behind me. I doubted the landlord would even let me back in. Onward, I trudged through the grimy streets, barely noticing the storm growing over me. Gusts of wind ripped through alleys, knocking over fruit carts and scattering flower bouquets.

Images of my mother came to me in heart-wrenching flashes—her chocolate brown hair bound at her neck as she cooked... her kind, dark eyes wrinkling up as she smiled at me. I'd never known my father—he left before I was born. My mother was all I had in the world, and now I felt utterly lost. I didn't know how long I'd been walking, but my legs were unsteady, forcing me to rest in a back alley. I cried softly, my salty tears mixing with the raindrops on my face. Despite the freezing rain soaking me, I eventually fell asleep.

I awoke shivering and shaking. Even with the afternoon sun emerging from the horizon, promising warmth and happiness, I felt as if my bones themselves were cold. The rain had thoroughly saturated my clothes, which clung to my chilled body.

"Hey! Are you okay?" a small voice called out from the open street ahead, drawing my attention. I looked up to see a young girl, her hair whipping wildly around her face in the wind. "Where's your mother?" she asked as she scooted into the alley.

"My mother is dead," I responded without thinking.

Something about saying it aloud brought my emotions to the forefront, and I struggled in vain to suppress my feelings.

An empty chasm stood before me, threatening to swallow me whole. I was so entirely alone without my mother. She was my world, and she was gone forever—taken by an aggressive lung-blight. Sobbing, I gasped for air as tears flowed down my rain-soaked face.

The young girl reached out and took my hand. Her fingers were cold and wet from the rain, but they stilled the shaking of my own hands. "My mom is dead, too," she whispered, her large blue eyes reddening with unfallen tears. "You aren't alone. Follow me. We should get inside."

I looked at the girl's hand in mine, and I felt as if I was being pulled out of that dark, gaping chasm. She helped me to my feet, and I clung to her like a lifeline. As I followed her down the streets, I hadn't even noticed the wind had stilled.

Potato soup had never tasted so good as I sipped from my oversized spoon. A tall, kind woman named Crysta had welcomed me and my new acquaintance into a small, run-down inn and served me some dinner. The young girl politely excused herself to change into dry clothes, leaving me alone with my soup.

The small windows and low ceilings in the inn induced a claustrophobic and pressing sensation, not unlike a cave. However, the burning candles and delicious smells countered it with their welcoming coziness, and I let my mind wander... I made myself stop thinking about my mother.

I wasn't sure how long I sat there, staring out the window, when the young girl came back out of the hallway. She inched forward and spoke softly. "My name's Francie," she said, sitting herself in the chair across from me. "Crysta is my aunt, and we run this inn together. What's your name?"

With hair like burlap and bright, inquisitive eyes the color of cornflowers, she was a radiant contrast to my somber mood. I found myself drawn to her, like a moth to a flame.

"Levick Roale," I answered, meeting her eyes.

Francie smiled at me. "I was thinking we could be friends, maybe?"

A thin ray of sunshine cut through the cloudy window, warming my hands. "That would be good, I think," I said, striving for a casual tone.

Francie sat with me for a while, and we began talking. Not about my dead mother, or about where I was going to live, but about little things. Silly theories about why some seagulls have red feet and some don't. Complaints about the constant stench in the slums. Arguing over which kinds of rocks skip the best on the water. I even laughed a little, and for a short time, I got to feel like a ten-year-old again. Before I knew it, the sun was setting.

After a while, Crysta popped her head in. "I've got your bed made up, dear. Come look?"

I cocked my head at Francie in confusion.

My bed?

She seemed to read my expression, because she nodded in encouragement. We both walked down the hallway, through the kitchen, and into a large storage room. There, next to a few bags of vegetables, Crysta had laid a pallet on the floor with blankets, a pillow, and a set of dry clothes.

"Would you like to sleep here tonight?" Crysta asked, kneeling down in front of me.

I was struck silent by relief.

I won't be sleeping on the street tonight.

I cleared my throat and spoke in the most grateful tone I could manage. "Yes, please! Thank you, ma'am."

Before I remembered my manners, I tossed my arms over Crysta's shoulders, nearly causing her to fall. I apologized, but she laughed and patted my shoulder. After I changed into the dry clothes, they said goodnight. Crysta tucked me in and they left me alone. Once the relief of sleeping indoors and not being alone wore off, I cried myself to sleep. I dreamed of my mother, and the songs she sang for me.

I dedicated myself to assisting at the inn over the next few days, despite my limitations. Crysta provided me with minor tasks, and Francie patiently mentored me like a loving older sibling. I eventually learned to clean the tables, wash the dishes, and sweep the floors before anyone even asked me to.

Days went by, then weeks, before I began to feel like a burden. Despite their assurances to the contrary, I felt undeserving and out of place. Crysta and Francie both lived in a couple of small bedrooms upstairs, but there wasn't enough space up there for another person—there was barely enough for them.

It was that train of thought that led me to go on a search for a new place to sleep. After fabricating an errand to run, I stepped out of the inn's old heavy door and into the bright morning sun. The mid-summer humidity hit me, and I instantly began sweating. The climate in Friese was mild, with warm, humid summers and bearable winters. Warm sea winds made snow and freezing temperatures infrequent.

I figured that the further I went out of town, the better chance I could find an unoccupied structure to take up residence in. Squatting was illegal in Friese, but people often got away with it if they were careful enough. I reached the edge of town and began walking along a minor road that bordered a forest. The trees outside of Friese were ancient and had massive trunks and sprawling branches. Moss draped off of them, creating a wistful scene when a breeze rippled through.

Through my daydreaming, I almost didn't notice an overgrown trail branching off the road. Looking each way down the street and seeing no one around, I ventured into the woods. I walked carefully, heeding the weeds and thorns jutting up around my feet. Just as I wondered if I'd made a mistake in following the trail, I rounded a small hill to see an old, rundown building. While it was small in radius, it was at least four or five stories tall, and a partially enclosed bell sat on the very top.

A twist of fear ran through me as I realized how alone I was there. If something happened to me, I would never be found. Although, from the looks of it, the place hadn't seen foot traffic in many years. So, pushing down my fear, I hesitantly crept closer to the front of the building.

Large double doors inlaid with intricate carvings stood covered in dust and grime from years of weather exposure. I tried to dodge the moss growing on the corners of the front steps as I climbed up and approached the doors. After taking a deep breath, I gripped the oversized handles and pulled backwards. To my surprise, the doors creaked and opened—the hinges groaning as they rubbed against themselves. Dim streaks of light came through the dirty windows, illuminating the mostly empty building. Dust-covered tiles spread from wall to wall, stained a dark brown color from years of built-up dust and grime. There was a cushioned bench sitting against the back wall, a small table next to the entryway, and a spiral staircase in the middle of the room.

I crept in, listening closely in case someone—or something—else was already occupying the place. I breathed the stale air in quick and nervous gulps as I made my way towards the spiral staircase. Resting my hand on the grainy banister, I began making my way up.

Peeking my head over the base of the top floor, I noticed there was significantly more light in there due to a large circular window.

This place rises above the trees.

The room was small, but in much better shape than the ground floor. There was no furniture left, and it needed to be swept, but it certainly wasn't below the standards of a young homeless boy. The air was stagnant and hot, but I noticed that the large window had a handle on one side and a thick hinge on the other.

It opens... like a door.

I carefully pulled the rusty handle on the window, and with a shrill squeak, it opened up. A refreshing summer breeze flowed into the tower, washing over me and filling my lungs. I took a timid step closer to the ledge and gazed upon the rolling forests of Friese. The window faced west, so I couldn't see the city, but I could barely spot a clearing nearby. I wondered what could be over there, but I couldn't make out any details from the hills and the distance. I put the thought from my mind, reveling in the comfort of having found a place to stay.

This will do.

That afternoon, I lied and told Crysta and Francie I'd found a distant cousin with a spare sleeping area for me.

"You're leaving?" Francie said, brows scrunched in disbelief.

"There's not much room for me here, and that's alright," I murmured. "I'll still come here every day to help, I promise." Before I could say more, Francie pulled me into a hug, catching me off guard.

Crysta had been unusually quiet. I assumed she'd known I couldn't stay there long term, and our separation was inevitable. "We're going to miss you, Lev," she said as she opened her arms wide. I extricated myself from Francie and let Crysta embrace me. She'd become like a mother to me; taking care of me and making sure I was safe. In those few weeks, I had a much better life than most orphans in Friese did. However, it was time for me to face reality: I needed to be self-sufficient.

I picked up a few old rags from the inn on my way out that evening. My new home needed some cleaning.

In just a few weeks, I'd transformed the bell tower into a makeshift home—functional, though far from luxurious by most standards. I'd scavenged some old blankets for a bed, and was slowly piecing together a second-hand wardrobe, thanks to the kindness of families who frequented the inn. Each day, my routine was the same: wake up with the first light of dawn, walk to the inn, spend the day working alongside Francie and Crysta, then return to my tower after dinner, tired but content.

It was on one of those normal days that I was discovered.

After dressing myself, I climbed down the twisting steps and exited the heavy doors. To my surprise, a young boy sitting atop an imposing gray horse stood about twenty feet away, staring at me in disbelief. He had tousled black hair and was clothed in immaculately clean and expensive-looking riding gear.

The boy broke his stunned silence. "What are you doing here?"

I racked my brain for plausible excuses, but came up with nothing.

Guess it's got to be the truth, then.

"I—I live here... my name is Levick Roale. What's yours?"

At that, the horse-boy's eyebrows shot up.

"This is my family's property. My name is Arturian Exley, and you can't just live here without permission." The boy puffed out his chest to give himself an air of authority.

It was nice while it lasted, I guess.

"How old are you, Arturian?" I asked on a whim. I figured I had nothing to lose, anyway.

Taken aback, Arturian answered, "I'm twelve. You?"

"I'm ten. I've never ridden a horse before. Is it hard?" I asked as I began inching closer.

Arturian's face lit up with excitement. "No, not really. Unless you're doing dressage. Or high jumps. Or a steeple-chase. Normal riding is really not that different from walking. Except you're up really high..." Before long, the previously aloof boy was explaining to me in long-form how to ride a horse.

Boy, he sure can talk, can't he?

"Would you like to try?" Arturian asked as he held his hand out. The offer surprised me.

Hesitating, I asked, "Are you sure?"

Arturian smiled encouragingly and motioned me closer. "Yes, come on! You'll love it."

Burying my reservations, I climbed onto the large horse with some help from Arturian and a conveniently placed stump. He sat in the saddle, and I sat right behind him on the saddle pad. "I forgot to introduce you—this is Smoke. You're going to have to hang on, you know. Unless you want to go socks-over-skull into the weeds."

I cringed at the thought and wrapped my arms around Arturian's midsection. "We aren't going to jump or anything... right?" I asked, voice trembling a bit.

"Don't worry, I won't let Smoke do any galloping... yet," Arturian responded with a sly grin.

"Yet?" I exclaimed as we took off at a trot into the woods.

Through the woods, Smoke raced. To me, it felt like a break-neck pace, but Arturian seemed completely unfazed. Smoke didn't seem to need much guiding as he easily trotted down the overgrown trail. This certainly wasn't his first time out there.

"Uh... Arturian? Where are we going?" I supposed I should've asked that question before I got on the horse—bailing out certainly wasn't an option at our speed.

"I'm going to show you around the estate. Don't worry, Father isn't here. No one will notice you," Arturian responded.

Estate?

What did he say his family name was?

Exley. Oh.

"Did you say your name was Exley?" I asked in what I hoped was a casual tone.

"Yes," was the only answer I got as Smoke kept us both bouncing along the trail.

I pressed further. "So... are you related to the Exleys who own the port?"

"Yes, that's my father, Augustus. But we don't own the port. We just do a lot of trade through there."

I wasn't sure I believed him. It sounded like the answer an obscenely wealthy heir-ling would give.

Before I could ask any more questions, the forest gave way to a large clearing covered in shining fields of grass. Glossy-coated horses grazed in groups in the distance, and I could barely make out a large mansion nestled against the woods on the other side of the clearing.

"Do you live there?" I asked without thinking.

"Yes," Arturian replied. "Father and I live there."

I scrunched my brow in confusion. "Just you two? All that room for two people?" I realized distantly that I was being rude, but such wealth was beyond anything I'd ever seen.

"Our family wasn't always just two people. A long time ago, the Exleys could've filled the whole house up," Arturian said with a tinge of sadness.

"I'm sorry. I was rude. I've just never seen such a big house before," I said wistfully.

"It's ok. I'm not mad at you," Arturian said after a pause. "I won't tell anyone about you living in our bell tower."

I shook my head a little, unsure if I heard him correctly. "You won't?"

"No. It's not hurting me or anyone else on the estate to have you living there. Father hasn't set foot over there in years."

If we hadn't been on horseback, I would've jumped in excitement. "Arturian... Thank you! I thought I'd have to find a new place to lay out my bedroll."

Arturian turned his head just enough for me to see his smile. "Don't mention it, Levick. Besides, it might be fun to have a friend living close by."

Friend?

A smile spread across my face.

"I agree, Arturian," I answered, still soaking in the relief.

After a few minutes, Arturian asked, "Want to take a quick break?"

"Sure!" I answered. The idea of sitting on stable ground excited me.

We came to a stop under a large oak tree, where we dismounted. Arturian laced Smoke's reins around a low-hanging branch. I didn't suppose it would hold up very long if Smoke gave it a yank, but Arturian seemed plenty confident of his horse's loyalty.

"You've been a pretty decent rider so far," Arturian said as he glanced over.

The compliment surprised me. "Thanks."

A few minutes passed by as we enjoyed the views of the estate. Rolling hills of grass dotted the landscape, occasionally broken by solitary, large oak trees. A herd of horses cantered by, keeping their distance. Leading them was a large stallion—even larger than Smoke. His coat was so smooth that it reflected light like a lake under the sun. Behind him were a pair of slender palominos and a gangly chestnut filly.

Such beautiful creatures. The horses I've seen before have all been dull compared to these.

"These are all yours?" I asked as I gestured to the passing herd.

"Yes, all of them. I guess you could say I collect them," Arturian replied, a hint of pride in his voice.

"Do you ride all of them? Do you even have time to?" I asked while pulling apart some wide blades of grass.

"The ones who are old enough, yes. Riding is how I spend most of my days," Arturian said quietly.

I nodded vaguely, still gazing into the distance.

He's out here all alone every day, just riding horses all the time? That's got to be lonely...

"Would you teach me how to ride? For real?" I asked hastily, surprising myself.

Arturian hesitated for a moment before saying, "I think I could find the time." He gave me a half-smile before standing and dusting himself off. "Come on," he said. "I've got to get you back home."

Later that day at the inn, I told Francie about my living situation in the bell tower.

"You're squatting in an abandoned building? Levick, you'll get caught!" Francie paced around the empty dining hall.

Tell her. Just do it.

"I won't get caught because the owner gave me permission."

At this unclear confession, Francie's head snapped up. I looked back at her hesitantly. "Well... don't keep me waiting in suspense! Who is it?"

I nervously picked at the hem of my shirt. "It's Arturian Exley," I said in barely more than a mumble. Francie's hearing was good—her mouth dropped open.

"Exley? Levick... you met an Exley? And he didn't kick you off of his property?" She was scratching her head in confusion.

I grinned a little. "Yeah, well... we're kind of friends now, actually... he's twelve years old."

Francie let out an amused laugh. "Levick! You let me believe he was a grown-up!" She gave me a playful shove in the shoulder. "I've never seen anyone make friends as easily as you do. Quite the charmer, aren't you?"

I turned to hide my blush and took a few steps over to the window, pretending to look out.

"I guess... but I think he's actually just really nice. You should meet him."

CHAPTER SIX
FRENZY

I am writing to you while holding back tears of relief. Our little boy had a close brush with disaster today. He was playing with the neighbor's three-year-old. While I wasn't paying attention, the two of them climbed halfway up that old oak tree by the docks. As is the way of our son, he got into a squabble with the other boy, and in the midst of their arguing, they both lost their grip. The neighbor's boy fell nearly fifteen feet, breaking an arm and a leg. But our son—by some miracle—walked away without a scratch.
- Unsent Letter from Elie Roale

Two weeks after Arturian's birthday, I'd only seen him once, so I resolved to go make sure he was doing alright. I arranged for mine and Francie's inn work to be covered, then got dressed and cleaned the bell tower. It wasn't often that Francie came inside, so I wanted to make sure it was in good shape. Over the years, I had gradually transformed it into a homey space. Arturian's assistance made a significant impact as well. There was a rug on the main floor, a few chairs, and I had acquired myself a proper bed.

When Augustus had all the beds replaced at the Exley estate, Arturian offered to smuggle me one of the old ones they were preparing to throw away. However, neither of us could figure a way to get it out without being noticed, or how to get it up the bell tower's spiral staircase. I ended up bringing supplies and materials up the stairs one at a time, and Arturian helped me build a bed for myself on the top floor. It wasn't nearly as nice as the one Arturian had offered to give me, but it was much more comfortable than blankets on the floor.

I was just putting my broom away when I heard a faint knock on the door, shortly followed by a familiar voice chiming, "I'm coming in!" in a sing-song tone.

Francie walked through the door with a warm smile on her face. She was wearing one of her best dresses; light sky blue, matching her eyes. It had quarter-length sleeves, and fit snugly through the waist until reaching her hips, where it fanned out and swayed around her ankles. Her dark blonde hair was collected in a long braid down her back, which flipped to the side as she cocked her head at me.

I quickly began fidgeting with my shirt, realizing I'd been staring. "Hey, ready to walk over?" I asked.

"I'm ready. When did you plan this with him?" she asked as we both walked back through the front doors.

"Oh... I didn't." I scratched my neck and shrugged. "He rides every day—he'll be out there."

"Levick..." Francie started. "What if Augustus is there? If he sees us, we'll never get to see Arturian again," she said, hesitating as we began down the well-worn trail to the Exley stables.

Arturian had gone to great lengths over the years to keep us separated from his father. The only things we knew about Augustus were rumors, reputation, and the tiny tidbits Arturian would tell us. Augustus was known to be ruthless, and capable of doing anything to maintain his position as the head of the most powerful house in Friese.

A few years prior, a rumor about Augustus had run through the inn. "I heard he uses his windblade to shave his face. That's just how good he is at using it!" a bearded man had said. A portly woman called out, "You misheard. He uses his windblade to shave the faces of the lesser Skylords! No one dares make a peep if he accidentally misses his mark!" Gasps had erupted through the dining hall at this supposition.

I shook the thoughts from my head and took Francie's hand. "He's never out there, Francie."

She nodded—still hesitant—but we kept walking in a comfortable silence until we reached the clearing. It was only then that I noticed I was still holding Francie's hand, and she hadn't let go either.

"Is that him out there?" Francie asked, taking her hand away to block the sun from her eyes.

I did the same, and could barely make out a black, glimmering form reflecting in the sun. "That's him, alright. Apparently he's feeling brave today."

"Why do you say that?" Francie asked, eyes still lost in the distance. The horse kicked up and bucked, but his rider showed no sign of losing his balance.

"He's on Hampton. Arturian only rides Hampton when he's feeling gutsy," I muttered, noticing the horse and rider were heading our way.

"Is the horse green? Is Arturian trying to break him?" Francie asked.

I chuckled. "He's been at it for six years now. Someone is broken, alright. But it's not Hampton."

Francie laughed incredulously. "I don't think I've ever seen Arturian beaten by something. That must be one hell of a horse."

I reflected on her words as Arturian and Hampton closed the gap between us. She was right; Arturian was the kind of person who never gave up. He possessed an unstoppable resolve that I found admirable. If I was honest with myself, it also fostered a small amount of unease. Despite our strong friendship, there was always some reserve on Arturian's part. I attributed it to his father and his high-society upbringing. However, despite my unease, I believed Arturian would choose the moral and good option if forced to make a hard decision. He'd taken countless risks over the years for me and Francie.

"You two are getting bold, showing up unannounced." His expression didn't match his tone as he rode up to us, showcasing his perfect teeth with a subtle grin. "What brings you to my humble side of the woods?"

"We thought you might do something stupid today. It looks like we were right," I said, gesturing to Hampton. The horse fidgeted and stomped, frustrated to be standing still.

"I hope you're being careful up there, Arturian," Francie chimed in.

Arturian gripped his reins in an attempt to calm the unsettled horse. "I don't know why I keep trying with him," he said between shushes and other horse-appeasing sounds.

Hampton, having had enough of the conversation, reared up, leading to many concerned exclamations from Francie and a couple from me. A less experienced rider would've fallen off, but Arturian appeared as collected and balanced as ever. "Looks like my time has run out. Meet me at the stables!" Horse and rider turned on a dime, darting back toward the magnificent building in the center of the field.

I could've sworn I heard a wistful sigh from Francie, but when I looked over, her expression was one solely of concern.

Maybe it's all in my head. She doesn't feel that way about him.

"I suppose we should get walking, Lev?" she asked as the wind brushed some of her hair against her face.

"Of course." I looked ahead and began walking. She fell into step next to me.

"Augustus must not be home if he's bringing us to the stable," I remarked.

"I hope he isn't. Although I'm sure Arturian has better judgment than to bring us out there while his father is home," she replied, squinting in the sunlight.

By the time we reached the stables, Arturian had saddled two other horses for me and Francie.

"You know I'm no good at riding, Arturian," Francie said, looking hesitant.

He emerged from behind the horses he'd saddled. "Don't worry, Francie, I took great care when choosing your horse. This is Satine." He scratched the cream-colored neck of the bored-looking animal. "She's slow, old, and too exasperated with life to make any sudden movements."

Arturian paused, looking Francie up and down. She apparently felt his gaze on her and cleared her throat.

"Are you wearing anything under that dress?" he asked, his cool tone a sharp contrast to the nature of the question.

I stood speechless, and Francie's light complexion turned red at the inquiry. "What kind of question is that?" she asked through disbelieving chuckles.

Arturian shook his head and laughed. "Can you ride astride without being indecent, Francie?" he asked, looking smug.

Francie threw back her head, an embarrassed smile on her face. "Oh! Oh, I see," she said. "Yes, I can ride. Sorry about that."

Arturian started patting Satine and beckoned Francie over to do the same. She hesitated, so Arturian reached to her and held out his hand. With only a moment's pause, she took his hand, and he brought her over to Satine. He placed her hand on the horse's neck and backed away. "Where are you going?" Francie said, giving Arturian an indignant look.

"You don't need me there anymore. Look, she likes you." Satine was swaying her head back and forth, enjoying the scratching Francie was giving her.

"My work is done. Now, Levick, this is your horse for today." On the other side of Satine stood a tall, muscled bay.

"Are you messing with me right now?" I couldn't hide my excitement. "You're finally letting me ride Frenzy?" He was Arturian's fastest and most prized horse.

"At long last, your years of pleading and convincing have paid off," Arturian said, obviously feeling magnanimous.

I approached the horse with a certain amount of trepidation; riding Frenzy had been my seemingly unattainable goal for three years. He was rumored to be the fastest horse in West Corlaea—another island nation to the east, known for their racehorses. The Exleys had acquired him in a business deal with a Corlaean house. Arturian had pleaded with his father for the horse, and in a stroke of generosity to his son, Augustus agreed.

"He won't bite you, Lev," Arturian said with a chuckle.

I smiled as I patted Frenzy on the neck.

"Who will you ride, Arturian?" Francie called over Satine's back.

"I'm not done with Hampton yet. I plan on tiring him out today," Arturian said in an unmistakably reluctant tone.

I could sense Francie cringing from a few steps away. Before anyone could object, Arturian declared, "Time waits for no one, friends. Let's ride." He led his restless horse out of a stall and out the stable doors. Francie and I followed with our horses, while grinning and nervously glancing at each other.

"I sure hope he survives this," Francie said.

With barely a warm-up, the three of us raced our galloping horses across the meadow. Of course, Hampton had taken off like a shot, placing Arturian in a comfortable lead. Frenzy was faster, though, so I was slowly closing that gap. Francie had been doing surprisingly well for someone who had very little riding experience. She had spurred old Satine to an impressive speed, but still trailed behind the two elite horses.

"Today's the day I'll finally outrace you!" I called as Frenzy and I crept up behind Hampton.

Arturian looked back, a determined grin on his face. "It'll never happen, Levick!" With a fresh burst of speed, Hampton took off.

I glanced backwards to make sure Francie was keeping up well enough, then urged my horse on.

"Well... I propose a toast. To the new fastest rider in Friese—Levick Roale!" Francie said as we raised glasses of expensive red wine in the air. Arturian lifted his glass with great reluctance. We were cooling off at a small table in a corner of the stables after spending the day riding and exploring the grounds. The sun had set just before we opened the bottle.

We all drank, and Arturian stood from his chair. "As the previous record-holder, I'd like to make it known that I am most bitter and resentful of this usurpation. That is all," Arturian said, followed by downing his entire glass of wine.

"A touching speech! Very nice," Francie said, clapping through bouts of laughter. "Winner's speech!" she called. "Speech! Speech!" Arturian echoed her as he poured himself a second glass.

I took a few deep breaths to stop my own laughter, put on a very serious face, and stood up. "I'd like to thank the losers here. Because without them, I would never have become the winner." My composure broke at the end as Francie and Arturian both booed me extensively. "Okay, okay! Proper speech this time." I took another deep breath. A moment of silence passed, and the mood of the group shifted.

"Arturian, you're the one who taught me how to ride. You coached me every day for years, even when I complained and whined about the humidity. You dragged me out of a ditch after I broke my ankle. You helped me make a home out of that dingy old shack you call a bell tower." That comment got quite a laugh out of my friends.

After they quieted down, I continued. "You're my brother, Arturian..." My friends got quiet. "That's why I revel so much in your defeat. Thank you all for coming, and goodnight." I sat down at the table, all three of us laughing. Arturian gripped my shoulder in congratulations and gave me a pat on the back.

We finished the bottle, all of us enjoying the time to forget about our duties and obligations. After relieving myself outside, I paused outside the open door to pet the barn cat that had ventured out. I could barely hear what Francie and Arturian were saying.

"Thank you for today. I needed it," Francie said.

"You don't have to thank me."

I walked to the door and looked around it, peering inside.

No.

I could barely see in the dim light, but Arturian had taken Francie's hand and was holding it on the table. I tensed upon noticing how they were looking at each other.

It's in your head.

"I always enjoy it when we spend time together... but I hope you understand that it can't stay this way forever," he said, looking into her eyes.

"What do you mean?" she asked. "Arturian... is something wrong?"

Before he could answer, an unfamiliar voice echoed from the other side of the stable. "Well, well, well. *This* is what you do while I'm gone."

Arturian pulled his hand away.

Augustus.

I could hardly make out his features in the faint candlelight, but his long black hair was bound behind his head and he wore a suit with long coattails. I was dumbfounded by his unexpected appearance; in all my years living on the Exley grounds, I had never seen Augustus in the flesh.

This isn't right... he's supposed to be gone.

"Father... I thought you had a meeting tonight?" Arturian said, standing from his chair. The shock of his arrival, combined with the effects of the wine, made their faces flush.

"I canceled it, and I'm glad I did. What an exciting night I've stumbled upon," he said, taking his time in approaching the pair. I stood still, knowing it would only make matters worse if I made my presence known.

"No, sir, this isn't what you think—" Arturian began, but Augustus interrupted him.

"Despite the darkness, I can tell she's *quite* beautiful." His voice was even—almost casual. "Why don't you open a fresh bottle for me, and I'll get to know her?" Augustus pulled a chair out and sat down at the far end of the table.

"Father—"

"Sit down," Augustus said to Francie, his voice edged with a well-practiced authority. She sat down. "Get my wine," he commanded Arturian, who followed the order with bated breath. He returned to the long table with a bottle and opened it for his father.

Augustus sat still for a moment, staring up at his son. "Hand me her glass," he said, and I couldn't help but notice the familiar surety in his tone. It was similar to how Arturian often spoke.

Arturian slid Francie's glass over to his father and poured. Augustus smiled suddenly, looking between Arturian and Francie. She kept her head down, her hair obscuring her face.

"I propose a toast!" Augustus held up his glass, staring at his son intensely. "My son has chosen a wife. That's the only reason you would have brought a young woman to our property, alone, *at night*. Am I correct?" He lowered the glass, eyes hardening. "I hope she has an impressive position... In society, I mean."

The temperature might as well have dropped twenty degrees. I held my breath as I remained hidden in the dark just outside the stable. The silence dragged on until Arturian put an end to it.

"She's nothing to me, Father," he said, and Francie's eyes flashed up to him for a moment. "She keeps me entertained when I can't travel," he finished with a callous disdain I had never heard from him.

Francie looked as if someone had slapped her. "Arturian... what are you doing?" Her voice was small—hurt. I resisted the overwhelming urge to run inside and take Francie out of there.

How could he say something like that about her?

A proud laugh escaped Augustus' lips. "It seems you've been misled, girl," he chuckled as he stood up, sipping his wine and turning to address Arturian. "Don't bring whores on Exley property. Don't create any bastard children." His tone was pure command—no room for argument.

Francie eyes darted between Augustus and Arturian in disbelief, and her expression collapsed into betrayal. She rose to her feet and made to run out the back door, but stopped in her tracks. "Now, now," Augustus called after her. "You won't want to miss this."

Augustus made his way over to Frenzy's stall and patted the magnificent horse's neck. "What a beautiful horse. I'm sure he ran well for you today."

I locked my jaw, my heart sinking as I witnessed the unsettling scene. Arturian and Francie waited in a paralyzed silence.

"I still remember when I got this horse for you... brought all the way from West Corlaea," he said as he led the horse out of his stall and into the middle of the stable, still stroking his neck and gazing in admiration. "You were so appreciative. You love this horse, don't you?"

Arturian responded with bated breath, "Yes, Father."

Augustus tied the horse's rope to a handle and walked to his son, placing a hand on his shoulder. "That is why I know this lesson will sink in." Without looking, Augustus swung his right arm to the side as if he were throwing something directly at the horse.

A sick squelching sound echoed out of the stable as a blade of wind as thin as a razor sliced through the horse's neck. Frenzy's head slid from his body and onto the floor with a thump; cut in a clean line.

Francie shrieked in terror, her hand covering her mouth.

Arturian dropped to his knees.

Frenzy's headless body fell sideways with an unsettling *thud*, and blood poured out onto the floor. It spread like a wildfire, soaking everything in its path.

My mind had difficulty processing what I was witnessing. A putrid, metallic smell wafted out of the stable doors, turning my stomach. My hands grew hot and sweaty as my heart pounded in my chest.

What is happening?

"Never again will you risk sullying our family name with slum trash," Augustus said, his voice cold. "Remember the words of our forefathers; 'That which a lifetime can build, can be felled In a single moment.'"

He let his words linger.

"Oh... and don't forget to send the maids out here to deal with this mess," Augustus said before walking out the way he came, stepping around pools of blood.

I couldn't stop staring at Frenzy's dead eyes. His exposed bones. I glanced away for a moment and saw Arturian rising from the floor, his eyes wide as he turned to Francie.

She bolted for the back door; terror written all over her face. "Wait!" Arturian cried out, but she didn't stop. She passed by without seeing me, but I followed her into the darkness and toward the trail in the woods.

As soon as I was sure we were out of earshot, I called out to her. "Francie! Wait, it's me!"

She gasped and turned, raising her arms in defense. After realizing it was me, she relaxed and wiped the tears from her face.

"Levick... oh, goodness," she said, trying hard not to choke up. She threw her arms around me, trembling uncontrollably.

She cried in my arms under the faint glow of the moon and I held her tight, as if that could stop her terrified shaking. I couldn't tell how long we stayed like that—time stood still.

After taking a deep breath, she pulled away from me and we continued our walk towards the woods. Her condition visibly improved as we distanced ourselves from what had transpired, but we walked in silence until we reached the forest trail that led to the bell tower. I stole occasional glances at her, but didn't speak.

"You saw everything?" she asked.

"I did." The sounds of our feet crunching on branches and stray leaves echoed through my brain.

"Why would he do that?" she said it so quietly, I almost missed it. I inched closer to her, and our shoulders almost touched as we walked. "I can't believe *that* is Arturian's father..." she mumbled.

"He *killed* Frenzy... just like that," I said, unable to get the image out of my mind.

"I'd never seen him in person before," she whispered.

Arturian always avoided talking about his father. He would take business trips and network with other noble families to please him. There was even a time when he attempted to get into the queen's social circle and forged a friendship with her son, Prince Harley. However, something must've fallen through, because he didn't continue that mission for very long. Arturian hated the political scene, so I always assumed he did those things for his father's sake.

The lie Arturian told his father repeated in my mind. He would rather his father think he was having a casual affair with Francie than to know the truth—that they're friends.

We made it back to the bell tower, and Francie paused near the doors. "I can walk alone from here, Lev. Thank you," she said, staring into the woods in front of her.

"You shouldn't walk alone at night, Francie. Especially after a night like this one." I began walking past the tower and towards the next trail, which led into town.

I felt her grab my hand before saying, "No, you don't have to go all that way..."

When I looked back, I saw her expression and knew what she was asking. She didn't want to go any further.

I turned and wordlessly led her into the bell tower.

"Don't let me be a burden, Lev. I can sleep down here!" She tugged at my hand as I led her toward the staircase.

"You're not sleeping on the ground floor, Francie," I said as we made our way up. As we reached the top, I silently thanked myself for having cleaned the entire bell tower.

"You'll sleep there." I gestured to my bed, next to the window.

"Levick, I won't kick you out of your bed in your own house," she replied.

I chuckled to myself. "Technically, it's Arturian's house..."

"You know what I mean," she said in mock exasperation.

I pulled down the covers and gestured for her to come over. With a grateful smile, she climbed into the bed, pulling the covers up and over her chin.

"Goodnight, Francie," I said with a soft smile, then headed for the staircase.

"Wait—where are you going?"

I turned back to her incredulously. "I'm going downstairs."

"To sleep where?"

"The floor, I suppose. I've slept in much worse places."

She shook her head. "If you're going to sleep on the floor anyway, can't you sleep on this floor?"

Being a gentleman in manners, I hesitated. However, one brief moment of staring into her pleading blue eyes was all it took for me to cave.

She gave me one of her blankets and I spread it next to the bed. After I laid down on it, she whispered, "Thank you," in a groggy voice.

After a few quiet moments, I responded. "I'd do anything for you, Francie."

The only reply I received was a light snore, and I smiled to myself.

Anything.

CHAPTER SEVEN
THE HEIR

ARTURIAN

The ancient kingdom of Friese has long stood as a titan of trade and commerce. Its bustling fishing industry and strategic, protected port ensure a steady flow of wealth and influence. Blessed with a mild climate and a large population, Friese commands both respect and envy from neighboring nations. But what truly sets this kingdom apart isn't its economic might—it's a singular, awe-inspiring phenomenon found nowhere else in the world.

Among Friese's noble elite, a select few wield a power both elegant and lethal: the ability to summon and shape razor-thin gusts of wind. Known as windblades, these invisible forces cut with the precision of a master's blade and the fury of a tempest. Each windblade is one of a kind, often designated with a personal name, and they are widely recognized as the deadliest weapons in human history. In the hands of their wielders—the Skylords—these deadly currents can strike unseen, severing steel, stone, and flesh alike, turning the noble houses of Friese into an unstoppable force on both the battlefield and in the shadowy games of power.

Whoever kills a Skylord inherits his windblade. *Therefore, most windblades are inherited through planned patricide. Near the end of a Skylord's life, whether he is dying by age or illness, his chosen heir is made to kill him before natural causes do.*

If a Skylord dies of a natural cause, or is killed by another Skylord, his power is lost. Many scholars theorize this power is absorbed into the atmosphere, eventually creating hurricanes and storms. Skeptics believe the windblade's power is simply gone, a diminishing resource never to be used again. The belief amongst the common man, however, is that this power is returned to Echna, the goddess of wind. When the time is right, Echna uses that power to create windwalkers—individuals nat-

urally gifted with a broad control of the winds. Unfortunately, these are largely unknown, with no documented cases in centuries.

- A History of Wind Control, Prof. Heliana Fromme

*A*lmost a bullseye.

I grabbed another knife from my set and launched it through the air.

Barely in the white.

I clenched my jaw, picked up another, and sent it into the bullseye.

There it is. In the red.

I stared down my target, which was looking like an overused pin-cushion. Throwing knives was one of my many methods of blowing off steam. It was also perfect practice for my eventual inheritance of Asgora, the ancestral windblade of House Exley.

The blade that just killed Frenzy.

I felt the weight of my grief and guilt as I replayed the scenes over and over in my mind.

I'm sorry, Frenzy. I was careless.

I walked over to the target and pried the knives out, spinning one in my hand as I finished the job.

Why? Why did he have to be there?

I arranged the knives back into their case. I'd been throwing for hours, but knife therapy hadn't been working like it used to.

For a moment, I wished I'd told my father the truth about my friends, but that moment passed in an instant.

It would've gotten them both killed.

I replayed the exchange over in my head endlessly. I'd lied and betrayed Francie, and my father decapitated my horse in front of her. She might never speak to me again. As much as that would crush me, I couldn't shake the thought that it might be for the best. I twisted my house ring on my finger, feeling the eight-carat black diamond at the center.

Father walked in right when I was about to tell her...

At breakfast, my father hadn't mentioned the previous night. But I could still hear the squelching sound of Frenzy getting cut in two... I could still smell the blood.

He had gotten his point across.

At nineteen years old, I was expected to participate in my house's business meetings as often as possible. Given House Exley's many enemies and few allies, it was logical for the sole heir to be prepared for unforeseen tragedies and the responsibilities that followed. Later that day, I was scheduled to join my father in a meeting at the port. However, I would be absent.

House Exley had cornered the market for metal importation for multiple generations. As Friese became more developed, the demand for metals continued to rise, cementing the Exley's position as one of the most powerful families in the kingdom. We shipped most of our imports across the Broad Sea from

Corlaea—a trade-wealthy nation with a powerful military. Our family's monopoly on metal trade had grown our influence over the queen of Friese, and she wished to stay involved in the proceedings as much as possible.

Queen Lesynna Ainsworth was the third of her family to rule the kingdom of Friese. For generations, their family controlled most of the local resources, including fishing and farming. Emboldened by their growing wealth, Lesynna's grandfather rallied the other houses to his aid and seized the crown for himself. The Ainsworths had controlled the Friesian throne ever since.

The queen was the first and only woman to wield a windblade—Friese was historically patriarchal, and only men were permitted to inherit windblades. As Lesynna's father, the king, was dying, she took advantage of his increasing blindness, and disguised herself as her older brother, the true heir. She slew her father and inherited his windblade, Ascheron, along with the throne.

I briefly wondered if I would miss an audience with the queen by skipping the meeting. Then, my mind took me back to the sound and smell of my horse dying a gruesome death. The look on Francie's face when I lied about her. The sound of her sobs as she ran away in terror.

I put the meeting out of my mind and continued on my way up into my rooms. As I sat in my bath, I wondered what Levick would think of me once Francie told him what had happened.

Have I just lost both of my friends?

"Levick? Are you awake?" I called through the doors of the bell tower. It was mid-morning, so it was likely he was already working at the inn.

Hearing no response, I began climbing the spiral staircase. Morning light flooded through the massive circular window on the top floor. A mess of hair stuck out of the covers of Levick's bed. *Blonde* hair.

Francie.

The sight hit me like a punch to the gut.

What did you expect after what she saw last night?

I stared for a moment too long—twisting the knife in my own wound. Tearing my gaze away, I climbed back down the spiral staircase. As I exited the tower and walked back to Satine, I saw Levick approaching in the distance. We both stopped dead upon seeing each other.

Even from afar, Levick's expression cut through me like a knife. I knew Levick could forgive a transgression against himself. But against Francie?

I broke the stare, mounted my horse, and took off into the woods.

Upon walking back to my house from the stable, I noticed a large black coach sitting in the drive, covered in silver silk ornamentation. Only one coach in Friese looked like that.

"My son, I see you've returned from your engagement?" My father's voice greeted me from the drawing room. While his tone would be unremarkable to most, I knew it well. Father was enraged by my absence at the port meeting.

Before I could answer, the corner chair came into view. Upon it sat Queen Lesynna, Sovereign Skylady of Friese. Her black hair had been arranged in intricate braids around her head and down her shoulders, and she wore a plunging dress of blood red. Her age was imperceptible—her skin seemed smooth as glass.

I attempted to shake off my shock at seeing her so casually seated in my drawing room. "My Queen, I am your humble servant." I knelt in front of her, but she quickly motioned me up. Her dark eyes studied me as I stood before her.

"I was disappointed by your absence at our meeting today. I would expect the sole heir of such a grand house to take more interest in the business affairs of Friese," she said, not breaking her gaze. The queen spoke precisely, measuring each word. I stole a glance at my father, whose expression remained perfectly controlled.

"My deepest apologies, Your Grace. I am at your disposal whenever you require me," I said, my tone deferential. I could almost feel my father's eyes rolling in response.

The queen broke into melodic laughter. "Oh Augustus, such obedience from a son! If only my children would follow suit!" The queen's two children—Prince Harley and Princess Eadlin—had reputations for being ruled by no one. Though unfamiliar with Eadlin, my experiences with Harley led me to concur.

Her laughter calmed, and with perfect poise, she resumed her intense stare at me. "Where do your loyalties lie, Arturian Exley?"

I was speechless for a moment; her question caught me off-guard.

What does she mean?

"With you, always, Your Majesty," I said with a respectful bow of the neck. A long pause passed between us.

After some consideration, she began speaking. "For many generations, even back to the days of our houses' great forefathers, the fates of Exley and Ainsworth have been intertwined. Agriculture and metal; food and industry; life and power. I hope you realize the gravity of this relationship—not merely for our houses, but for all of Friese."

I understood her meaning. I'd suspected my father of colluding with the queen for some months, but hadn't been sure. *That* was the purpose of her visit... to confirm my loyalty and discretion for the future.

But what are they colluding on? Why would the queen feel as if she had to work with us at all?

Father must have leverage over her.

His expression was one of warning. My involvement wasn't optional.

"Of course, Your Majesty. What is good for the throne is good for Exley," I said, earning a very reserved but satisfied look from my father.

"I'm glad to hear it," she responded, standing to leave. Her guards opened the doors for her and followed her out.

"Father, please explain to me why the queen of Friese was in our drawing room, interrogating my loyalty," I said, using my well-practiced self-control to maintain a respectful tone.

I had my suspicions, but I'd avoided dwelling on them. My ignorance had been blissful—I had no desire to be involved in whatever shady business my father was conducting. However, my hand had been forced.

"I'm sure you've had suspicions; you would be a fool not to. But the truth goes beyond what you can imagine," Father said, sitting down in one of our ornate chairs. I sat down opposite him.

He swirled his glass of salt rum, staring at it with sharp eyes, dark as coal. "House Ainsworth has been losing relevance for decades. They disregarded the importance of trade across the Broad Sea for years. They've poured money into production of products that are cheaper to import, and now they are paying for their obstinance."

"Their isolationist bent has been public knowledge for years, Father. What does this have to do with us?" I asked, checking my tone again.

"We've surpassed Ainsworth in both wealth and influence. They are no longer the force they once were."

My jaw dropped.

"Father... how? When did this happen?" I asked, my throat going dry.

"Our house controls all metal trade in Friese, and metal is all anyone wants to build with anymore."

I put my forehead in my hands. The implications of the news were mind-boggling. The throne of Friese had always belonged to the wealthiest house. With wealth followed power, and with power followed influence. The allegiance of the lesser houses was largely influenced by wealth and power.

She's scared and trying to prevent a power-grab.

"On top of that," Augustus continued, "a rebellion group that calls itself the 'Revolt of the Common Man' has been a thorn in Lesynna's side for a year, now. They've ransacked half a dozen of the new Ainsworth trade ships at port, and she's made no headway in stamping it out. She uses all of her resources to keep the other houses from knowing, but there is blood in the water."

A rebellion in Friese?

My chest felt tight. "What does this mean?" I asked.

"The queen is desperate to keep control, but she senses a threat from us. She has waived taxes and inspections on our imports in an attempt to keep us comfortable and satisfied," Augustus responded, taking a light sip of his drink.

I jerked my head up. "Father... if the other houses find out—"

"Yes. They would levy charges of collusion."

I played the odds out in my mind. "But... no one will find out. The queen will never let it slip because it would expose her and her house's weakness."

Father stood. "Now that you know our... advantageous position, I expect you to behave accordingly." Father cleared his throat in an unusual display of anxiety. It was so out-of-character that I found it more unnerving than if he'd yelled at me.

What is he not telling me?

"Our talent at strategy may not be from Exley blood, but it is invaluable to our success," he said, his tone uncomfortable.

"What do you mean by that? I thought Grandfather was a brilliant man?"

"Whoever said that was woefully misinformed..." Father said under his breath. "But that is beside the point. There's something I've meant to tell you for some time now. Once learned, I hope this truth will show you the risks of not fully committing to this house's success," he said, walking closer.

"You are not a legitimate heir."

The words didn't register.

"You are not a legitimate heir, because *I* am not."

CHAPTER EIGHT
CURSED LINEAGE

Titles are inherited. True power is earned.
- Augustus Exley

I was known for my meticulous scheming. Every move and every detail were carefully planned and executed. If a variable existed, I rigged it or removed it entirely. Despite inheriting a windblade, I still felt the relentless need to prove myself and earn my position. Because I carried a damning secret. One that would certainly ruin me and my house if it were made public.

I was a bastard.

Like myself, my mother Prosé had a reticent nature, masterfully concealing her true thoughts—and secrets—from everyone. It was this quality that successfully hid her indiscretions from even her husband, the leader of House Exley. It was only by happenstance that I discovered the truth of my parentage in my early teenage years.

Twenty-eight years ago

It was one week before my thirteenth birthday, and I'd come home early from a trip abroad to surprise my parents. I'd learned from a guard outside that my father had been called away on business—deflating my excitement. However, I could still surprise my mother. Upon entering the master's wing of the house, I heard an unfamiliar voice. A *man's* voice.

Thinking quickly, I crept along the hallway, nearing the parlor. I peered around the corner, and witnessed my mother arguing with a tall, thin man with alabaster skin and jet-black hair. She stood in front of one of our many plush velvet couches, her deep brown hair cascading over her shoulders in glossy waves. She was a stunning woman, whose dark brown eyes complimented her warm, autumnal complexion.

"He deserves to know. He's almost thirteen, for stone's sake!" The stranger hissed, standing from his seat to approach my mother. She stood her ground, unafraid of him.

"If you tell him, he'll lose everything! His house, his name, his *father!* If you truly cared about him, you would never jeopardize his future like that," she responded, her voice firm.

The man shook his head and stared into the lit fireplace. "He's *my* son, Prosé. Not his. I've missed *everything.*" His countenance became anguished and his breathing quickened. The fire glowed and reflected off the man's face, highlighting the few wrinkles beginning to form near his dark blue eyes.

Mother approached the man and raised a tender hand to his face. "I wish it didn't have to be this way," she said, so softly that I could barely hear her from my hiding place.

"He would kill me, Julius. You know it's true," she whispered. Silent sobs finally erupted from his chest, and he leaned into her touch.

My heart pounded.

It can't be...

I fought to remain silent, barely suppressing a gasp. Their quiet murmuring no longer audible, I slowly backed away from the corner and made my way back down the hall. A hundred thoughts raced through my mind as I neared one of the smaller back doors. I opened it and made my way back over to my horse. My hands shook as I grabbed the reins, mounted, and urged him forward. My heart thundered, matching the hoofbeats as I retreated into the Exley grounds.

I rode my horse through the rippling fields, the rhythmic pounding of hooves against the earth barely registering in my mind. The wind swept past me, carrying with it the scent of freshly turned soil and the faint sweetness of distant wildflowers. But even the beauty of the landscape, the whisper of the breeze, the earthy texture of the air, couldn't quiet the storm raging inside of me.

I am a fraud.

The thought gnawed at me, each repetition digging deeper into my chest like a sharpened blade. My fingers tightened around the reins, but the grip felt distant. The land of my upbringing suddenly felt foreign to me. How had it come to this? How had I allowed myself to believe that the title, the wealth, the power, were truly mine to wield? Despite my relentless hard work at just thirteen, my success was built on a foundation of lies.

I am unworthy of my name.

The renowned name of Exley, heavy with expectation, smothered me; a legacy I felt unable to bear. What had it all been for? The walls of my own identity seemed to close in, the reality of my existence fraying at the edges. I was to inherit the Exley windblade, a symbol of power and authority, but now, in the solitude of the fields, it felt more like a mockery of my true self. Could I, in good conscience, carry the name of Exley when my bloodline was so... corrupted?

Wild with anger, I whipped my horse on. I rode for miles until I reached my place of respite: an old bell tower on the edge of the Exley estate, abandoned when I was an infant.

I slammed opened the door and sprinted up the stairs, not stopping until I reached the top.

"No one can know," I spoke aloud. My favorite thing about the bell tower was that I could work through my thoughts and feelings out loud, as there was no one around to hear them.

"No one can know," I repeated, still panting from exertion.

As I gazed out through the large circular window, a hawk flew nearby, carrying a field mouse. He flapped his wings, hovering high in the air. Then, to my surprise, the hawk dropped the mouse, letting it fall forty feet to its death.

"No one can know," I said for a third time. "There can be no living souls who know this truth."

The death of Lady Exley was an unexpected tragedy. None of her close friends knew she was going through such serious troubles. After all, only a very troubled woman would throw herself head-first off of the roof of the Exley mansion.

Chapter Nine
Prelude to a Tragedy

ARTURIAN

My breath came in ragged gasps. The ground beneath my feet seemed to spin, the edges of my vision blurring as the weight of the revelation crushed down on me, relentless and suffocating.

My father... killed his own mother. To hide his true lineage.

"That means... the true Exley bloodline ended with Grandfather," I thought aloud.

"Yes," my father replied.

A concerning question dulled my emotional response. "Your true father... what happened to him?"

Father took a deep breath. "His name was Julius, and I never found him. He disappeared. If he meant me harm, he would've done it by now." I couldn't help but feel like he was trying to convince himself of that, too.

Father lowered his voice and stared into my eyes. "*A single moment.* Never forget that. A single moment to rise, and a single moment to fall. *Do not* be the downfall of this house, Arturian." He turned to leave, but paused in the doorway. "That means

no more port slum sluts. You must remain marriageable."
With that, he left.

Hampton hadn't been very tamed from the previous day's
ride. I held on tightly as my horse galloped beneath me,
barely under control.

A good metaphor for how my life is feeling right now.

The setting sun illuminated the field in bright orange as
we barreled on toward the forest trail. I didn't have a plan for
when I got there, I just needed to get away from my father.
On and on we raced, hitting leaves and small branches as
we went. We emerged from the familiar thicket into the bell
tower's clearing, and I pulled Hampton to a sudden halt.

Francie was sitting under the old tree next to the tower,
a book in her hand. She stared at me, her mouth opened in
surprise.

"Francie…" I started, not sure what to say. No words
seemed sufficient. "Is Levick here?"

She stood up and held a guarded posture. "No… he isn't.
I'll tell him you stopped by."

I dismounted and walked toward Francie until I was only a
horse-length away. Contrary to my expectation, she didn't back
away from me. As we stood under the shade of the vast and
richly-blooming tree, a thousand unsaid words hung between
us. I couldn't help but feel as if she had ventured beyond my

reach. Her eyes were distrustful, but I could've sworn I saw a slight flash of something else there. Hope, maybe?

Hampton reared up and let out a whinny, breaking the moment as I calmed the wild animal.

"Why did you lie about me?" Francie asked, coldness returning to her face.

I meditated on the question for a long moment. "He would kill you, Francie. Both of you."

Pursing her lips, Francie looked down at her feet and nodded.

I closed the gap between us to take her hand, but she snatched it away and backed up a few paces until her back touched the tree trunk. Those simple actions were a knife in my heart.

"Francie... it's the only thing that would've worked. His assumptions about the slums made it believable for him," I said through a strained throat.

She stared at me for a long moment before asking, "What do *you* think of me, Arturian?"

My heart stopped for a moment. "You know what I think of you," I said, absently taking a few steps closer.

"What if I don't? Not *really*..." Insecurity crept into her features.

"*Francie,*" I said forcefully. "You know."

Regret pinched at the corners of her eyes as she stared at me. "What were you going to say to me? Before your father came in?"

I glanced at the ground, my jaw clenched. I was hesitant to delve into the subject—I'd planned on telling her I was going to be unavailable for a while due to official house duties. While it bore a touch of truth, my primary reason was my concern that I'd act on my growing feelings for Francie. As much as I wanted to, doing such a thing would put a target on her back. The previous night had only confirmed that.

However, I didn't want to inflict any more suffering on my friends. But before I could stop it, the image of her sleeping in Levick's bed flashed through my mind.

"What does it matter anymore?" I asked, a dark smoke swirling through my emotions.

She furrowed her eyebrows, cocking her head. "What do you mean?"

"You and Levick will be just fine without me," I said as I walked past her. To my surprise, she grasped my arm, sending my heart racing at her touch.

"What do you mean 'without me'? Are you leaving?" she asked with a look of genuine sadness that struck me to the core. I looked down at her as she held me there.

"I won't let go until you answer me," Francie whispered as she stared at me, eyes just inches from mine.

Before thinking, I said, "I saw you this morning. In the bell tower."

My words caused an immediate reaction, and I regretted the confession immediately. Her expression turned from sadness to confusion, and then to suspicion. "Why didn't you say something? Or talk to me at all?"

Why did I have to bring it up?

"You were sleeping," I murmured, searching her eyes. I watched her blue eyes widen as she realized what I'd assumed.

"He wouldn't let me sleep on the floor. I told him I would, but he wouldn't have it."

"It's not my business what you and Levick do," I said distantly, hating myself for it.

Her eyes darkened in betrayal—an expression that had become all too familiar to me. "We didn't *do* anything, Arturian. Are you saying you don't believe me?"

I did believe her. But I saw how it would play out. How it *should* play out. Regardless of how I felt.

"Arturian?" she asked again, as she waited for a response. After taking a deep breath, I wrapped my arms around her. I tried to savor the moment as much as I could—feeling her hair under my hands, her heart beating against my chest.

The leaves on the tree above us rustled softly, their gentle whispers blending with the songs of the resident birds. But as the melody carried through the air, it began to twist, taking on a sorrowful tone—like the haunting prelude to a tragedy.

CHAPTER TEN
THE REVOLT

I didn't know how to react as Arturian held me close under the oak tree. I sensed he was hiding things from me, but for a moment, my desire to mend our friendship was stronger than my anger and suspicion. I let my face rest against his chest, and he rested his cheek on my head. My heart raced as he held me in his powerful arms, exposing my years-worth of denial. His black shirt was soft and smelled like well-oiled leather. I briefly noticed that his top buttons were undone.

After a few silent moments, he kissed my hair, sending my heart racing once again. To my displeasure, he soon broke away. His long dark hair swayed in the breeze as he looked into my eyes with an expression that seemed like deep sorrow. Then, with no explanation, he turned, mounted his horse and disappeared into the woods.

With conflicted emotions in every step, I continued through the old-growth forest, subconsciously headed towards the path leading out of the grounds. As I strode away, tree limbs and thorns tore from my path at the flicker of my windblade. Using my windblade always helped to clear my mind when it became muddled or overwhelmed.

It feels like we're losing him. Why did that hug feel like a goodbye?

Arturian had been my friend since I was young—same as Levick. However, the gulf between our stations felt like it was broadening by the day.

I was no longer a young girl, blind to the mounting tensions between the social classes. Sometimes I felt guilty for spending time with Arturian on his lavish estate. I'd hold my tongue while watching him feed his gourmet leftovers to his dogs, and then I'd go back home and watch families starve in the slums. I'd been holding a small amount of resentment toward Arturian for a long time—offset by more complicated feelings I knew could never bear fruit.

Then there was Levick. Though he'd refused to acknowledge the events of the previous night, I could see his jaw clenched as he stewed about, completing minor tasks in the bell tower before heading into town some hours earlier on "errands."

I'd reached the edge of the trail when I saw Levick walking towards me. His mousy hair had gotten long—it was about time for me to cut it. I noticed with some bittersweetness that there weren't many vestiges left of the boy I'd found in the rain so many years ago. His boyhood nearly behind him, Levick was starting to fill out his clothing as his younger gangly-ness gave way to a strong frame.

"Hey, I'm heading to the inn. Did you check in with Crysta?" I asked as he got closer.

"Yeah, she said she's good today," he responded in a skeptical tone. Crysta had a habit of taking on too much work because she wanted to let us "be kids and enjoy youth."

"I'll go in and check on her," I said, pausing in front of him. I almost began walking past him to the slums, but he looked like he was deciding whether to say something.

"I won't tell you what to do... but I might keep my distance from Arturian for a little while. Especially if Augustus has become suspicious..." he mumbled.

I sighed in resignation. "I think we might not see as much of him for a while."

Levick breathed in deeply, shaking his head. "Arturian is already so alone out there,"

I nodded. "Maybe this isn't forever... maybe he just needs some time for things to settle," I said as I took his hand. He stared down at me with a look I wasn't sure I'd seen before.

"I'll let you get going, then. Crysta is worried about you," he said, backing away towards the forest trail. "I'll see you tomorrow!" He waved at me.

I said goodbye and began my walk to the slums.

The next few weeks passed uneventfully. Levick and I worked at the inn with Crysta and spent our free time outside enjoying the summer weather. Arturian made no contact with us, which was unsurprising but disappointing. I wasn't sure how long it would be before either of us saw him again. I tried to ignore the aching in my heart.

Over the last few days, the demand for free dinners at the inn increased, placing a strain on us. A fire had broken out on one of the docked cargo ships and injured more than a dozen dock workers, leading to more hungry families, unable to earn a living.

At least the dockmasters salvaged the luxury silks for the noble houses.

Never mind the seven fatherless families and the dozen or so badly injured men, the worst of whom were left disfigured and permanently unemployable. Those sorts of accidents seemed to be occurring more frequently as the port struggled to meet the demands of a rapidly growing city.

After finishing hours-worth of cleanup, I removed my apron and tossed it in the kitchen laundry basket. I could feel the weariness weighing on me, threatening to close my eyes before I made it upstairs.

A knock sounded from the front door and I threw my head back, pressing my eyes closed. "You'd think the sign on the door would be enough..." I muttered to myself as I walked over. It had been a long and discouraging week.

I'd barely cracked the door open when someone shoved it ajar. He might've been the largest man I'd ever seen, but he moved so quickly that I couldn't discern much more about him.

He forced me down and shoved a gag in my mouth, holding off my defenses as if I was a small child. I kicked away from the stranger, my screams muffled and lost in the dirty tasting gag. I landed a kick to his head, but it did nothing to slow him. He was upon me again in seconds, flipping me over and pressing me onto the wooden floor. I thrashed as he straddled me and tied my hands together behind my back, rendering my windblade useless.

My mind raced with a thousand questions.

Is this about my windblade? How would he know? What does he want with me?

My ribs ached from his massive weight on me. When he was done tying my hands, he pulled a burlap bag out of his pocket. After forcing it over my head, only faint patches of light remained visible. Hefting me onto his shoulder as if I were a sack of flour, he disappeared into the night.

He's making circles.

I shook uncontrollably as I bumped along in the back of a cart, fear having sunk its poisonous claws into me. I'd been laying there for at least half an hour, trying to piece together how anyone could know about my windblade.

Dear Echna... I'm going to die. I'll never see Crysta again. I'll never see Levick or Arturian again.

Bitter regret twisted in my heart as I thought of them.

I thought about how Levick deserved honesty and openness from someone who claimed to be a dear friend. He possessed an extraordinary goodness, a stark contrast to his harsh beginnings, yet I *lied* to him. Every day, for years.

Then, there was *him*. The object of my forbidden desire, and the storm brewing under the surface of my every thought. Like a bolt of lightning, one passionate strike could engulf me in flames and burn everyone around me. Even so, I couldn't help but wonder how it would feel in those brief seconds before the burning devastation... when there was only *heat*.

The cart's stop jolted me from my thoughts, then my kidnapper heaved me over broad shoulders. I winced as my head hit what I assumed was a doorframe.

"Sorry 'bout that," my abductor said in a surprisingly casual tone.

What kind of kidnapper apologizes to his victim?

Warmth enveloped my body as we entered the building, and a small amount of soft light filtered through the sack over my head. My captor lowered me into a cushioned chair, and I immediately pulled my knees up and shrunk back from him.

"Did we have to do it this way?" a feminine voice asked.

"We talked about this ad nauseam. This is the only way," a masculine voice said from a few feet away. "You can take the sack off, Ress."

The first person I saw was a burly man in his twenties, hair shaved short and clean. He had tattoos of vines weaving all around his muscular arms, and a few up his neck as well. As he stood up straight, I figured he was the one who'd captured me—his head nearly touched the ceiling.

He backed away, revealing three more people standing in a fire-lit room—two of which I recognized from the inn. In the center stood a middle-aged man in a utility vest, an older gentleman to his left, and a small brunette to his right.

"Before I remove your gag, I'd like to explain who we are and why we brought you here," the man in the vest said. "My name is Orin Strickland. This man is my father, Tangier," he said, motioning to the older man.

That's the man who mistook me for someone else. Someone who used to work in a noble house...

I hoped it wasn't my mother he was recognizing.

"Tattoos over there is Ress, and to my left is my wife, Nina." Orin walked closer to me and sat on a stool in front of me. I did my best to look fierce, but I could tell I was failing.

"You may recognize my father and I from your inn. My father certainly thought he recognized you. I didn't believe him, but I had you followed for a little while—just in case. You're very talented with your *bow*," he said, leaning in close. "How long have you been keeping *that* little secret?" He cocked his head and motioned to my bound hands, smiling. He leaned back and motioned to someone.

I felt Ress untie my gag from behind my head. I cleared my throat before asking, "My arms too? They're in a lot of pain."

Orin laughed in my face. "You think I was born yesterday? Piss off. Now tell me. How well do you use that windblade of yours, *Skylady*?" His dark eyes stared me down hard. I swallowed, unsure of what to say.

No use in lying at this point.

"Why don't you untie me and find out," I growled. "Why am I here?"

Orin stood and walked over to the fireplace, then turned back to me. "The noble houses have doubled their wealth in the past four decades. As a fellow slum-dweller, I'm sure you already knew that—you're feeding more impoverished families from your inn's kitchen than you ever have before." He ran his hand through his long hair, pacing as he spoke.

"Meanwhile, the Yorkes sit on their fat asses counting gold in their marble banks, and the Exley brat is probably on his fifth foreign prize horse." I bristled at the mention of Arturian, but no one seemed to notice.

"There is only one way to break up the large monopolies of wealth in Friese." He came over and leaned close to me, hands gripping the armrests of my chair. "Inter-house civil war."

I stiffened. "You want to set the houses against each other?"

"That's where you come in. When the nobles have the only windblades, we have no chance. But here you are." He leaned in until I could see the gleam in his eye.

"We are the Revolt of the Common Man, and we are planning to overthrow the Queen of Friese. Will you help us?"

Orin summoned his wife, Nina, who then sat on the chair opposite me. He nodded to her, and she cleared her throat. "Corruption is rampant in our aristocracy. Our spies, as anticipated, have revealed countless inconsistencies from the ruling houses. There are few true guarantees in life, but corruption is one of them." She chuckled, brushing away an errant lock of hair. "So you can imagine our surprise when one of our sources uncovered a surprisingly generous tax break with one of the influential houses. It seems our queen has exempted all import and export taxes, including fees and sales taxes. Although she's managed to conceal it from the other houses, we suspect they'll object to this preferential treatment."

Orin sat back down in front of me and stared at me expectantly. Despite my fear, I nearly scoffed at their nerve.

"You've just had me bound, gagged, and thrown over the shoulder of a giant. Please, tell me why I should listen to a word you say instead of whispering your plans to the closest Crown Police officer? I've heard information on potential treason can fetch quite a price." I stared him down.

"Quite bold of you to assume you'll have that opportunity." He leaned closer. "There is a much *simpler* way of acquiring your windblade than convincing you to join us." His tone was low and even, and sent shivers up my spine. "In fact, the queen and the High Skylords would be *much* more interested in where you got your windblade than what we're doing. I think the queen relishes her false notion of being Friese's first and *only* Skylady... I wonder what she'd do to avoid sharing that title with anyone?"

My breathing quickened. We were at a stalemate—bound by mutually assured destruction. I felt the walls closing in on me as my agency disappeared.

The words escaped me in a breathy hiss, "I *will not* be your assassin." I shuddered as I considered the various violent ways they might employ me in their schemes.

Orin sat back in his chair, looking vexed. "That was never what we wanted from you."

"Bullshit."

"That isn't how we operate, despite my protestations. There are some members of the RCM who find murder and assassination a... *distasteful* tactic." His tone was light, but I didn't miss his subtle glance at his wife.

I looked between them, scanning for deceit, but found none. "You've not even told me your goal. What do you hope to achieve from all of this? Friese is a monarchy and always has been. Rule by the Skylords is unavoidable while they exist—they serve as our protection from foreign nations."

Nina looked at Orin, letting him answer. "We'd like to establish a new form of government where Skylords are *only* military leaders—not aristocratic overlords. It's the only way we could ensure the common folk got a say in anything."

I balked at him. "That would be a tall task, and I highly doubt any of you are up to that challenge. You may be soldiers and tacticians, but politicians? I think not," I said, scanning the room with a raised brow. Some looked offended, but Ress shrugged, nodding his agreement.

Orin smiled, a knowing look in his eyes. "Don't you feel it in the air? The season is changing, and times are ripe for the harvest." His lips twitched at the corners. "Let's just say we share common interests with some *very* influential backers who will ensure our success once the dust has settled."

I narrowed my eyes in suspicion, but could tell I wouldn't get any more information out of him. The idea of a fundamental change in Friese appealed to me, despite my distrust of the organization. As much as I hated the idea of conflict, I hated the seeing the sick children and dying fathers more.

"What would be my role?" I asked, to the enthusiasm of the rest of the room.

"Well, that didn't take long," Ress chuckled, smirking as he leaned against a door frame.

"If you're sure you're in, we'll get you briefed as soon as possible," Orin said with a tight smile.

"Honestly, I'm not sure. I've been tied up, tossed around, and threatened in the span of a few hours," I said, contempt heavy in my tone. "I'll only participate if I'm certain that my friends and I are safe."

I might be able to prevent the deaths and poverty, rather than just dealing with the aftermath.

"Well then, welcome to the Revolt of the Common Man," Orin said, gesturing to Ress to remove my restraints. I sensed a collective sigh of relief from all the members in the room.

"You're a Volty now," Ress said with a wink as he released my hands from their binding.

I glared at him before turning to Nina. "I forgot to ask... which house is it that's colluding with the queen?"

Nina smiled and laughed, clearly enthusiastic about having a Skylady in their ranks. "Oh, yes...It's the Exleys," she responded.

Well.

Shit.

CHAPTER ELEVEN
THE BREAKING POINT

We could benefit from your help these days. Something strange is happening here, but I don't know how to put it into words. It is almost as if the air in our home can't lay still... I'm uneasy. This may sound silly, but I feel haunted.
- Unsent Letter from Elie Roale

A cacophony rang through the inn as four bloodied men were carried in on stretchers. Surprised families moved their chairs aside to make room as screams echoed through the halls. Children cried and ran to their mothers, eyes wide in fear.

"We cleared some rooms, bring them up!" Crysta called out. I helped push chairs aside as men carried the injured workers up the stairs.

Anguished groans accompanied the screams of panic from their loved ones. Francie emerged from the back room, carrying her emergency medical kit. It was smaller than I remembered. It wouldn't be enough.

"I don't have the supplies to treat these men, and I *certainly* don't have the qualifications," Francie said, her voice tense as we rushed up the stairs. The stress seemed to have her on the verge of hyperventilating.

At the port, a dropped container crashed through multiple decks of a ship during unloading, injuring multiple men on the way down. The slum's hospital was full, and the queen recently passed laws barring slum residents from higher-class hospitals. The results were frequent bed shortages, and people dying from infection and blood loss in their homes.

Two men working below deck had their legs crushed by falling debris during the accident. One of them would require amputation. The third man fell into the sea and inhaled a large amount of seawater, but rescuers resuscitated him, and he was recovering. The fourth man was crushed from the waist down by debris, and his chances of survival looked slim. However, even in his dying moments, he maintained a white-knuckled grip on a sword, and was wailing incoherently. It was a sword the likes of which I'd never seen in Friese.

A foreign sword found on a trade ship...

Francie rushed past me to check on the other men, but I paused, peeking through the dying man's doorway.

"Import—" the man wheezed through agonized moans. I approached the man's bedside, kneeling down to be at his eye-level. Color was leaving his face—draining from numerous gashes and leaking into his bed sheets in crimson splotches.

"Important?" I asked, clasping the man's shaking hand. It was deathly cold.

He shook his head with the little strength as he could muster. "Sword—" he started, a ragged cough interrupting him, spewing blood over the bed. "Importing... weapons."

Swirling unease filled my stomach.

Someone is importing weapons into Friese. But who? And from where?

Pain pulsed through my hand—the dying man was squeezing it, staring at me with wide, bloodshot eyes. A disturbing gurgling erupted from his throat, sending blood bubbling from his mouth and down his chin. Clutching the man's hand, I heard his last breath whisper: "Thousands."

My jaw went slack.

Thousands of weapons?

The man's grip loosened, and I took a moment to process what I just experienced. I sat in silence, eyes pressed closed for a few long minutes, controlling my breathing before it became panicked. After taking a deep breath, I straightened up and gently closed the eyes of the deceased.

Wooden floor panels creaked behind me. Crysta appeared in the hallway, sleeves rolled and ready to help. She briefly checked the rooms and the wounded before rushing to me, a serious look on her face.

"He's gone," I said, clenching my jaw. Crysta bowed her head and pressed her eyes shut, wringing her hands together. After a moment, she shook her head and leveled her shoulders.

"Francie, would you secure a tourniquet for me?" Crysta called down the hall. Francie rushed over, nodding. Crysta motioned to the room across from us. In it lay a man with open, bleeding fractures. "That one will need an amputation."

Francie began walking over to his room, but froze mid-step, a contemplative look on her face.

"Secure the tourniquet on him, and we'll come amputate after we set his friend's leg," Crysta said, an authoritative firmness to her voice.

Snapping into action, Francie rushed into the room, but I grabbed the door before she shut it.

"I can handle a tourniquet, Lev," Francie said as she leaned over the man's mangled-looking calf, studying it.

"You don't need help? Where are the tourniquets?" I asked, eyes scanning the room.

"I've got it! Please, go help Crysta!" she cried in an urgent tone I'd seldom heard from her.

"Alright..." My instincts told me something was amiss. However, Francie was louder at the moment. "I'll come back as soon as I can," I said, closing the door behind me.

By the time I'd come out, Crysta had moved on to the last room and was waiting for me. "Help me set it," she commanded. Pink, blood-smeared bone protruded from a gory gash in the unconscious man's leg. Steeling myself, I complied.

As I walked back down the hall toward Francie's room, a glimmer in the first room caught my eye… the sword that the crushed man had been clutching in his arms. It was propped up next to the bed, which had since been cleared of the man's body.

Unable to control my curiosity, I made my way over to it. The sword was unlike anything I'd ever seen. Strange geometric symbols were inscribed along its long blade. The hilt was straight, forming into a diamond shape at the base of the handle.

"Crownies! They're heading this way, fast!" a young boy called up the stairs. I stepped into the hallway and looked down at the frazzled boy.

"How soon?" I asked. A heavy pit formed in my stomach as I thought of the sword.

"Minutes, and they look pissed!" The boy promptly disappeared down the stairs.

Down the stairs I raced, the sound of footsteps nearing. I cursed under my breath. Making a snap decision, I ran back up the stairs, grabbed the blade, and darted into the room across from it. I could hardly believe my actions—men had been killed for less in the port slums—but something told me I couldn't let them take that sword.

There was a shriek as I shoved open the door. Francie sat on the bed next to the wounded man and looked up at me like I was a ghost. One thing was clear immediately.

"You amputated *alone?*" I gasped. The man was still unconscious, but the lower part of his left leg was gone. I caught a glimpse of a perfectly clean cut just below the knee before Francie began wrapping it up with clean towels. There was a tourniquet fastened tightly above the amputation.

"I have it under control," she said quickly, before looking at me in confusion. "Why are you holding a sword?" she asked, clearly trying to redirect.

"The Crownies are coming and I think they're looking for it," I responded, shutting myself into the candlelit room and stashing the sword in the small closet.

"That's the sword from..." Francie trailed off, then looked at me with wide eyes.

"Yes, he's gone. I'm sorry, Francie. There was nothing we could've done. He was already standing on death's threshold when he arrived," I whispered. I could sense she was reaching a breaking point with the accidents and deaths occurring. "You amputated by yourself?" I asked, sitting on the foot of the bed.

"Yes, I did. There was a saw." Her voice broke a bit. "I used a saw." With careful, delicate motions, she finished wrapping the last towel over the tourniquet.

Why is she acting so dodgy?

There was a commotion outside—shouting and clattering sounds. I looked at Francie, mouthed "Crownies," and brought my index finger up to my lips. She nodded in acknowledgement, then gently held the injured man's hand.

I put my back against the door, barricading it. As I leaned against it, I found myself admiring Francie's nature of being so caring toward complete strangers. The bed was a bloody mess that would surely stain her light green skirt, but Francie didn't seem to notice. She held the unconscious man's hand, her eyes distant and distraught.

"Francie?" I whispered.

"It's not right. This man probably has a family—one that won't be able to feed themselves now. The Skylords... they're so flippant with our lives," she choked out as she wiped her tears away, inadvertently smearing blood across her cheek. She noticed too late and looked at her bloody hands in horror.

I felt helpless, unable to move from the door to comfort her without risking our safety. "We'll take care of the families, we always do. They won't starve." I tossed her a handkerchief.

She shook her head, as if that could clear it. "I don't know what I'm saying." She wiped the blood from her face with a trembling hand.

Suddenly, a series of loud bangs erupted from the door. "Open up! Crown police!" The blood drained from my face as Francie and I stared at each other. The handle turned, and someone pushed the door from the outside.

"This is a private room; we have an injured man in here," I yelled as I held the door shut.

"I have five men waiting outside—we'll get this door open," the guard threatened. "I'll count to five, and if I reach it, every-one here will be executed for obstruction," he growled, his voice audible through the crack in the door.

"One,"

Francie gestured for me to open the door.

"Two,"

If they find us hiding the sword... we'll be as good as dead, anyway.

"Three,"

"Levick!" Francie cried out.

"Four,"

Finally, I gave in and opened the door. The guard looked disappointed. He was tall, muscular, and outfitted in the pristine, dark blue garb of Friesian officers. He was of higher rank than most patrolling guards.

"What's the meaning of this?" Crysta's voice sounded from behind him. He turned to look at her, irritated.

"This man has just had his leg amputated!" She gestured to the bed and shoved past the guard. "Where is your pity?"

The guard's lip curled up in anger, but one of his subordinates rushed to his side before he could speak. I watched as the guard's brows furrowed at the report he received through hushed tones. He nodded in frustration and dismissed the younger guard. He narrowed his eyes, glaring at me in suspicion, before rushing out of the room and down the stairs.

When we heard the front door click shut, we all breathed a collective sigh of relief. Crysta stood before us—color completely gone from her face. "Thank goodness," she muttered. As she surveyed the room, her expression became one of concern. "You *amputated* without me?"

After a few hours, the amputee woke up, and in no small amount of pain. He told us his name before falling into a restless, alcohol-induced sleep. Crysta hated resorting to liquor to ease their pain, but it was all we could supply them.

The Crownies had nearly torn the rest of the inn apart, refusing to say what they were looking for. I'd been cleaning up and organizing for an hour when I realized I hadn't seen Francie since we left the amputee's room. I tried to appear casual as I brushed past volunteers helping to clean up.

"Hey Crysta, have you seen Francie?" I asked as I entered the dining room. She looked harried as she wiped down the bloodied floors. Her frizzy blonde-gray hair had been tied back and secured with a faded old scarf.

"Now that you mention it, no. Not since earlier." She looked up at me and raised an eyebrow. "I'm sure she just stepped out for a bit. Try not to worry about her too much. She's two years older than you, remember?" She smiled that knowing smile of hers. Crysta had always been very observant.

Or maybe I'm that obvious.

"Do you need any help in here?" I asked, eager to change the subject.

"No, no. You've done enough. Get some sleep. I'll see you in the morning," she said as she finished her scrubbing.

I breathed a subtle sigh of relief and made my way out into the dark streets to look for Francie.

CHAPTER TWELVE
BLOODED

While there is often some confusion about the distinction between the windwalkers and the Skylords, the differences are marked. Windwalkers had the ability to project strong, wide gusts of wind, unlike the extremely thin gusts of the windblade. Windblades are inherited through murder, while the inheritance of windwalking is largely speculation. Some claim it was hereditary and passed on to their genetic children. Others claim the windwalkers' line of succession was controlled by Echna herself, and therefore seemed to manifest mostly at random. The truth of it, however, is irrelevant. There hasn't been a known windwalker in Friese in centuries.

*- A History of Wind Control, Prof. Heliana
Fromme*

Traversing the rooftops unnoticed was much easier to do at night. I could take more liberties with my helpful wind gusts—sometimes clearing gaps of eight or ten horse-lengths. I made my way north across the slums and into the wealthier side of Friese.

Friese's slums and port sat on the eastern side of town, while the wealthier Friesians lived inland. The noble houses dominated the outskirts, wrapping around Friese like a chokehold. The Exleys were situated in the south, and the Ainsworths—the queen's house and palace—loomed in the north, just inland of the sea-cliffs. Some of the other major houses, such as the Yorkes, the Wemberleys and the Draughtons, buffered Friese to the west.

I made my way north. All three of us knew most of our meeting places. Not this one, though. This place was just between me and Francie. A large arboretum sprawled along the edge of the queen's estate, for use by the wealthier citizens in the northern business districts. The Crownies would never allow slum-dwellers into the gardens, but I learned they didn't monitor them closely at night.

After glancing around to make sure no one would witness, I approached the hedges that surrounded the garden, walked along the edge until I found a small gap, and crept through. I emerged into a small courtyard surrounding the famous austoria bushes. The flowers were in full bloom, wafting a pleasurable fragrance into the air.

Pale moonlight shone down on the engraved stone benches that surrounded the bushes. Upon one of those benches sat Francie, whose ethereal beauty struck me like I was seeing her for the first time. Her dark blonde hair was bound in a long braid down her back, and her smooth skin seemed to be made of perfect marble.

In the faint lighting, I could barely make out the figure of someone approaching Francie from the bushes. A short, grizzled man who, based on his silvery hair, appeared to be in his forties. I nearly ran out from my hiding place to interrupt the stranger, but before I could, Francie waved at the man in greeting. My eyes narrowed as I watched the scene play out in front of me. Their body language was relaxed, betraying a familiarity between them.

Fighting my instinct to disrupt the pair, I remained concealed and watched the interaction. The older man spoke urgently to Francie, to which she responded with nods and a tense posture. A couple of minutes of conversation passed before the man motioned north and beckoned Francie to follow him.

I furrowed my brows, an intense feeling of unease growing in my stomach. Francie and the stranger began retreating north through the gardens, and without a moment's hesitation, I took off after them. I followed along behind them just far enough to ensure they didn't notice me—ducking behind trees, shrubs, and statues at every opportunity. Massive statues loomed over me as I crept my way further north. The plants thinned out, stone walls and structures taking their place. The further they went, the heavier my dread became.

Turning around a bend, my fear was confirmed. A colossal iron gate stood before us, covered in embellishments. It trailed off in both directions, as if swallowed by the night itself.

The palace grounds.

Francie stopped and knelt before it, glancing left and right. The older man flicked his arm to the right, signaling for Francie to follow him. She nodded, and they snuck along the fence, heading east. I trailed behind them, making sure I remained quiet.

The fence led into dense foliage—any semblance of a clear path was gone. Despite being so far from the front gate, rotations of guards patrolled the grounds inside the fence. The dense trees and shrubs were the only things concealing us from sight.

Nearly half an hour had passed by the time Francie and the stranger had stopped in a slight dip next to the fence up ahead. The moonlight streamed through the trees, vaguely illuminating their forms. My heart raced as they whispered to each other, motioning to the fence. I clenched my fists at my side as I realized what they intended to do.

In that moment, my body was pure coiled, tense energy. Tight streams of air spiraled and twisted through my flexing fingers, coursing with power. Bursting from my position, I used a powerful gust to propel myself forward. The man's head jerked in alarm before taking up a defensive position in front of Francie. I knew I'd made a mistake by dashing full-speed at someone I didn't know, but I'd already set things in motion and was nearly upon him. The man's right hand swung backwards and over his shoulder. He flung it forward and released.

Throwing knife!

"Levick!" Francie hissed from behind her partner, eyes wide in recognition as the knife passed through my sleeve, grazing muscle.

Raging gale—

My shoulder exploded in pain, and I felt blood dribble in a warm mess down my arm. I groaned as I stumbled to a stop and grabbed a tree trunk for support.

"You know him?" My assailant turned and asked Francie, but she was already crossing the distance to me.

"Dak! What have you done?" she cried out, her voice breaking as she placed a shaking hand on my shoulder. "I'm so sorry..." She tilted her head, searching my expression for signs of distress.

"I'm okay, Francie. It's just a graze," I said, glaring at the man she called *Dak*. Calling it a *graze* was certainly an understatement, but Francie didn't need to know that.

"There's no time for this," the older man said, earning an icy stare from Francie.

"We make time for this, Dak. We can't just leave him here after you've thrown a knife through his arm." She clenched her jaw and turned back to me. "If you sit down, I'll wrap it." She gently pushed my shoulders down as she tore a long strip off the hem of her skirt, then began diligently wrapping it around the bloody wound. "Why were you following me?" I could barely see her through the darkness, but I could tell she was eyeing me in suspicion.

"If anyone owes explanations, it's you," I said, looking at her through fresh eyes. She was hiding something from me. Something big.

She looked back down at my shoulder as she wrapped it, waiting a long moment before speaking. "I can't say."

I raised my eyebrows, indignant. "You 'can't say?' You're wandering around the palace perimeter with a trained fighter and you expect me to just let it go?" I blinked in disbelief.

After seven years of friendship, she hides things from me?

I caught myself before I continued on my hypocritical thought process.

Stop it. You're a windwalker and a liar.

"If I tell you..." She sighed as she finished wrapping my arm and tied it up. "If I tell you, I can't protect you if something goes wrong."

"Nothing will go wrong if we move *right now*," Dak said in an irritated tone.

"What is he talking about?" I asked Francie, hoping she could see how serious I was. "What are you doing here, and who is *he*?"

Francie rose slowly and offered me a hand, which I declined. "Tell me," I demanded as I stood. A chilly wind blew through the ancient trees, giving me goosebumps as it slid over my skin.

"I've joined the Revolt."

"You can't be serious," I hissed, staring daggers at Dak.

She'd hastily explained that she'd joined the "Revolt of the Common Man,"—an organization that I'd never heard of—and then refused to give details about how she contributed.

"This is Dak. He's our infiltrator." She motioned to the older man, who stood next to the fence, completely still. "We received a tip that the queen is taking part in trade and tax collusion, and we're here to gather solid evidence from the palace."

My stomach dropped. If caught, they would certainly face execution. "The palace is the most patrolled place in Friese. What the hell are you thinking?" I struggled to keep my voice down.

"Watch it," Dak said, anger edging his voice. "We're doing the messy shit *everyone* knows needs to be done. You want to keep standing idly by as people die in the slums? Or will you do something about it?"

I worked my jaw, staring the older man down. "I don't want to watch Francie die, which is apparently more than can be said for you," I bit back.

"Enough," she said, stepping between us and levelling a serious stare at me. "I've made my choice, Lev. You can either come with us or stay here, but we don't have much time."

"He can't come with us!" Dak nearly shouted. "The RCM doesn't let just anyone join—Orin makes sure to only accept people that are discreet, useful, and never liabilities. He's not one of us," he finished, throwing an exasperated hand in my direction.

"He's trustworthy." Francie turned to face Dak. "I've known Levick for over seven years, and trust him with my life."

"'Trustworthy' and 'fast' are not the same thing, Francie. He'll get us killed," Dak said, still glaring at me.

Swallowing the bitter unease in my throat, I made my choice. "I'll come. You don't have to worry about me—I'll keep up."

Dak looked like he wanted to object, but deferred to Francie. I briefly wondered why he didn't put up any more of a fight, but I let it lie. Best not to look a gift horse in the mouth.

Dak motioned us over to the fence and we peered through the bars. A large sloped meadow laid before us, and at the top of the hill stood a grand structure the likes of which I'd never seen. The palace put the Exley mansion to shame. Six towers rose from the corners of the building, which appeared to be broken into wings. Dak backed up a few paces and revealed a broken bar on the fence. "Let's go. The guards will be coming around on their patrol any minute now," he said urgently.

I shook my head in frustration. "We'll be spotted out in the open."

"It's dark out here, and the guards are on changeover. You can stay and keep watch, but we need to get this done tonight," Francie said as she moved past me, obviously resolute. She gripped the broken fence, staring at me expectantly.

"I'm coming with you," I said, knowing I couldn't stay behind while she put herself in harm's way.

She nodded before crawling through the gap, followed closely by me and Dak. As we crept closer to the palace, I felt completely exposed out there. There was no cover at all. Our only ally was the darkness. After racing across what felt like the longest field I'd ever been on, we reached the ornate gray brick walls of the palace. Rose bushes surrounded much of the wall, which finally supplied us with a bit of cover.

We crept along the wall—Francie and Dak looking and feeling for any weak areas or old doors. "Here," Dak said, stopping suddenly. He was leaning over a small window that was situated barely above the ground.

"A basement?" Francie asked.

Dak nodded and began pulling on each corner of the window. There was a faint creaking sound, and Francie gave Dak a nervous smile. The window was unlocked.

I couldn't ignore my growing sense of foreboding. I looked over to Francie in the faint moonlight, only to find her staring at me. Her eyes were fiery with hope and passion, and it was contagious. "Are you sure about this?" I asked, coming close enough that only she could hear.

She smiled and nodded her head. "Something needs to be done, Lev," she tapped my chest. "I can't watch any more of them die."

"Any day now," Dak grunted in annoyance. He hunched over the window, looking uncomfortable in the position.

I took a deep breath and sighed in resignation. "Lead the way," I said over her shoulder.

Dak pulled the window open as far as it would go and slid through with Francie close behind. I followed, hoping I wouldn't regret it.

We landed in a dark, musty room. The moonlight through the window gave us just enough visibility to know the room was empty. Francie fumbled with her skirt, pulling out a match and a small candle from her pocket. Once it was lit, it became clear that we were in an old storage room.

"There's nothing in here. We should keep going," Dak whispered. The candlelight illuminated his face, his wrinkles more pronounced under it. He led us to the door and opened it into a hallway that smelled as dank as the storage room.

After sneaking through hallways and multiple rooms, the basement proved to be mostly empty. I still wasn't sure what we were looking for, but it seemed like Francie didn't know, either. When pressed on the subject, Dak brushed me off.

"There's nothing down here." Francie stated the obvious after we'd looped back to the first room we were in. "We need to find her trade and tax documents..." She glanced over at the dark staircase at the other end of the hallway, leading up.

"No! Absolutely not, Francie," I said, grabbing her hand. "We're already lucky no one came down here. Let's go."

Even Dak shook his head at her, agreeing with me.

Francie hesitated, obviously wanting to go upstairs. "We need solid evidence of special treatment if we want to expose her..." she trailed off.

What kind of scheme has she been sucked into?

"We'd get caught immediately, and we'd be too far from the window to escape," I said, tugging her hand toward the storage room.

"He's right, Francie," Dak said from behind us. "We should go. Every extra second we spend here is an unnecessary risk."

"Okay," she conceded, disappointment in her eyes. "Let's go."

Francie and I were nearly walking through the door to the storage room when a creaking sound echoed from the other end of the hallway.

Shit.

A guard in light leather armor stood at the foot of the stairs, pure alarm written across his face. Suddenly, the gravity of our transgression fell on me in full-force. We had broken into the queen's home. The ancient palace of Friese.

What were we thinking?

After regaining his composure, the guard swiftly drew his sword and charged toward us. Dak, who stood closest to the staircase, ran at the guard, knives drawn.

A horrific slicing sound echoed through the basement as the guard's sword emerged from Dak's spine, coated in dark blood. He coughed and choked, the blood already diffusing through his system.

"Dak!" Francie cried out. The guard shook Dak off of his sword and stepped over him.

"You're under arrest," he growled at us as he moved closer, sword raised.

I was about to step in front of Francie when she raised her hand and flung it at the guard, as if she was throwing something at him. The guard's eyes bulged—a clean puncture to the neck dribbling blood as he choked. He teetered for a moment before falling forward, bloodied sword clattering to the ground beside him. A wet cough sent blood spurting onto my shoes as the man gasped and gurgled on the floor. In a moment that would forever be etched into my memory, the guard's movements finally stilled.

For a few seconds, the only sounds in the basement were two hearts pounding like galloping horses.

I was standing next to Francie, her hand still outstretched. The guard laid in front of us—an unmoving mess of blood.

"Francie, how did... what just happened?" I stammered.

Her eyes were distant—nearly vacant. "I killed him."

She killed him... with no weapon.

We stood in stunned silence for a long moment before Francie turned to me. "We have to move them."

I shook myself out of my shock, trying to understand what she said. "What do you mean?"

"It has to look like they killed each other, or they'll come looking for us," she said, already walking over to Dak's body on shaking legs. She pried a small throwing knife out of his hand and proceeded to plunge it into the guard's throat, where it was already sliced open. My jaw dropped at the sight of it.

My mind was reeling from what I'd experienced—my breathing was ragged, and my pulse raced faster than any of Arturian's racehorses. Dak's body was completely lifeless, eyes staring into the void.

"Don't step in the blood—you'll leave tracks. We'll have to hope this looks convincing enough..." she said, her voice cracking. She looked like a ghost who was in denial about her own death. I forced myself to help her and dragged the guard's body by his shoulders until he was laying directly in front of Dak.

"Francie..." I started, but she cut me off.

"We can't talk about this now. We have to get out of here." She turned away, rushing into the storage room.

My hands were sweaty, and my chest tightened.

Who is this girl?

I snapped myself out of it and ran through the door to the storage room, following her up and out of the window. Silently, we sprinted into the woods, not slowing until we'd passed the damaged fence. There hadn't been any noise or commotion behind us, so we allowed ourselves to walk as we made our way back along the fence line and toward the gardens. The moonlight suddenly felt brighter than the sun—illuminating us in its cold, deathly light. Dak's dead expression hung in my mind like a permanent fixture.

"He's dead because of me," she said suddenly as we walked through the dense trees and brush. I said nothing, but a pit formed in my stomach.

She doesn't carry knives... and I definitely didn't see one.
And the way she threw her hand forward...

There was no other explanation. Francie had a windblade. However, that explanation left an even larger question.

"How did you get it?" I asked, speeding up to follow closer.

A minute passed, and I began to think she didn't hear me.

"I don't know," she said without turning, still looking at the ground as she walked. "I've had it for as long as I can remember." It was obvious she was having trouble controlling her voice.

She was a Skylady. However, not wanting to upset her, I let it go. Neither of us spoke again that night.

CHAPTER THIRTEEN
THE PERCH

Sleep barely came to me after I'd returned to the bell tower. It embraced and released me sporadically, like a conflicted lover. My senses betrayed me—replaying the night's events in vivid theatricality. I saw the guard laying on the stone floor, heaving and gasping as he choked on his blood. Dak's lifeless eyes stared up at me, open wide as if they were gates into the void itself. And before it all, stood Francie. Her delicate hand was outstretched, as if trying to catch someone before they fell. However, if I'd learned anything in the past twenty-four hours, it was that looks could be deceiving.

I shook those thoughts away, only for memories of the injured dock workers to come surging into my mind. I'd been trying not to think about the incidents, but they were occurring more and more frequently. There was only so long I could continue to bury my head in the sand. *One* family had control over the vast majority of trade in and out of Friese. The Exleys.

I wondered if Arturian even knew how bad things had gotten there. He hadn't attempted to speak to me since the night Augustus had discovered him with Francie, and despite my frustration with him, his absence felt like a twist of the knife. I couldn't help but feel a twinge of unease as I thought of my friend, but I knew the lives of the dock workers were more important than my pride. *Francie's* life was more important.

The trail from the bell tower to the Exley fields had grown over a bit during the previous few weeks, and was crawling with golden-tipped weeds. The spring rains had fostered bountiful growth, and I hadn't been cutting it back like I usually did around that time of year. I brandished an old knife and hacked away at thorns and weeds. With every strike through those thick, woody branches, I wondered whether I should even bother—if Arturian would risk his father's ire for the sake of lowly dock workers.

If he won't risk it for them...

He might... for Francie.

I clenched my jaw, suspicions creeping into my mind. I thought of the way Arturian had held her hand that night at the stable—how he'd *looked* at her. It was far from simple friendliness. Stamping out my jealousy, I thought of what would happen to Francie if she were caught. My chest tightened.

Surely Arturian knows what's going on at the port, and if he could stop these mishaps and the poor treatment, he'd have done it already...

Despite my warring conscience, I continued on through the thicket until it opened up to the rippling green field. I jogged across it and slid through the heavy stable doors.

"You shouldn't be here," Arturian said from his stool. He was facing away, his shoulders tense and tight under his black shirt as he oiled a saddle.

"That's all you have to say to me?" I asked, cocking my head. "After what happened that night?" The horrifying image of the decapitated horse remained as fresh in my mind as if I'd witnessed it yesterday.

Arturian shook his head as he worked. "It happened. There's nothing more to say."

I stood just inside the doorway, feeling foolish for trying. The despondency in Arturian's voice almost went unnoticed. Almost.

"How is she doing?" he mumbled before turning to meet my eyes. Just slightly, his brows were upturned—an undeniable marker of sincerity.

I ignored it, tilting my head forward and giving him an icy glare. "You don't get to ask about her. Not after what you put her through."

Even Arturian, known for his fortitude, looked away. He flexed his jaw and began rubbing a bridle clean.

"Did you hear about the latest dock accident?" I asked, disregarding Arturian's question.

He met my eyes again, brows furrowed in confusion. "Accident?"

"Yes, yesterday," I answered, unable to restrain the impatient clip in my tone.

"What do you mean by 'latest?'"

"Is this a joke, Arturian? Are you trying to be funny? Because hundreds of starving families think it's pretty damn serious."

My tone set Arturian off. Suddenly, my childhood friend was gone, replaced by the highly trained, unnaturally fast Skylord heir. He rose to his feet, smooth and silent. "You'd be wise in checking your tone when you're in *my* stable," he growled, his voice low and smooth.

I scoffed, but bit my tongue. I knew our conversation would go nowhere productive if I let my bitterness overtake my sensibility. "Arturian, it's getting so frequent. This latest incident caused so many injuries that the clinic was overflowing. There were men dying in pools of blood in the inn. Francie, she..." My voice faltered. "She had to *amputate* a man's leg by herself. That's how dire this is."

Arturian's eyes widened, but otherwise his expression remained constant.

"We've been friends for seven years, Arturian. I know things are rough right now, but for old time's sake, can you look into this? I can't say why, but Francie's safety is at stake here, too."

Arturian displayed a nearly imperceptible flinch, but a second later his eyes narrowed in suspicion, and he sat back down on his stool. "Our business at the port has never been more profitable than it is now. I can't compromise that." He turned to resume oiling his saddle. "It's not safe for you to come here anymore. Goodbye, Levick."

Biting my cheek to keep from saying something I'd regret, I stormed out of the stable, feeling my anger radiate all the way to my fingers and toes.

What is wrong with him? Is he turning his back on us forever?

Cool drops of rain hit my skin as I made my way back to the trail. With every drop, I felt my options dwindling.

Drip, drop.

"She's going to get herself killed," I muttered to myself. The image of Francie walking to her execution weaved through my mind like an invasive weed.

Drip, drop.

"Arturian doesn't give a shit," I said louder, feeling my anger and frustration bubbling to the surface. Execution by windblade was a gruesome thing to watch.

Drip, drop.

"What choice do I have?" I cried out in frustration as I picked up and flung a large rock into the woods. A powerful gust of wind followed it into the trees, bending them and shaking many of their leaves off.

I stopped in my tracks, stunned.

That came from me.

My outburst created an entire patch of trees that leaned over, as if they'd sustained years of constant resistance.

Coming to my senses, I glanced around to make sure no one saw, and darted into the woods in search of my trail. As I waded through the underbrush, my mind raced. I'd only ever been able to control the wind during jumping, but I'd never *projected* it from my body like that before.

It's changing. I'm changing.

Maybe this could be useful.

Four uneventful days later, I made my way to the center of the port slums. Francie had been acting aloof and refused to detail much more about the RCM or her involvement. She looked exhausted and seemed like she wasn't getting much sleep. I rounded a curve, approaching the large washing fountain in the center of the common area. I eyed a familiar purple-frocked woman as I made my way closer.

"What do you know about the 'RCM?'"

The grizzled old woman looked me up and down, squinting in suspicion. She chuckled in dismissal and returned to washing her clothes.

"Plumeria, please. It's urgent. I figured if it was real, you would know," I pleaded with her. The wind was blowing from the east, bringing the port smells over the city in a thick, putrid wave, adding to my unease.

Plumeria was an old friend of Crysta's and a frequent contributor to the inn. Her son ran a vegetable farm outside the city, and they often donated from its produce. With deeply wrinkled hands, she rubbed sopping wet clothing up and down the washboard.

"I've always liked you, dear. I've got nothing to say about the RCM." She waved me away and continued her task.

After stewing for days about my tense exchange with Arturian, I was entirely out of patience. "It's Francie!" I exclaimed, desperation leaking into my voice.

Plumeria froze mid-scrub, pale hands shaking as they held a sopping wet scarf against her washboard.

"Is she one of them?" she asked, lowering her gravelly voice.

I didn't know how to answer—Francie had implored me to keep quiet. Instead of answering, I stood in a regrettably implicating silence.

"Salted sea..." the old woman muttered, shaking her head and causing some of her white-gray hair to flutter around her weathered face. She turned to look at me with pleading eyes. "If I tell you what I know, you must *get her out of there*. The things they do—it's suicide." Her thin, bony shoulders shuddered under her faded shawl.

My stomach dropped. "I'll do everything I can to keep her safe, Plumeria," I responded tactfully—not wanting to lie to her. It was enough.

"Their leader hangs around some shifty pub near the docks. What was the name... the Prawn? The Pelican? No, no... it's... the Pike; that's it!"

The signature sounds and fishy smells of the docks greeted me as I made my way to the pub. It was an unseasonably warm day, even for the Friesian summertime. Grimy men unloaded colossal ships, barking orders at each other. A warm sea breeze distorted the reflections of the ships on the water, glistening as each wave caught the sun.

After walking along the edge of the docks, I found my destination. Ship bells rang in the distance as I ducked into a small pub called "The Perch." The odor struck me—snaking through my nose and making my lip curl back. It was the smell of sweat, dead fish, and poor hygiene hanging in stagnant air. Someone sang a famous Friesian pub song on the other side of the room.

> *"Her lips are so soft, those eyes blue and wide,*
> *She knows she's every man's weakness.*
>
> *Despite her suitors and my countless flaws, it's me*
> *she clings to all night."*

The drunkard's friends laughed along at the poor singing, urging him to keep on. He obliged them and continued to belt out the increasingly vulgar lyrics.

"Dark rum, please," I said to the bartender, a woman who looked like she could have grown from the place. She grunted and poured me a glass. After she slid me my drink, I passed her a sizable tip.

She raised her eyebrows, lingering beside me. "D'you need anything else?"

I leaned in closer, holding my breath a bit, and murmured, "I have some business with the RCM. Is this the place for that?"

The bartender narrowed her eyes, looking me up and down.

"I'm a friend of Francie's, if that means anything to you," I said, hoping it wouldn't backfire on me.

Without another word, the bartender turned and left through a door behind the bar. I resisted the urge to bolt while I had the chance. Drumming my fingers on the bar top, I downed the rest of my rum. The calming effects didn't set in as quickly as I'd hoped they would.

After what felt like hours, a brawny hand gripped my shoulder from behind. "Looking for our girl, are you?"

'Our girl?'

After taking a deep, controlled breath, I turned and faced the stranger with a neutral expression. My composure almost broke when I saw who stood there—a towering, muscled brute of a man glared at me, gripping me tight with a tattoo-covered hand.

"I'm looking for your leader, whoever he is," I responded, measuring my words. "I'm a friend of Francie's."

At that, the large man stepped back, releasing my shoulder. "Follow me."

We made our way through the bar until we got to a set of stairs going down into a basement. Rows of dusty shelving lined the walls, piled with produce of dubious freshness and dry goods. I wondered how serious of an organization the RCM must be if it met in a dingy cellar.

After reaching the bottom of the stairs, the tattooed man stood aside as I wandered over to one of the shelves.

Is he ever going to tell me what we're doing down here?

"So... is this where the group meets?" I asked as I picked up a jar, trying to hide my disappointment.

The man chuckled from behind me. "Hell, no. This is just a cellar."

Then my world became darkness.

"Hey, time to wake up."

A gruff voice broke through the nothingness.

"I don't want to smack you again. But I'll do it if I have to."

My thoughts were in complete disarray.

Where am I? What's happening?

"Alright, here it comes—"

I jerked upright, opening my eyes to see the man from the bar standing in front of me in an unfamiliar room. He was flanked by a middle-aged man in a vest, and a slight woman with dark hair and complexion.

"He put up less of a fight than Francie did," the tattooed man chuckled to the older man next to him.

"That's not entirely fair, Ress. It sounded like you had the drop on him," the older man responded, his dark eyes studying me as if he was expecting me to sprout wings and fly.

We seemed to be in a living room—a fire crackled and glowed in a hearth behind them. The ceilings were low, and the walls were paneled with faded, dark wood. I could smell the aroma of cooking herbs coming from a kitchen.

Stew? Is this someone's house?

"Where am I?" My voice was hoarse as I tried to ignore the throbbing pain in the back of my head.

The older man stepped forward. "The question isn't 'where', but 'why?'" Ress moved aside, allowing the older man to take a seat in front of me.

"Why are you here?" he asked, his dark gaze boring into me.

I did my best to straighten up and appear impressive. "I want to join. Francie is a good friend of mine and she would vouch for me."

The man cocked his head in coy curiosity. "Two things: First, she wasn't supposed to tell anyone about us."

Oops.

"Second, if she'd vouch for you, as you claim she would, why didn't she come with you?"

I swallowed hard, hoping the truth would get me where I needed to go. "She doesn't know I'm here. For some reason, she thinks she has to do this alone... but I'm worried about her," I said, prompting a few raised eyebrows.

"She's not alone," Ress grumbled from a nearby chair, with no attempt to hide the resentment in his voice. "She has us."

"You can trust us when we tell you," the older man interjected, "she can take care of herself."

"Damn straight," Ress said with a sly smile that I didn't care for.

"I've been her friend for years. I am very aware of how capable she is."

My words brought a silence over the group. The air in the room was thick with implication and curiosity. I could feel Ress's stare on me, hostile and distrustful. I focused on the man in front of me—who I presumed was their leader—and stared right back, unblinking.

In that moment, I knew I was close to winning some respect. They hadn't taken me seriously—they'd seen me as a boy, desperate to impress a girl. But my tenacity and knowledge of Francie had clearly given them pause. For a moment, I contemplated demonstrating my power over the wind, then decided against it. It wouldn't impress them, and it wasn't worth the risk.

"Let me in. I know I didn't lead with this, but I *do* sympathize with your cause and will help however I can. I'm quiet, quick on my feet, and can disappear faster than anyone I know." I leaned in towards the leader. "Give me this chance."

A long moment of silence passed, making me wonder if I'd wasted my time and efforts.

"Let him in, Orin," a quiet voice chimed in. It was the dark-haired woman standing next to the hearth. I'd forgotten she was there. "It would benefit us to bring someone new in. Especially after..." Her expression grew solemn as they all exchanged mournful glances.

Before anyone else spoke, a tall young woman with short blonde hair emerged from the hallway. "After that bitch let my father die?" she drawled, her voice thick with resentment as she glared at me. "That's what you were going to say. Right, Nina?"

I shot to my feet, jaw clenched, before Orin stepped in front of the hostile woman. "Not now, Iliana."

"We don't need her," she growled, looking past Orin at me. "And we sure as hell don't need any friend of hers."

Orin spoke in a serious murmur, but I could still pick up what he said. "You heard Francie's debrief. Your father acted *heroically* and saved her life. He wouldn't want this from you."

Dak...

"You have some nerve telling me what my own father would've wanted," she spat.

"Out. *Now,* Iliana," Orin said in a tone so deadly serious, it gave me chills. Iliana took one last look around the room, nostrils flaring in anger. A long, tense moment later, she spun on her heel and marched out.

Francie clearly hadn't told them I'd joined her on the palace mission. I sat back down, schooling my emotions as Orin turned around. Doubt clouded his gaze as he looked at me.

Nina broke the heavy silence. "Francie has mentioned him before, and he's being genuine. I can tell."

Orin sighed and threw his head back in frustration. "Please don't make me regret this." After a moment, he pursed his lips as he leaned forward to remove my restraints.

CHAPTER FOURTEEN
ORIN STRICKLAND

Francie wasn't surprised to hear that I had joined the RCM. She did, however, seem disappointed.

"I just wish you had talked to me about it, first," she said for what was probably the tenth time as we walked to my first official RCM meeting. The sun was rising over the glistening bay and a humid breeze was blowing in from the water. I let myself enjoy it for a moment before walking through a cloud of gnats.

"Francie, I know you're concerned, but I also need you to remember I'm capable of making my own choices."

Francie had the tendency to treat me with the protective-ness of an older sibling. I tried not to let it irritate me too much—it came from a place of love. However, sibling-love was *certainly* not the type of love I felt for her.

"I know, Lev. I just didn't want to drag anyone else into this," she said, wrapping her arms over her chest in the wind.

"You didn't drag me, Francie," I said, inching closer to her as we walked.

I could tell she was cold, and I was tired of second-guessing myself. I put my arm around her shoulder, pulling her closer to give her some warmth. Although a bit surprised, she eventually huddled in closer to me, and we continued walking together down the street.

Her warm body pressed tight against mine—a perfect fit that sent my heart racing. It was so normal... so *good*. Just a young man, sharing heat with the woman he loved. For a moment, I let myself pretend it could be so simple.

As we approached Orin's house, I spotted Ress staring down at us from the second-floor window, looking displeased. Nina quietly ushered us through the front door, then looked outside to check if anyone was following. I'd made it a habit to check myself for tails, so I knew we were safe.

Francie greeted Nina with a hug—exchanging pleasantries as if they were friends. She then moved on to greet a few more people I hadn't met yet. The group dynamic seemed more like a friendship than an assembly of people with a common mission. I couldn't help but feel a sense of unfamiliarity from Francie—she had an entire social circle I didn't know about.

"There she is, in the flesh! Come here, you," a familiar voice echoed from the hallway. I turned to see Ress smiling at Francie as she walked in. "How's our favorite Skylady?"

To my surprise, Ress took Francie in a hug and spun her around multiple times—earning many mock protestations and laughs from Francie. The size contrast was a bit jarring—Ress stood a head taller than her and was built like a bull. He lifted her like she was a doll.

"Ress! I'm getting nauseous!" Francie said through bouts of laughter.

"Don't tell me you're getting soft now. Especially after that raid last night. I don't think I've ever seen someone get so close to a Crownie without being seen," he joked as he set her down.

Raid?

That's why she's so exhausted... she's been doing night raids?

"I don't think you've met Levick yet—" Francie began, but Ress cut her off.

"We've met."

I gave Ress a polite nod, which he returned.

"Ress was the first Volty I met," I said.

"Mine, too," Francie replied, "and he could've been gentler. I feel like my head still hurts from hitting this door frame," she said, tapping the wood door frame she was leaning against.

"I wouldn't have had to carry you like that if you hadn't fought back so much," Ress mumbled. "You were like a feral racoon."

"That racoon could dissect you like a frog, Ress," Orin said, approaching us from the living room. "Levick, it's good to have you back. Are you ready to get started?"

We sat in a circle, making small talk while we waited for everyone to settle. There were around fifteen people there, and Francie seemed to know most of them.

"Listen up, everyone!" Orin's usually soft voice boomed over the conversations. "It's time to get started." A hush grew over the room as he began to pace slowly in front of us. While a physically unremarkable man, something about Orin's demeanor commanded attention.

"Today, we plan what will be our most ambitious operation yet. The Queen of Friese and her corrupt police force have spent far too long abusing us. Her desperation to maintain her chokehold on Friese will be the cause of her undoing. We've already made a significant dent in her wealth through our trade ship raids, which have been an undeniable success."

A few people chanted their agreement before he continued.

"However, it's time for us to make a pivotal move. We've received a tip on some evidence that would implicate the queen in a scandal. A scandal of preference, bias and *collusion*. We all know how seriously the noble houses of Friese take accusations of collusion. The queen must *always* treat the houses equally, with no partiality. To show favoritism to one house is to invite civil war between them." He paused his pacing, turning forward. "Thankfully for us, our ranks have grown, and we're ready to move forward with our plan."

Francie reached over and patted my arm.

"Our next step is to raid the port headquarters for unimpeachable evidence of collusion. For this mission, we'll need someone quick and light on their feet," he said, looking directly at me.

After a moment of silent confusion, I spoke up. "I'm sorry, I must've missed it. Which house is colluding?"

"My apologies... I forgot this is your first meeting. House Exley, of course."

"I won't do it, Francie," I said, pacing back across the patio. After hearing who their target was, I'd stood abruptly and walked out the back door, earning many surprised looks. Francie had wasted no time in following me out. We stood on the small stone patio behind Orin's home as the sun crept higher, casting long shadows over us.

"I'm not asking you to, Levick! Please, listen—"

"I know we're frustrated with him, Francie, but do you understand the consequences of this? He could be *hanged!*" I had to stop the urge to pace, in case any curious eyes were watching.

More lies from Francie... she knew *of their plan to target the Exleys, and didn't tell me.*

The only thing stopping me from pressing the matter was the guilt I felt for keeping my windwalker identity a secret. I knew I had no ground to stand on.

"I know, and I'm not going to let that happen. We'll target the Yorkes instead," Francie said, stepping closer and grabbing my hand. "We'll find something on the Yorkes, and Arturian will be safe."

"That's not what their leader said." I avoided her eyes, knowing what they'd do to my resolve.

"I'm going to change his mind. I just need time." She squeezed my hand, and I looked at her directly. "Nobody in there knows about our friendship with Arturian, but they'll figure it out if you keep this up," she whispered.

"Why didn't you tell them?" I asked her, my eyebrows knitting together in confusion.

"I like these people, but I don't think they could resist the temptation of exploiting it," she said with a tinge of regret. "He doesn't deserve to die for the crimes of his father," she said in such a hushed tone that I could hardly hear her.

"Can I talk to Orin? I think I could change his mind," I said, moving closer to avoid any curious eyes from lip-reading. A plan was already taking form in my mind.

Francie nodded and mouthed a 'thank you.' I was hyper-aware of how close we were. The bright flecks in Francie's blue eyes glistened like white doves flying across a clear blue sky. I forgot what I'd even been talking about... until Ress interrupted.

"Is this urgent, or can we get back to the meeting?"

I hate this guy.

Francie moved away, embarrassed. I couldn't decipher what she was thinking, but I kept my frustration buried beneath a layer of feigned seriousness.

Orin Strickland, Head of the Revolt of the Common Man, and "Chief Volty," was not easily convinced of anything. It took all of my persuasive abilities to avoid getting shut down in the first two minutes. I'd waited until the meeting was over to ask to speak to Orin privately, and had been appealing to him for the better part of an hour with very little progress.

"The Exleys are the obvious choice; their wealth surpasses every other house except that of the queen herself, and maybe the Yorkes," Orin said as he sat at his desk in his small home office, pinching the bridge of his nose between his fingers. "Not to mention my sources are already suspicious of them."

"House Exley is too strong. If the collusion was discovered, the queen and her house would double down and ally with Exley. They would be too strong to defeat together," I replied, sitting in a chair in front of the desk. The conversation had drained me.

"I don't appreciate how you—our newest member—think you can come to your very first meeting and presume to tell me how to run my organization. Don't get me wrong, I always appreciate input from my Volties, but this is too much," Orin said, exasperated.

Come on, Levick. Drive it home.

"Queen Lesynna is a tyrannical oppressor, right?" I asked.

"Yes... we've established that."

"Her Crownies commit unspeakable injustices and violence upon the people in the slums, right?"

"Yes, but—"

"Wouldn't it stand to reason that adding Augustus Exley to the power dynamic would be a net negative?"

Silence.

I leaned forward on my elbows, staring at Orin. "Augustus Exley is the most wicked human being in Friese. Even more than Lesynna Ainsworth. If you think things are bad now, just wait. He would level the slums and send us to the depths of the Broad Sea if it would add a cent to his wealth."

Orin stared at me, eyes narrowed. "How does a slum-kid know so much about Friesian politics?"

Yikes—set myself up for this one.

"One of our regulars at the inn has a daughter who works in the Exley estate. She overhears all sorts of gossip," I lied. The truth was that Arturian would sometimes confide in me when the tensions between the noble families got high, and I had a good memory.

While maintaining a skeptical look, Orin said, "We'd have to start from scratch..."

"I think someone is importing weapons into Friese," I blurted out. It was about time I told someone about the sword I had hidden away at the inn. If nothing else, it could serve to redirect some of the attention off of the Exleys.

"Why would you think that?" Orin sat up, eyes wide.

"During a dock incident, a man got fatally wounded and was brought to the inn for medical attention. Before he died, he mentioned something about imported weapons..." I shuddered at the memory, "thousands of them."

Orin sat still for a long moment, but eventually granted a slight nod. "That's interesting. I'll inform my... sources." With that, Orin motioned me out.

I was feeling very accomplished on our walk home from the meeting. Francie had thanked me countless times for my help—her conscience had been weighed upon by the plans to target the Exleys. With that weight removed, she was nearly skipping along next to me.

"What a relief, Lev! I feel so much better about this now. I'm so grateful." She took a deep breath and let the sun shine down on her face. "I'm going to consider this your early birthday present to me."

It was coming up in four days—I never missed it.

"Are you excited to turn nineteen?" I asked. Although I was excited for her, I enjoyed the few months after my birthday and before her own. It felt like we were only one year apart instead of almost two. But who was counting, anyway?

Me. Always me.

"I'm a little excited, but nervous," Francie muttered, fidgeting with her long hair.

"Why is that?"

"This year I've worked up the nerve to ask Crysta about my mother. About the kind of person she was, before... you know," she said, dropping her hair to pick at her nails as she walked.

"I know, Francie," I said, giving her a soft smile. "I know what it's like to miss a person I barely knew... and I imagine it's much harder to miss a person you didn't know at all."

She nodded, eyes lost in thought as we arrived back at the inn. I took a deep breath and tried not to let the memories of my mother haunt me.

CHAPTER FIFTEEN
ORIGIN

The sun rose over the city of Friese, heating the damp ground. Steam wafted up from the road and swirled around in hypnotizing patterns from the sea breeze. To most people in Friese, it was an unremarkable late-summer morning. To me, it was the day my life could change forever.

I had woken up early and couldn't fall back asleep, so I was just returning from a scenic sunrise walk. Alone in the crisp, fresh air outside, I found a type of serenity that eluded me elsewhere. The chance to learn more about my mother felt like a looming presence, akin to the ominous sea cliffs in the north—drawing me in with magnificent scenery, but from a lethal height. I kept finding myself speculating on what kind of person she was. Sweet, and selfless? Strong and brave? Or was she weak and self-serving?

As if I wasn't tormented enough, I couldn't stop think-ing about Arturian and Levick. Mourning the unexpected pulling-away by Arturian... and trying to understand why Levick had begun treating me differently.

Arturian had always been friendly, but distant with me. After a while, I'd begun to see him as someone I deeply cared for, but was ultimately unreachable. His lifestyle of opulence had disillusioned me on multiple occasions, although I tried to be gracious because it was the only lifestyle he'd ever known. It was his demeanor that drew me to him. He exuded a quiet confidence that was rare and... *irresistible.* Not to mention the way he looked at me. The way he *touched* me. I could still feel his hands on my waist... his lips against my hair. In those moments, I felt like he knew me better than anyone.

I figured I must be misinterpreting it.

Levick, on the other hand, was someone I'd known closely for years. I'd seen him through many childhood stages and into adulthood. His honesty, courage, and self-sacrificial qualities had become more pronounced as he grew older. The moment I shared with him outside of Orin's house threw me for a loop.

When did he start looking at me like that?

"What are you doing out here so early?" Crysta called from the front door of the inn. Despite her pale, wrinkling face, she radiated a rare beauty that exuded wisdom. I tried to clear my mind of Arturian and Levick so I could prepare for the conversation I planned on starting.

"Any preparation I need to get started?" I asked as I walked past Crysta's tall frame and through the inn's front door.

"No, I'm keeping it simple today. I'd hate for a certain girl to be caught up with work on her nineteenth birthday." She gave me a knowing smile as we made our way to the back office where we kept a couple of small padded chairs. "What do you have planned with Levick today?" she asked, her tone elevated in a poor attempt at sounding casual.

"I don't spend every moment of my free time with him..." I said, sitting on the edge of my chair.

"Don't be silly, Francie—" Crysta paused as she saw my expression. "Dear, is there something wrong?"

Deep breaths. You've rehearsed this.

"I'd like to know more about my mother. The only thing I know about her is that she died while giving birth to me. But it's my nineteenth birthday, I'm a grown woman, and I'd like to know more about who my mother was."

Breathe.

"And maybe... who my father was."

Crysta shook her head and looked away. "Some truths are better left buried, dear."

"Crysta." I reached out and took her hand. "I *need* to know."

The weary woman leaned back in her chair, resigned. "This isn't the birthday gift I wanted to give you, but I suppose you deserve to know..."

Twenty Years Ago

Corsa Hanover

Working at the country estate was a privilege only bestowed upon the most skilled servants. However, Corsa didn't feel privileged. She didn't understand why she, a girl of only eighteen, had been selected for such a grand opportunity. She felt out-of-place working amongst older, more mature maids.

They resented her, and they didn't care to hide it. Many servants assumed that she must have been carrying on an affair with an important member of the staff or noble family. While these rumors were simple speculation at the time, they eventually held a grain of truth.

As she sat huddled in the corner of her master's bedroom, Corsa realized why she had been hired at the country estate.

The room exuded grandeur and elegance. The hand-carved dressers, velvet curtains, and ornate chandelier would lead most people to assume the owner was a gentleman. Corsa, however, knew better. She trembled uncontrollably, fear having taken hold of her earlier in the night. Her eyes refused to budge from the snoring figure laying on the grand canopy bed.

Could I sneak out without waking him?

No, the heavy wooden doors were far too loud to allow a discreet escape. The last thing Corsa wanted to do was wake him, but she didn't have another option, and she *had* to get out of that room.

Legs shaking, Corsa stood and began creeping toward the door. Every step terrified her—the old floors couldn't be trusted not to creak. After what felt like hours, she made it to the door and slid a gentle hand over the handle.

A splitting crack echoed through the room. Horrified, Corsa looked down and saw a split floorboard beneath her feet.

"Where do you think you're sneaking off to?"

Gasping, breathy sobs erupted from her mouth. She turned to see him climbing out of bed. Tall, muscular, and dark—he was a terrifying specimen. But it was his *smile* that struck fear into Corsa's very being. It was a broad and nefarious thing, glinting with the clean polish of an ocean pearl... only shaped like the teeth of a shark.

Corsa shrieked and huddled against the door as he crossed the room in an instant. He grabbed her by the shoulders and tossed her away from the door as if she were nothing but a doll.

She felt herself slam into an end table—the antique gold vase she dusted the day before clattered to the floor.

"I hadn't dismissed you yet. I could consider that a fire-able offense..." he said casually, as if he hadn't just woken up seconds ago. "Although I may overlook it for another hour."

He was crouching down in front of her when there was a loud crash in the hallway, diverting his attention for a moment.

Thankfully, that moment was long enough for Corsa.

Echna, forgive me.

She hefted up the vase and smashed it into her master's head with all of her strength. Blood sprayed onto her face, and he went limp, falling to the floor.

Still kneeling next to the end table, Corsa stared at her assailant's body. His head poured out blood, ruining a carpet worth more money than a housekeeper could make in a lifetime.

Suddenly, Corsa felt unnervingly cold.

A strong draft gusted through the room, causing the curtains to sway. The draft progressed to a gale and spun around her at terrifying speed. She tried to scream, but the torrent sucked the air out of her lungs. One last gust of wind struck her in the chest, causing her to stumble back into a dresser. Trembling violently, she took a deep breath of perfect air.

The windows and doors are all closed—where did that come from?

There was a distant commotion in the hallway outside. This brought Corsa back to her current, very dire situation.

I've just killed a man.

She leapt over the body and ran to the door. She took one last look at the horrific scene and bolted.

Still in her ripped and tattered clothing, Corsa sprinted out of the mansion and toward the stables. She had been lucky no one noticed her sneaking out of the house. She had the forethought to wipe the blood from her face in a washroom, but it wouldn't be long until someone found the body.

Barefoot, with her long blonde hair blowing in tangles behind her, she ran across the grass. Breathing in ragged gasps, she got to the stable, mounted the first saddled horse she saw and took off down the road. Faint screaming erupted behind her—they'd found him. Turning in the saddle, she saw a couple of men mounting horses to pursue her.

If they catch me, they'll kill me. I have to make it into the city where I can disappear.

Panicked, Corsa nudged the horse to move faster. She nearly tumbled off the back as he shot forward with a jarring burst of speed. She clung to the stallion for dear life—he was *much* faster than she'd expected. Despite her terror at their increasing speed, Corsa felt overwhelming relief.

This is a racehorse.

It didn't take long for her pursuers to realize it was a lost cause. The speed of her horse and her significant head start made it impossible for them to catch up. She disappeared into the woods and braced herself for the long ride to the city.

After riding for two hours, Corsa entered the city center of Friese during the busy hours of the afternoon. Merchants bustled around her, trying to sell their goods to weary travelers. The food was tempting, but she needed to find her sister and hide. Her master's guards would soon have their people in the city looking for her. She whispered her sincere thanks to the horse who saved her life, sold him, and pocketed the generous proceeds. As she walked on, she struggled to keep herself upright through her dizzy spells. Thankfully, her tattered clothing helped her blend in with the commoners. The noble families left little for the rest of the populace.

Turning down a dark street, Corsa spotted a dingy but familiar looking door. She glanced around to make sure she wasn't being followed, and entered. The smell of rosemary, thyme, and sage immediately overpowered her senses, wafting through the warm air. The small room was cast in a dim light by a couple of lanterns on the wall and a fireplace in the corner. A frazzled-looking figure emerged through a small doorway from another room.

"No open rooms until later this afternoon! I still have some cleaning to do—"

The woman stopped abruptly upon seeing Corsa, who was closing the door behind her. Color drained from Crysta's face—they hadn't seen each other in over a year.

At first, she smiled, but that smile faded into a look of concern when she saw her sister's state. "Corsa! What happened?"

Corsa rushed into her older sister's arms, feeling relieved for the first time since she escaped the estate. "Crysta—I had a job... but it didn't work out," she said through quiet sobs. The reality of what had happened to her, and what she had done, settled over her like a heavy, cold blanket.

Sensing her sister's mood, Crysta stroked her hair and held her close. They embraced in silence for a few moments before Corsa's shaking had subsided, and she felt able to speak again.

"Would you have room for one extra person here? I'd work in the inn every day, doing anything and everything you need. Please... I have nowhere else to go." Corsa hated asking her sister to take on more responsibility, but she had no other options.

Crysta backed away and took her sister's face in her hands. "I would never turn you away. As if I could send my sister into the streets—I'll hear nothing of it." Crysta lightly brushed the dirt from her sister's clothes and led her into the kitchen for a long-awaited meal.

Corsa made good on her promise to her sister by working long hours at the inn every day. The dining area was often full of hungry families, making her busy days go by quickly.

Despite their recent food shortage, it wasn't long before Corsa started filling out her apron. Her traumatizing encounter with her master had left her with more than just repressed memories. Before she knew it, many of her work duties grew difficult, and her condition was impossible to hide. At Crysta's insistence, she spent her last month hidden away in their rooms above the inn.

Once Corsa's time had come, she knew almost immediately that something was wrong. The entire ordeal lasted only four hours, and Crysta could barely revive the baby girl after she was born an alarming gray color.

Is my baby alright? Just give me my baby, please.

Corsa could feel herself growing colder. There was blood everywhere. Crysta placed the baby on her sister's chest and stepped back for a moment, letting them bond. Corsa stared into the eyes of her fussing daughter, in awe that she could've produced such beauty.

My sweet girl. How could such a horrendous act give me such a perfect gift?

The new mother smiled down at her child, holding her tight in her shaking arms, before slipping away into darkness.

Present Day

Francie

"My mother..." I said, voice cracking, "was *assaulted*? *That's* where I came from?" My voice broke—sobs threatening to break loose. I'd thought about my father before—I'd wondered who he was and what kind of man he'd been. I'd naively assumed that I was conceived through a passionate love affair.

"What was his name? My father's name?" I asked, desperate.

Crysta shook her head, mouth down-turned in contained anguish. "She refused to tell me, but I know he was a Skylord. Corsa and I hadn't seen each other in a year when the incident happened, so I didn't know who she worked for..." She trailed off for a moment before raising a trembling hand to her brow. "I shouldn't have told you—I'm so sorry." She wrapped her arms around me, bringing my head to her shoulder.

Why does reality have to be so cruel? Are the good assumptions always wrong?

I sobbed into my aunt's shoulder until my tears ran dry. Crysta kept whispering her apologies and regrets as she gently stroked my arms.

"No, Crysta," I said, straightening myself despite the brokenness in my voice. Crysta had been crying too—her strong features were red and wet with tears. "It's better to know."

Crysta dried her tears on her sleeve and took a deep breath. "There's something more. As a Skylord, your father had a windblade... and Corsa *killed* him." Silence hung between us as I realized the implications. "She inherited it, but she refused to use it. It must've been lost to the atmosphere when she died."

My mouth went dry. There was only one way to inherit a windblade. It was passed from the victim to their killer. I tried to think of any alternative scenario that could explain how I acquired my windblade. There was none except the glaringly obvious one.

My birth killed her. That's *how I got the blade.*
I killed my mother.

Making a hasty excuse to Crysta, I burst from the inn and ran towards the port. An early morning storm was brewing over the water, and I felt myself being drawn to it. My emotions churned within me, bringing me down with the undertow. I'd always assumed my windblade was a gift from some unseen force, to be used to save lives. After learning how I'd gotten it, it felt more like a curse.

The undeniable proof of matricide.

Clouds coalesced above Friese as I made my way closer to the water. Tiny drops of rain landed on me, rolling down my skin.

I felt the pressure dropping... that ominous lightness. That feeling of *knowing* something disastrous was coming—something no one could control. A sudden gust of wind hit me from behind, pushing me along with every step.

I'm not scared of you. You've always been on my side.

I clung tightly to those feelings; doing everything in my power to stop the tide of resentment I knew was coming.

But... you belonged to him. The monster who hurt my mother.

Words couldn't quite convey the complex series of emotions I was having as I walked down an old wooden pier, jutting into the tempestuous port waters. I stopped at the edge, watching the boats rock against their anchor lines. How could I hate my father when I owed my existence to him? How could I *not* hate him for what he did to my mother?

Chimes made a frantic chorus in the wind and flags nearly ripped from their poles. Waves splashed up on the pier, soaking my shoes and ankles. Someone shouted at me from a distance. He was ignored.

"Why did I have to ask?" I whispered into the storm. It had no answer for me.

I don't know what I expected to hear.

The shouting person persisted in his attempts to get my attention.

"I'm fine! Please leave me alone," I called over my shoulder. Wind whipped against my hair, blowing it across my face and obscuring my vision. The rain began falling harder, running in chilled rivulets into the neckline of my dress.

Both of my parents are dead. My mother lived a terrible life and my father was the cause of it.

My entire purpose was a lie. My windblade wasn't a gift to make a change, but a reward for a grisly, contemptible act. Whether it was another gust of wind, or from simple, inescapable despair, I felt myself falling forward. I closed my eyes and waited for the cold rush of water, hoping it would bring me one step closer to meeting my mother.

But it never came.

"Francie, what are you doing?" a familiar voice called out as muscular arms wrapped around me from behind, shaking me from my stupor. He lowered both of us down until we were sitting together on the pier, leaning against a piling. Over the wind and rain, I heard his even, low voice.

"Why?"

Arturian. He found me.

"It doesn't matter," I said, finally feeling the chill in the air. Forgetting our recent divisions, I let myself feel soothed by the warmth of his panting chest against my back, and leaned my head against him. I could feel his heart pounding.

"Yes, it does," he whispered into my ear, and held me tighter. I soaked in the moment. Despite the anger and bitterness that had been clawing at me... I felt safe. The pressure of Arturian's arms wrapped against my own seemed to release some of the crushing weight upon me.

I opened my eyes to look up at him and noticed his brows were furrowed in concern. His long, wet hair stuck to his face and neck. Rain poured down on us and wind whipped past our faces, but Arturian's eyes remained fixed on mine, churning like the depths of the Broad Sea itself.

"Please, let me get you inside," he whispered. He was so close that I could feel his breath against my lips, and the sensation sent a warm wave up my spine. I nodded, and with little effort, he rose to his feet, carrying me in his arms.

CHAPTER SIXTEEN
SALT RUM

The Exley's port office was a complete contrast to the chaos taking place outside. Fine, dark wood furniture and detailing accented the various rooms. Sleek leather couches sat arranged in a circle, divided by small tables set with expensive liquors and glasses. Arturian and I sat alone on a plush rug in front of the fireplace, warming ourselves. He'd covered my shoulders with the softest blanket I'd ever felt, in the color of perfectly creamed coffee. I absently ran my fingers against it as I stared into the dancing flames.

"What were you doing out there?" Arturian asked from beside me, his voice even and controlled. As usual.

"I could ask the same of you," I responded in a quiet, clipped tone. He'd not reached out to me or Levick in a while, and it bothered me more than I'd wanted to admit.

"I was walking to this office when I saw you," he said, without an ounce of defensiveness. I wondered how he maintained it. I sighed and shook my head, gripping my blanket closer.

"I know you're still upset with me... for what happened with my father." His voice was low and expectant as he turned to look at me.

I said nothing.

"He wouldn't have let you live if he thought you meant something to me," he said, leaning closer.

I shook my head. "Why do you put up with it? He controls every aspect of your life with an iron grip." I wasn't one to speak so frankly, but the events of the day weighed on me, lowering my inhibitions.

"What choice do I have?"

"Run away!" I said, my voice an exasperated scoff. "If you wanted to, we'd go with you."

He cocked his head. "We?"

"Levick and I."

He turned back to the fire, blinking slowly. "You would never leave Crysta, and I don't blame you. Besides, I can't run away, Francie. I'm the only Exley heir."

I sat up straighter. "Does that matter, Arturian? Does that life make you happy?" I knew it didn't. I saw it in his eyes.

His lips turned up in a sad smile. "I think it could... someday. But there is more to this life than my own happiness. I have obligations; a duty to my house."

"You don't owe your father anything. Please, at least consider it," I mumbled. Running away from my own problems sounded very appealing.

Arturian sat quietly for a while, staring into the fire. Thunder boomed outside and lightning bolts lit up the windows—the storm was hitting Friese in full force. I dared a long, searching glance at Arturian. His hair had partially dried and hung around his angular features. The light from the fire cast warm tones on his face, accentuating his dark blue eyes. I tried not to stare, but the fluttering in my heart was becoming difficult to ignore.

Arturian finally spoke. "My duty isn't only to my father. It's to every Exley who came before me. The survival and success of our house is my responsibility."

Despite my disappointment, I nodded. His loyalty to his house was entirely undeserved, but I let it go. "As much as I wish you'd change your mind, I respect your steadfastness."

He turned again and met my eyes, and the openness in them nearly took my breath away. "Thank you, Francie. That means a lot to me. Especially after... recent events."

I found myself speechless for a moment, as if all of my thoughts had slipped away.

"I'm sorry, I didn't mean to bring that day up again—" he started.

"It's okay, really," I cut in, my sense returning. "You might've saved my life today."

A tense silence enveloped us as I listened to the storm outside and watched embers crack and fly in the fireplace. I could feel his gaze on me, bringing warmth to my cheeks. We'd rarely spent much time together without Levick, and his absence completely changed the atmosphere between us. I was hyper-aware of how Arturian's shoulder brushed mine—his thin white shirt still damp. In spite of that, it was warm.

"Francie..." he began, lowering his head towards me. The few inches of air between us felt electric. I kept my eyes on the fire, as if it could give me strength to resist what was coming. The problem was, I didn't want to. If I was being honest with myself, I knew we'd have to address what had been swirling under the surface of our friendship for a long time.

"I'm sorry I've been distant... but if my father hurt you because of me, I'd never be able to live with myself," Arturian said, his voice nearly a whisper. "I've only ever wanted to protect you from that."

I shuddered as I recalled the brutalized horse; his severed head leaking blood across the floor. Arturian was right. He may have hurt my feelings that night, but he also may have saved my life.

My emotions had been stirred up and unsettled by the revelations of the day. The walls I had carefully constructed around my heart for years were crumbling down, and I lacked the strength or desire to rebuild them. The culmination of years of silent longing had worn down on me, like the torrential rain coming down on the roof outside. Acting against my better judgment, I turned to meet his gaze.

His eyes were like a raging ocean—an endless deep blue, swirling with danger and adventure, sending my heart pounding. In a reckless instant, I abandoned my caution, letting all of my hidden desires show on my face. For a split second, a steely cast took over Arturian's countenance, and he backed away, as if he wanted to resist. The next second, he slid his hand up the nape of my neck and into my hair, and pulled my lips to his.

Stars exploded behind my vision.

Winds above...

The kiss was gentle, but had no hesitation. I fell into it, letting him pull me in closer as I reveled in the moment.

However, too soon, he pulled away. The firelight shone on half of his face, illuminating the embers sparking deep in his eyes. "I've wanted to do that for years," he said, sliding his hand from my neck and threading it gently into the hair above my ear. For a moment, I thought my heart might explode.

"Me, too," I whispered, running my fingers up his arm.

Pure, hungry desire burned in his eyes, freshly ignited by my admission. He pulled me back in, his mouth hot and desperate against mine. I was overcome... *overwhelmed* with longing for him. I was completely consumed in the moment, but it still wasn't enough. I needed *more*.

Arturian sensed my eagerness and grabbed my waist, pulling me onto his lap. He pulled away from my mouth to plant soft kisses down my neck, leaving a trail of burning pleasure behind. I leaned into his hands as they ran over my back, pulling me ever closer to him. My fingers wound in his damp hair, and I felt him groan against the crook of my neck. Thunder boomed outside and wind whistled in the windows, but I only wanted to hear *him*.

"Francie..." he said my name desperately, as if it was the only thing keeping him tethered. "Francie," he repeated, but his tone shifted, and he pulled away from me. I had to use every bit of self-control not to whimper at the separation. Confliction painted his handsome features; his jaw was set, and his brows were furrowed.

"We can't." His words didn't reflect his expression—he remained the picture of lust. His chest heaved under his thin shirt, which stuck to him with rain and sweat. His jet-black hair hung by his face, framing his sharp features in ways that made my heart skip a beat. "We can't," he repeated, obviously more to himself than to me.

I made myself pause for a moment before asking, "Why not?"

He ran his fingers up and down my waist, making me tremble. I could've sworn I saw him bite the inside of his cheek at the movement. He took a deep breath and tilted his head as he met my eyes. The genuine concern on his face made my heart clench. "I don't know what brought you to the edge of that pier today," he said, his jaw twitching slightly. "But whether or not you're ready to talk about it, you're obviously still reeling from it."

My throat tightened as my mother's story played over in my mind. I said nothing, but knew my anxiety was obvious.

"I won't take advantage of that," Arturian mumbled, "no matter how much I want to."

Damn chivalry.

I sighed in disappointment, but nodded. I knew he was right. My emotions were in complete shambles, and I wasn't thinking clearly. Arturian pulled me down against him, wrapping his arms around me. I ran my fingers through his hair as he rested his cheek against my shoulder.

A perfect gentleman. One I'll never get to have.

Damn this aristocracy.

"Stay with me, today," he murmured against my neck, his warm breath reigniting my ache for him. "I'll lock the doors and we'll weather this storm together."

I didn't know if he was talking about the storm outside, or the storm he knew was raging in my heart. Regardless, nothing sounded better.

Well, except...

Off the table. Stop thinking about it.

"I'd like that," I said as I pulled away. Sliding my hands over the back of his neck, I leaned in and brushed his lips with a delicate kiss.

I love you.

I didn't say it. But I meant it with all of my heart.

After Arturian added some logs to the fire, it burned brightly through the room. The flickering flames cast dancing shadows over me as I hung a damp shirt over the back of a chair. *His* damp shirt.

"I found it."

Just hearing his voice brought warmth to my cheeks. My face almost lit on fire when I turned to look at him. He walked in from the hallway carrying a white box with black lettering, his toned chest and arms completely exposed. I looked away, hiding my blush.

"You can look, I don't mind," he purred, and I could nearly *hear* the suggestive smirk on his face.

"That's a bit unfair," I murmured, staring at the fire as a smile crept onto my face.

I heard him drop the box on an end table before stopping behind me. He was so close... I could feel his body heat against my back. My skin was electric, anticipating his touch.

"If fairness is what you want..." he whispered in my ear as he tugged on my flowing skirt.

I spun around and met his playful stare. "Didn't anyone ever tell you it's cruel to tease?" I said, a coy smile on my face.

The playfulness disappeared from his expression. His eyes roamed over me as if he'd been trapped in the desert for weeks and I was a cool glass of water. His mouth pulled up at the corner in a sly smile. "Let's play a different game."

"You're cheating," I accused him as he took my king yet again. It was our seventh game of chess and he'd won handily every time. I sat upright and began braiding my hair, which had finally dried.

"Although my father didn't directly teach me much, he made sure I learned chess," he chuckled, clearing the board once more. It had been hours, but the storm still raged outside. We lounged on the plush rug next to the fireplace and periodically took breaks from our chess games to engage in more pleasurable games of testing each-other's self-control.

"I think it's in that Exley blood," I quipped as he set our pieces up and arranged them with care.

He said nothing, and his expression took a dark hue.

Did I say something wrong?

Lightning flashed in the windows, making me jump despite its frequency that day. He remained silent as he finished his work, but his brows were knit together in deep thought.

"Is everything alright?" I asked, scooting closer to the fire to get around the chessboard.

He straightened up and leaned his back against the couch behind him, and motioned for me to sit next to him. I crawled over and settled against the couch, and he wrapped an arm around my shoulders, pulling me closer. I felt him press a soft kiss against my head, exhaling deeply.

"I have no Exley blood," he said, his voice almost sounding... nervous. "I learned that Adolpho didn't sire my father, rendering him—and myself—illegitimate."

I stifled a gasp. My heart hurt for him; his family line had always been important to him... and to have that taken away? It was probably devastating.

I hadn't realized I'd been silent until he spoke up, his voice low and strained. "Please say something."

My throat tightened. He was *worried* about how I'd react. "Arturian." I turned to face him and looked into the deep tides of his eyes. His expression was partially concealed under one of his well-practiced masks of indifference, but I'd finally gotten to where I could see through them. I slid my hands through his hair and cupped his neck. "Your last name has *never* mattered to me, and it never will." I took a moment to appreciate his unequaled perfection, and leaned in and sealed my promise with a kiss, which he returned with enthusiasm.

After a heart-stopping minute, Arturian pulled away, leaning his forehead against mine. "If the other Skylords find out, our house would be in danger. Despite my father's power with his windblade," he whispered, and I knew what he was asking.

"They won't hear it from me."

I danced and sang my way around the living area of the Exley's port office, a half-empty bottle of salt rum in my hand. Arturian had found it in the early evening, and we made *quite* a time of it.

> *"She begged me to take her to the temple and make her*
> *An honest and upstanding woman.*
> *But when the time came for our vows to be made,*
> *we were too distracted for goin'."*

The famous Friesian pub tune echoed through the common area, eliciting a rare laugh from Arturian. "I can't believe you know a song like this," he said from a bar stool at the edge of the room, taking another sip from his glass.

"It gets even better, trust me." I sang the words as I spun over to him. He caught me between his legs, gripped my chin, and pulled my lips to his. He slid his tongue over my lip and I immediately opened myself up to him and began engaging in a more intricate dance than the one I'd just finished. As our bottle of rum had emptied, so had my inhibitions. I couldn't get enough. The taste... the sound... even the *smell* of him was magnetic. However, my good sense returned, and I pushed myself out of his clutches, twirling away in a mess of skirts and flirtatious looks.

"Come back, I'm not finished with you," I heard him say, his voice smooth as the priceless salt rum we were drinking.

"I suppose it's *my* turn to be chaste, is it?" I said, giving him a sultry wink. "Besides, my song isn't over yet."

A soft chuckle sounded from across the room. "Where did you even learn it?" he asked.

I stopped next to the fireplace, leaning on the mantle. "Levick and I used to go to this seedy little pub over by the Weigh Anchor..." I froze, and my heart leapt into my throat.

Levick.

The subject we'd very obviously been dodging all day. Where did this leave him? Where did it leave *us?*

"It's okay. We've been avoiding it."

I nodded as I stared into the flames. My buzz was gone.

"What do we tell him?" he asked after it became obvious that I wouldn't be the first to ask it.

I pressed my eyes closed and prayed to Echna for a simple answer. I worked with Levick every day at the inn. For the RCM. If he learned about this...

"Nothing," I said, perhaps too quickly. "I don't see what good it would do."

I was met with a long moment of silence, so I turned around. Arturian was staring down into his empty glass of rum, his face contemplative. "You're probably right," he said, glancing up at me. Something about his countenance concerned me—his eyes seemed to stare at nothing as he pursed his lips.

I crossed the room and stopped when I stood between his knees once again. Taking a deep breath, he looked up to meet my gaze, and I poured another splash of rum into his glass before setting the bottle on the bar behind him. "It's getting late. Let's not waste the time we have left."

He smirked before gripping my hips in his hands and pulling me against him.

I felt like I was walking on clouds after our night—or day?—together. It was getting late, and if I didn't return soon, someone would come looking for me. The question I'd been avoiding loomed in the back of my mind... What next? Was there even a 'next' for us?

Arturian brushed a strand of hair over my shoulder and took me in his arms, then leaned down to kiss the crook of my neck. "You are my very own summer storm, Francie," he whispered in my ear, sending a rush of warmth over my skin. "I'd stay wrapped in your tempest until the breath left my lungs."

But you can't.

The reality of Arturian's rank loomed over me. Friese would never allow us to be together. *Augustus* would never allow it. He'd have me killed. I said nothing as I leaned into him, but my heart cracked.

A cool metallic sensation slid over the ring finger of my right hand.

"Keep this safe for me."

He broke apart from me, took my head in his hands, and kissed me. It was a desperate kiss, but of a different sort than the countless others we'd shared that day. Instead of a desperation to take things *further*, this was a desperation to cling to something fleeting. I held on to him, willing the moment to last forever... but I suspected it was his kiss goodbye. I wanted to remember the feeling of his hands in my hair, his breath on my skin. I'd just had the most incredible day of my life.

And my heart was shattered.

CHAPTER SEVENTEEN
PRINCESS EADLIN

ARTURIAN

I always hated having strangers in my home, and tonight, there were hundreds of them. Romantic music floated through the air, played by professional musicians. From above, the Exley ballroom looked like a hive of well-coordinated ants moving around in rhythm. It was on one of my perfectly situated balconies that I hid from my guests.

Memories of the day I spent with Francie in the port office occupied my mind, and I was having a hard time focusing on anything else. It had been a constant struggle to resist shirking my responsibilities, finding her, and reliving it.

"Why is our host up here all alone?" a familiar woman's voice purred from behind me.

I sighed before forcing myself to turn around and put on a practiced smile. "Miss Wemberley, it's a pleasure to have your attendance tonight." I took her pink silk-gloved hand and gave it a light kiss.

"I've told you to call me Rynne, you know," she said, her icy blue eyes dancing, contrasting against her dark red hair. Rynne Wemberley had a way of blurring lines or crossing them altogether. Her family controlled most of the fertilizer in Friese, as well as the trade of many food items through the port. Our paths seemed to cross often, to my consternation.

"And I will continue to show you the respect a lady of your rank deserves," I said with a sly smile. She giggled, hiding a blush with her hand.

Such was the game I played at every social event. Engage them enough to keep their interest, but not so much as to welcome an unwanted attachment. I was seen as the most eligible bachelor in Friese aside from Prince Harley, causing balls to be an excruciating experience. Every family was desperate to be tied to the Exley name, and there was only one Exley son. A son whose heart was already claimed.

"Let us join the others, shall we?" I offered my arm to Rynne, eager to avoid any more time alone together. She seemed disappointed, but took my arm and let me lead her down the stairs.

"Is the queen in attendance tonight?" I asked.

"Oh, you haven't heard?" Rynne giggled conspiratorially. "The queen is here, alright. And she brought her entire family!"

Echna, spare me.

"When you say, *entire*—" I began, but Rynne cut me off enthusiastically.

"Yes! The prince and princess are here!" she whispered in what might've been the shrillest tone I had ever heard.

Damn.

Queen Lesynna had made a few not-so-subtle hints that she expected me to court her daughter, Princess Eadlin. My father, however, had made it very clear to me that he didn't wish to tie the Exleys to the royal family. Those conflicting desires had left me in a very precarious position. If I was too familiar with the princess, my father had endless ways to make me pay for it. If I was too distant with her, the queen could get suspicious of me and my level of commitment to our *arrangement*.

Upon Rynne's tenacious insistence, I led her to the ballroom for a dance. The crowd moved in synchronicity with the waltz that was being played, making grand ball gowns flow and sparkle. Rynne was quite a talented dancer, so I much preferred dancing with her than listening to her endless gossip.

As we moved along to the music, my mind drifted again to Francie. I thought of her beautiful voice as she sang to me. The taste of her skin under my lips. How soft her hair was as I ran my fingers through it...

A familiar glare caught my eye, pulling me from my memories. Prince Harley Ainsworth, heir to the Friesian throne, stood on the edge of the ballroom. He was tall and formidable—clad in a full royal dress uniform, and even deigning to wear a golden crown. Harley's wavy chestnut hair hung next to his dark eyes, which were narrowed on me. I bit back the disgust that threatened to show on my face and looked away. I mentally noted to check on my maids and make sure they hadn't been subjected to any of Harley's unwanted flirtation.

Before I lost myself to my disgust, the song ended and someone grasped my hand from behind. I turned to see Her Royal Highness, Princess Eadlin Ainsworth. Pitch-black hair fell straight down her back, framing her angled face. Her unnaturally light grey irises gleamed as she studied me.

"Your Highness! I apologize, I failed to sense your approach!" Rynne wheezed, executing the lowest and clumsiest curtsy I had ever witnessed.

A corner of the princess's mouth turned up, amused by the display in front of her. "The apology is mine, Miss Wemberley. I've been told I have the tendency to sneak up on people." She spoke in a low, confident voice, eyes locked firmly on mine. "May I borrow Mister Exley for a dance?" she asked.

Rynne wheezed yet again. "Oh—of course, Your Highness!" She said goodbye and made her way out of the crowd.

"Shall we?" I asked, looking at the princess with caution.

She only smiled at me and took my hand. A new song began, and we fell into our roles. Unable to resist, I showcased my dancing expertise with sweeping dips and twirling my partner. She played along, matching my skill and enthusiasm. Her wine red, draping silk gown—which was quite a departure from the grand ball gowns that were typical among the elite Friesians—contoured every curve as she danced, rippling like water. I could tell that we were attracting eyes, but the competitive air she displayed was irresistible. It may have been a mercy to us both that the song ended, and a slower, more intimate song began.

"If you are as smart as your reputation would lead me to believe, I'm sure you know why I've sought you out," the princess whispered.

Here we go...

"I have absolutely no idea," I said with a slight smile.

She looked up at me, one eyebrow raised. "You're going to play coy, then?"

I stared back at her, letting my silence be my answer.

The princess sighed. "In recent months, Mother has done nothing but implore me to deepen our acquaintance. I have reason to believe she's done the same to you," she said in a suppressed tone.

"You would be correct," I replied.

How am I going to survive this conversation?

"I will be frank with you, because I don't believe in wasting people's time. I am uninterested in a marriage alliance between our houses, no matter what my mother thinks."

My jaw nearly dropped. "Your Highness..." I balked for only a moment before I realized the implication in her words. "Why not?" I asked.

"Am I to believe you *want* this alliance?" Her perfect eyebrows rose in taunting disbelief.

"That's not what I mean to say. My question is, why are you trying to avoid a connection to my family?" I asked, my tone hushed as I tried not to give away my concern. In Friese, a house's reputation was everything.

"Color me shocked; you sound offended! I suppose the rumors of you being unflappable are unfounded," she said as she moved closer to whisper in my ear. "If you are solely worried about your house's reputation among the high society of Friese, you may rest easy. Exley remains untarnished."

I spun her out, then pulled her closer and dipped her low. Often, when an unfamiliar dancer lowers his partner for a dip, she will tense up as a natural reaction to having to trust a stranger. The princess, however, tilted her head back and embraced the moment. Her body was completely relaxed in my arms.

After I brought her back up, she gave me a feline smile. "Do you realize you just used my hair to sweep your floor?"

"Then it's fortunate I found the largest pile of dirt to stand over before dipping you," I retorted.

Her eyes shot wide for a moment before rolling. "That wasn't funny."

"Why are you opposed to a marriage?" I asked pointedly, pulling her close.

She leaned in closer. "I am not opposed to marriage, Mister Exley. I'm simply not interested in a marriage to you."

Ouch.

Even though I was also uninterested in a marriage to the princess, the jab still hurt. Being labeled "one of Friese's most eligible bachelors" had inflated my ego, and our conversation punctured that image.

"Why?" I insisted.

She sighed, obviously preferring to avoid the explanation. "I am dubious of our houses' recent closeness. Something about it doesn't feel right."

She must not know about the secret arrangement the queen has with us.

"I can assure you, Your Highness, that nothing untoward is occurring between Exley and Ainsworth. All of our dealings are open," I lied.

She looked up at me, doubt written on her face. "Even if there was, I'm sure I wouldn't be informed of it. My mother tells me nothing."

I wish my father told me nothing.

"I am well-informed of all Exley dealings, so my assurances are reliable."

Liar.

The song ended, and the princess stepped backwards. "Be that as it may, I shall continue to trust my instincts in this realm. I hope you don't take offense, as I surely don't mean to give any."

To my surprise, she took my hand and led me through turning heads before stopping behind a pillar.

"What are we doing back here, Your Highness?" I asked, confused.

"I want my mother to assume I am making an effort in a courtship," she said, eyes roving over the crowds. "If she sees us spending some time together at public functions, she might ease her constant insistence."

I found it ironic that the exact thing the princess needed to please her mother was what would displease my father.

"I'm sure we've attracted enough attention with our dance, Your Highness." We certainly had. People were whispering to each other, hiding their faces with fans and gloved hands.

She nodded, sure enough that the queen had seen us together. "Well then, Mister Exley, I bid you farewell. Until the next social event, that is."

I bowed, and she made her way up to the royal table.

No sooner did the princess walk away than I felt a firm, unsettling grip on my shoulder.

"Library. Now."

"What were you thinking?" My father asked in an even, suppressed tone. He'd brought me to his library, where he now stood close to the shelving, facing away.

"I was—"

He cut me off. "This had better not be one of your sentimental excuses."

"There is no courtship, Father."

"Does she know that? Or is she going to run to her mother and beg for an autumn wedding?"

"No, she isn't interested in marrying me." As soon as I said it, I wished I hadn't.

Father turned his head, revealing furrowed brows. "Why not?" he asked, his voice sharp as a knife.

"She suspects the alliance between our houses," I answered. Father always seemed to sniff out blatant lies—deceit would be futile.

He began pacing back and forth along the wall. "She doesn't know, then? Of our... special arrangement?" he asked.

"It would seem not. Isn't that a good thing? One less person to leak it?" I asked, hoping to ease the tension.

Father chuckled. "The princess's exclusion from this information shows the queen doesn't trust her with it. She would try to put a stop to our advantageous business dealings, or expose us altogether." He stopped, turning to face me. "Don't trust her. Tell her nothing. I have some plans in the works that I would hate to be delayed."

Don't ask. Don't ask. Don't ask.

"Plans, Father?"

Idiot.

"Trenica has expressed interest in exporting their goods into Friese," he said, watching me with a measuring stare.

Air rushed from my lungs. Friesians had been trying to convince Trenica to export to us for years. Considering their long and complicated history with Friese, Trenica was considered an untappable market. It was on the same continent as Friese, but situated far in the north, separated by barren wastelands. Its natural resources were seemingly endless metal deposits and gemstones, which were very desirable by Friesian high society.

"How did you do it?" I asked, unsure if I wanted to know the answer.

Father smirked. "There's no need to get into that right now. We do, however, need to focus on how we will make it happen. Our house now has an exclusive opportunity to monopolize this."

My head was swimming with the implications of such a large expansion. "We'd need more ships, more docks, more warehouses..." There was no way to make the increase in trade efficient with our current infrastructure.

"I also have considered this," he said, leaning against his imported mahogany desk. "There happens to be a large, perfectly situated piece of land just west of the docks. It's perfect for development, and its current use is a waste of its potential." He let his words simmer, staring intently at me.

I racked my brain, thinking of alternate possibilities from the very obvious one.

Surely, he doesn't mean to...

"The slums?" I choked out.

Father smiled. "I knew you'd figure it out. My genetics weren't a waste, after all."

"But, Father—there are hundreds of people living there, if not *thousands*. Where would they go?" I felt like I was on a sled going down a hill that was getting steeper and steeper. I'd lost control—I was incapable of stopping it now.

"Where they go is none of our concern. I've already acquired the land. My next step is to delegate."

"Respectfully, Father, whichever employee you delegate this to is none of my concern. I will take my leave." With that, I turned on my heel, making a bee-line for the gardens. Before I made it to the door, I heard an ominous chuckle from behind me.

"You should be very interested in whom I delegate this task to," my father called.

No.

I will not.

I spun around. "I won't do it, Father. I refuse to oversee the displacement of hundreds of people—many of them our own employees!" I shouted. "This time, you go too far."

Father scoffed and stood up. "Then I suppose you will have to decide where your priorities lie. I'd rather leave my windblade to the atmosphere than to an ungrateful and insolent child."

"There is no way you'd let our house collapse purely to spite me!" I growled, my throat constricting.

"And there is no way I would let someone hold my plans hostage!" he yelled, waving his arm and throwing his windblade into a shelf. Books exploded and bits of paper floated to the ground.

He cleared his voice and stepped closer to me. "Let me be clear. Your wishes are irrelevant. If you execute my plans, you will have proven your loyalty to the success of our family, and shall therefore inherit my windblade when I die. If you refuse, Exley might as well be ash. The blade will go to the atmosphere."

Deep down, I'd always assumed that my father would give me his windblade when he died, regardless of our conflicts. I was his only heir and the only hope of our house continuing on. It was only then, however, that I realized my father was not bluffing.

"I think it's time," he sighed, circling me. "You need to know about what happened to your grandfather. You might learn a little something about sacrifice.... about doing whatever it takes to secure our future."

I furrowed my brows. I'd been told my grandfather took ill and died just after my father had married. "What do you mean?" I asked, rooted to where I stood.

"I've told you the very heartfelt story of his passing. Unfortunately, that was a necessary fabrication to preserve your untarnished view of your ancestors. For all of his good qualities, unfortunately, discernment was not one of them. He became smitten with one of our lowly housemaids, who had hidden her true motives. In a fatal moment of vulnerability, she killed him." He paused, letting me process it. "I've found myself grateful to be without his genetic influence," he muttered.

"If that's true... she took Asgora? Our blade..."

How could Grandfather let something like that happen?

"But you got it back, of course."

Father laughed. "No, I never did. That little slum cat disappeared. However, I couldn't let the other houses know I was without a windblade—that would mean ruin."

My stomach sank. "If you didn't get it back... whose windblade do you have?"

CHAPTER EIGHTEEN

ESESTIA

Twenty Years Ago

There can be only one windblade within a bloodline.

Long ago, when the windblades had first been bestowed upon Friese, multiple Skylords attempted to consolidate power by having their sons and brothers kill the Skylords of other houses and steal their windblades. While this may have seemed like a surefire way to control Friese indefinitely, the result was far from desirable.

Within a year of claiming their blades, every additional Skylord died until there was only one left. A tree fell on one, and a disease took another until all of those additional Skylords were gone.

Very few other families attempted this sort of power grab over the years, but the results were always the same. Within one year of adding another windblade to the bloodline, its wielder would die. No one knows why this phenomenon occurs, but it is the sole reason Friesian houses don't consume each other to hoard windblades amongst their own family members. It would seem that Echna, the goddess of wind, doesn't allow the monopolization of her power.

- A History of Wind Control, Prof. Heliana Fromme

Twenty Years Ago

The sun rose over the vast Exley countryside. Rolling hills dotted with grazing cows and horses went on for as far as the eye could see. Mazes of ornate, colorful gardens surrounded the sprawling mansion. The building itself was a feat of architecture—three ballrooms, two fully staffed kitchens, two libraries and sixteen bedrooms. Only a select few Friesian families held such amounts of wealth.

As I pondered my wealth alone on my balcony, the only conclusion I could reach was that it was not enough. Wealth without power meant little to me.

I'd spent years being ridiculed and mocked by my father, whose shame of having only one son was exacerbated because this son was wispy, slight, and spent all of his free time practicing games of strategy. No, wealth was not enough for me. I stood to achieve greater power than my brute of a father could have imagined.

Upon my father's death, my plans had been rendered obsolete. The problem wasn't the fact of his death, but the cause of it. The power that was supposed to pass to me had slipped away, disappearing into an untraceable horizon. This was the crux of my bigger problem: House Exley had no windblade. The even distribution of windblades among the noble families was the only thing deterring us from destroying each other whilst clamoring for power and influence. If it became public that House Exley had no windblade, it would be the end of our superiority—maybe the end of the Exley family altogether. I wouldn't let that happen.

The sound of bare footsteps on the marble floor distracted me from my planning.

"Come to bed, Augustus," a mischievous voice purred from behind me. I turned and gazed upon my new wife, a devastating beauty made up of sharp amber eyes, blonde hair and a figure that most of her peers hated her for. A figure that was completely exposed.

"Naked on the balcony again, Adriana? We've talked about this." My words were firm, but she noticed my eyes lingering.

A smile formed on the edge of her lips as I moved closer to block her nakedness from any curious onlookers below. Eighteen-year-old Adriana Clarendon married me only two weeks ago. She was full of a youthful exuberance that both excited and frustrated me. On one hand, I found her forward nature to be very convenient. That trait, however, cut both ways. She was strong-willed, which was a decidedly problematic quality.

"Afraid the horses will see me?" She slid a hand over my belt, but I pushed it away.

"Not today. Something's come up." I gripped her shoulders, spun her around, and pushed her inside.

She flinched, rolling her shoulders under my grip. "Too tight, Augustus."

I rolled my eyes. She was so naïve. "Don't be soft," I commanded before releasing her.

She scowled as she slid a pink silk robe over her shoulders. I knew it frustrated her when I reminded her of her place. A wife served two important functions: to satisfy her husband, and to produce an heir. Adriana—while very enthusiastic about fulfilling both functions—seemed to expect something more from me.

She walked in front of me, blocking my way to the door. I stopped just before colliding with her.

"You left last night."

"I came back." My mouth twitched at the memory.

"Then you left *again,*" she said, her tone verging on pleading. Her robe slipped down her shoulder, exposing the marks I'd left on her.

"I've told you before—I keep my own room."

"So you can't stay for *one night?*"

I didn't have time for another argument. Unbeknownst to her, our house was in a crisis, and I needed to remedy it as soon as possible. Reaching up, I slid my hand under her chin, gripping her jaw. Her eyes widened slightly, the familiar glints of fear and desire flashing through her amber irises. I slipped my other hand under her robe, taking her hip and digging my nails into it. She squirmed, but didn't back away.

I slipped her robe off her shoulders, leaning in until my lips brushed her ear. "Fine. You'll get what you want." I wrapped my hand around her throat. "But you'll regret it."

Reston Orrick

The magnificent city of Friese hummed with activity in the crisp morning air. Birds sat in the sun atop the walls of the Friesian Archive building, chirping and enjoying what many city-folk were saying was the coolest day yet in the autumn season. Merchants passed by with pumpkins, gourds and chrysanthemums piled high in their carts.

A beautiful day, indeed, thought Lieutenant Reston Orrick of House Exley's guard. He was grateful for a peaceful morning after the week he had. Lord Augustus Exley sent word that they were to be on high alert, hunting for a small, blonde-haired girl. Lieutenant Orrick was no fool—he knew a noble family would have very few reasons to be so intent on finding a young woman of familial insignificance, and the elder Lord Exley's reputation was widely known amongst the high-born. Therefore, it didn't dismay Orrick when no trace of the girl had been found. As a kind-hearted man, it relieved him. But he wasn't so naïve as to display those feelings. A sharp voice shocked him out of his reverie.

"Lieutenant, a word," snapped Augustus Exley as he climbed down from his carriage which had just come to a stop in front of the Archive. Augustus was tall and wore a dark, unadorned suit. His long black hair blew next to his sharp face, providing a stark contrast to his alabaster skin.

The flustered lieutenant scrambled to attention, embarrassed to be caught daydreaming. "Yes, My Lord. What can I do for you?"

Augustus stared at Orrick with a steely expression, making the soldier inwardly squirm. Even the tall nobleman's posture and countenance evoked unease in him. "Still no sign of the girl, I presume?"

"N-No, Sir," Orrick answered.

Something about those piercing black eyes... What's happened?

"You were in charge of the search?"

Orrick got a sinking feeling in his stomach. "Yes, sir."

Out of the corner of his eye, he saw a glint of silver flash from under Augustus's coat. Hot pain overcame Orrick as the dagger plunged into his side—a fatal placement.

"That's too bad. I hate to make an example of you, but it seems I had no choice."

Orrick collapsed to the ground, barely hearing what Augustus was saying. He stared up at his murderer and found only cold indifference.

His voice rang through the courtyard. "My father is dead. I am your new Skylord, and I will not tolerate any level of incompetence in my guard. Is that understood?"

The other guards in the courtyard, who had congregated nearby to observe the spectacle, snapped to attention. The last thing Orrick heard was their faint disharmonious echo: "Yes, Skylord!"

Augustus

I handed the bloody dagger to my carriage driver before climbing back in. As the carriage started down the cobbled Friesian roads, I stared out the window, contemplating my upcoming meeting. I didn't have time to reflect on my actions—all that mattered was what I would do next. The answer to my problem lay only a few miles away, and I intended on exploiting it for all its worth.

House Merton, being of minor significance amongst the nobles, sat near the edge of the city. The Mertons held control over the fishing exports and land in the nearby Friesian-ruled coastal village, Bureneau. This was of little consequence compared to House Exley, which controlled all industrial trade in and out of Friese. Most sources of building materials, metals, and lumber were owned and controlled by the Exleys, which gave us a heavy influence over Friese and its queen. Minor houses like the Mertons held very little influence over city affairs and thus were largely ignored.

Until their debts were called in.

The Skylord of House Merton, Frederick, had an unfortunate spending problem. He'd furnished his residence with the latest fashions, and his gardens boasted the finest flowers and trees. The meager Merton income could never support his lavish lifestyle, and the Exleys never turned down an opportunity for control over another noble house. One never knew when said control may come in handy.

The carriage came to a stop in front of a small but pristine residence. Fence pillars of gray stone bricks buffered a heavy black gate, which had already been opened for me. Late-blooming austoria bushes grew beside the cobbled steps, exuding a sickly sweet scent which was carried through the air by a cool autumn breeze. My lip curled up in distaste. The accompanying carriage stopped behind me, and two of my guards got out and headed toward the house.

A well-manicured butler eyed the guards, but greeted me before leading me up the marble steps to the door.

"So good to see you again, Lord Exley," the butler said while opening the door for me.

"Yes, yes," I replied, looking around in disdain at the garish fashion in which the entryway had been decorated. It was no wonder how the Mertons had become so deeply indebted to me. As I was ruminating, a portly man in his mid-sixties, clad from head to toe in purple velvet, trundled around the corner.

"Augustus Exley, my goodness, it has been too long! You must be nearing twenty years old now! How's the new wife?" Frederick Merton slurred through his jowls.

This fool has the nerve to get half-drunk before meeting his creditor. Although I don't suppose it will change the outcome for him.

"She's well." I didn't try very hard to hide my disgust, though I considered it unlikely Frederick would notice. The large man started leading me down the hallway and into a study.

"Please, take a seat, dear boy. We keep our finest leather couches and chairs in this room. Go ahead, take a seat!" Frederick said as he plopped down on a jewel-encrusted loveseat. I ignored the comment and remained standing, wearing an impassive expression.

"Lord Frederick, I am here to collect the debt you owe House Exley."

Upon hearing this, Frederick's expression transformed to disbelief with the delayed sluggishness that came from intoxication.

"B-But... Sir! House Exley has never asked for more than a small interest payment from us! Surely you don't expect us to come up with that kind of money on such short notice?" Frederick sputtered, his face turning a shade of red that put his gaudy decor to shame.

I slipped my black gloves off one at a time as I walked around the room. "Of course I don't expect that, Frederick. That is entirely the point."

The fat nobleman didn't seem to hear me, as he'd buried his face in his hands and started muttering about selling assets. After a few seconds of this, he jerked his head up, eyes bulging in desperation.

"This is unprecedented! Let me speak to your father! Where is he?"

I came to a stop behind Frederick's chair and rested a hand on his shoulder. Leaning in close, I whispered, "That's the problem, you fat, useless, money-grubbing codger."

Before Frederick could respond, I'd buried my dagger through the side of the old man's neck. Blood spilled out of the wound as I pulled it back out, staining the loveseat. Frederick clawed at his throat, trying to scream, but only managing bloody gurgles.

I walked around to face my victim, smiling as I noticed a small gust of wind brush through Frederick's thinning hair.

"My father is dead, and not by my hand," I said, loud enough for the dying man to hear. Realization dawned on Frederick's face, and his bloody chokes became more desperate. The air spun around him like a tornado, sending papers flying around the room. Frederick's blood leaked into the torrent and flew in circles around the room, resulting in bright red spray shooting out in every direction. I didn't cover my face.

Frederick's body finally slumped back into the bloody chair, and the tornado redirected itself—flying straight into me and pushing me backwards onto the floor. The air in the room stood still as I sat there, stunned.

That tingling sensation... is it adrenaline? Or something more...

With shaking legs, I pushed myself up off of the floor. The room laid in absolute disarray. On pure instinct, I flung my arm in a throwing motion. A wall of books split open—a long tear through their spines. I smiled as I flexed my fingers.

"This... is what true power feels like."

As I stared at my hands, lost in thought, one of my guards dragged the Merton heir into the room, holding a knife to his throat.

"I just caught this one trying to sneak in." The burly guard shoved the young man down to his knees. Unlike his father, Robert Merton was a muscular man of average height and decent appearance. I presumed Robert owed his handsomeness to his mother.

A startled cry erupted from him as he laid eyes on his dead father.

"You bastard! You killed my father over a debt?"

I directed a predatory gaze at my victim's son, making him shrink back a bit. "Dear, Robert. I have more money than I could ever dream of spending. Why would I go to such an effort over a small debt?"

Robert furrowed the brows on his red face as he pieced together my true goal. "You stole Esestia," he roared, referencing the heritage windblade of House Merton.

I started slow-clapping. "Ah, there are those quick Merton wits I've heard so much about. Figured it out, have we? That's wonderful—just in time, too. Decker, step aside a few paces if you please."

The guard wore an ominous look on his face but complied, knowing better than to make me repeat myself.

"If Lord Exley is dead, you should have Asgora... why would you want Esestia?" Robert mumbled, shaking his head in confusion. His eyes remained locked on his dead father's body. "You major houses are always playing games with the lives of those born lower than you. You'll pay for that one day." His hateful expression held firm.

"Tell your father I said 'Hello.'"

CHAPTER NINETEEN
NOBLE BLOOD

ARTURIAN

Friese is the only known place in the world to have individuals with wind-control. There are many theories as to why, but many believe that the goddess of wind, Echna, holds dear the Kingdom of Friese. Windblades can be used outside of Friese's border, but not inherited. On the rare occasions a Friesian Skylord is killed outside of Friese's border, his power is not inherited. This phenomenon has caused Friesian Skylords to be very averse to foreign travel unless they deem it absolutely necessary. Conversely, for centuries, Friese has been essentially immune to foreign threats because of the Skylords. There is no weapon created by human hands that can match the deadliness of the windblade.
- A History of Wind Control, Prof. Heliana Fromme

Shame had been a recurring theme in my recent life. Upon hearing my father's story, I felt ashamed of my father's cruelty. However, that cruelty had kept House Exley alive. Conversely, I felt guilty about what I would have to ask of my friends. Although the actions of my father disgusted me, I wouldn't let them be in vain.

I walked along the darkening, pungent streets of the port slums, clad in my best attempt at disguise. Mine and my father's faces were well-known to most Friesians, so I made my way along in a faded old cap, oversized coat, and my oldest pair of riding pants. I looked odd, but not wealthy. I'd only been to the inn once, and I'd been a young boy at the time. Father had found out I'd been in the slums, and the repercussions had been severe. I took extra precautions to ensure no one followed me.

As I approached the door, someone pushed past me with an aggressive shove. I turned to face the assaulter, barely glimpsing his face. He was a tall, muscled man, covered in tattoos. I palmed my throwing knives under my coat, but thought better of it.

No, I shouldn't draw unnecessary attention.

I took a deep breath and pushed the inn's door open. The room was lit with an array of candles, casting a welcoming light on the tables.

A soft voice called across the room. "I'm sorry—dinner ended an hour ago. Breakfast is just after dawn."

I turned to see Francie, clad in a tattered work dress and a blue scarf over her braided hair. As always, she was breathtaking.

After turning to look at me, she dropped the ladle she'd been drying.

"What are you doing here?" she whispered, glancing around the room in alarm. Before I could answer, she turned and bolted through the door behind her.

Not a good sign...

I stood in the entryway for a moment, not knowing what to do. Right as I turned to leave, Francie came back through the door.

"Levick will return any minute," she said with an apologetic look on her face.

Jealousy burned in my heart. Levick spent countless hours with her while they worked.

"I need to talk to you," I said, taking a few steps closer. "Somewhere we won't be seen."

I watched as her expression softened. She grabbed a candle from a table and took my hand. My heart thundered at her touch. She turned and led me back through a dark hallway and into a storage closet. Upon entering, she released my hand and stepped away, setting the candle on a small table. I faltered.

What is that... distance?

"What do you need?" she asked with an air of polite formality. As if that day we spent wrapped in each other's arms never happened.

"Francie," I said through bated breath. She stared back at me with an unreadable expression.

Without thinking, I closed the gap between us, taking her face in my hands. She relaxed into my touch, but I still sensed her tension. Her soft blue eyes were guarded.

"Do you think about it?" I whispered, needing to know if she was as consumed with me as I was with her. "Do you think about that day?"

Her beautiful features twisted in incredulity at my question. "Of course I do." Her voice broke.

"Francie..." I whispered, brushing a knuckle over her cheek. I had to know if it was all just a momentary lapse in judgment for her. A dream.

Just as I started to second-guess myself, she tilted her head up to mine, her lips parting ever-so-slightly.

I knew it.

Without another thought, I brought my lips to hers in a deep, passionate kiss. She melted into it immediately, nearly sighing in my arms. The tightness around my heart loosened as I lost myself to the moment. My only thoughts were of her... of *more.* Francie ran her hands over my back, and cans rattled behind her as I pressed her against a shelf. She arched against me, hands pulling at my shirt—unbuttoning it. I had her dress ribbon in my fingers, about to pull, when she pushed me away. She leaned on the shelf, panting. Her breathing was ragged, as if she was about to cry.

"What's wrong?" I asked, backing away to give her the space she clearly needed.

A dark thought entered my mind—one that had been festering below the surface since our conversation at the port office. When she made it clear that she didn't want to tell Levick about what we'd done. I voiced it before I could stop myself.

"Is this about Levick?"

Her head jerked over at me, looking hurt. "It's about *you*," she choked out. Straightening up and composing herself, she looked directly into my eyes. "Someday, I am going to watch you marry someone else."

Her words cut like a knife. I'd been in denial, but the future was a dark cloud hanging over me wherever I went. To marry a commoner would be unheard of. My father would kill her.

"That's why..." she started, her composure deteriorating, "that day was a mistake."

I said nothing, but noticed her clutching the necklace she was wearing... an ornate platinum ring with a massive nine-carat black diamond at its center. I couldn't see it clearly, but I knew exactly where the intricate letters buffered each corner of the square stone.

The ring of House Exley... all is not lost.

"You should repair things with Levick," she whispered, and without another word, she turned and left.

I took a few minutes to gather my composure before leaving the storage closet and searching through the hall. I went through the first door I came to, which led to the prep kitchen. Francie scrubbed the counters, her tension palpable. She turned and saw me, pausing her work.

"Francie—" I started. But just then, Levick came through the back door, smiling at her. He stopped dead when he saw me.

"Why are you here?" His words were clipped. He still hadn't forgiven me for what I said about Francie on the night my father killed Frenzy.

Francie stared at me, her eyes pleading with me. I raised my hands in a conciliatory gesture.

"I'm here to apologize."

Levick scoffed, but Francie placed a hand on his arm before he could speak. She gave him a look that was so familiar; I felt out of place. My heart ached.

"Let's sit down," Levick said, leading the three of us out of the prep kitchen and to a table in the back, away from the windows.

Wise.

I cleared my throat and tried to think of Francie's wishes. "I realize I haven't been a good friend, but you two are very important to me. One of my primary concerns is that you're both safe and stable." I paused and took a deep breath, remembering the initial reason I sought Francie out. "That's why I'm asking you to trust me and move out of the slums." Upon hearing that, Francie's eyes widened. However, Levick's eyes narrowed.

"Why?" Francie asked. "What's going on?"

"I can't say," I said, hoping it had an air of finality.

"People don't choose to live here, Arturian. It's where they end up when they can't afford anything else," Levick said. "There is no other place to go."

"Does your aunt have any connections, Francie?" I asked, grasping at straws.

She put her head in her hands. "Her only connections are here in the slums..."

My father's requests of me added a layer of stress to my life, and learning about my grandfather's unfortunate death had only made it worse. In a moment of sentimentality, I decided that if I wanted my friends to trust me, it was time for me to trust them with something.

"My father recently told me a family story; one that I'd never heard. It made me realize how valuable it is to have trustworthy people in your life," I said, hesitating slightly. "Twenty years ago, my grandfather, Adolpho, was betrayed by someone he knew and trusted. A few months before I was born, one of his house-maids at the old country estate seduced him and caught him by surprise. She—" I stopped myself before I said "murdered." I knew better than to let anyone—even my friends—know the windblade was stolen.

"She injured him, and stole something from him, and was never caught." My voice grew tight. "Unfortunately, he died shortly after. At my father's hand, of course," I added, hoping it didn't sound suspicious.

Francie gasped, bringing a hand to her lips. It wasn't unusual for people to be unnerved by how the windblade must be passed down.

I continued, "The wealth and status that comes with my rank can lead people to exploit it, but I know I can trust you two. I really appreciate that—it's rare."

Francie

I frantically did the math in my head.

No, no, no.

There are dozens—if not hundreds—of Skylords in Friese. Surely there was another major murder of a Skylord twenty years ago? There's just no way...

The evidence was undeniable.

The timeline was irrefutable.

After exhausting everything I knew about recent noble history, I knew I couldn't deny it. The odds were against me. The *seductress* in Arturian's story was my mother.

My mother killed Adolpho Exley.

"That means a lot, Arturian. Although, I'm not sure if I can fully trust you if you can't tell us *why* we should leave the slums," Levick said. I barely heard it—my head was buzzing.

Adolpho Exley is my father.

Augustus is illegitimate.

That makes me...

The only blood heir to House Exley.

Arturian

"Air!" Francie gasped from across the table. Her hands shook and her eyes were wild.

"Are you alright?" I asked, resisting the urge to reach for her hand.

Francie's eyes shot to mine, blinking rapidly before composing herself. "I need some air—I dissected a few too many rabbits today." She laughed awkwardly. "We'll think about what you said, Arturian. But I'm going to step out." With that, Francie stood and rushed off into the prep kitchen.

Francie's odd behavior threw me off. I briefly considered going after her, but there was no way to do it discreetly.

Levick stared at the prep kitchen door in concern. "She's probably just tired," he said, thoughts obviously occupied.

I couldn't help but feel resentment for how Levick spoke about Francie. Like he knew her *better*. I quickly stamped out the jealousy, remembering Francie's plea that I mend things with him.

He placed his hands on the table. "We'll consider your suggestion, Arturian, but I don't like the secrets. They've never ended well for us."

"Of course," I responded as Levick stood up.

"I should check on her." Levick was obviously keen on making a quick escape.

It should be me.

"I'll see you around?" Levick asked. Despite the knot in my stomach, I felt encouraged by the familiarity.

"Yes, and tell Francie I hope she feels better soon," I said with a wave. As I got up to leave, I felt the weariness of a lifetime settle upon my aching heart. Francie's words echoed in my mind.

"That day was a mistake."

CHAPTER TWENTY
THE ARCHIVE

As soon as I walked into the prep-kitchen, I sprinted to the back door, swung it open, and burst into the alley. I suspected where Francie was going, so I followed my hunch.

Bounding into the alley, I took off like a shot, harnessing gusts of wind to speed my every stride. I'd recently honed the ability to use wind gusts to increase my running speed, a task that used to be nearly impossible without constant tripping. To an onlooker, I'd appear to have unusually long strides. In reality, I was using a powerful burst of targeted wind to propel myself after every forward spring. I'd made it to the trail leading to the bell tower when I saw Francie jogging ahead.

I called after her.

She glanced back, exposing her tear-stained face in the broken-up moonlight. "I can't do this right now, Levick." She slowed to a walk. "I can't."

I approached her in the woods, but didn't get too close. "I won't interrogate you, Francie. But please—don't make me leave you alone like this," I said, my voice pleading.

She stopped next to an old oak, placing her hand on its trunk. Hands trembling, she toyed with her necklace before tucking it back into her neckline. "It's okay. I should tell someone." She shook her head, then looked over her shoulder at me. "The girl in Arturian's story—the one about his grandfather?" She paused, looking down. "That was my mother."

I tilted my head. I'd been worried her distress had something to do with Arturian... but not at all like *that*.

"Your mother seduced and stole from Adolpho Exley?"

"No, no. Augustus twisted the story to cover things up. The actual story is much more... disturbing," she said, her voice growing quiet. "He... *assaulted* her. She defended herself and killed him by accident."

"*Killed*?" My mind began swarming with the implications of it.

That means... Francie's mother must've inherited Asgora. She had his windblade.

"You still don't understand, Lev," she muttered.

"I know, but I can try. Please, let me try?" I pressed. I hated seeing her like this—so anguished by the past.

She turned and looked into my eyes, shame written across her fair features. "He *assaulted* her. Adolpho Exley is my father."

It hit me like a punch to the gut—knocking the wind out of me and sending me spiraling backwards.

Francie is an Exley.

"I wield Asgora, the windblade of House Exley—the blade that was meant for Augustus, and one day, for Arturian," she said, voice shaking. "Do you want to know how I got it?" she asked, her composure crumbling as she held in broken sobs.

I clenched my fists—I figured out the answer before she said it.

"Because my mother killed Adolpho, and then *I* killed my mother. As I was being born, I killed her." Francie collapsed under her despair, falling to her knees in the dirt.

I sat down and held her in my arms as she cried. A storm was forming overhead, lowering the pressure and dropping light rain on us. The revelation burned in my mind as I brushed her damp hair with my fingers.

"That means Augustus is your *brother...*" I said, working through it. "Shit. Arturian is your *nephew.*"

Francie shook her head. Denial, maybe?

My chest tightened as I held her shaking body in my arms. I'd known there would come a time when things could never go back to how they were in our youth. My friends would grow up, maybe lose touch, and the weeds might overtake our well-trodden trail. But as I stared it in the face, I couldn't help but dig my heels in. The woman I loved was a member—albeit illegitimately—of the most powerful noble house in Friese. She held the heritage windblade of House Exley. If that was discovered, she would become the most wanted person in the kingdom, and be purged by one of the many Skylords. Augustus would be the first in line.

Things will never be the same again.

Then something occurred to me.

"Francie, if you have the Exley windblade... where did Augustus get *his*?"

She wiped her eyes and lifted her head. "I don't know."

"Wasn't there an entire noble family that dropped off the map at around that time?" I racked my brain.

Francie looked at me, confused.

"I suppose it doesn't matter right now," I said, not wanting to be insensitive.

I helped her up, and we walked towards the bell tower to seek shelter from the brewing storm. As we walked, I searched through my memories.

Skelton? No...

Melton? No, that doesn't sound right, either.

Merton.

I watched the storm rage outside from the oversized windowsill at the top of the bell tower. I'd insisted Francie stay overnight rather than try to walk home in the wind and rain, so she slept in my bed as I pondered the day's events. As I watched the rise and fall of the blankets, I couldn't help but wish I could see it every night. It gave me a warm peace, having her there, safe and sleeping in my bed as the storm pounded against the window. Occasionally, lightning would light up the night sky, illuminating the forest trees bending over in the wind.

As raindrops ran down the window, I recalled the tragic story of the entire Merton family being killed in a catastrophic house fire; their windblade lost to the atmosphere.

The timing lines up too conveniently. But would Augustus risk the eradication of his house through something like this? If he massacred an entire house to steal their windblade, the other houses would unite to destroy him. The houses denounce windblade theft and strictly punish it. So strictly, that it hasn't occurred in centuries. Supposedly.

Suspicion slunk through my mind like an uninvited pest. Every memory, every anecdote, tainted by the new knowledge. The stories of Augustus' duplicitousness made more sense than they ever had. His conscience had been completely seared. He was a man who was reigning by the threat of a stolen power.

A man with a secret.

A secret that could destroy life in Friese as we knew it.

The next day, Francie had sheepishly apologized for her *intrusion* and flitted off to the inn. I could tell she was embarrassed by the vulnerability she'd shown me.

Maybe someday she won't be embarrassed around me anymore. It'll be natural... as easy as breathing.

I didn't let myself daydream too much before setting about my mission. My curiosity had overtaken my thoughts. Carrying nothing but my resolve for the truth, I set off for northern Friese.

The House Archive sat at the northernmost tip of Friese, just south of the queen's palace and north of the business district. When the Ainsworths took the throne of Friese two generations ago, they barred lower-class Friesians from many market districts and public places, such as libraries and the Archive. I knew some acquaintances who could help me, so I made my way down dirt roads until I recognized a large, well-maintained farmhouse, surrounded by vast gardens and crops.

As I reached the top of the steps, I took a deep breath. "It's okay to ask for help," I told myself before knocking on the front door. Commotion rang inside—children yelling and a feminine voice telling them to quiet down.

The front door swung open to reveal a beautiful woman in her thirties wearing a farmer's apron and her hair in messy braids. Her eyes lit up, and she smiled upon seeing me. "Levick! How are you doing?"

"I'm well, Gemma. Your mother-in-law has been keeping us busy, as always," I joked, wearing a charming smile. She was Plumeria's daughter-in-law, and a frequent donor to the inn.

Gemma laughed. "That doesn't surprise me in the least! She somehow manages to keep us busy, too, even from a distance." She smiled at me, her tan cheeks rounding under her eyes. "Can I help you, Levick? What brings you all the way out here?"

I breathed deeply and hoped she was feeling generous. "I know your husband has business up north, and I was wondering if he'd be willing to lend me some clothes?"

She cocked her head, intrigued. "Toren is outside. Let me go and fetch him." She invited me inside to wait, where multiple small children swarmed me. They were apparently starved for new climbing surfaces.

I had a toddler on my shoulders and a pair of five-year-olds hanging off of my legs when Toren came in the door. They were all laughing hysterically at how much they slowed me down. "Kids, why are you treating my friend as if he were one of your sheep?"

It had been a long time since I'd interacted with small children, and I found their endless energy to be infectious. I lifted the toddler, a little boy named Adrian, up and over my head, and handed him to his father. The five-year-olds were harder to shake off. They were twins, a boy and a girl named Lyon and Kiera. They giggled as I tried to lift my legs to shake them off, but their grip was impressive.

"Alright, kids, that's enough!" Toren grunted, prying the giddy children away. I couldn't help but laugh along. "Go help your mother!" Toren said, patting them on the head as he sent them off.

"My wife says you're in need of some nicer dress?" Toren asked, beckoning me to follow him down the hallway.

"Yes, if you don't mind lending me some?" I responded in what I hoped was an appropriately respectful tone. Toren and Gemma had been consistently generous to the inn, and I didn't want to take that for granted.

"I'd do anything to help one of the inn workers. Our kingdom desperately needs more people like you and your friends," he said, opening his armoire and rustling through the contents. "We're about the same height... what kind of clothing are you seeking? Formal? Business?"

I wasn't quite sure what I needed. "I need to blend in. My current clothing would stand out in the business district... I wouldn't last long before the Crownies chased me out."

Toren nodded as he continued his search. "You're right about that. One whiff of the slums on you and they'll send you right back. Ah! This one will work," he said triumphantly as he held out a steely-blue ensemble and a dramatic black tailcoat.

"That will help me *blend in*?" I asked, voice heavy with doubt.

"You really haven't been up there much, have you?" Toren replied as he handed the clothes over. "I meant to ask... what business do you have up there?"

"I'm visiting the Archive," I said in the most casual manner I could manage.

A gleam of curiosity shone in Toren's eyes, but he simply said, "Ah. The Archive." An awkward pause hung between us. "Well, I'll let you change," he said as he walked out of the room.

I took a deep breath and began the tedious task of dressing myself in the complicated outfit. After fastening what felt like my one-hundredth button, I turned to face the mirror.

A different man stood in my reflection.

Two vertical rows of gleaming silver buttons graced the surface of the pitch-black tailcoat, highlighting its snug fit. The back of the coat hung over the dark grey riding pants, which were tucked into tall, black boots. My blue shirt was barely visible under the tailcoat's high collar. I'd only ever worn slum-fare clothes... and I looked like an entirely new man.

There was a light knock on the door. "Levick, how is it fitting?" Gemma asked from the hallway.

"Surprisingly well," I responded. "You can come in. I'm dressed."

Upon seeing me, Gemma's eyes lit up. "You look so handsome!" she said, clapping her hands in excitement. The twins rushed into the room, gasping and clapping along, followed by Toren.

"It certainly fits," he said as he scanned me for any need for improvements. He stopped at my head, cringing. "Gemma, dear, would you mind working some of your magic on his hair?"

My hair was slightly overgrown, with the top strands hanging longer than the sides. I brushed it when I had the chance, but I usually just swept it out of my face and tried to keep it from becoming matted.

Gemma approached me, and I lowered my head for her. "It's not so bad, it just needs some work," she said as she ran her fingers through my hair. I took a seat and she began her work.

After some intense brushing—with a real hair brush—and some styling, I looked completely at home in my suit. "You look perfect!" Gemma said, standing back to admire her handiwork.

This will do.

"I wish you'd tell us why you need to go to the Archive," Toren said, prompting Gemma to nudge him in his side.

"It's not my secret to share. I hope both of you know how grateful I am, though," I said as I shook Toren's hand.

"You know..." Toren began, scratching his head. "I have plenty of suits, and this one seems custom-made for you. Keep it."

I resisted, but Gemma put her foot down. "Keep it! Who knows? Maybe you'll need it for a wedding or something..."

she trailed off with a sheepish grin on her face. We said our goodbyes, and I continued my walk further north.

Gemma's words haunted me as I walked. What could my future look like? What could *our* future look like? My thoughts drifted to our last RCM meeting, when Francie and I were outside together.

If that damn Ress hadn't showed up...

I had to suspend my reverie as I made my way into wealthier sector of Friese. Immaculately maintained cobbled streets lined the way, and large baskets of flowers hung from the front of most buildings. Women wore long elegant gowns and stylish hats that did nothing to block the sun from their squinting eyes. The men wore clothing very similar to what I wore. That was a relief, as I'd felt conspicuous in my fine clothing. Although my suit seemed perfectly appropriate for the area, I noticed I was attracting stares.

Why are they looking at me? What am I doing wrong?

I did a mental checklist of accessories I could be mis-wearing, or possible outlandish behavior I could be displaying, but nothing came to mind. Eventually, I noticed something about my onlookers.

Only the women are looking.

Oh.

Just then, a young woman with an elaborate red updo walked across my path. I barely side-stepped in time to prevent a collision with her.

"Good morning, sir," she said with a wink, red lips pressing together in a sensual pout. I barely contained an incredulous laugh, but winked back at her.

"Rynne, you're a menace!" I heard the friend hiss as she tugged the redhead away.

I chuckled and wondered if I might be attracting more attention in my current clothing than if I'd dressed as a slum-dweller.

Too late for that, now.

I rounded the corner of a tall bank and saw a magnificent architectural feat standing in front of me. It was nearly as grand as the queen's palace. A circle of broad pillars acted as the foundation of an enormous dome. It appeared as if the building had once been open between the pillars, but walls had been erected between them to protect the archives from the weather. Lush vines covered in yellow flowers traveled up each pillar and draped around the border of the dome. I could only see the front half of the building, but it appeared as if the vines traveled around the entire dome. The vines had been trimmed to make way for the arched entrance, whose steps were bordered with grand pots of tropical plants blooming in every color.

I realized I'd been gaping at the grandeur of it, while most people simply walked past me without even bothering to look up.

They're so accustomed to such beauty... they don't even appreciate it anymore.

I took a moment to straighten my coat, then walked up the steps and into the grand building. The bookshelves were arranged in semi circles; the smallest on the inside, and the largest running parallel to the walls. The ceiling was painted with scenes of famous Friesian stories depicting love, death, and joy. Feeling overwhelmed, I looked around for a guide or sign.

I scanned the room, but stopped short upon seeing a familiar face.

Arturian.

My stomach dropped, but I straightened my collar and strolled over to one of the innermost shelves and peeked out. Arturian was standing with two women—one of them being the redhead I almost collided with earlier. He wore a sharply tailored suit that was open low in the front. He'd left his shirt buttons unfastened as well, exposing part of his chest. The look was quite different from most of the attire I'd seen so far. The redheaded girl didn't seem to mind—in fact, she seemed to be throwing herself at Arturian. She was leaning in and laughing, placing her hand on his arm familiarly. However, it seemed to me like Arturian wasn't entirely smitten with his very forthcoming friend. His posture was stiff and uncomfortable.

Just as I was wondering how to accomplish my goal with Arturian hanging around, the trio made their way towards the exit. Breathing a sigh of relief, I turned and noticed the small labels on the shelf in front of me. I began weaving through the semi-circle shelves, checking the labels. The outermost shelves contained the archives of the noble families, arranged in alphabetical order. While working my way through the alphabet, I noted that House Exley had an entire shelf to itself. I tried not to let that intimidate me as I continued my search.

K...

L... almost there.

M.

I rustled through dusty books until I found a lone book labeled "Merton." Rustling through the pages, I found the page dedicated to the demise of the family.

That date...

I did the math. The entirety of House Merton had been killed in a tragic, accidental house fire *nine months* before Francie was born. If my theory was correct, that would mean Augustus killed their Skylord and stole their windblade almost immediately after Francie's mother killed Adolpho.

Feeling unsettled, I turned the page. However, that page did nothing to ease my nerves. Apparently, the house had been burned so completely that nothing could be salvaged from it. Four skeletons were recovered and were presumed to be the bodies of Frederick Merton, his son Robert, his daughter Aurelia, and his butler. They'd been the only living Mertons, and they had all died on the same day—conveniently leaving their windblade to the atmosphere.

It was irrefutable. The timing, the circumstances.

Francie was an Exley, and Augustus was a mass murderer.

My instincts told me to find proof of the crime and let Augustus be killed by the other Skylords. However, there were two glaring issues with that plan. At the moment, my only evidence hinged on Francie and her mother's story, and if her true parentage became known, every Skylord in Friese would converge upon her. Second, if Augustus was killed, Arturian would undoubtedly be brought down as well.

As much as I wanted justice, I could never sacrifice my friends for it. So, from that moment, I decided I would do anything in my power to maintain the secret of Francie's parentage. Her life depended on it.

CHAPTER TWENTY-ONE
THE YORKES

I was a solitary man. Most upper-crust Friesians would never know it because I spent much of my time networking and mingling with other house leaders, but I despised them. I saw them as a means to an end, but they *did* provide some occasional entertainment. But the only thing that brought me true satisfaction was the acquisition and wielding of power to further the goals of my house.

I was determined to be the most powerful Exley who ever lived, despite my lack of true Exley blood. I'd bring my house higher than it's ever been, without any of Adolpho's poisonous genetic influence. House Exley would be created anew... stronger, more ruthless, and more cunning than ever. And despite his recent failings, I was certain that Arturian would fall into his teachings and carry on that legacy. He was my son, after all.

On that day, I was meeting with the queen. I'd requested that we met at my port office and she'd resisted, knowing the port to be a place of low-class brutes and disease. However, I put my foot down, and the queen folded. I let myself revel in my own power for a few moments. I dictated where the queen went. She had no choice but to indulge me. It was *that feeling* that kept me striving when I began feeling fatalistic.

I'd just finished gathering my thoughts as my manservant opened the door to my office. The queen was already there, and had been waiting for me alone. A dark grin pulled at my lips—it never hurt to remind someone of whose timetable they were operating on.

"I hope whatever delayed you was important," the queen said from her chair, visibly perturbed. For all of my disdain for her, I had to acknowledge that she was stunningly beautiful. Her status as the first and only noblewoman ever to wield her family's windblade was enough to terrify most men into silence. For me, it only made her a more tantalizing opponent. A fair match, so to speak.

She wore her hair in elaborate curls atop her head, and her structured dress was of pure white, rising high around her neck. It was only when she stood that I noticed that the dress was backless.

I disregarded her initial jab and redirected. "A backless dress, Lesynna? Use caution, or your behavior may be seen as erratic, *Your Majesty*."

The queen scoffed. "Surely, Augustus, you are not so bold as to think you can address me in such a way. I am still the Queen of Friese, lest I remind you more directly," she said, her words as sharp as a windblade.

I let the corner of my mouth pull into a smile. "I believe we are past the point of pleasantries, wouldn't you agree?" I said, refusing to break eye contact.

She broke first. "What do you want, Augustus? It had better be important."

I stood silently for a moment, making her wait. It was all a part of the game. "I'm razing the port slums."

She raised her eyebrows. "Why would you do that?"

"I require more room for my business."

"What business?"

"None of yours."

The queen took a step back and crossed her arms. "No. If you can't tell me why, my answer is no."

I couldn't stop myself from laughing. I held my hand to my mouth and shook my head. "Oh... dear, Lesynna. You've misunderstood me," I said as I walked over to an end table near the hearth, picking up an apple that sat in a fruit bowl. I turned it around in my hands a few times and offered it to the queen. She looked at me with suspicious eyes, but took it. I walked back to the other end of the room with my hands in my pockets.

"Are you going to eat it?" I asked.

She said nothing, but continued to stare at me in suspicion. After a tense moment, she brought the apple closer to inspect it, and pressed it for any evidence of tampering.

I flicked my wrist from my side, directly at the queen. The apple exploded in her hands, covering her in juice and pulp. She shrieked, her lip curling in a very satisfying display of indignation.

"Would I stoop to poison, Your Majesty? Or have you forgotten why no one ever dares to cross me?" I asked.

I'd worked tirelessly to refine my skill with my windblade for decades, earning the respect and fear of my peers. Most Skylords didn't bother to strengthen their skill beyond basic aim training. Their comfort kept them content... docile. I, however, knew that throwing a windblade was so much more than aiming. The strength of the throw, the curve, even the position of the fingers would affect the outcome. Queen Lesynna Ainsworth experienced that outcome with as much dignity as I had ever seen.

Her guards had rushed in, but the queen quickly indicated that I was not to be touched—she knew where the power lay in our relationship. She shot me looks of hatred and disbelief as her guards cleaned the apple gore from her clothing. I helped myself to another apple from the bowl, biting and chewing until the guards finished and left.

"You can't oppose me now, Lesynna. I have our mutually assured destruction in the palm of my hands. All I have to do is open my fingers, and the entire kingdom will know the lengths to which you will go to maintain your stranglehold on Friese," I said as I tossed the apple into a waste bin.

"I don't believe—" the queen started, but I cut her off.

"You think I wouldn't do it? Really?" I shook my head, sitting myself in one of my luxury chairs by the hearth. "Based on everything you know about me—everything you've seen me do—what makes you think I wouldn't go to the *farthest possible extreme* to get what I want?"

She stood, her jaw jutting in contained outrage. I felt a surge of satisfaction watching the indelible marks dry on her pristine dress. It would surely be noticed when she returned to the palace.

"I will start my slum project immediately. Thank you for meeting with me, *Your Majesty.*" I couldn't stop myself from sneering at the last words. I nodded towards the door, and Her Majesty, Queen Lesynna of Friese, walked out. A successful meeting, indeed.

Later that afternoon, I made my way to my second important meeting. This one, however, would require more negotiation and persuasion than the first. I was on my way to meet Nestor Yorke—Skylord of the house that controlled all the banks in Friese. They lived in northwestern Friese, amongst the wealthiest and most profitable families and businesses. I mentally gathered my plans as I approached the Yorke mansion, and stepped out with confidence.

Their mansion was exactly how one would expect a house of a banker would be. Tall, extravagant, glowing... but lifeless. There were no flowers, plants, or life of any kind ornamenting the front of the Yorke mansion. They were a cold people, with an appreciation of timeless things. Plants could die and wither, but diamonds shone without a need of water or fertilizer.

I climbed the marble steps of the grand edifice, my servants trailing behind me. The mansion was supported by thick, spiral pillars, and was somehow still a beautiful glistening white. Friesian weather made it difficult to maintain a clean exterior due to the humidity and storms, but it seemed that House Yorke could afford to have their mansion cleaned regularly.

Upon approaching the double doors, my guard gave it a firm knock. Within seconds, a stern-looking woman opened the doors.

"Good afternoon, Skylord Exley. Skylord Yorke is awaiting your arrival. Please follow me," she said in a monotone voice. She led me through the grand entryway, the walls inlaid with gold streaks. Diamonds encrusted the door frames, sometimes with more colorful stones mixed in.

After navigating through increasingly grandiose architecture, we entered a large, open room lined with bookshelves. The library of House Yorke could nearly put the Friesian House Archive to shame. The domed roof had been constructed with an iridescent material, allowing light to flow in but no visibility out. Somehow, the Yorkes had created a space that was both luxurious and restrained. I didn't appreciate it, but I respected it.

"To what do I owe the pleasure?" Nestor Yorke said as he entered the room from the other side. He was a tall, lean man with a ruggedly handsome face. He kept a well-manicured beard and mustache, graying slightly in his fifties. His coat was a stately dark blue, and the only ornamentations were his diamond cuff-links.

I smiled, walking forward to greet Nestor with a traditional Friesian grip of the arm. Despite our houses' decades of feuding, I'd spent the last few years attempting to forge a bond between us. "I have a proposition for you, but it is the kind that is best made while sitting."

Nestor laughed. "Oh, Augustus! My day just got more complicated, didn't it?"

We took our seats next to a grand statue of gems, portraying the mythical goddess of wind, Echna—the original giver of the windblades. As I settled, something moved in the corner of my eye. I turned to see a young woman standing in the doorway, whose hair was the lightest blonde I'd ever seen, and fell to her knees in shiny waves. She wore her hair pushed behind her shoulders, revealing an array of very expensive-looking jewels piercing the entire length of her ears. Even her head had been adorned with a chain that dangled a sapphire on her forehead, enhancing her austere looks. Her beauty was striking, and of a rare kind in Friese. Her eyes sat farther apart than most women, and were large and sensual.

"I hope you don't mind, Augustus, but I've invited my daughter to join us. She is of the age where I'd like her to learn some things about inter-house relationships," Nestor said, motioning his daughter to come and sit.

The young woman complied, her long silver dress flowing as she walked with perfectly trained form. She silently settled on one of the chairs.

"This is Eliandre, the only child of my late wife, Elspeth," Nestor said. Despite the rigid formality, his tone was gentle and loving.

"May her soul find rest in the breeze," Eliandre said in a calm, level tone.

Nestor leaned forward to squeeze his daughter's hand, to which she conceded a small smile. "So, Augustus, what brings you here today?" he asked, leaning back in his chair.

I hesitated for a moment. Nestor had displayed genuine love and affection for his daughter, which made my proposition much more delicate. Nevertheless, this step was long overdue.

"Nestor, I am here to propose a marriage alliance with your daughter."

Nestor chuckled, brows furrowed in incredulity. "You can't be serious... my daughter's age—"

"I'd hardly consider that an issue," I replied coolly.

"Not an issue?" Nestor yelled. "She is eighteen! You must be in your forties!"

To her credit, Eliandre remained calm while watching it play out in front of her. I almost laughed, but instead I lowered my head and took a deep breath. The idea of remarrying had entered my mind a few times, but I'd always seen it as more trouble than it was worth.

"Nestor... I was speaking on behalf of my son, who is nineteen."

Nestor let out a relieved laugh. "Oh, dear! What a misunderstanding." He reached over to pat the hand of his daughter, whose expression was stoic as ever. Her blue eye makeup would have accentuated her facial expressions if she had shown any.

"I have to be frank, Augustus... I was not expecting this. I'd assumed your son was intended for the princess," Nestor said, head tilted forward and eyes expectant.

The time had come for me to reveal my hand. I was relying on Nestor Yorke being as politically wise as his reputation made him to be.

"You're not mistaken. Long ago, Princess Eadlin had been my first choice for my son. No offense intended, Miss Yorke," I said with a look at Eliandre. She simply nodded. "I have, however, noticed something akin to... *instability* amongst the Ainsworths," I said with a meaningful look at Nestor. "I figured it might be wise to link arms with our house-peers... in case that instability rears its head," I finished, letting my words linger.

Nestor, thankfully, picked up on it. "Yes, *stability* is of the utmost importance in times such as these."

The way Nestor finished his sentence, I knew he was of the same mind. The rumors of the rebel raids on Ainsworth ships had reached him. The queen's weakness was being exposed, and we needed to unite in the face of it. The Yorkes and Exleys were known to be the two wealthiest houses in Friese, excluding the queen's. In reality, we had become the wealthiest, but Nestor didn't need to know that.

I locked eyes with Eliandre, who looked pensive. "What do you think of this alliance, Miss Yorke?"

She blinked and tilted her head. "I appreciate your consideration of me, Lord Exley, but it is not my place to weigh in. My only wish is for my father to do what is best for our house," she said with perfect formality.

As I wondered whether I was a fool to let my son marry Eliandre instead of marrying her myself, Nestor chimed in. "It sounds like we have a wedding to plan, Augustus."

Eliandre cleared her throat and straightened her posture. "May I ask one question, Lord Exley?" she asked, clearly uncomfortable to speak up.

I tilted my head. "I suppose so."

"Does he know?"

"My son's loyalty to our house is undying—I expect his full cooperation."

It was obviously not the answer she wanted to hear, but she accepted it with a nod.

The carriage ride from northern Friese and back to the Exley estate felt especially long. I was eager to make official our alliance with the Yorkes. The longer I pondered my earlier meeting with the queen, the more I wanted to be done with all of my dealings with her. I knew I was playing a dangerous game, and if I didn't diffuse it myself, it would blow up in my face.

The carriage came to a stop, and I went about finding Arturian to inform him of, and congratulate him on his impending nuptials. It didn't take long to find him.

I stood at the edge of the estate along the meadow, and it wasn't long before Arturian noticed me. He'd likely been riding all day, as usual.

"Father—give me a moment!" he called before swinging himself off of the moving horse. As soon as he was off, the horse calmed and stood still.

"You shouldn't be jeopardizing the Exley family line by riding horses who mean to kill you," I said, scowling. Maybe marriage would mature him.

"Yes, Father. I will be more careful."

"Speaking of the family line, it's about time ours is continued."

"Are you remarrying, father?" Arturian asked, still out of breath.

I scoffed. "No—don't be foolish. It's your turn."

He went silent at the news, standing completely still for a few long moments.

"Who?" he asked.

"Eliandre Yorke." I stared at my son, searching for a reaction. *Will he fight it?*

Arturian bowed his head. "So be it."

CHAPTER TWENTY-TWO
WHEN THE BILL COMES DUE

ARTURIAN

Three Years Ago

It was a cold winter's day by Friesian standards when I rode my new horse, Frenzy, for the first time. Father had just returned with the prized racehorse whose successes had made him famous in the renowned West Corlaean racing circuit. At seventeen hands tall, with rippling muscles and a glistening bay coat, he drew eyes everywhere he went. I was well-aware of that effect, and I fully planned on exploiting it that day.

Frenzy and I approached the bell tower, feeling very confident. I had dressed in my nicest competition clothes, and Frenzy was freshly bathed and tacked in my most expensive saddle. Behind us trotted a cranky Satine, whom I led along with a lead rope. As we emerged into the clearing, I spotted Levick and Francie attempting to climb the large oak in front of the bell tower.

"You might as well give up," I called out to them. "That tree is unclimbable." My friends beamed at me, thrilled to see Frenzy for the first time.

"Is this your new horse?" Levick asked as I stopped in front of them. Francie looked a bit cautious, staying near the tree trunk.

"Yes, he was brought off the ship yesterday! Isn't he magnificent?" I asked with a smile.

"I'll say!" Levick said, inching closer. "May I?" he asked, holding his hand up. I nodded enthusiastically, and Levick began to stroke Frenzy's immaculate coat.

Francie was still standing nervously by herself, so I beckoned her over. She shook her head.

"Come on, Francie!" I called. "He's harmless."

At this, she slowly made her way over. She stood next to Levick, who gently took her hand and placed it on the horse's shoulder. "He's bigger than most horses, but he's friendly. See?" He said as they gently patted the horse together. Even though Levick was only fourteen years old while Francie and I were sixteen, I couldn't deny that Levick somehow kept us all together.

"Father is gone for the day, so I brought a horse for you to ride," I said, motioning to Satine. Levick nearly jumped for joy.

As Levick clambered onto the docile mare, Francie hesitated. "Why don't you ride with me?" I asked, lending my hand.

"He won't go too fast?" she asked, her eyes pleading.

"I won't let him. Now, get up here!" I said, heaving her up. She used my stirrup as a foothold and swung herself up to sit behind me. She immediately wrapped her arms around me so tightly that I could feel her shaking.

"Francie..." I began, my voice hoarse. "I need to breathe, please."

"Don't kill him, Francie!" Levick called from Satine's back.

She reluctantly loosened her grip.

"Don't worry, I won't let anything bad happen. I promise," I said softly, so only Francie could hear. She nodded in response, and we began to make our way to the Exley fields.

It pained me to hold back my new racehorse, but the last thing I wanted was to traumatize Francie for horse-back riding. We rode at a slow canter around the perimeter of the field, watching the other horses graze in their herds. After a few minutes, I was relieved to feel Francie start to relax. I let myself feel some accomplishment for that.

Eventually we stopped under a grove of trees to let the horses rest and drink out of a nearby stream. Levick helped Francie dismount, then I swung myself off. On the way down, my leg caught on a buckle, tearing a hole in the calf of my riding breeches.

I swore in frustration, leading my friends to approach in concern. "Are you hurt?" Francie asked, crouching to see my leg.

"No... I'd prefer that over these breeches being torn, though," I muttered.

"It's just clothes, Arturian." Levick patted me on the shoulder.

"These clothes are worth half a carriage," I said, earning a gasp from my friends. I should've known better than to wear competition breeches out on a whim. My father would be livid if he found out. Sometimes I felt like my father would use any excuse he could find to punish me. The torn breeches would certainly fit the bill.

"I can fix them," Francie said. "My aunt will help me if I need it."

I breathed a sigh of relief. "Thank you so much, Francie." I surprised her by taking her into a tight hug.

"I suppose I should go and change them quickly," I said as we broke apart. "I'll ride Frenzy to the house, and I'll be back soon."

Levick and Francie agreed and made themselves comfortable by sitting under the tree, and I mounted Frenzy once again. We took off like a shot across the field, towards the Exley mansion.

As soon as we approached, I heard a commotion on the other side of the house. Shouting and crashing sounds erupted as I urged Frenzy to a gallop, quickly rounding the large mansion. The chaos taking place in the courtyard was unlike anything I'd ever seen.

My father, Augustus Exley, stood on one end of the courtyard with his feet planted slightly apart, arm raised to throw his windblade. On the other end stood Leon Draughton, head of House Draughton, in a similar stance. Many of the various statues and plants that had once graced the borders and walkways of the courtyard had been cut to pieces and laid scattered across the ground. One of them was a statue of my mother, but it had been decapitated.

"I told you not to come, Leon. There's nothing I can do for you now," Father called across the courtyard.

Leon's eyes met mine. "So, you *did* have your heir waiting in the wings?" My father's head snapped around to me, his expression both enraged and concerned. "To think—you had a problem with my bringing Victor! I always knew you were a hypocrite, Augustus!" Leon shouted, flinging his arm forward once again.

Father dove to the side, dodging the windblade that ultimately shaved the top of a very well-maintained rose bush. "Get out of here, Arturian! You're lucky he didn't aim that blade at you!" he yelled before turning and throwing a slice of wind at his opponent.

Leon cried out as blood spewed from his left arm, now a bloody stump with no hand. "Bastard!" he managed to choke out between screams.

I sat atop Frenzy, completely frozen. I'd never seen such violence, and I'd certainly never seen my father participating in anything approaching combat. The gore, the screams, the chaos—those were foreign things in my life up until that moment. My father had always seemed like a cold, distant man who would never debase himself with violence if he could avoid it. For the first time, I realized that I didn't know my father at all.

After jumping over a strike aimed at his legs, Father ran up to Frenzy and grabbed the horse's bridle, barking Corlaean commands at him. Frenzy spun around and took off around the other side of the mansion, and I clung onto the horse for dear life, still stunned by what I'd seen.

As we cleared the corner, I'd recovered enough sense to slow the horse to a stop. I dismounted, tied Frenzy to the marble banister, and clambered up one of the thick vines that scaled the house. I carefully made my way to the edge, peeking out around the corner.

The fight was essentially over—it had been since my father severed Leon's hand. That certainly hadn't prevented him from putting up a fight, though. Father had earned a slice across the bicep, and his shirt sleeve hung off in bloody tatters. Leon was in much worse shape and was barely sitting upright. Part of his scalp hung off of his head from the side, and his thigh had been slashed through, severing the artery. He wouldn't live much longer.

I could barely make out what the men were saying. "I wish you hadn't come, Leon. I hate settling things like animals," Father said, out of breath.

"You're a snake, Exley," Leon managed to choke out amid gasps of pain. "Victor! It's time, son!" he cried out, hunching over and groaning.

A freckled teenage boy emerged from behind a statue of my father, looking like he was barely holding himself together. He walked nervously towards his father, obviously unprepared for the task before him. A Skylord could never tolerate being killed by an enemy. Losing their heritage blade would spell the end for a noble family.

Father climbed the steps towards the back doors and turned to watch.

"My knife—grab it! It's on my belt," Leon shouted weakly at his son. With shaking hands, Victor pried the stiletto knife out of its sheath, staring at it as if it was alive.

The boy spoke in panicked tones, quietly enough that I couldn't hear exactly what was being said. All I saw was Victor shaking his head and holding the knife weakly. Leon caressed his son's face, spoke softly to him, and closed his hand around the knife's handle. A moment of silence was shared by all as the teen boy said his goodbyes to his father. When he was finished, he held up the knife and plunged it into his father's chest.

Life wasn't supposed to be that way. I was a privileged heir of a noble house. Heir to a massive fortune. For my entire life I'd been told that I was so lucky to be born into such wealth. Such power.

It certainly didn't appear lucky.

I couldn't stop myself from imagining the day I would inevitably have to take my family's windblade. To pick up the torch of House Exley and lead it into the future. To kill my own father.

I never experienced real bonding with my father. I'd often been pushed to the side and seen as a distraction. My father had intentionally excluded and isolated me, leaving me to the company of my horses and my secret friends. Even so, the human heart was a difficult thing. No matter how neglected or rejected I felt by my father, there remained an innate need to be *known* by him. To be appreciated, validated, *loved*. I would've settled for simply being wanted. Therefore, the idea of one day finally dealing the death blow to end my father's rule of terror was daunting.

"Are you going to speak? Or will you continue to sit there silently like a stone?" Father asked me as I sat in the corner of the study.

Father was sitting in his leather chair, hand-sewing the gash in his arm closed, and I couldn't make myself look at it. Every few minutes he would make suppressed sounds of discomfort. I wondered how he stood the pain.

"I didn't know..." I said through a cracking voice, still staring at my feet.

"Well?" he said through gritted teeth, holding one end of the string he was sewing with. "Didn't know what? That there is a cost to everything?" He snipped the ends of the string and began to wipe the blood from the surrounding area. "The Exleys didn't achieve our position by sitting idly by and watching the world play out in front of us." He stood to retrieve a black shirt that had been left out for him.

"If there is one thing you need to learn from what you saw today, it is this: there is *no such thing* as success without sacrifice. The bill always comes due. My job—and your job, someday—is to ensure the bill is paid without hesitation." He pulled his long hair out of his shirt and tied it back loosely.

"I would sacrifice *anything* to maintain the power and prestige of our house. Do you understand what I'm saying?" he asked, standing over me.

I forced myself to meet my father's gaze. The scene of my father shooting his blade at his enemy, dodging, and continuing even after sustaining the deep wound in his arm had inspired me. I would live up to my family's legacy. I would lead House Exley with the strength of a warrior and the tact of a general. As difficult as my relationship with my father was, I silently committed to learn whatever I could from him—for the glory of Exley. To live up to such a man was certainly going to be a challenge—but I had always loved a challenge.

CHAPTER TWENTY-THREE
RECOGNITION

I massaged the scar in my bicep as I rode in my carriage toward the slums. It was time for me to inspect the exact area I needed for my port and warehouse expansion. The sights, smells, and sounds of the slums repulsed me, but I kept my focus on my goal. I was *so close* to holding the ultimate power in Friese—I could nearly taste it. Lesynna's days in the sun were nearing their end. I'd almost be sad to see her go.

Almost.

The carriage came to a stop, and I climbed out into the slums' common area. It was mid-afternoon, and the streets bustled with peasants pulling carts, carrying children, and bargaining for cheap goods. A tall boy jumped from a roof and onto a fence pole, and proceeded to run along the posts.

I had taken only two steps from my carriage before people began staring. Most of them were wise enough to duck their heads and turn away once they recognized me. Flanked by two of my personal guards, I walked through the main thorough-fare, crowds parting as I approached.

I understood my public image. I'd carefully curated my reputation to ensure the population remained respectful of me. Most of the slum peasants worked at the port, which was controlled almost entirely by me. They knew where their meager paychecks came from. In addition to my reputation, I always took care to dress in a subtle but dignified manner. My black suit coat was thin and tailored, accentuating my height and broad shoulders. The silk lining of my pockets was visible and a bright blood red. I kept my dark hair long, as a mark of privilege. I'd never needed to secure my hair to perform menial work, and I never would. Overall, I stood out, even amongst other noblemen. Fashions and trends changed, but I did not.

As I walked, for the first time in years, I looked at the people of the slums. I was not merely glancing, but looking and *seeing* the faces of the people who maintained the Exley wealth—often at the cost of their own well-being. Yet, still, I saw only what they lacked. They had no wealth, power, or any basic control over their lives. I wondered how they made themselves go on.

Whilst pondering the sad existence of the lowly dock worker, I experienced the disquieting feeling that someone was watching me. I scanned the crowd, catching the eyes of a beautiful young woman with dark blonde hair and wearing a light green dress. Something about her seemed strikingly familiar. As I searched my memories, the girl looked away and rushed toward an alley. At that moment, I *remembered.*

The girl from the country estate... the maid who killed Adolpho.

My heart thundered in indignant anger.

Wait... where else have I seen her?

Shelving my thoughts, I beckoned my guards, and began following her through the crowds. The girl noticed she was being pursued and sped up. I cursed to myself, knowing there was no way we'd catch up if we lost sight of her. As we followed, it occurred to me that she hadn't aged at all since I saw her in my youth.

It's not her. It can't be—it's been almost twenty years.

On a hunch, I ordered my guards to go back to the carriage and wait for me there—I knew I'd be faster alone. This girl wasn't the one who killed Adolpho, but she'd seemed *very* interested in me, which was suspicious enough.

I hid myself in shadows and followed from a distance along shop fronts and shabby houses. After glancing around in every direction, she finally slowed to a comfortable walk. I sped up, preparing to apprehend her, when a boy dropped from a roof and landed behind her. Evidently friendly, he approached her and took her hand. She jumped in surprise, but after recognizing him, smiled and swatted at him. They walked together, talking quietly until they entered a small, run-down building with a hanging sign that read, *The Hanoverian.*

I leaned against a brick pillar in the shadows. My mind told me I was being paranoid, but my instincts urged me to investigate. Even the *notion* of Adolpho having a blood descendent made my blood boil. I didn't abide loose ends. While turning to leave, I decided to have someone follow her in the coming days.

I won't forget about you. In fact, I'll keep an eye on you... and I have the perfect man for the job.

CHAPTER TWENTY-FOUR
17 GRIFTON STREET

ARTURIAN

I wiped the sweat from my brow after leaping off the last pillar on my obstacle course. Years ago, I'd built it behind the mansion for training, and it had become a place of respite for me when I got overwhelmed. It was arranged in a large oval, and on one of the long ends stood a high rising pier with gaps and divots, along with a couple of steep climbs. When I built it, I had to dig deep holes as if I was building a foundation or a dock in the water, and then used Smoke, fitted in a driving harness, to pull the logs into place.

The log pier slanted down to the end of the oval, where I'd built a wall. I opted out of attaching the traditional rope to the top and instead etched small divots into the planks so that I'd have to use my fingers and hand strength to pull myself up. On the other side of the oval were four boulders I'd alternate between stacking and removing before reaching the end, where I'd throw five knives in succession into a distant plank.

I finally let myself sit down on a nearby log, dripping with sweat. Training had become a bigger part of my life in the previous year. My father was healthy and not at any imminent risk of dying, but the political climate we found ourselves in was worrisome.

It was also an excellent distraction from my troubles with my friends. The familiarity Francie shared with Levick bothered me more than it ever had. I wasn't sure if they'd become closer, or if I was just noticing it more. My mind wandered to our meeting at the inn, and how strangely Francie had behaved near the end.

Francie. How am I going to tell her I'm getting married?

The idea of loving another woman made my stomach turn.

I stood and began a jog to the end of the course. I leapt up onto the pilings, jumping from one to another until I was fifteen feet in the air. With every step, my thoughts came into sharper focus.

Despite my jealousy, I wrestled with guilt where Levick was concerned. He was in love with Francie, and had been for years. He knew I was aware of it—it was an open secret between us. If Levick found out about what happened between me and Francie, he would feel betrayed.

But it was hard to feel too guilty when Levick was the one spending all of his time with her.

I shook off my conflicted feelings and began climbing the wall for the fifth time that morning.

Later that day, I sat in my bath and let myself relax. I'd trained for hours and accumulated countless new bruises and strains. I'd almost fallen asleep when my father entered the room.

"I have a task for you, son," he said from the doorway.

On top of the port warehouse expansion?

"Yes, Father. What shall I do?" I tried to hide the incredulity in my voice.

"I'm sure you recall the story I told you... about your grandfather," he said, lazily pacing the other side of the room. "As it turns out, I may have found a lead on the murderess."

I sat up, splashing warm water onto the floor. "Here, in Friese? She's in the city?"

"I'm not sure it's her, but I'm still suspicious. She's too young, but the resemblance is... uncanny," he said, taking a seat near the fireplace. "You will keep an eye on her while you're starting your expansion work. It's quite convenient for you... this girl lives in the slums—on Grifton Street. Number 17, to be exact."

My stomach dropped.

That's the inn.

Could it be Crysta? No... he said she's young.

Francie?

My mind raced as I tried to make sense of what I was hearing. Maybe my father recognized her from the night he saw us in the stable? The night he killed Frenzy...

No... it was so dark...

If he did recognize her from that night, he'd mention it, wouldn't he?

"Are you drowning back there?" Father asked.

"No, sir. I'm sorry. I'm just confused..." I stammered. "How do you think she's connected to the woman who killed Grandfather?"

"Adolpho had a reputation for... *womanizing*." The way he said the word made me think it wasn't as simple as marital infidelity. "I think the slum girl could be a product of such behavior."

I emerged from the tub, struggling to process the new information. "You think that this girl," *Francie!* "is Adolpho's daughter? The heir to the Exley fortune?" I stumbled as I began drying myself and dressing behind the partition.

If that's true... she'd be the only *blood heir.*

"Make no mistake. *We* are Exley. Adolpho be damned." My father's tone was cold and heartless. "Follow her. Ensure she isn't his bastard."

"I'll do as you ask, Father," I muttered as I stepped out from the partition, mostly dressed. "But... if she is?" I asked, knowing I'd regret it.

"I'm disappointed. If you don't already know what needs to be done, then you're no son of mine," he drawled, boring his icy eyes directly through me. I felt as if I might freeze over.

"Get to it, then."

With that, he left, closing the door behind him.

I finished dressing myself in haste after shooing away my valet. After fastening the buttons on my slim coat, I brushed my hair and checked my reflection. I wore a coat of a militaristic style—buttoned up to a rounded collar around my neck. Technically, all male noblemen were officers in the Friesian navy, but we hadn't needed a true service in centuries. After smoothing out non-existent wrinkles, I made my way through the marbled corridors and out the double doors. I'd just made it down the first step when my shoulder collided with something.

"Mister Exley!" Eliandre Yorke exclaimed. She stumbled backwards, but I caught her arms before she fell.

"My apologies, Miss Yorke!" I said as I helped stabilize her. She was wearing a sleek gown of dark blue that seemed to ripple in the sun... almost like oil. Her platinum blonde hair shimmered as it blew in the breeze.

"Please, don't apologize," she said, her tone calm and even. "The fault was mine."

I'd known Eliandre since we were both children, but she'd always been isolated from the other youths of Friesian society. I'd assumed that was because she was the only child of House Yorke, and her mother had passed away. Nestor Yorke seemed to be very protective of her.

I would have invited her inside, but my mind had been clouded with questions about Francie and I wanted to get to the slums to investigate.

"To what do I owe the pleasure of your visit?" I asked, trying to mask my impatience.

"I assume your father has spoken with you?" she asked, but before I could answer, she said, "Something urgent has come up—quite time-sensitive. Our arrangement may need to be accelerated."

The wedding.

I couldn't think about that at the moment. My current predicament left me with little concern for any woman besides Francie.

"Miss Yorke, as pleased as I am by your visit, I'm afraid you caught me at a bad time," I said, bowing my head in apology. "I must take my leave."

With that, I hastened to my carriage.

CHAPTER TWENTY-FIVE
THE LIE

The inn's kitchen was quiet except for the sounds of my sponge against the dishes, splashing water around in the sink. It had been a long day of work—I barely saw Levick, and got yelled at *twice* by guests. On top of that, my encounter with Augustus had left me paranoid and nervous. He'd looked directly at me, and followed me a long way down the street before I'd shaken him off. The look in his eyes when he saw me... it was recognition. Did he recognize me from the night he caught me in the stable with Arturian? I shuddered at the memory. A much more haunting theory had recently invaded my mind, taking root like a weed—what if he recognized my *mother?*

Crysta always said I looked just like my mother. Augustus had likely seen her on multiple occasions before the incident with Adolpho occurred. If he suspected the truth—that I was the daughter of Corsa Hanover, a former housemaid on the

Exley country estate—he would guess my age and do the math. Adolpho's reputation would make the theory of my parentage *very* believable.

If he knows I'm Adolpho's daughter... he might know that I have Asgora. The windblade that was supposed to be his.

"Looking good, Skylady," a gravelly voice purred from behind me.

I jumped, despite recognizing the voice. "Ress," I gasped as I turned towards the door. He was leaning against the doorframe with his muscular tattooed arms folded in front of his chest, a smirk tugging at his handsome face.

"Who else would it be at *this* hour?" he asked with a wink.

I shook my head, fighting a smile. "What's going on?" I asked as I dried my hands on a towel.

"I'm looking for a sparring partner. Maybe we can get out of here and you can toss me around a bit," he said, his smile turning mischievous. "Who knows? Maybe you'll end up on top."

"Ress!" I stifled a laugh, my face turning red. "What did you *really* come out here for?" As much as Ress teased, he'd never made any real advances. Despite his endless streams of innuendo, he kept a respectful distance. I was convinced he simply enjoyed embarrassing me.

Ress pushed himself away from the door and sauntered over to me. "I'd love to tell you if you'd stop flirting with me for *one second*."

I raised my eyebrows at him, hanging the towel back up. "Ress."

The corner of his mouth pulled up in a smile as he looked down at me. "Orin needs you tonight. It's urgent."

I gaped at him. "Urgent? You should've led with that," I said, unfastening my apron and securing my hair in a braid.

"And miss my chance to see you squirm? No way," Ress chuckled at me, the sound echoing through the quiet kitchen.

I settled onto the bench nearby to pull my boots on. "What's the mission?"

"I don't know," Ress said as he toyed with some of the hanging utensils, looking bored.

Those were my least favorite missions. Sprung on me out of nowhere, with no information or warning as to what I'd be facing. Unfortunately, it was how the RCM often had to do things because of Orin's shadowy unknown sources tipping him off at random times.

"Your hair is fine, come on," Ress said in exasperation, tugging at my hand as I tucked a strand behind my ear. "Fit for the Exley mansion."

Ice ran through my veins as I followed after him, my joints going stiff. "What do you mean?"

"I shouldn't have said it. I don't know anything more. Orin will explain." He went silent as he led me out into the dark streets.

It was almost midnight by the time Ress and I made it to Orin's house, and my nerves had only doubled since we'd left. I had to school my emotions lest they suspect me of caring *too* much about a noble house. I had no intention of letting anyone at the

RCM know about my history with Arturian, but it was getting very difficult to hide my distress at the thought of targeting the Exleys.

Clouds hung low over Friese, obscuring most visibility as we waited outside of Orin's front door. The door swung open shortly after Ress knocked, and Nina welcomed us inside with a severe look on her face, her posture bent and wearied.

"What's wrong, Nina?" I asked, resting a hand on the thin woman's shoulder.

Nina sighed, shook her head, and motioned for the two of us to follow her into Orin's study. Our leader sat at his desk, his elbow propped on his shabby desk and holding his head in his hand. Ress and I sat on the pair of chairs opposite the desk and waited.

"Thank you, Ress. That will be all," Orin mumbled without looking up. I glanced over at Ress to see his eyebrows raised in incredulity at being dismissed. "It's *need to know*. Not even my wife knows the true objective tonight," Orin said, looking up at Ress with a sharp expression. Ress sighed, but took his leave. The door shut, and Orin and I were alone.

"I'm going to ask you to do something very dangerous tonight, Francie," Orin said, leaning forward on his elbows. His eyes were serious as a storm, his mouth pressed into a thin line.

My stomach sank. "What is it?"

He steepled his fingers together, meeting my eyes. "There are rumors that the Exley family collects *ancient texts*."

No, no, no.

"My source thinks they're in possession of a banned book, *The Chronicle of the Caelators.* It's about the origin of the windblades."

I said nothing, but recognized the name. The Exleys did, in fact, have the book in question. Arturian had let me read some of it once while he and Levick were out on a ride, and I remembered a great deal of it. He'd told me it was very valuable, and I needed to be cautious. When I was done with it, I'd seen where he'd returned it.

And now, I was surely going to be asked to steal it.

Orin continued, oblivious to the chaos reigning in my mind. "If that book details how Skylords were first created, theoretically..."

Stop this, Orin. Don't make me do this.

"It might contain information on how to *destroy* them."

My throat went dry. "Why would you want to destroy them, Orin?"

He leaned back in his seat and cocked his head at me. "They're tyrants. That's why." His eyes were as hard as the marble of the Yorke mansion.

This is a test. A test of loyalty to the cause.

He was on a very dangerous path. While the Skylords *had* devolved into tyrants in recent decades, they also served as the ultimate powers protecting Friese from greedy neighboring nations. Friese was the only known kingdom with windblades, and their existence kept us safe.

The northern nation of Trenica had a centuries-old grudge against Friese, and would surely take advantage if the windblades suddenly disappeared. However, as it stood, no nation would ever dare to challenge Friese while hundreds of Skylords held the power of the wind in their fingertips.

I shifted in my seat. "What about me? I have a windblade..."

"Obviously, you wouldn't be included in this reckoning... if the information is true and useful," he said, waving a nonchalant hand.

Reckoning.

The word sent a wave of nausea through my gut. A seed of doubt burrowed itself into me, spreading its vines through every corner of my being.

Orin leaned forward on his hands, continuing. "Augustus is in a meeting at the palace with the rest of the Quorum of the High Skylords. They often go all night and into the morning, so he won't be at the house."

It took me a moment to realize what he was implying. "Wait... you want me to break into the Exley mansion *tonight?*" Shrinking smaller and smaller, the wooden office walls closed in around me. Even the air felt stagnant and lifeless.

"This might be our last opportunity for a while. Right now, we know for *certain* that Augustus isn't there. He is your biggest threat, and he's gone." Orin's voice was like fingernails on a chalkboard.

How could I refuse? What reason could I give? Danger couldn't be my excuse—I'd already broken into the palace, for Echna's sake. I certainly couldn't tell them about my connection to Arturian. I *wouldn't.* For all of Orin's admirable qualities, he was a pragmatist. He would use me against Arturian in an instant if he knew the truth.

Gritting my teeth, I forced myself out of the spiral I was careening into. A plan formed in my mind, easing some of the anxiety threatening to eat me from the inside.

"Francie?" Orin's voice broke through the dense fog that had settled over me. "Do you understand your mission?" I nodded before he became too concerned and started asking questions. "My source thinks the book is stored in Augustus's study—in a hidden drawer in the back of his desk."

It wasn't. I remembered *exactly* where the book was. I swallowed the lump forming in my throat and nodded. "Yes, okay."

Orin spread some floor plans on his desk and stood from his chair. "This is the general layout of the mansion, but the study shouldn't be hard to find. I'd think the best points of entry would be the hinged windows, but that sort of intelligence was Dak's job..." A somber silence filled the room as we thought of our lost friend. "Study up a bit while you get dressed... quickly. You don't have much time," he said with a firm pat on my shoulder, and left me alone in the office.

I couldn't believe how poorly timed the mission was. Augustus Exley had just followed me through the slums, and I'd recently spent most of a day tangled in the arms of his son. The last place I wanted to be was sneaking through those halls, intent on stealing from them.

My black trousers hugged my waist, along with the hooded black top I wore. In any other situation, there would be no way

I'd go outside like that. However, stealth was of the utmost importance when sneaking through the halls of Augustus Exley's home. My breathing became panicked as my shaking fingers tied my boots. Memories flashed through my mind of the day Arturian let me borrow that book—almost a year ago.

It was the first and only time I'd been inside the Exley mansion. Augustus was on a two-month trip to Trenica, and Arturian had been eager to show us around his family's ancestral home. I remembered how breathtaking it was... how grand and pristine. Gleaming hallways with marble tiles and gold, swirling moulding. Even the air in the house smelled of cedarwood and bergamot, enchanting my senses as we explored.

We hid from the occasional guard or servant as Arturian led us around the house until we'd made it upstairs to his bedroom. It was larger than the entire ground floor of the inn, and was adorned with red velvet curtains, black leather couches arranged around a grand golden hearth, and a bed so large that I couldn't avoid looking at it.

Arturian had remembered how much interest I'd shown in the history of the windblades and Skylords, and presented the weathered old tome, *The Chronicle of the Caelators,* to me as we sat on the priceless couches. "Read it while we ride for an hour. Stay in this room—you'll be safe once I lock the door."

He locked the door behind them, and off they went. I spent a peaceful hour poring over the ancient text, holding it as gently as one would a newborn child. I learned a great deal of hidden knowledge from the book, and only gawked at Arturian's enormous bed for a few minutes before my rogue thoughts interrupted my concentration. When the boys returned from their ride, I thanked Arturian for letting me read the book. He'd flashed that heart-stopping smile at me, and placed it right back where he'd gotten it from.

The drawer of his nightstand.

Ress escorted me through the dark streets of the slums. Orin hadn't liked the idea of anyone accompanying me at all, but Ress had put his foot down. "If you're going to send a doe into a forest of wolves, the least you could do is send one wolf with her," he'd growled at Orin in a rare display of insubordination.

I insisted I was *far* from defenseless, but he'd shot me a look that said, *it's the principle of it, Skylady.* Regardless of whether I truly needed the protection, I was glad for the company to distract me from the gaping maw of darkness I was about to crawl into.

"I don't know what kind of crazy shit Orin has you chasing after," Ress muttered as we approached the edge of the forest, "but do me a favor. Unless the survival of Friese hangs on it, please... don't die for it." He stopped by the tree line and turned to face me. I had to crane my neck to meet his eyes, which were ringed with concern. He didn't like this mission any more than I did.

"I won't," I said, giving him a soft smile. "If I died, who would keep you from hitting your head on every single door frame in Orin's house?"

Ress's smile morphed into a familiar smirk. "Be safe. It would be a shame to lose such a nice a—"

"It's a wonder you don't have a woman in your life, Ress."

He chuckled at me. "I don't think there's a woman in Friese who could handle *this*."

I rolled my eyes but patted his arm fondly. "On that, we agree. I'll meet you at Orin's in the morning." I gave him one last wink, which he returned, and made my way down the tree line.

I forced any doubts from my mind as I padded through the forest, my footsteps silent. Approaching the bell tower's clearing, I skirted its edge to reach the next trail. No need to drag Levick into what very well could end up being a suicide mission. Augustus might be gone, but his army of guards would be there. Arturian would be there. Sleeping right next to my target.

I shook the thoughts away before I began spiraling again. Clouds hung ominously over the Exley meadows, but to my relief, they withheld their moisture. It would be difficult to be stealthy if I was sopping wet.

The Exley mansion came into view in the distance; candles lit in a select few windows. It stood tall and imposing, but never austere like the Yorke mansion or the palace. Thick, woody vines and flowers climbed up the walls, snaking back and forth along the windows and doors. Some of the vines made it all the way up to the fifth-floor windows. My mouth pulled up in an exuberant smile.

I dug into my memories, trying to remember which of the fifth-story windows belonged to Arturian's room. I was almost certain of it by the time I approached the mansion, and laid a delicate hand on the cool, gray stones.

Such grand beauty. For only two people.

I walked along the wall, careful to sneak past windows, until I found a thick cluster of vines trailing up. My chosen set of vines wrapped around multiple jutting structures, such as oil lamps and statues, which made them much more likely to bear my weight. Closing my eyes, I took a deep breath and prayed to Echna that I wouldn't die while stealing from the man I loved.

After multiple tests of weight bearing, I took my first step up the thick collection of vines. It held, and I tilted my head back in relief. My plan might work, after all. I gripped multiple woody stems in each hand as I climbed, thanking Echna for every step. As I made my way higher, I had to force myself not to look down. After passing the third-story window, I caved to the feeling and glanced below. My stomach dropped, and I cursed myself for being foolish.

Keep going, Francie. Keep going. You can't stop now.

At long last, I crept up on the fifth-floor window. Steeling myself, I lifted my head up just enough to peek through the window. The bedroom was dim, illuminated only by a faint glow of dying embers in the fireplace. The decoration was just as grand as I remembered. His couches, the gold moulding... his bed.

Alone, in a bed four times the size of mine, Arturian slept. He was shirtless and lying on his stomach, his muscular arms under his pillow, and his hair resting in dark, gleaming strands over his face.

I gritted my teeth in an infuriating mixture of longing and frustration. I'd been hoping that he'd gone with his father to the meeting, though I'd known the chances of that were slim. Only Skylords were allowed entrance to those meetings. In a moment as heavy as the Exley mansion itself, I gripped the vines with one hand, and used my other hand to curl my fingers under the window frame.

Please, for the love of all things good, don't squeak.

After a moment of pure anxiety, I tugged at the frame with the gentlest force I could conjure. To my relief, the window was unlocked. It tilted open silently, craning out into the air like a door. In a moment of panic, I glanced back over to the bed, but Arturian was still sleeping.

Get in. Get the book. Get out.

Using every bit of strength and control I had, I hauled myself through the window. Warm air rushed over me, welcome and comforting as my boots met the soft rug on the floor. I took a deep breath to calm my nerves—watching Arturian the whole time—and crept my way over to his nightstand.

Please be a heavy sleeper.

I repeated it in my head a dozen times before reaching the drawer. Unfortunately, Arturian was facing the nightstand as he slept. From where I knelt, his face was half a horse-length from me. A strand of his hair moved gently against his face as he breathed.

I cleared my mind of the suffocating guilt and gripped the delicate handle on the drawer. It slid open, smooth and quiet, revealing a set of black razor-sharp throwing knives. The blood drained from my face, but I kept on my task. After a moment, I spotted it. Lying in the back of the drawer, tucked behind a loose cravat, sat the book. *The Chronicle of the Caelators.*

With one last glance at the peacefully sleeping Arturian, I pulled my hood lower over my face and slipped the book out of the drawer, closing it. I tucked it under my shirt in the tight sling bag I'd worn and smoothed my shirt back down.

Thank goodness.

I let myself breathe a soft sigh of relief as I glanced back up at the bed.

The *empty* bed.

He was upon me like a jaguar upon his prey. He swung around one of the bed posts, feet angled at my head. I rolled away just in time, but he caught my arm in an iron grip.

"Who are you?" he growled, but before he could see under my hood, I leveled a powerful booted stomp onto his bare foot. He groaned, breaking his concentration just enough for me to wiggle out of his grasp and dart for the window.

I only made it to the couches before he crashed into me like a tidal wave, tackling me. The air rushed from my lungs as we fell onto the couch, and I could've sworn I heard a *crack.* The impact buckled the couch shortly after, splitting one leg into a jagged point.

I twisted under Arturian, but he had me pinned on the sloped sofa, straddling me under his muscular legs. To my horror, he reached under the couch and pried the broken leg from under it, and raised it over me.

It came down upon me slowly—as if time had suspended itself for that moment. Arturian Exley, the man I was in love with, sat atop me and swung a weapon directly at my head.

He doesn't know it's me. He doesn't know—

Just before it could collide with my face, I shot my arm up, slicing the wood in half with my windblade. However, as I lifted my arm, it pushed my hood back.

I witnessed every one of his emotions as they flashed over his heart-stopping face. Eyes wide in horror at what he'd been about to do to me. Brows furrowed in confusion... why was I there? Stealing from him in the middle of the night? Then, finally, the hardening of his entire expression as it fully registered with him. I had a windblade.

I'd been lying to him.

"Francie..." My name escaped his lips in a breathless gasp, his bare, toned chest heaving from exertion.

Commotion sounded down the hall, and he jerked his head to the door for a split second before looking back down at me. His eyes softened before he leaned over, picked up the pieces of the broken couch leg, and tossed them into the fireplace. The sounds outside grew closer, and I tried but failed to squirm out from under him. Those were guards. They'd heard the commotion upstairs.

Arturian leaned low over me, lips brushing my ear, and whispered, "Don't kill me."

With that, he grabbed the front of my shirt with both hands and ripped it apart from the center. I yelped in shock, but before I could attempt to flee, he lifted me up, carried me across the room, and threw me onto his bed as if I weighed no more than one of his saddles. My heart thundered in my chest, and my head was swimming. It was all wrong.

What is he doing?

He climbed onto the bed, gripped my knees, and forced them open.

"Arturian!" I shouted, but he lowered himself on top of me until his breath brushed my ear.

"Play along if you want to live," he whispered, hot breath tickling my skin.

I would have cried with relief, but the sounds in the hall were getting closer. Arturian didn't spare another moment, and brought his mouth against mine in a frenzied, desperate kiss. I wrapped my legs around him and responded in kind, dragging my fingernails down his back.

For a blissful moment, I let myself imagine my life was simpler. That I'd been *invited* into Arturian's room instead of breaking in, and our kisses were purely out of passion, and not part of a curated display.

I could feel his hot skin against mine through the gaping hole he'd torn in my shirt... and his heart was pounding. I knew it was all a ploy—an act—but the way he moved against me... there was no way that could be a lie.

It wasn't five seconds before the bedroom door burst open and a panicked guard stormed in. Arturian continued his attentions for a moment, dragging his mouth down my neck to leave a few *very* pronounced marks on my collarbone. Even after pulling away a bit, his grip on my thigh would've been impossible to shake. To my frustration, I didn't want to.

"Sir, I heard a crash!" the guard exclaimed as he surveyed the room, narrowing his eyes at the broken couch. However, once his eyes made it over to the bed and onto the bright red claw marks running down Arturian's back, and the large tear in my shirt, his suspicion turned into embarrassment. "Oh—sir. I didn't realize…" he stammered.

"It's fine, Coran. But we'd like to finish what we started," Arturian said, his voice low and commanding as he tilted his head towards the door. The guard took the hint and turned to leave. "Coran," Arturian called after him, and he paused in the doorway. "I hope I can count on your… discretion."

The guard gave a curt nod. "Of course, sir," he mumbled, then left us alone.

Arturian sat perfectly still, eyes still trained on the door. The open window allowed a soft breeze to flow in, sending chills over my exposed skin. A burning question haunted my mind, and I couldn't stop myself.

"Why did you cover for me?" I asked, my eyes lingering on the marks I'd left on his back.

He hates me, now. I know I would.

He turned slightly, but his hair still obscured much of his face. "If you don't know by now, then it was truly hopeless from the start." His voice was raw—edged. "It's one of life's cruel tricks that I can't stop myself from loving you."

My heart swelled.

He loves me.

"Get out. *Now,*" he growled, meeting my eyes with an expression so hostile, I never would've believed his previous statement if I hadn't just heard it. His eyes, usually made of deep pools of mysterious ocean, were tumultuous and cold. My throat tightened as I felt my heart break in two. Forcing myself up and off the bed, I walked over to the window. I spared one last glance at him, but he didn't meet my eyes. He simply stared at his door.

I clenched my jaw, stifling the sobs that threatened to break through. Without another word, I leapt out the window and began my climb down the vines.

Drops of cool rain ran down my chest, exposed by the wide rip Arturian had left in my shirt. I was cold and shaking, and my lungs heaved from exertion as I continued my sprint across the meadow to the cover of the trees. I dared not stop for even a moment.

He knows. He knows.

Despite having let me go, I kept glancing over my shoulder, expecting to see a fleet of guards or Arturian himself racing after me through the blackness, but I was alone out there. Alone with a void of self-loathing expanding so rapidly that it threatened to swallow me completely. Memories of our time together at the port office swirled through my mind like a suffocating smoke.

"You are my very own summer storm, Francie. I'd stay wrapped in your tempest until the breath left my lungs."

Tears stung my cheeks as I thought of him. How he'd just told me he *loved* me. Right as I was betraying his trust, stealing from him, and exposing the fact that I'd hidden something from him for almost a decade. Cursing myself, I pushed on as I entered the trees, relieved for the cover of darkness.

I took the western route into the slums, avoiding the spot where Ress had left me earlier in the night. I anticipated a long night of flipping through the book, ensuring that it had *no* method of destroying the windblades hidden within its texts. As much as I respected Orin, I knew eliminating the windblades in Friese would only sow chaos and death, leaving us vulnerable to the enemies who'd been deterred by the Skylords for centuries. Doubts swirled in my mind, only comforted by the weight of the book in my—

The book.

The book I had nearly died for. The one I revealed myself to Arturian for.

It was gone.

CHAPTER TWENTY-SIX
KNIFE THERAPY

ARTURIAN

I stood twenty horse-lengths from my target. Drawing my arm back, just as I'd seen Francie do, I flung my knife into the bullseye. I was a perfect shot, despite the half empty bottle of salt rum in my other hand. Walking over to the table, I poured myself another.

Torchlight illuminated the Exley courtyard, making the shadows of the statues dance. My aristocratic façade was gone, replaced by a shadow of a man. Most Friesians had already been asleep for hours, but sleep didn't come to me.

Memories haunted my every moment. Memories that had previously excited me, now only devastated me.

Francie. The one person I thought would never lie to me.

The early fall breeze blew over my bare chest and abdomen, carrying with it the briny scents of the port. I looked to the sky, as if I could find answers amongst the stars. The constellations hung overhead, glowing in glistening displays of red and blue.

Despite their dazzling beauty, I could only scowl at them. My father had been right. Francie was the daughter of Adolpho Exley. She sliced that couch leg apart with Asgora, our house's own windblade... and no amount of alcohol had dulled the questions swirling in my mind. How long had she known who she was? Did she know at all, or had she no idea how she'd gotten her windblade?

Had she been playing with me the whole time?

No.

I had to believe some of it was real. How her eyes glistened when she looked at me... the gentleness of her fingers running over my chest. How relaxed her body was as she sighed in my arms. Betrayal washed over me again, souring my heart.

Maybe this will help.

I tipped my glass back, draining the rum before throwing another knife at my target. It hit the bullseye, knocking the other knife to the ground.

CHAPTER TWENTY-SEVEN

SELECTION

I raced through the midnight streets of Friese while covering myself from the late summer rain. I was running late for my very first pre-mission brief, and there was a rumor Francie and I had been chosen for an important job down at the docks. Orin kept us in the dark until right before our missions, so I had no idea what I could be getting myself into. Orin said he was keeping it quiet due to *sensitive information* and the *risk of potential sabotage.*

Lightning flashed as I approached the house, illuminating the stern face that looked down on me from the second-story window. Ress still hadn't warmed up to me, undoubtedly because of his affection for Francie. He was very protective of her, which I tried to appreciate considering the amount of dangerous places they ventured into together.

Multiple RCM members greeted me as I came in the door. Orin's wife, Nina, made her way over to me. "How are you feeling, Levick? Did you sleep well last night?" she asked, her dark eyes scanning me.

Her tone and energy made me anxious. "I slept fine... why do you ask?" I replied as I slipped off my boots.

"That's good to hear. Please, come and sit by the fire," she said, leading me over to the hearth. Even in summer, fires were a common sight in Friese to combat the chilly nights and brighten homes.

I'd only just made myself comfortable on the old sofa when, out of the corner of my eye, I saw Ress descend the last few stairs and yank open the front door.

"There you are. I was starting to worry about you," he said warmly as Francie came inside and shook the rain from her hair.

"I'm sorry for being late. It's been a long couple of days..." she trailed off as she searched the room. Finally, she met my gaze and her eyes softened. I smiled and beckoned her over.

"Do you know any details yet?" Francie asked as she sat down next to me. Her eyelids were heavy, and I wondered if she hadn't been sleeping well.

"Nothing more than you told me yesterday," I replied.

She hummed in disappointment, her expression wearied. The other members of the RCM mingled and chatted, but the general unease in the room hung like a fog. I hadn't received any contact from Orin since our initial meeting, which Francie said was unusual for him. I'd asked her if she'd heard from him, and she claimed that we'd been told to lie low while Orin planned our next move, and to wait for direction. Thankfully, for my patience's sake, it wasn't much longer before I received the summons for our current meeting.

"Gather 'round, everyone," Orin said from next to the fire-place. He was all business in his usual utility vest and lace-up boots. Nina took her customary seat right next to him.

"I'm sure you've all wondered what I've been up to these last few weeks," he said, to a modest cheer from the room. Ress hooted in excitement. "I had something in the works. It would've revolutionized the Revolt and given us an unbeatable edge…" Murmurs floated around the room. "However, that plan fell through." I could've sworn I felt Francie shift uncomfortably beside me.

Orin continued, "Thankfully, I often have more than one iron in the fire. I have another plan ready… and it's one that could change everything. A plan to destabilize. To shake their entire hierarchy to its core." A few people mumbled in excitement.

"I received a tip that may change our strategy completely." Orin paused, looking at me and Francie. "I've obtained sensitive, but reliable information, which leads me to believe that one of the major houses is planning something *big*." His tone seemed to unsettle everyone in the room. "I won't be too specific about it until we get solid proof. However, if my information is correct, Friese will soon be engulfed in chaos." Gasps erupted from the other RCM members.

"Tonight, our plan is to recover hard evidence. For this mission, I've chosen two of our members who I believe will be thorough, swift, and most importantly—inconspicuous," Orin said, before holding his hand out towards me and Francie.

Ress cursed, storming out of the room.

"Levick, Francie. Will you please join me in my office for a pre-mission brief?" Orin asked, ignoring Ress's theatrics.

Francie shot up out of her seat. "Of course. Let's go," she said, taking my hand and following Orin to his office. My head was still spinning. Despite the rumor Francie had told me, I couldn't believe we'd been chosen—we were the two newest RCM members.

I couldn't stop myself from questioning Orin before we even sat down. "With all due respect, Orin... why us? We're your newest members. Wouldn't more seasoned members be a better choice?"

Orin smiled. "I've put a great deal of thought into my choice, Levick. You'd be best served by trusting my instincts," he said with a look that said, *don't try me tonight, boy.*

I took the hint and sat myself down.

"We should get started—the cover of darkness won't last forever. The port headquarters building is where the Crown keeps track of all imports and exports. You'll be looking for the Royal Imports office, which is controlled by the queen, and documents every shipment into Friese. Bring back all the recent ledgers so we can inspect for any major shifts in the amount or nature of shipments. If you find anything else suspicious, bring it back to me, along with the ledgers. I can't emphasize how serious this new threat may be. I need you to look through every major house's import shipment information, *without bias,*" he finished with an emphasis that made me suspicious.

Francie was about to chime in with a question before Orin cut her off. "Keep in mind that the port headquarters building is the most heavily guarded building at the port. You'll have to use every method of stealth you have. I'm counting on you two tonight."

I found myself relishing the idea of a challenge. "We'll handle it, Orin," I said, surprising myself with my confidence. I turned to see Francie smiling in nervous excitement.

"Let's get moving, then."

THE PORT AUTHORITY

I pulled a long, black shirt over my head, taking care not to loosen my braid. Levick and I were in Orin's office alone, donning dark clothing to make ourselves blend in with the night. It had only been two nights since Arturian caught me in his bedroom, and I'd barely slept since then.

"Can you still pick a lock, Lev?" I asked as I secured a couple of locks of hair that had gotten loose.

Levick chuckled, embarrassed. "I'm not proud of that skill, Francie, but I hope it will be useful tonight. I only hope they aren't using advanced, expensive door locks. My expertise doesn't extend that far, unfortunately..." he trailed off as he pulled his shirt over his shoulders.

I grasped the Exley house ring I wore on a chain around my neck, as if touching it would bring me clarity. Lately, it brought only guilt.

Stop thinking about him.

My heart felt like it was twisting in knots as I recalled the look on his face as he told me to leave. I tucked the necklace back into my blouse's neckline.

Stay focused, Francie. This is the real thing. No distractions.

"I suppose you could always just slice the door open," Levick said, grinning and looking at me over his shoulder.

I had trouble remembering what we were talking about, but I cleared my thoughts and replied, "I think that might violate our instruction of being inconspicuous, don't you think?"

"Ah, that's too bad," he said as he ran his fingers through his messy brown hair.

"Are you ready?" I asked after lacing my boots up tight. I stood by the door, ignoring the dark, inescapable cloud hanging over me.

"As ready as I'll ever be."

He smiled at me, and I wished I felt as optimistic as he seemed.

We hurried through the slums, careful not to attract any attention from the Crownies. As we made our way closer to the docks, Levick gestured for me to follow him into an alley.

"What are we doing?" I whispered into the darkness.

"Over here," he replied, leading me to a stack of crates leaning against a building. They'd been arranged into steps.

"No, Levick! That's your realm, not mine!" I hissed as I realized what he had planned for us.

Levick took my hand and looked into my eyes. I could barely make out his boyishly handsome features in the faint moonlight. "The Crownies would be suspicious if they saw us walking the streets this late at night."

"I can't do that, Lev," I said, shaking my head. Despite my penchant for tree-climbing, the idea of running across rooftops was not something I relished. I clung to his arms, panic threatening to steal my nerve away.

Levick's eyes darkened, and his expression took on a look that I'd never seen in him. His eyes darted to my hands, gripping his sleeves, and then landed on my lips. A nervous lump formed in my throat when I noticed how close we were. I knew what he wanted... and to my surprise, I wanted it, too.

I should stop him. He doesn't know about me and Arturian. It wouldn't be right.

But my heart raced as I stared at him.

Don't I deserve to be happy? Don't I deserve to have a love that makes sense?

Arturian is marrying someone else.

I seized the moment, forcing anything and anyone else from my mind. I took a step closer and slid a hand over Levick's chest, meeting his gaze with an open, inviting stare. His green eyes burned hot, and without hesitation, he took my face in his hands and brought his lips down to mine.

In an instant, Levick and I were sharing a moment I'd only ever shared with Arturian. The kiss was gentle and warm—an embodiment of our years of cherished closeness. He pulled me in tighter, deepening the kiss, and my heart thundered in my chest. I wrapped my arms around his neck, the heat between us undeniable.

Even so, my traitorous hand reached for Arturian's house ring tucked into my shirt. Any warm feelings I had began drowning under a flood of heartache.

The kiss lasted only a few heartbeats before Levick pulled away. I stood completely still. I'd been subconsciously clinging to the hope I'd be able to love Levick like I loved Arturian. I wanted *so badly* to make him happy—to give him what he yearned for... but I couldn't lie to myself. My heart belonged to someone else, and Levick deserved more than half a love.

Thankfully, he didn't seem to notice my distress. "You can do this, Francie. I'll be right here with you," he whispered against my lips.

Heart still reeling from whiplash, I pressed down my emotions. I nodded and climbed the crates, Levick following close behind. As I stood up on the roof, I was immediately dazzled. The openness of the rooftops was a stark contrast to the narrow Friesian alleyways that didn't allow for much light. The moon shone its silvery rays down on Friese, casting a blue hue over the northern sea-cliffs. I could see the bay in the distance—the moon's reflection shimmered off of the rippling surface.

"It's something, isn't it?" Levick said as he emerged onto the roof next to me.

"You see this all the time, don't you?" I asked.

"A few nights a week."

For a moment, I stood in awe. In awe of the beauty of our kingdom, and in the mystery of my friend. I'd known Levick for years, but there was an entire side of his life that was unfamiliar to me. I looked over at him and saw his pure, uninhibited freedom. His exuberance of the moment.

"Are you ready to jump?" he asked, jolting me out of my thoughts.

"Jump where?"

Levick chuckled. "How did you think we'd get to the port from here?"

"I guess I was hoping there was some sort of bridge system up here..." I trailed off, realizing how silly the notion was as I said it. My heart raced as I came to terms with what I'd have to do.

"The rooftops... they're not too far apart?" I asked.

"They aren't that far. Don't worry, I'll... help you."

I doubted how useful Levick's moral support would be when I was twenty feet from the ground, but I let it go.

"On my count of three, run and jump onto that roof over there," Levick said while motioning to a shabby-looking neighboring roof.

He knows what he's doing. He does this all the time.

Taking a deep breath, I looked over at Levick and nodded.

"One.

"Two.

"Three!"

Before I could doubt myself, I took off across the rooftop. The night breeze blew through my hair as I bounded exultantly across the roof. I picked up speed as I approached the ledge, knowing I would need all the momentum I could create.

This is it. Just jump.

My foot struck down on the wooden ledge, and I pressed down with all the strength I could muster. Just as I leapt, a strong gust of wind hit me from behind, pushing me even faster. I yelped in shock, but landed safely on the neighboring roof.

I bent over, hands on my knees and panting for air. "Levick! I did it!" I laughed partially in relief, but also in disbelief.

I can't believe I just jumped off of a roof.

I could barely see Levick motioning a thumbs-up from the other rooftop. I watched him take off across the roof, running confidently and with perfect form.

Like he's done this countless times.

He smiled as he jumped—his expression was completely devoid of fear or anxiety. His dark clothing rippled in the wind as he *flew* through the air. I couldn't look away, even after he'd landed.

"What?" he asked, his breathing barely elevated.

"How have I never seen this side of you?"

He smiled. "I'd love to talk later, Francie, but we have a mission to accomplish. We have a few more rooftops to get across, and I think you might be *almost* as fast as I am," he said with a snarky grin.

I could never resist a challenge, so we bolted through the darkness, racing towards our objective.

From rooftop to rooftop, we bounded and flew across the open air. Levick followed closely until we both landed with a soft thump on the main thoroughfare that bordered the docks. Despite the hour, voices could be heard from the ships, as well as hollering from outside the seedy port pubs. Thankfully for us, the road was mostly empty.

"Which building is the Royal Port Authority?" I asked as we hunched under an overhang.

"Right there," Levick said, pointing to a centrally situated building with a tall steeple at the top.

It was obviously one of the better-funded architectural projects at the port. The ruling class of Friese would never accept one of their government buildings being shabby. They were satisfied with leaving all the shabbiness to their underpaid and overworked slum-dwellers. The disparity between the districts of northern Friese and those of southern Friese was so marked that if someone walked directly north from the port slums and into the wealthy business district, one would assume they entered a different kingdom entirely.

"We should get closer to find a suitable point of entry," I whispered.

Levick nodded in agreement, and we crept towards the Port Authority building, taking care to stay near the shop fronts for cover. As we got closer, I noticed a guard patrolling the front of the headquarters building. The light of the guard's torch glimmered off his pristine silver buttons and illuminated the stiff structure of the black military uniform he wore. That was no simple guard.

Echna, save us.

I took Levick's hand, stopping him behind a shop's sign. "Lev, that's an Exley man."

He looked out, narrowed his eyes, and then opened them wide as he recognized the uniform.

"This complicates things," he whispered.

We stood silently for a moment until I placed a hand on Levick's arm. "We are getting what we came for, Levick Roale," I said, my voice bolstered by determination.

He nodded hesitantly. "Alright, but we need to be very careful not to alert that guard. I'd bet my bell tower that he's not the only one there."

We worked out a plan to get inside quietly and resumed creeping towards the building. We turned down an alley to approach it from behind. Tiptoeing past a few unconscious drunkards, we made it to the side of the Port Authority building.

Empty barrels had been left in the alley, so we dragged one over to the wall, and placed it directly underneath a second-story window.

"This thing better be unlocked..." I muttered as I hefted myself up on top of the large barrel.

Levick stood watch, facing the main street where we'd seen the guard. Seeing his uniform had unnerved both of us. It was highly unusual for anyone except a Crown Police officer to be guarding a government building. Why would Augustus feel the need to guard this building? Why would the queen allow it?

I shook away my distracting thoughts. "Are you coming?" I whispered, kneeling on the barrel and offering my hand.

He nodded and leapt up onto the barrel.

"The window is unlocked," I whispered, pulling the glass out to open it.

"That's lucky," Levick responded, but I couldn't help but feel decidedly unlucky. Something was amiss.

You're just being paranoid. It's probably nothing.

We found ourselves in a large office. I produced a small oil lamp from my satchel and lit it. The dim orange light filled the room, illuminating large maps displayed on the walls. Friese sat on the southern end of our narrow continent, while the mountainous, cold nation of Trenica sat in the north. The nations were divided by a large swath of unnavigable, desolate land—the Wastes. Crossing the Wastes was generally considered unsafe and unnecessarily time-consuming, so most travel between Friese and Trenica took place by sea.

"This is a cartographer's office, Francie. We won't find what we need here," Levick said as he motioned for the door.

I nodded and followed him out. We snuck from room to room, and eventually came to the conclusion that the second floor was devoted mainly to navigational purposes. We looped back through the hallways and found a staircase. It took every bit of my patience and balance to keep from making the boards creak.

Coming around the corner of the last few steps, I spotted a patrolling Exley guard walking away from us. The building was arranged in a circle—the hallway went all the way around, with rooms and offices on either side of it. That meant that the guard would be coming back by the staircase soon. Avoiding him would be a challenge.

I turned to Levick to make sure he saw, and he responded with a grimace. He understood.

"There's a patrolling guard up here for a reason," he whispered, leaning in close.

I nodded. There would be no reason to actively guard innocuous information. This was where we needed to be.

We snuck into the hallway before the guard could make it all the way around, ducking into offices and rooms. We searched each one, diligently leaving each room exactly as we found it. Every time we finished in a room, we had to listen carefully by the door to be sure the guard wasn't passing nearby.

We eventually finished all the smaller offices without success. Rounding a corner, we came upon a large, executive-style office, the furthest office from the stairs. The room was furnished with fine chairs and a desk made from imported wood. We quickly threw a small towel over the base of the door as we'd been doing throughout the night, covering the light of our lamp from the passing guard in the hallway.

"This is it. The Royal Imports office," Levick hissed at me, and I immediately rushed in and began rummaging through a trunk.

"It appears so…" I said, pausing what I was doing. "Are we sure we want to open this box? We really don't know what we'll find," I said suddenly, picking at my fingernails and glancing around the office.

There could be evidence in here. Evidence that could sign Arturian's death warrant.

Levick cocked his head in confusion. "Francie… this is about Arturian, isn't it?"

I looked over at him, my face draining.

"We have to look. Even if there's a small chance Augustus is plotting something," Levick said resolutely.

I knew he was right. "I think there's a very high chance. That's what I'm afraid of."

A long silence settled between us.

"You're right. If Augustus is planning something illegal, Arturian would go down, too," Levick acknowledged. "But we have to think of Friese."

I nodded stiffly. Augustus was a cold-blooded killer, and I couldn't risk Friese's safety to keep Arturian from the consequences. "Can you pick this lock?" I asked, kneeling next to an ornate desk.

Levick hesitated for a moment, but sighed and inspected it. "Probably..." He retrieved a couple of picks from his pocket and got to work.

The lock put up a strong defense, but Levick's tenacity won out, earning a satisfying *click* sound. He opened the drawer and revealed a thick, leather-bound ledger.

"That's it... the ledgers." I sighed in relief. I gripped the heavy book and quickly stashed it in my satchel as Levick hastened over and listened by the door for the guard.

I won't lose this *book.*

"I think he just rounded the bend," Levick whispered over to me.

I nodded. "I'm ready."

Levick opened the door slowly, peering out. *Clear,* he mouthed.

The Royal Imports office was situated on the opposite side of the circular hallway from the staircase—we didn't have much time before the guard rounded the other side. As we crept down the hallway, I cringed at every creak and crack the wood floors made. After what felt like forever, we made it to the staircase. The guard was nowhere to be seen. I breathed a sigh of relief.

We were fast enough.

My relief was cut short when Levick nearly ran head-first into a broad-shouldered man coming out of the staircase.

No!

Without hesitation, the guard swung back and punched Levick square in the jaw, sending him spinning.

"Stop, please!" I called out, stepping between Levick and the guard.

He was dressed in an unmistakable Exley uniform, but of a more tactical style. Heavy-looking black metal armor protected his chest and abdomen, and black chain mail covered his muscular arms. Even his light hair was shaved down, completely contrary to Friesian fashions. He bore no rank or identification marks.

This is no simple guard.

"You are trespassing on Her Majesty's property. Lay face-down on the floor and your life *may* be spared," the guard replied in an emotionless monotone.

Please don't make me do it again. I can't do it again.

I held my hands up, ready to throw. "Please! I don't want to hurt you."

The guard nearly laughed at the notion—his ruddy features twitching in amusement. He had no idea that he wouldn't be my first.

Please don't make me kill you.

Levick stood up slowly and leaned over to me. "There's a window at the far side of the hallway," he whispered into my ear.

"Quiet!" the guard barked. "Get down onto the floor, now!" He had his hand on his sword's hilt.

Just then, the patrolling guard sprinted towards us from the other end of the hallway, sword drawn. I swiveled to face him. "You're surrounded, thieves!" he yelled. He looked young—almost like a teenager.

"You're surrounded. If you comply, no harm will come to you," the tall captain said to me, obviously not including Levick in that promise.

I breathed in deeply, knowing I had no choice. My heart already grieved for them... and for myself. The young, innocent girl from the inn died the night I killed the palace guard.

Fly true, blade of wind. Our lives depend on it.

I brought my arms up and over my head and flung them out in opposite directions.

Blood spewed onto the walls as the young guard's head fell from his body.

Look away. Look away.

By the staircase, the captain's shoulder gushed from a deep laceration, but he remained standing. I had to stifle a scream at the horrors I inflicted.

"Run! To the window!" Levick shouted as the captain drew his sword and lunged at us. I charged ahead, jumping over the corpse lying in the hallway.

"Stop!" the captain called after us. Despite his wound, he was gaining on Levick.

He'll catch us. We'll never make it out.

We were a few lengths from the window when Levick suddenly stopped and turned around.

"What are you doing?!" I shouted at him.

The injured officer's blade was mere inches from Levick when he suddenly thrust both of his hands forward.

A gust of wind *exploded* down the hallway, throwing the captain all the way back into the staircase. A grotesque *thump* signaled his landing.

I stared at Levick, dumbstruck.

"What are you doing? Jump!" Levick yelled. "Don't worry, I'll catch you!"

Was that a windblade?

"Go!" He pushed me towards the window.

He'll catch me.

I turned and leapt out the third-story window.

CHAPTER TWENTY-NINE
THE BASTARD DAUGHTER

"I hope I'm hearing you wrong, Lieutenant. I hope you aren't saying what I think you're saying," I said, my voice tight with tension as I paced back and forth in my study. The implications were astonishing.

"His head had been severed from his body, sir. It was the cleanest cut I've ever seen," Lieutenant Coran Trust responded, his expression grave. "Captain Stone is lucky to be alive. He has a deep laceration on his shoulder, and was knocked out from being thrown down the stairs."

I paused my pacing, my head jerking up. "Knocked unconscious from one flight of stairs?"

Lieutenant Trust hesitated for a moment, his expression dour. "We believe he was... *projected* into the wall of the stairwell, then fell straight down. There is an... imprint on the wall." His last words were clipped, as if he didn't want to think about it.

Projected?

"Is he awake now?" I asked. I could feel my blade's energy surging inside me, responding to my fury.

"No, sir. Our doctors think he won't wake for hours, at least."

"The thieves—did they take anything?"

"Your office desk had been unlocked. We're assuming things were taken, but our investigation is ongoing," the officer said, looking uncomfortable.

"Dismissed," I hissed through my frustration.

The lieutenant had the good sense to rush out of the room before I sliced an ancient tapestry to shreds.

It would take a directed gust to throw a man down a hallway.

Inherited windblades didn't work that way. They could slice and stab, but never directed, controlled gusts. I had occasionally disrupted the wind if my mood grew sour, but I had no control over it. There was only one type of person who could throw a full-grown man down a hallway with nothing but a strong gust of wind.

There is a windwalker in Friese.

To make matters worse, this windwalker appeared to be working alongside someone with a windblade. Blades of steel could never sever a head with such precision.

I felt my control slipping as I tried to think of who they could be.

Which of the Skylords would dare something this brazen against me... Lesynna? No, she wouldn't risk exposing herself.

It couldn't be Nestor Yorke, not with the wedding being arranged. And he just caught that deathly lung blight...

Then, the realization hit me.

"Her. The bastard daughter," I said aloud. I thought of the girl at the inn who had a remarkable resemblance to Adolpho's killer. My mind pieced together the implications.

I was right. She must *be Adolpho's daughter. The daughter of that thieving, murdering housemaid. She passed the Exley wind-blade to her daughter.*

I walked out onto my balcony and looked down on my expansive property. I could see the very edge of my military camp.

"This changes nothing," I said, resolute. "The plans commence."

It's time for Arturian to prove his worth.

CHAPTER THIRTY
THE WINDWALKER

"You have a windblade?!" Francie was nearly screaming as we leapt from rooftop to rooftop. I heard her, but I was completely focused on keeping both of us aloft as we jumped between roofs.

"Francie!" I hissed, landing on a ledge and rolling. "We can't talk about this right now!" I glanced over my shoulder to make sure we hadn't been followed. Relief overcame me upon seeing only empty rooftops behind us. Francie's anger seemed to boost her forward, keeping up with me. For the first time in my life, I wanted to outrun her a bit.

I can't have this conversation and keep us alive at the same time.

Francie used someone's chimney to gain some height, then jumped off, landing in front of me, still sprinting. I didn't need to boost her that time.

"If I beat you back to the bell tower, you tell me *everything*!" Francie cried out over her shoulder. There was no room for negotiation in her tone.

She's forgotten who she's challenging.

I smiled to myself. "You're pretty bold for someone who needs my help to clear the gaps across these roofs!" I couldn't help but laugh as I said it.

Francie slowed down just enough to meet my eyes. "You'd never let me fall."

I leapt off of a fence that divided two gardens, somersaulting in the air before landing on a ledge.

"Show-off!" Francie called from a roof nearby. Her skirt was slowing her down as it billowed behind her, but it made for an enchanting display. My rogue thoughts ventured to the kiss we shared earlier that night. The sensation of her hands sliding over my shoulders... the taste of her mouth as she parted her lips for me... I'd *finally* done it.

After stumbling near a ledge, I shook the memories from my mind. If I thought about it too much, I might very well fall to my death. Surging with a new wave of energy, I flung myself up onto the bottom of a temple steeple. The moon glistened off the cobbled roof as I jumped onto the vaulted peak of the sanctuary and ran along the center. Francie's footsteps echoed behind me.

"You can try all you want, Francie, but I've been doing this for years!" I said with a breathless laugh. I only hoped she wouldn't notice my increasing fatigue. As we made it closer to the edge of the slums, the buildings had gotten taller, and it took most of my focus to ensure both of our safety.

Thundering on like unstoppable forces, we ran towards the last building in the slums before the forest began. The roof stood at least five feet higher than the one we were currently on.

Uh oh.

I'd never needed to boost two people that high before. To assuage my doubts, I tried to remind myself of the guard I'd just thrown down a hallway.

If I can do that, I can get us up on this roof.

"Lev, are you sure?" Francie called from behind me, having just noticed the height difference.

"I've got us! Just be sure to jump as hard as you can!" I desperately hoped I was right.

Too late to stop now.

I pushed off the brick ledge with all of my strength, while simultaneously summoning a jet of air beneath me. My shirt flew up, almost impeding my sight. Ignoring every bit of sense in my brain, I looked down. My stomach felt like it dropped all the way to the distant ground.

Shouldn't have done that.

Blessedly, my feet slammed against the last rooftop. Without a moment's hesitation, I jumped to the side and turned around, only to see Francie in midair and not even close to the ledge. She let out panicked shrieks as her arms flailed in the air.

"Francie!" I cried out, lifting my arms and summoning the strongest gust of wind I could manage.

Francie's hair blew straight up, along with her skirt and shirt, exposing her black trousers and undershirt. The absurdity of the sight would have made me laugh if not for the seriousness of the moment. She started tumbling through the air, end over end.

"Levick!" she yelled as the wind blew her hair across her face. I realized my error as she flew towards me, her head almost colliding with mine.

"Hang on!" I said, contorting my hands to tame the raging tempest. The gale finally died down, lowering Francie until she hung horizontally over my outstretched arms.

"About time," Francie huffed as the winds dropped her.

"At least I caught you," I said, grinning at her. Her hair had been twisted into knots, but her clothes had fallen back down to an appropriate position.

She rested her head on my shoulder as she caught her breath. "That was *terrifying*. Maybe we should practice together."

"Excuse me," I began, my indignation only slightly exaggerated, "I just helped you jump three horse-lengths through the air *and* lifted you up about ten feet. I believe the words you're looking for are 'thank you.'" Francie raised an eyebrow at my embellishment.

Still, she muttered a "thank you" before pinching me on the shoulder.

"Hey!" I laughed as I set her down.

"Really, though, Lev. That was incredible. I've never seen someone use a windblade like that. I don't think I could ever get mine to do that," she said, brushing her tangled hair out of her face. I leapt down from the tall warehouse, using my wind to cushion my landing. Francie followed without hesitation, letting my winds swirl around her as I lowered her to the ground. My heart jumped at the smile on her lips.

"I don't think I have a windblade," I mumbled. The moon shone down through the forest, illuminating the trees as they rippled in the breeze.

"What do you mean?" she asked. "That looked an awful lot like wind-control to me."

"I was born with it, Francie," I said hesitantly, while admiring the view.

She paused, as if she were remembering something she'd learned long ago.

"Oh. *Oh.*" She turned to look at me, eyes wide. "You're a windwalker."

We walked the forest trail in silence, but I could feel Francie looking over at me every few minutes. It was making me anxious.

"Do you have something to say to me, Francie? I can't take this anymore," I said, breaking the unbearable silence.

"I have about a thousand questions to ask you, Lev," she said, sounding frustrated. "But, if I'm being honest, I'm hurt that you didn't tell me after all this time."

"But—" I cut in, but Francie stopped me.

"I know, I know. I didn't tell you about my windblade until recently. I realize how hypocritical my feelings are, but it's hard to ignore them." Suddenly, Francie stiffened, staring at me with wide eyes. "Does Arturian know?"

I shook my head. "No, you're the only one."

"Why haven't you told him?"

"For the same reason you haven't told him about your blade." Francie nodded, but remained silent. "He's from a different world than we are. Who knows how he'd react... or who he'd tell? He might think just like *they* do. *The wind is reserved for nobility,*" I finished, bitterness creeping into my voice.

Out of the corner of my eye, I caught Francie bristling at the notion. She held her hand up to her chest, clutching at her blouse. She clearly didn't want to assume that of Arturian.

We walked in a heavy silence for a while—I was unsure of what to say. Something felt unusual about the way she reacted when Arturian was mentioned, but I put it out of my mind.

The moonlight barely filtered through the trees, illuminating the trail just enough to follow it. I dodged some stray branches, then held them aside so Francie wouldn't walk into them. She absently flicked her fingers and sliced them off with her wind-blade. I almost flinched.

"I'm still not used to that," I muttered as I dropped the cut branches. I hoped Francie could see my conciliatory smile in the darkness. "I'm sorry, Francie," I said as we continued on the trail. "I should've told you a long time ago."

"So why didn't you?" she asked.

"I could be hunted down and exterminated, along with any-one who knows about me," I said, looking over at her as we walked. She was staring at her feet, silent. "The Skylords would kill us if they found out. They guard and preserve wind-control for themselves, and I didn't want them to execute you if they discovered me. I was trying to protect you." I shook my head in frustration. "Although I suppose we're in similar situations now. Your windblade is just as illegal as my windwalking," I said, a grim undertone in my voice.

Francie went unusually quiet and had no response for a while as we walked. After the silence became unbearably tense, she said quietly, "I know stories about the Caelators."

I furrowed my brows. I didn't know much about them, and neither did most people in Friese. According to legend, they were Friesian windwalker generals from centuries ago, but their histories were destroyed by the Skylords.

"Where did you hear them?"

"I've always been very interested in the subject, and a few years ago Arturian found an old Friesian history book in Augustus's study. It was a banned book, secretly kept by the Exleys for generations. He let me read through some of it on one of the days you went out riding." In an uncharacteristic lack of coordination, she stumbled a bit, but caught herself with a branch. I chuckled from behind her, earning a glare from over her shoulder.

"I remember that day... only you would prefer reading a dusty history book over riding," I said, smiling at the notion. Memories of our shared adventures ran through my mind, making me miss the summers we'd go riding together. "What did the book say?" I asked, tucking away the nostalgia.

"From what I remember, the Caelators were what the Skylords were intended to be. When Echna bestowed her gift of wind control upon Friese, there were no windblades—only windwalkers. There were still very few of them, but instead of being hunted down and exterminated, they were embraced. They went through rigorous training from the time of childhood so that one day they could earn the right to defend Friese as elite, esteemed warriors. Some of them even became kings and queens." She trailed off a bit, becoming lost in thought.

I, however, felt starved for information. "If there were no windblades back then, where did they come from?"

"The Caelators became greedy and were unsatisfied with wind-control. They wanted more, and had heard musings of a dark power hidden away in the Trenican mountains... the Midnight Zephyr." She paused, taking a deep breath. "The Friesian Caelators brought tornados and storms of ice to Trenican cities in their search of the Zephyr, killing thousands of innocent people. Echna, in her rage and disgust at the perversion of her gift, cursed the Caelators by stripping them of their vast control of the wind, replacing it with the windblade, and making it transferable *only* through murder," Francie finished, her voice shaking at the end. She was undoubtedly thinking of her mother.

A worthy power and a fitting punishment for a bloodthirsty, greedy people.

"That's not all, Lev," Francie said, her voice becoming ominous. "I remember... there was a prophecy about Echna and the windwalkers. It was only mentioned briefly, but if it's true..." Her shoulders shook.

"What was it?" I asked, speeding up and taking her arm. She stopped to look at me, worry ringing her eyes. "Francie?" I whispered.

"It said that one day, Friese will face an existential threat like no other. A threat that could permanently end the powers of the Skylords and leave Friese in rubble." She swallowed nervously and tore her eyes away from me to stare at her feet again. "When that time comes, Echna will bestow a windwalker upon Friese as an act of mercy; as a champion for her survival. *Only a Caelator—a windwalker general created by Echna herself—will be able to stop the bloodshed.*" She raised her eyes to mine as tears welled in her eyes. My throat tightened as the implications sunk in. "That's you, Lev. You must be the last Caelator."

"But that would mean..." I said, my voice barely audible.

Francie bit her lip, the moon casting a pallid, haunting sallowness over her face. "War is truly upon us."

The bell tower's large doors creaked as I opened them. I stopped short when I realized Francie wasn't following me. She stood a few feet from the door, looking conflicted.

"Come on, we should look at the ledgers," I said, waving her forward.

She nodded in agreement, but remained where she stood, staring at the threshold. Her entire demeanor was unsettled—almost forlorn.

"No one can find out about you." She looked up at me, her face drawn with worry. "The queen and the Skylords will hunt you down and kill you." Her voice faltered and cracked. "And if that prophecy is true... you might be our only hope."

My heart ached to see her that way. "Francie," I said, meeting her gaze with steady, assured eyes, "we don't even know how reliable that book was. The histories are notoriously varied. You should put it out of your mind. We're going to stop Augustus *together*."

She took a deep breath and nodded at me, a smile touching her features as she reached for the neckline of her blouse again. "Let's go inside. We have ledgers to investigate."

I smiled back, fighting the growing sense of unease building in my heart. Her words floated through my mind like a haunting refrain: *a dark power hidden away in the Trenican mountains... the Midnight Zephyr.*

As soon as we'd walked through the doors, Francie had already begun unpacking the ledger from her satchel. I knew what she was worried about. She didn't want to hand-deliver damning evidence about Arturian to the RCM.

I bit at my cheek in frustration, but I knew she was right. I nodded at her, and we settled on the floor together under the light of her lamp. We flipped through pages upon pages of mundane trade material.

"The Yorkes like gems, no surprise there," Francie muttered as she read on. "The Wemberleys import enough dresses to clothe half of the slum's population... shit," she gasped.

I knew it had to be bad. Francie rarely swore. I bent over her shoulder to see what she'd found and glimpsed a figure that made my head spin.

"The Exleys are importing weapons..." she muttered.

"By the *tons.*" I shook my head in disbelief. I recalled the memory of the wounded man at the inn who'd been clutching the unusual sword. I still had it hidden away.

It's Trenican. Augustus is importing weapons from Trenica.

"What does Augustus need these for?" Francie asked, flipping through more of the ledger.

"I think I have an idea..." I said, my voice ominous as I prayed to Echna I was wrong.

"It's dated at *two years ago,*" Francie hissed, panicking.

I saw the planned delivery location of the weapons and had to rub my eyes to make sure I was reading it correctly. "Augustus is going to stage a coup, and he's been preparing for it just a few miles from where I sleep every night."

CHAPTER THIRTY-ONE
IT COULD FIT TWO

Does Arturian know?

Above all other thoughts, that question burned in my mind like a furnace.

No... there's no way.

I thought back to his strange request that we move out of the port slums with no explanation. I'd nearly forgotten about it after later finding out I was the daughter of Adolpho Exley.

Could his request have something to do with the massive amounts of imports? With the coup?

Suddenly, I felt more distant from Arturian than ever before. He was keeping so many secrets from me. But then again, so was I. Before he'd caught me in his bedroom, he'd never have suspected I had a windblade... or that his best friend of seven years was a windwalker.

"This is so far beyond tax breaks," Levick said, his tone heavy with solemnity. We sat together on the cold stone tiles of the bell tower's ground floor.

A pit opened up in my stomach. Even if he didn't know about his father's plans, there was no way to shield Arturian from the consequences. "We never should've searched that room..." I said, stifling panicked sobs. I had to lean on my arm to keep from crumbling to the floor. My heartbreak over Arturian seemed so trivial as I imagined the downfall of his house.

His execution.

I brought my hand to my chest to feel the familiar imprint of the Exley house ring resting on my sternum. The weight of the evening's events threatened to suffocate me. Just that night I'd decapitated a man, learned my close friend was a windwalker, and learned that the man I loved might be complicit in a nascent takeover of the Friesian throne. I just wanted everything to *stop*.

Levick wrapped his arms around me. "Francie... I know we don't want to hurt Arturian, but his father *has* to be stopped. If Lesynna Ainsworth is a tyrant, could you imagine what Augustus Exley would do on the throne of Friese?"

I trembled at the thought as memories of Arturian's dismembered horse flashed through my mind.

"Maybe we can protect Arturian—shield him from the consequences. Maybe he doesn't know about it," Levick finished, sounding as if he needed to convince himself as well.

I won't let Arturian go down for his father's crimes. Maybe I should warn him.

But doubt crept into my mind.

But what if he does *know? What if he's complicit?*

In an excruciatingly painful moment, I resolved to do whatever it took to protect the innocent civilians in Friese. Even if Arturian *was* complicit. I wiped a tear from my eye and stood up straight. "We have to tell Orin tomorrow. This news changes everything."

"I've inconvenienced you enough, Levick. Please don't sleep on the floor for me," I said, guilt eating away at me. Moonlight shone through the large circular window at the top of the bell tower, illuminating the soft bed draped in animal furs.

It could fit two.

I shook the thought out of my mind. I cared deeply for Levick, but I couldn't lie to myself. My thoughts always returned to *him*. Being in a dark room with another man had only brought my memories flooding back—memories I'd tried desperately to avoid.

Arturian's dark hair hanging over my face... tickling my shoulder as he kissed my neck. His strong arms as he held me close. Despite the day we'd spent locked in the port office together, I never knew for certain what was going on inside his head. Since finding the damning evidence on Augustus, and the moderate likelihood that Arturian was involved, I was only certain of one thing.

I love him.

But is that enough? Would he even want me if he knew where I got my windblade? My identity... my very existence is a threat to his position.

My dour thoughts had surely darkened my expression, and I was suddenly very thankful for the blackness of the night.

"What's troubling you?" Levick said, approaching me from behind. I took a deep breath and watched it fog up the large window.

"It's just... been a very long few days."

I trembled as he wrapped his arms around me, bringing my back to his chest. "You should get some sleep," he whispered.

My heart undeniably skipped at the warmth against my back, but a deep sadness took hold of me, anyway. I knew I couldn't give Levick what he wanted from me.

Things could've been simple with him. No lies...

You still haven't told him about Arturian.

Arturian.

As much as I craved a steady and safe answer, Levick deserved honesty. He deserved *love*.

Before I could pull away, his hands slid to my waist and turned me around. Moonlight barely lit up his sun-kissed face and messy hair. The look in his eyes was dangerous. I became hyper-aware of my position—backed up to the window, the window frame on either side of me.

He must've noticed my hesitation, as he slowly eased away from me. "I'm sorry. I shouldn't be up here with you... alone." Despite the darkness, I could see his downcast expression.

"I trust you, Lev. You wouldn't do anything to me," I said as he backed away toward the stairs.

"I would, though. If you wanted me to," he said without hesitation, causing my eyes to widen and warmth to rush to my cheeks. He maintained eye contact with me—it was completely disarming.

Did he really just say that?

"It's just..." I started, but I lost my words. This wasn't how I wanted to tell him.

"It's okay," he said, stepping down the first step. "Whenever you're ready to talk, I'll listen. Goodnight."

His footsteps echoed up the stairwell, and I settled into Levick's bed. Despite all the questions swirling in my mind, my thoughts settled on the guard I killed. The sound of his head hitting the floor after I sliced it off. I cried myself to sleep.

"Wake up!" I said as I jostled Levick for a third time. "How do you sleep so heavily?" I muttered in frustration. After my night of fitful and broken sleep, I envied his peaceful slumber. However, as the sun had risen, I'd been filled with new purpose. We needed to prepare for the storm that was inevitably coming.

"Why?" Levick grumbled, turning over on the small couch that sat in the front room of the bell tower.

"I want to see if I can train you!" I exclaimed. "What if you could get your wind gusts narrower, like mine?"

Finally, Levick craned his head back and opened his eyes. "You think that's possible?"

"We won't know unless we try. Also, I was thinking about trying to broaden my gusts like yours. It might be really useful for both of us to have both abilities." I could sense myself rambling a bit, but I was still feeling a bit awkward after the previous night. Thankfully, he seemed to be acting as if nothing had happened.

"Okay, let's do it," he said before standing up and turning around to fold his blanket. He was shirtless.

How do I keep landing in these situations?

His toned back and shoulders flexed as he folded and laid the blanket down. I tried to look casual as he turned to face me, but I was sure my blush was visible. He didn't even seem to notice his state of undress.

"I'm going up to get dressed. I'll bring some bread and meet you out there?" he asked as he walked to the staircase.

I quickly said yes and made my way outside, my stomach growling at the thought of breakfast. The summer was finally coming to an end, and I could feel it in the air. A light breeze tousled some stray hairs from my long braid and ruffled my blue skirt. I was lucky I'd left a change of clothes at the bell tower a few months prior.

After walking over to where the clearing was the widest, I began collecting sticks and logs. I'd piled a few into makeshift targets when Levick met me outside, already tearing his loaf into chunks for us.

"Good idea," he said, nodding at the targets.

"Thanks." I smiled and nodded in thanks as he handed my portion over.

After we'd finished eating, Levick helped with the larger logs, and it wasn't long until we had five targets placed at varying distances. I walked until I was roughly five horse-lengths from the closest target and dropped a line of stones on the ground.

"This is where we'll throw from," I said, standing behind the line. "Come here." I gestured Levick over. He nodded and stood at my side, and I began explaining the intricacies of my throwing method.

"It took me a long time to control it well, which made it very dangerous. For years, my windblades were always very long and inaccurate. I couldn't hit a target from this distance without brutalizing everything around it," I explained. Levick took in a sharp breath. "Don't worry, there's nothing near your target that is off-limits. Even if you miss, there's no risk of any real damage out here," I finished.

"Could you demonstrate a few times? I'm not sure I know where to start..." Levick said, looking uneasy.

I nodded, straightening my posture and adopting my throwing stance—my left arm extended in front of me, and my right arm held up by my head, as if I held a throwing knife. I focused on the closest target—a few sticks propped up to stand as tall as a person. My pulse raced, and I felt the power surge through me, quickening my breathing. Exhaling, I flung my right arm forward.

A precise strike sliced the very top of the target off, and it fell silently to the grass. "Kind of anticlimactic, isn't it?" I said, laughing as I glanced at Levick.

He stood, mouth agape, staring at the target. "I know this isn't the first time I've seen you do this, but I forgot how terrifying it is."

I blanched.

He noticed my expression and quickly amended his statement. "It's just that... that could be someone's chest." He gestured at the target. "All it takes is a flick of your wrist." His eyes settled on me, a look of wonder on his face. "I had no idea how much power you held."

I then realized that he wasn't speaking with *disgust*, but with admiration. He was impressed. I let myself sigh in relief.

"Keep going," he suggested, pointing at the other four targets.

After slicing the tips off of all the targets except the farthest one—which I couldn't quite hit—it was Levick's turn to try.

"Remember to envision a throw, not a push," I said, stepping back.

Levick adopted my throwing stance, eyes narrowing on the target. He flung his arm forward with an amount of force I could never conjure, but it flew over the top of the target. "Seem's my accuracy isn't perfect..." Levick mumbled.

"In your defense, you usually *want* large gusts of air. You've never needed to be very accurate," I said, regretting how the last bit sounded. Levick shot me a glance, his mouth turning up in an amused smile.

"Sorry," I said, smiling awkwardly as I approached him and took his dominant hand. "Instead of holding your fingers splayed out, try pinching your fingers together like this, and release at the pinnacle of your arc," I said, manipulating his fingers to match how mine looked when I threw. When I looked back up at him, he was watching me with deep interest. He nodded, backed away, and made a second attempt at the target. He missed again, just to the left of the target.

After half a dozen throws, Levick was as tenacious as ever. He was the type of person who somehow became more determined after failing, instead of getting discouraged. I admired him for it—I wished I could emulate that quality.

After ten tries, his aim was true, and it blew the target into pieces. I yelped in surprise, but Levick had a grin on his face.

"Not quite a blade..." I mumbled in shock.

"That was *much* more focused of a blast than I've ever made," he said, looking proud. "I've knocked things over plenty of times, but *completely destroyed?* That's new," he chuckled. "That gust looked to be only a few hands' width."

"That's tremendous progress, Lev!" I laughed, still shocked by what I'd seen.

The two of us continued our training throughout the morning until finally calling it quits at lunchtime. Levick had seemed to hit a wall with his throwing, but he'd shrunk the gusts down to fist-size.

I, on the other hand, had become incredibly frustrated by my inability to broaden my windblade into a gust. The only thing I'd accomplished was throwing a blade as long as a carriage and slicing two targets at once. I doubted I would ever use that ability, though—far too high a risk of collateral damage.

To my relief, our morning of training had eased some of the tension between us. As we walked the forest trail to the slums, we joked about Crysta's frustrations with the new volunteers at the inn. According to her, some of them seemed like they'd never held a butcher knife in their lives. Crysta loved to complain, but deep down, I could tell that she loved teaching them.

A breeze blew my hair into my face, and I realized I'd forgotten my hair scarf at the bell tower.

"Oh... I left my scarf. I should go back and get it," I said, stopping and turning.

"I'll come with you," Levick offered.

I shook my head. "Crysta is probably worried about us. You should go ahead, and I'll meet you there."

Levick hesitated, looking unsure.

"You just watched me slice solid blocks of wood apart for hours. I can defend myself," I said with what I hoped was a reassuring smile.

Levick nodded. "Stay safe, Francie. See you soon."

CHAPTER THIRTY-TWO
A TIGHTENING CHAIN

Use caution when cutting through years' worth
of lies. The blade of truth is double-edged.
- Augustus Exley

After waving goodbye to Levick, I turned on my heel and made my way back towards the bell tower. I reached it in a few minutes and made my way inside. It didn't have the same inviting feeling it usually had when Levick was there. I shook off my sense of unease and made my way up the stairs to the top.

A tall, dark figure stood by the large window, looking out. He wore one of his fine black suits, with a blood red cravat around his neck. His hair had been combed neatly and fell past his shoulders. One thing didn't match—the blue scarf he held in his hand.

"I figured you'd come back for this," Arturian said without turning.

"What are you doing here?" I asked, my heart pounding in my chest. The room seemed to close in on me—the very air felt thin. I'd known it was only a matter of time until I saw him again, but I wasn't ready.

Why is he holding my scarf?

It was probably in Levick's bed...

My heart leapt into my throat as he looked down at it. "You've been lying to me." His voice was smooth and even.

I had to slow my breathing before I could answer. My chest felt like it'd been wrapped in ropes, and they were tightening. "About the other night..."

I trailed off, and finally, he turned to look me in the eyes. He clenched his jaw, and his eyes stared right through me. "You have a windblade." His voice cracked—famous composure, breaking. The air in the room felt like it had dropped ten degrees, bringing goosebumps to my skin. "Does Levick know?" he asked, taking a step closer.

I nodded without thinking.

He gripped the scarf with white knuckles. "You'd tell *him*, but not me?"

Undeniable guilt sat upon my shoulders, pressing down on me with its weight. "I didn't tell him. He found out." I bit at my cheek. "There's a reason I didn't tell you..." I began, my voice shaking. I wasn't even sure of what I was going to say.

"Does that reason have something to do with the identity of your father?" A cold edge slipped into his voice.

No, no, no... how does he know?

"I didn't want this, Arturian. You have to believe me." I clutched my hand over my chest, hoping desperately that the familiar shape of the Exley house ring would comfort me. However, at that moment, it only made me feel like a thief.

When he looked up at me, it was as if I were a stranger... his jaw set, his eyes distant. "Father had suspicions, but I didn't believe him. I couldn't imagine that *you* would hide something like this from me. But after I caught you the other night..."

Before I could react, he closed in on me, caging me between his arms and against the wall. "You are the illegitimate daughter of Adolpho Exley. Do you deny it?" His voice was barely a whisper. He radiated energy—muscles tensed, eyes afire with intensity. His sudden proximity stole my breath, but it wasn't the kind of closeness I'd longed for. This was something else... all anger, jealousy, and bitterness. And it was entirely my fault.

I looked for any hint of tenderness in his eyes while I blinked away my tears. "I wanted to tell you, especially after—"

"After our day in the port office?" His stare softened for a moment, as if he was remembering how good we were together. For a split second, he glanced down at my lips... as if he wanted to relive the memories. However, the softness was gone as fast as it appeared, and his expression turned stormy again. "Or after I told you that my father and I are illegitimate?" he growled, pushing himself away from the wall. He ran a hand through his hair as he took a few distracted steps away. The polished, stony mask I saw moments ago was gone, replaced by tousled hair and a heaving chest.

Panic clawed at me—my years of deceit were reaping their heartbreaking harvest. "I knew I was the daughter of a Skylord, but I didn't know it was Adolphu until—"

"Until I told you about what happened to him." He paused by the window for a moment as he put the timeline together.

I took a small step away from the wall. "If this is about your inheritance, you don't have to worry…"

"You think *that's* why I'm angry?" He spun around, his voice a cold, unfamiliar sound, cutting me like a knife. "You grossly misunderstand my character if you think I'd put my inheritance above someone I love." He shook his head and his expression became tight—drawn. My heart somehow swelled and broke at the same time, and I wished more than anything that I could cross the distance between us. But the price of deceit was steep.

He stood silently for a long moment, staring at the bottom of the windowsill. "Tell me something, Francie. Did you ever think, for even a moment…" He turned his head to look at me, his hair falling beside his eyes, "That I would kill you? To hide my illegitimacy?"

The breath rushed out of my lungs at the question, but I didn't hesitate. "No."

"Then why—"

"Your father would."

"I'd never tell him, and I'd never let him hurt you. I'd die first." He said it so resolutely that my guilt doubled.

"I was scared—we both know what's happened to every commoner who's ever had a windblade."

Arturian's expression became one of resigned disbelief, brows furrowed and head tilting back. "Don't insult our shared experiences with such a lie. You don't live your life in fear—you never have. This lie wasn't about your safety. It was about *us*."

His words cut me deep with their truth. All the time I'd claimed to trust him, I kept him at a distance. I had no way to counter him because he was right.

Arturian glanced back at Levick's bed, then at the blue scarf he still held. "I found this on his bed," he said, clearly using great effort to school his emotions. "Did you sleep with him?"

"No," I whispered.

"Do you love him?"

"No," I responded truthfully, and I noticed his shoulders relax at the answer. I cared deeply for Levick, but it differed from what I felt for Arturian. "I wish I did," I said, and his eyes shot to mine, but I didn't regret the statement. "Everything would be simpler if I loved Levick."

Arturian looked down, working his jaw. Bitter regret filled me completely as we stood in a heavy silence.

If I'd trusted him... maybe I wouldn't be so close to losing him.

I was interrupted from my guilty thoughts when Arturian met my eyes and began walking towards me—his steps slow and measured. An enigmatic ocean swirled behind his irises, unreadable and unreachable. I set my jaw and fought against the instinct to back away. If he wanted to yell, swear, or accuse, so be it. But I refused to run from the consequences of my actions.

He didn't stop until he stood mere inches away. I lifted my chin as he stood over me, his eyes still a mystery. Something soft and light fell upon my shoes... my hair scarf. He'd dropped it. My throat tightened as I felt his hands slide over my waist, his thumbs brushing light circles over my dress. Just as he'd done in the bay on his birthday, before everything had fallen apart. The contact sent a hot wave up my spine, and I silently cursed myself for being so easily affected by him. I could smell the expensive cologne on his suit, affecting me in ways I'd never expected.

"I don't know what's real and what's a lie anymore. Do you even love *me*?" he asked, his gaze so piercing it crumbled my defenses.

No more lies.

"Yes."

His chest fell—a sigh of relief. He lightly ran his fingers up and over my ribcage, summoning chills along my skin. With steady fingers, he began pulling my necklace from the neckline of my dress. I tried to ignore the electric sensations he elicited as his fingers brushed against my skin. It was such intimate contact, but I had no instinct to stop him.

"You still wear it," he whispered, holding the Exley house ring. He stared at it for a long moment, eyes ringed with longing and sadness.

I noticed a sudden dark shift in his gaze as he stood over me. He clutched the ring tight between two fingers and began twisting—deliberately wrapping the chain around them. I felt my heart rate rise and my skin grow hot as it became tighter.

Clink. Clink. Clink.

In that moment, he seemed so different from the man who caressed me while whispering poems of love in my ear. I'd let myself forget about his unpredictability—his steely nature, but I felt such guilt for lying and assuming the worst about him. A small part of my mind told me I deserved whatever consequences came my way.

As the chain tightened around my throat, Arturian leaned in and whispered, "I wish I could trust you." His lips brushed my ear, sending a shiver up my spine. The chain was tight, but not painful.

He wouldn't hurt me.

As if sensing my thoughts, he lowered his head and pressed a hot kiss against my neck, lingering for a long moment. My knees nearly buckled, and I hated myself for not pushing him away. I felt the chain loosen as he lazily unwound it and brought his eyes back to mine. After taking one last look at the ring, he tucked it back into my dress.

"You could've stopped me. You could've pushed me away... or eviscerated me where I stood." His words were an accusation.

He knows I couldn't hurt him, either.

He let me stand speechless for a moment before turning on his heel and walking to the stairs. Pausing abruptly, he turned his head, not quite looking at me.

"Something built upon lies is equally false as the lies themselves." He looked up at me... and I was *devastated*. The anguish in his eyes took my breath away. "You should've trusted me, Francie."

I blinked away the tears threatening to fall down my cheeks.

"I'm getting married."

With that, he disappeared down the stairs.

CHAPTER THIRTY-THREE
HER WINDBLADE

ARTURIAN

I woke up feeling like a rag that had soaked too long in alcohol. Light streamed in through the red velvet curtains, worsening my headache. My body was drenched in sweat, so I dragged myself out of bed to strip off my wet clothes. My servants must've noticed my state, as they'd filled a bath for me and left it in my room.

I should thank them later.

After washing up, I dressed myself in a lightweight shirt and pants and went in search of a guard. It didn't take long for me to find Lieutenant Trust walking down the front steps. I sped after him.

"Coran! Wait!"

The lieutenant didn't hide his surprise well. He snapped a quick salute before standing at attention.

"Good morning, sir. What can I do for you?"

"At ease, Coran. I need you to find some men to keep tabs on someone," I said before I could second-guess myself.

"Of course, sir. Who is it?"

"She's a young woman who lives in the slums."

I slunk through the port slums, disguised in a dark coat and cap. Ever since I'd caught Francie attempting to steal *The Chronicle of the Caelators* from my bedroom a few weeks ago, the mystery had consumed me. What made her want the book so much she'd risk stealing it? Why wouldn't she simply ask to borrow it? And the most concerning question—who was her employer? Who would have her break into the Exley mansion in the dead of night?

Over the previous weeks, my guards had reported a "suspicious man" coming and going from the inn late at night. They described him as young, unusually large, muscular, and crawling with tattoos. A mixture of concern and burning jealousy ran through my veins, pushing me forward. My guards informed me the man was currently at the inn and had been there for hours already. I settled against a wall in an alley, watching the door. I ran my fingers along the outlines of my throwing knives, safely in their holster under my coat.

I waited, twirling a knife, until the door finally opened. A man built like a boulder ducked out through the front door before turning around and kissing someone on the cheek.

Francie.

My stomach felt like it dropped to the ground and somehow kept falling. I gripped my knife as if it could save me from what I saw. It had been weeks since I confronted her in the bell tower, and I'd known no peace since then. My every thought revolved around her. I could tell my guards were getting suspicious from how much I asked about her.

Francie's perfect dark blonde hair glowed in the light of her candle as she smiled and laughed with the giant man. He nodded to her, and she waved back, then he set off down the road. I set upon the pursuit before my good sense could catch up with me.

"Who are you?" I asked from a wet alley as the large man walked by. He immediately took on a fighting stance—trained in hand-to-hand, so it seemed. I maintained my casual posture against the wall.

"Who wants to know?" the man growled, entering the alley but keeping his distance.

He is huge.

"Let me rephrase my question... who are you *to Francie*?" I kept my tone smooth and easy.

The man tensed up. "What the hell do you want with Francie, jackass?"

Struck a nerve, there.

"You've been visiting an inn at strange hours, but rarely staying all night. So, I'll ask you one more time: what business do you have with her?" I said, sure fingers gripping my knife.

The man lunged forward, and I silently thanked my years of Skylord training. With little effort, I dodged the attacks, moving faster and ducking under punches.

Get some distance and throw. You can't match this guy's muscle.

I slid away from another powerful punch before spinning around, running into the road.

"Running away, you coward?" the boulder-man yelled out while running after me.

I surprised him by stopping in my tracks, turning, and launching a knife directly at him. My aim was true; the knife plunged into the man's shoulder, eliciting a furious groan.

An unnerving slicing sound made me stumble backwards, and the very front of my cap came free, falling to the ground with barely a sound.

"Get away from him!" a familiar voice called from down the road. I froze, my heart in my throat.

No. Don't come over here. Please, don't.

"Ress! Oh, no—don't touch it!" Francie cried out as the injured man moved to pull the blade out. She ran in front of him, putting herself between us.

"You'd be wise to get away from us unless you want to see me aim to kill," she shouted in my direction, standing in a throwing stance. Her hair fluttered in the night breeze—her work dress covered in food stains. The contrast between her looks and her stance would've been amusing, if not for my clear understanding of a windblade's brutal capabilities.

Before I could turn and escape into the darkness, she stepped forward—a knowing look in her eye. She almost spoke my name, but stopped herself.

"What are *you* doing here?" she asked, voice bleeding with indignation.

"You know this guy, Francie?" Ress called from behind her, wrapping his shirt around the knife to stop the bleeding.

She nodded, then walked over to me, her stride long and confident. I'd never seen her look so sure of herself.

"I could ask that same question to you," I said, my voice low as she came closer.

"Yes, I know him."

I fought the urge to roll my eyes at her sarcasm. "I got that part."

"So why don't you tell me what you're doing in the slums in the middle of the night?"

"How about you tell me why you tried to steal my book from my nightstand?" I said, painfully aware of our proximity.

She winced, but crossed her arms over her chest. "Don't you have a wedding to plan? Or will Eliandre handle all of it?"

Ouch. I suppose I deserve that.

My betrothal had just been made public, and it seemed the identity of my betrothed had made its way to Francie.

"In case you've forgotten, Arturian, I live here. The company I keep is none of your business, and I *certainly* don't want you throwing knives at my friends anymore."

Ignoring the coldness in her words, I tilted my head forward, fixing her with a knowing look. "He's just a friend, then?"

It had the desired effect—a blush crept its way up her neck. "You don't get to be jealous, Arturian. You're the one getting married, not me."

"It's all political."

She scoffed and shook her head. "Not to me, it isn't."

"Hey, Francie. Bleeding out over here," Ress called over, surprisingly calm for someone with a knife buried in his shoulder. Francie glanced back, then took another step towards me. She tilted her face up at me, mere inches away.

"You've made it clear there's no future between us. If you mean that, do us both a favor and *stay out* of the port slums." She leaned in closer, pressing a finger to my chest. "You don't belong here."

I glanced down and noticed a necklace chain trailing into her bodice. "You don't belong here, either." I still held so much anger at her for lying, trying to steal from me, and for assuming I would take her life for the sake of my inheritance.

But love is a stubborn thing.

"You belong in the Exley mansion," I whispered.

Francie's eyes softened for a moment as she attempted to discern my meaning. "I have to go. I meant what I said—it's not safe for you, Arturian," she said before turning and jogging back to Ress.

She helped him up, and he put an arm around her protectively, even as his other arm dripped with blood. I tried to ignore the grief building inside me. The words of my father echoed in my mind.

That which a lifetime can build, can be felled in a single moment.

CHAPTER THIRTY-FOUR
THE RIDER

"**I**'m just saying—he looked familiar," Ress grumbled as I pulled a needle and thread through the gash in his shoulder. He had an impressively high pain threshold. We sat in the dining area of the inn, multiple candles burning to illuminate my work.

"He's just someone I knew when I was younger," I said, telling myself it was technically the truth.

Ress tensed for the first time since I started stitching him up. "He seemed pretty territorial. Something happen between you two?"

I paused my work. "Honestly? Yes." I surprised myself with my candor, but I needed to vent. I couldn't talk to Levick about it, so I'd just been stewing for weeks. "Something *did* happen between us. But it's in the past."

Why don't you try telling your heart that, Francie? It doesn't feel like it's in the past.

"Why?" Ress asked, stone-still even as I resumed my stitching. He clenched his strong jaw, his dark eyes impassive.

"He's getting married. That's all I have to say about it," I said, ending that line of questioning.

I finished my work in silence; Ress was seemingly lost in thought. He was lucky the knife was short, or he might have bled out. However, his only concern was whether it had pierced his tattoos.

Ress and I had grown close after Orin assigned him to protect me a few weeks prior. He often slept outside my bedroom door, or on our sitting-room couch. I'd insisted that I didn't need protection, but Orin overruled me. He'd told me he suspected I was being watched, and my windblade was too important to risk. I tried to shake the disquieting feeling that Orin saw me only as a weapon.

"You won't be able to join us on the mission tomorrow night," I said as I packed up my medical supplies. Ress was very useful to have on missions—he could dispatch enemies with remarkable speed and efficiency. However, I was sure that using his arm would break the stitches and open the wound.

"It's okay, Orin already benched me," Ress muttered as he stood and stretched.

"Wait—why?"

"He thinks I wouldn't *blend in well* at a ball. I can't say I disagree," he chuckled.

I dropped my thread.

"A ball? I thought we were infiltrating another shipment?" I asked in disbelief as I fumbled on the floor for the spool.

"There's a masquerade ball at the Exley mansion in honor of some rich Corlaean emissaries. I thought he told you already?"

I shook my head.

No... I can't go in there again.

"What's the objective?" I asked.

"Intel we've gathered is telling us Augustus is having a secret meeting with someone from Trenica. Something to do with all the weapons he has flowing in. Orin wants you to attend the ball undercover to listen in on it. I'm sure he'll give you more information at the meeting tomorrow night."

"Like the guest list?" I asked, hoping my desperation wasn't obvious.

Wishful thinking. It's Arturian's house—he'll be there.

"I think he mentioned one," he said, as he carefully shrugged his jacket on.

I could feel myself panicking.

A ball? At the Exley mansion, of all places?

At least it's a masquerade...

"I'll see you tomorrow, then?" I asked, handing Ress a cheap bottle of salt rum for the pain.

He popped the cork out with his teeth, took a generous swig, and smiled at me. "No one could keep me away, Skylady," he said, biting his lip as he flashed a sensual wink at me.

I rolled my eyes and pushed him out the front door. "Goodnight, Ress."

He blew me a kiss before disappearing into the darkness.

After a mere four hours of sleep, I woke up to go see Levick at the bell tower. The forest trail that had once felt safe now felt haunted. I kept my head on a swivel as I walked. I'd left earlier than Levick expected me, so I took a detour. Venturing from the main trail, I began down an overgrown path, making my way deeper into the woods until I came to a large, old tree. Its thick branches extended in every direction—but only one direction mattered to me. I climbed the trunk and stood up on the large branch that stretched over the tall wrought-iron fence I'd crossed so many times. With cautious steps, I walked over the top of the fence, sat down on the branch, and let my legs dangle over.

The last time I was here, things were so much simpler. Arturian invited me to tea, and I'd assumed he was just lonely.

The memory cut me deep, remembering a time when there was no bad blood between us. I thought of his birthday, when we swam in the bay together, and he held me for just a moment too long for it to have been casual. Gleaming, silvery stars had shone in his eyes that night.

Before he caught me in my lie.

I buried the memories before my throat could tighten any more.

He threw a knife at Ress. He is part of the enemy.

My run-in with Arturian in the slums the previous night had unsettled me—he must've been keeping tabs on me. Ress thought he'd noticed some watchful eyes near the inn, but I had assumed he was just being paranoid. I decided to tell Levick not to train at the bell tower anymore. I knew Arturian or his men could be watching, and I didn't want him discovering Levick, too. Thankfully, our suspicions of Arturian's complicity in Augustus's schemes would likely be enough to convince Levick to use caution on Exley property.

There's no way he'd actually have me followed... would he?

If I was lucky, he was simply a jealous ex-lover, and knew nothing of my involvement with the RCM.

Ex-lover...

My chest tightened. The day he confronted me in the bell tower, I almost asked him if he knew what his father was scheming, but thought better of it. That question would only reveal my involvement with the RCM. Besides, I enjoyed my blissful ignorance in assuming he wasn't complicit in staging a coup.

We'll stop it before it happens. It won't matter, anyway.

My mind drifted to Levick and the late-night kiss we'd shared on the roof. While my heart ached to keep so many secrets from him, I saw no way around it. Our ability to work together on missions was too vital. If I told him about my history with Arturian, I worried he'd distance himself from me. I knew he'd feel betrayed by how long I'd kept it from him, and he'd be justified in feeling that way.

Thankfully, Levick had noticed my hesitance with him and had kept our relationship friendly. There were no more lingering touches, expectant gazes, or flirtatious jabs. His disappointment was palpable, but he didn't ask for any explanation. Though my deceit made me feel unworthy of his friendship, I was still deeply grateful for it.

My legs swung in the air as I stared through the trees, watching the Exley meadows ripple in the wind. Silhouettes of grazing horses wandered back and forth across my vision, and a bittersweet nostalgia fell over me. I'd give almost anything to relive those memories... riding across summer fields, swimming in the bay, dancing at our pretend soirees. I cocked my head when I noticed one horse was standing unusually still. He wasn't grazing—he just... stood. Facing my direction.

My breath caught in my throat. The dark, peculiar horse had a rider.

There's no way anyone could see me through these trees...

The horse reared up, tossing his head back. The expert rider remained steady and unfazed... before taking off at a gallop *straight towards me.*

I shouldn't have come here.

I walked back across the branch and over the fence, and disappeared into the forest.

"How is your practice going?" I asked Levick as we stretched together in the clearing in front of the bell tower. We'd taken to going running together, and the exercise had worked wonders for my stress.

"Really well," he said, placing his hands against the wall of the bell tower and doing a lunge. His lean muscles flexed as he stretched. "I'm not making blades, but I'm packing a punch."

From what I'd seen, narrowing his wind to a blade almost seemed unnecessary. His wind gusts had enough power to knock a person unconscious, which seemed more than enough for our purposes. I envied him—my windblade was impossible to use as a non-lethal force. There was no way to throw a razor-blade at someone safely.

"You've been great. I'm starting to feel superfluous," I joked as I lunged, earning an incredulous scoff from Levick.

"Don't say that—we're a good team. I wouldn't get far without you," he said earnestly as he bent down to stretch his hamstrings. He'd stripped his shirt off after our run, and I couldn't help but feel jealous. Sweat soaked through my blouse, making me feel sticky as I touched my toes.

"I appreciate your trust in me, Lev," I said, hoping he'd understand the insinuation. He'd become more confident in my abilities, and therefore was less protective of me. He still watched over me, but he began prioritizing the mission. I found it incredibly refreshing.

He gave me a genuine, warm smile, then left to go rinse off in the pond.

CHAPTER THIRTY-FIVE
MASQUERADE

"I feel ridiculous," I complained as Orin's wife, Nina, helped me with my gown. "Are you sure this is the style of dress the princess has been wearing? It seems scandalous..."

"Relax, Francie. You look beautiful," Nina said as she worked on the buttons on the back. There weren't very many. The dress was made from fine Corlaean blue silk, gleaming like a calm river under the sun. The fabric in the front had been braided in intricate knots that wrapped around my neck, but left my shoulders bare. As if that wasn't enough, the dress was backless, revealing almost my entire spine.

At least it covers my legs...

"You're perfect for this mission, Francie. Guards will be checking everyone entering the mansion for weapons, but you won't need any physical weapons. Although I hope you won't need any weapons at all..." Nina trailed off, as she often did.

"Where did you even find this dress, Nina? It feels expensive," I asked as she finished the buttons. A floor-length mirror sat in the corner of the bedroom, showcasing the exquisite gown.

"We don't have to share *all* our connections with you, you know," Nina said with a coy look in her eye. "Now sit down. I need to braid your hair."

After what felt like an eternity, my hair was completed with smooth braids twisting into a sapphire-studded bun on the crown of my head. Nina left the back half of my hair down to cascade over my back in sleek waves. The detail was breath-taking. "Where did you learn how to do this? It's incredible," I said as I turned back and forth in front of the mirror, admiring the handiwork.

"Thank you. I spent some time as a lady's maid," she said, clipping her words to show she was unwilling to elaborate. "Time to meet your chaperone."

Nina and I emerged from the bedroom only to see a small crowd of RCM members huddled around the door, Ress being the most obvious.

"Damn, Francie. You were holding out on us," Ress said through a chuckle, a devilish grin on his face as he stepped aside for me.

I rolled my eyes, shaking my head until I saw Levick. He was clad entirely in dark gray, as attendants traditionally were. His usually messy hair had been combed to the side, and his coat buttoned all the way up to his chin. His lips pulled into a smile as he stared at me.

"You look great, Lev," I said, stifling another blush before reaching out for his hand.

"There are no words to describe how you look, Francie," he blurted, eliciting quite a few whoops and *aww*s from the others in the room.

"Are you going to escort me or not? We have a ball to attend."

Levick and I rode in a coach befitting even the great houses. The RCM had spared no luxury for our mission. However, just like Nina, Orin had refused to say where he'd gotten access to it.

"Here," he said, pulling something from his coat pocket. The mask was small and ornate, and meant to only cover my eyes. Its light blue color matched my dress, and small, dark blue gemstones encrusted its eyes and edges.

I took it from him and tied it on with the silk ribbon. "It's beautiful, but I'm not sure it will do much good if *he* is there," I said with an ominous scowl.

"His name wasn't on the list," Levick said for the fourth time that night. "He won't be there. He always hated these things, anyway."

"Right, right..."

Anxiety spiked through my veins as I remembered how Augustus followed me in the slums that day. How he'd seemed to *know* me.

Please work, little mask.

I buried my anxieties and went over my cover-identity again. "My name is Lady Julianna Forsythe, of the Eastern Shore of West Corlaea. My father's name is Jeras, my mother's name is Lilianna, and I have four brothers." I must've repeated it twenty times.

"Your accent is good. You remember their names, don't you?" Levick asked, raising an eyebrow at me.

"They're not real. I'll make them up as I go."

"It will be obvious if you do that. You should invent them now and memorize them."

It was my turn to raise an eyebrow at him.

"Fine, fine... I trust you. I hate to leave you alone in there, but Orin doesn't trust me to lie." Levick's tone was innocent, but I felt convicted by it.

I lie entirely too easily.

Too soon, the carriage pulled to a stop, and Levick leapt up like a good attendant and reached for the door handle. "You can do this. Lie low for a while, follow Augustus, and get the information. Then, *get the hell out*," he said with an intense stare. I brought my forehead to his for a moment, then motioned for him to open the door.

It was only two hours after sunset, but the ball seemed in full swing as I climbed down the steps of our carriage. Ours was one of many carriages parked outside of the Exley mansion, letting beautifully adorned aristocrats out of their cabs. I was already receiving stares as Levick helped me down and nodded at me. I returned the nod, took a deep breath, and walked up the marble stairs into Arturian's home.

Please don't be here. Please don't be here. Be anywhere else.

I sent silent prayers to Echna as my heels clicked against the stone. The mansion's open doors were three times taller than the inn's, and inlaid with swirling gold filigree, climbing along the edges like shining, priceless vines. A pair of strapping guards stood at the entrance, wearing the immaculate black and red uniforms of House Exley.

"Good evening, my lady." One of them smiled at me, looking me up and down. I regretted the dress already.

"We need to check you for weapons, if you don't mind stepping aside over here..." he motioned to a dark corner behind a thick pillar, and I fought the urge to cringe.

"That doesn't seem routine," a low, but feminine voice purred from around a pillar nearby. "Where could she be hiding a weapon in *that* dress?"

A luminous young woman approached us, and the unsettling guard promptly dropped to his knee.

"Your Royal Highness! I didn't see you there..." he stammered.

"They rarely do."

Her dress was made of similar silk to mine, but was a light lavender purple, and bore a deeply plunging neckline encrusted with gemstones. Her black hair had been partially woven into a low braid, flowing down her back and nearly touching the backs of her knees. A delicate tiara of intricate platinum adorned her head, and she wore no mask.

"Back to your post, reprobate. Keep your hands off of the guests unless you'd like Lord Exley to hear of this." Her voice was sharp—dripping with authority.

That threat resonated with the guard, and he turned back to the door on trembling legs.

That's Princess Eadlin. She was definitely *not on the guest list we received... I have no idea how to interact with this woman.*

I panicked and dropped to an unstable knee in front of the princess, nearly ripping my dress in the process. "My sincerest apologies, Your Highness."

An amused chuckle sounded from in front of me, and I dared to look up. The princess was smiling as she beckoned me to stand.

"I suppose they don't teach the curtsy in West Corlaea," she said as I rose from my awkward kneel.

Shit.

"You *are* Corlaean, are you not?"

"Yes, Your Highness. I am Lady Julianna Forsythe, of the Eastern Shore."

Princess Eadlin cocked her head, eyes inquisitive. "Lovely to make your acquaintance, Julianna." She offered her arm.

I wasn't sure I liked the curious way in which the princess said my fake name. However, she *did* just save me from an unnecessary body inspection. I gently took the princess's arm.

"I'm not delicate, you know." Eadlin smiled sideways at me as she led me into the vast ballroom. "You won't break me with your hand."

I could, though.

"My apologies, Your Highness," I said, maintaining my Corlaean aristocratic accent.

"No more apologies, Miss Forsythe," the princess ordered as we made our way through the extravagant party.

The entryway was draped in artificial vines made of gold and silver, crawling up the walls and around pillars. After walking beneath a glistening archway adorned with hanging crystals, we emerged into the ballroom. Women in shimmering gowns spun around the dancefloor with their partners, who wore their finest suits and vests. The dazzling spectacle blew me away.

The princess led us deeper into the ballroom, stopping in front of a string quartet accompanied by a woman playing a grand, golden harp. She rocked back and forth as she plucked at the strings, eyes closed as if she was in a trance. A smile grew over my face—I had never heard a song so beautiful.

"Have some wine." Eadlin handed me a glass I hadn't noticed her carrying. "Go mingle—relax. I expect to see you dancing later." She winked over her shoulder as she glided into the crowd, her gait as smooth as a ship in glassy waters. Despite my nervousness around the princess, I was sad to see her leave.

Alone again.

Augustus's rumored meeting wasn't scheduled to occur until later in the night. In the meantime, I aimed to keep my head low and attract as little attention as possible. The music shifted into a waltz, and people began pairing off. Desperate for structure to hide next to, I made my way to one of the small tables that bordered the ballroom dance floor. The gilded table had intricate designs running around its edge, reflecting the light from the chandeliers. I'd almost forgotten how wealthy Arturian was... his life couldn't be more different from mine. The gulf between us grew ever-wider.

A short, stout man in a black suit eyed me from across the room.

Here we go. You can do this.

I downed the rest of my wine as the man approached me. He was older—brown hair thinning at the front. "Care for a dance, miss..."

"Julianna. Yes, I'd like to dance," I said with an amiable smile.

Arturian had taught Levick and I how to dance when we were younger, but I hadn't thought I'd ever use the skill—we'd just done it for fun. However, the lessons were paying dividends as the stout Lord Hendricks led me around the room. We maintained pleasant, if not shallow, conversation until someone cut in, stopping us in our tracks.

My breath caught in my throat as I beheld him. The stranger wore a military uniform of crisp white, with golden knots at the shoulders and medals hanging from his chest. He looked to be slightly older than me—maybe mid-twenties—and was just as handsome as his reputation made him to be. He wore a crown of twisted golden vines atop his head, and no mask.

Prince Harley.

"Lord Hendricks, may I steal away your dance partner?" he asked in a deep baritone with a posh aristocratic accent.

The poor, plump Lord Hendricks tripped in surprise. "Of course, Your Highness!" he exclaimed as he handed over my arm.

It was all I could do to still my breathing. My job was to blend in and not attract attention, but I already had hundreds of eyes on me, many glaring in jealousy. The prince stood taller even than Arturian, had shining waves of chestnut-brown hair, caramel-tan skin, and dark, intense eyes. In his royal uniform and crown, he looked like he'd been plucked straight out of a Friesian folktale... undeniably dashing.

"Tell me, what is your name?" he asked in a tone slightly too commanding. He slid his arm around my waist and we merged with the other dancers.

"Lady Julianna Forsythe, Your Highness," I said, focusing more than ever on maintaining my accent and dancing form. I'd been there for only an hour and had already met the princess *and* the prince.

So much for lying low...

"Ah, I figured you must be Corlaean. I've never heard of you." He aimed narrowed eyes at me.

"Yes, Your Highness. I knew I'd be unknown here—news travels slowly across the Broad Sea."

He nodded as we danced our way across the room, occasionally glancing at me with curious eyes. I could feel myself stiffening, but I couldn't help my discomfort at how many stares we were attracting.

Not good.

"Pay them no heed," he said, leaning in closer. "It's only natural to be mesmerized by such beauty."

I blanched, but quickly composed myself.

"Although it's a shame to hide half of your face under a mask..." he purred, lifting his hand from my waist to run a finger across my mask's jeweled edge. As we turned, a flash of red and black shot across my vision.

Amongst the spectators stood a tall, broad-shouldered man in a sleek ensemble of black and dark, wine red. He wore a black mask, structured in angles and harsh lines around his eyes, but I knew that stormy shade of blue better than I knew my own name.

Arturian.

CHAPTER THIRTY-SIX
RECKLESS

There was no mistaking the direction of Arturian's stare. He was looking *right at me.*

The prince lifted me by my waist and spun me in time with the song, shocking me out of Arturian's hold over me. The movement was surprising, but I recovered my wits as he set me back down and brought me close again.

He's here.

"You dance well. I didn't think you'd keep up." The prince smiled at me.

"I'll admit it's been difficult while dodging your feet. You've nearly stepped on me three times," I responded with a coy smile, but my mind was racing.

His smile broadened. "I surely won't make that mistake again, Miss Forsythe," he said with a chuckle.

I became so absorbed in our dance that I didn't notice the crowd had thinned and collected at the edge of the floor to watch. The prince pulled me closer, his dark eyes locked on mine. The rhythm vibrated through my bones, spurring an undeniable euphoria inside me and chasing away my anxiety. My partner noticed my enthusiasm and twirled me out, making the bottom of my blue dress fan around me as the song reached its climax. An exuberant laugh escaped my lips at the absurdity of the situation, but I made sure to enjoy every second of it.

The song slowed slightly, coming to an end. When Prince Harley pulled me back in, his expression took me by surprise. A soft smile had crept to the corner of his full lips, and his eyes had a glow of playfulness to them.

"A worthy partner."

I smiled back, panting but proud of myself. "You were... *suitable*, Your Highness."

"Please," he began, sliding a finger over my jaw, "call me Harley."

My lips parted in surprise, and I felt heat rush to my face. Poorly stifled gasps erupted from the spectators, and the musicians shifted to a slower, romantic tune. Harley slid both hands down my waist, brushing the bare skin of my back. He pulled me tightly against him, but someone interrupted before we began dancing.

"May I cut in, Your Highness?" The smooth, dangerously level voice came from behind, sending chills up my spine.

"Exley," Prince Harley said through gritted teeth.

I turned to see Arturian, as arresting as ever, staring at Harley with a cold indifference. Similar to the prince's, Arturian wore a uniform of military style, but black and opened slightly at the collar. The magnificent Exley crest was emblazoned in red on his chest, over his heart. The blue in his eyes seemed cold and turbulent, like the waters along the coast of Trenica. Even after the closeness I'd shared with him, I was nearly affected by it.

A long, tense moment hung between the two men. The crowd watched, some murmuring to each other.

"I suppose I could use some fresh air," the prince said, looking simultaneously intrigued and annoyed as he glanced between us. There seemed to be no love lost between them.

Harley slid his fingers from my wrist to trail up the inside of my arm, making me tremble. He leaned in close, his lips brushing against my ear. "I'll see you again, darling," he promised before turning and leaving the dance floor.

Tearing my eyes from the prince, I looked up and gazed upon the exposed portion of Arturian's face. Even under the mask, I could see that his eyes were narrowed in veiled disdain at the retreating prince. With a trained smoothness, Arturian pulled me close as the dancing resumed. The crowds spread apart, returning to their own business.

"*Miss Julianna Forsythe*, you are the talk of the party," he murmured. I didn't know how to respond—my words had left me. I tried to gauge his thoughts, but his expression was perfectly neutral, and the mask certainly didn't help.

"Did you really think that tiny mask would shield your identity from me?" he asked in a low, husky tone that made my pulse race. He pulled me closer as the sensual music floated through the ballroom, only adding to my nerves.

"You can't hide from me. What are you doing here?" he whispered as he slid his finger down my bare spine, his touch drawing the breath from my lungs. The cold seas of his eyes crashed upon mine, leaving me breathless.

My jaw clenched, and I was grateful he couldn't see my red cheeks under my mask. "You weren't supposed to be here," I said before thinking better of it.

"In case you've forgotten, this is *my* house," he said, pulling away slightly. "Give it up, *Julianna*. Why are you here?"

Time to obfuscate.

"I'm not sure your betrothed would appreciate the display you're putting on," I leaned in and whispered provocatively, staring evenly into his eyes. "The way you're touching me—people might think we know each other."

His hands only gripped my waist tighter, sending a hot wave through my body that made me feel like I might melt. "She's not here. Besides, there's quite a crowd shielding us now," he said dismissively, briefly glancing at the mass of couples swaying around us. "Your choice of clothing—or lack thereof—is providing spectacle enough as it is," he said, running his eyes over me.

"Yes, *Harley* certainly didn't seem to mind," I said, making a display of looking through the other dancers for the prince.

I could nearly feel Arturian's body temperature rise. "I'll cut off his hands if he touches you again—allegiances be damned," he said, his voice a low, steady growl.

Allegiances? No... they are *colluding with the queen. And Arturian knows.*

My heart sank. "I didn't realize there was an alliance between your houses..." I said, hoping I sounded innocent enough.

"Never mind that. Let's talk about you," he said, dipping me low. I leaned my head back, savoring the feeling of his hot breath on my neck. He pulled me back up, twirled me into his arms, and held my back against his chest.

Slowly, he leaned over my shoulder. "I knew you were up to something when you tried to steal my book, but this little stunt of yours makes me think I might've underestimated the scope. I hope you're not here to carve up any of my friends."

His grip tightened like a vise. Suddenly, I felt cold, sharp metal against my right hip. Arturian had pushed my dress aside and held a knife against me. The way we were standing, no one in the crowd would be able to see it.

No, no, no...

"Don't pretend like you're friends with any of these people," I whispered, trying to quell my rising panic.

Arturian scoffed quietly, his breath tousling my hair. "Maybe I *will* be. I'm in the market for some new friends. Who knows? Maybe they won't lie to me for seven years."

I took the jab like an adult. I knew I deserved it. "I apologized, and I'll do it again. I'm sorry."

He ignored it.

"If you swear to me that no one here is in danger, I will put the knife away," he said, squeezing my other hip in his left hand.

"You wouldn't do it."

"Francie," he warned, his voice low and ominous as he pressed the knife harder. All he'd have to do was turn the blade to draw blood.

I drew a sharp breath. "I swear it, Arturian. I don't kill innocent people."

"Good," he said, removing the knife and smoothing my dress in one fluid motion. He spun me back around so I was facing him again. "Then why are you *really* here?"

"Maybe I just wanted to dance with you." I glanced around the room, hoping someone would cut in so I could escape.

He noticed my wandering eyes. "If you think anyone in this ballroom would try to steal you from my arms, you're mistaken. Enough of your distractions." He placed his hand on the small of my back and gave me a firm push towards the edge of the ballroom.

"People will talk," I said, turning my head so he could hear me.

"Let them."

I relaxed my posture, ensuring my movements were fluid and unconcerned. Better to seem like lovers sneaking away than enemies plotting against each other. I wrapped my hand around his arm, and he led me towards the library. There was no avoiding the stares as we entered the room alone, closing the doors behind us.

In less than a heartbeat, Arturian had me up against a bookshelf, arms on either side of me.

"Tell me why you're here!" he growled, eyes ablaze behind his mask. "You already haunt my every thought, and now you show up at my house wearing *this*?" He brought his hand up to the braids of my dress.

My throat tightened.

"I can't tell you."

"Why not?"

I paused, choosing my words carefully. "There is more occurring under the surface than you may realize," I answered, hoping against hope that he didn't pry further.

Arturian looked as if he was about to ask another question but paused, tilting his head.

For a reckless moment, I reveled in the situation. I was alone with the man I undeniably loved, and he had me trapped between his arms. He was so *close*. I could sense his desire, despite everything that happened between us.

Forgetting all thoughts of my mission or doubts about his loyalties, I grabbed Arturian's suit and pulled his mouth down to mine. He reciprocated without hesitation, taking me in his arms and pulling me against him. My heart soared, and I wondered why we let anything keep us apart. The lies, schemes and politics all seemed so trivial compared to the moment we were in.

I wound my fingers in his dark hair before sliding them over his neck and slipping them under his collar. I was completely lost in the moment, and would do *anything* to stay in it. Memories of our day in the port office flooded my mind, lowering my inhibitions. That day, we'd been patient and practiced restraint. Tonight, however, we were on borrowed time. As if reading my mind, he pressed my hips against the shelf, knocking a book to the floor.

The sound of the doors opening jolted us out of our passions, and Arturian broke away from me.

"Am I to defend you from every hot-blooded man tonight, *Julianna?*" the familiar, smooth voice echoed through the library. Princess Eadlin stood next to the door, the light from the party streaming into the dark room around her.

"Your Highness," Arturian bowed his head in her direction.

"I thought better of you, Arturian," she said as she closed the doors behind her. "Don't worry, I won't tell anyone. For Eliandre's sake."

I bristled at the mention of Arturian's betrothed, but the feeling was quickly replaced by guilt.

"Fix your dress and be on your way," Eadlin commanded.

I glanced down to see my dress had been pushed open along the back, exposing a significant portion of my side. I pressed my eyes closed, willing away the mortification.

"Yes, Your Highness," I said, smoothing my dress and walking over. Once I reached the door, I spared one last look for Arturian. I expected to see anger or frustration in his eyes, but all I saw was dark suspicion.

"Julianna," the princess urged, eyebrows raised.

I curtsied and went out the doors.

As embarrassed as I was, the princess might've inadvertently saved my mission. I could still feel his hands on me—his intensity. I never would've been able to get away from him if it weren't for the princess's intrusion. At the moment, I hadn't wanted to.

I forced the memories from my mind and walked through the large corridors of the Exley mansion until I spotted Augustus. He stood tall and austere at the edge of the ballroom, engaged in conversation with a man in a bright red suit coat. The man was pale and wore his blond hair in a long braid. Trenican men often wore their hair in braids, usually to keep it out of the way of the heavy furs they had to wear in their harsh climate.

I assessed the area, devising a way to get nearby without seeming suspicious. Luckily for me, Prince Harley stood alone, somewhat near Augustus, drinking a glass of salt rum while watching the dancers. I sidled up to him, keeping Augustus and the Trenican man in my peripheral vision.

"I'm glad to see you've escaped Exley," Harley said, slurring his words. How many glasses had he drunk? "Fate is cruel, isn't it?"

His words puzzled me, and the prince noticed. "It's not your fault, darling. I can tell you're new to this scene," he said with a crooked smile. He straightened and took my hand, pressing his lips against it. "It's time for me to return north. Please send my regards to our host," he finished, his voice heavy-laden with sarcasm. I watched him leave with curiosity, his words echoing through my mind.

After glancing at a clock, I began strolling down a large hall-way, adopting the posture of someone who belonged. Head high, back straight, steps sure. I glanced in the rooms as I passed until I glimpsed one with a large framed painting of Adolpho Exley. I froze at the sight.

Hello, Father.

A bitter taste swirled in my mouth as I looked at him. His brow was low, and his jaw was strong and wide under a neatly cropped beard. Taking a deep breath, I strolled into the room with a false air of purpose. Thankfully, it was unnecessary, as the room was still empty. Its decor was obtrusive and disturbing—it was certainly Augustus's study.

I glanced around, looking for somewhere to hide. The large room was bordered mostly with bookshelves and windows, but my eyes landed on something promising. The corner held a tall ivory armoire, just the right size for me. I approached it and climbed inside, closing the doors behind me.

I only waited a few minutes before I heard Augustus's edged, harsh voice echo in the room. I spared a glance through the crack in the armoire's doors and saw the Trenican man with him.

This is it.

They all sat down at the table and poured themselves drinks. I hadn't accounted for the thickness of the armoire's doors, and I could barely hear their words as they murmured to each other. However, after a few minutes, I heard a chair scratch against the floor.

Someone is standing up.

A very distinctive, purring voice traveled across the room as it spoke, weaving tapestries of deceit with his words. I couldn't even understand what he said, but I knew who it was.

Augustus.

His voice carried through the room like a sensual siren song, making promises behind veiled threats of retaliation. He walked uncomfortably close to the armoire I was hiding in, and I caught a few unsettling words: "shipment," "weapons," and "destabilize." As their conversation shifted and became agitated, one phrase from Augustus rang out like a bell.

"It's scheduled to make port on October tenth. That will be the day we start."

Thankfully for my strained joints, the meeting didn't last much longer. I watched and counted their heads as they all left through the doors. After I was sure they'd all cleared out of the room, I emerged from my hiding spot. While I was disappointed with how little information I gathered, the nearness of the date concerned me.

October tenth. That's four days from now.

I assumed they spoke of a weapons shipment arriving from Trenica, and the date of Augustus's takeover. Suddenly, I felt a jolt of panic.

He won't stop with the queen and king. He'll kill Prince Harley and Princess Eadlin, too.

The way Arturian had glared at Harley rose to the forefront of my mind.

Surely he doesn't know. Surely...

I made my way out of the study unnoticed, and walked along the edge of the ballroom, intending to make a subtle departure. A grand waltz was playing and a large crowd of people moved around the room in perfect coordination. I couldn't deny the beauty—the glamour of it all. It was mesmerizing.

I made it out the enormous front doors and down a couple of marble steps when I felt a dark, icy presence upon me. I stopped dead in my tracks, the breeze ruffling my dress and hair as I looked up at the mansion behind me. Arturian stood alone on the grand balcony, the moon shining down on him as he watched me.

To my surprise, he reached up, unfastened his mask, and pulled it from his face. He tilted his head forward, and I could nearly hear his words in my mind.

My mask is off. It's your turn.

It was an offer of honesty. I bit at my lip, raised a hand to the silk ribbon behind my head, but hesitated. With all of my heart, I wished I could tell him everything. But the stakes were too high, and he was the son of our enemy. My hand fell back to my side.

Arturian tilted his head back—disappointed, but resigned. I held his eyes for a long moment before tearing myself away and continuing down the steps, desperate to find the carriage that waited for me.

As I approached, Levick tried to open the door for me from the inside, but I motioned for him to stop. He listened, and let me open the door from the outside.

He breathed a deep sigh of relief as I sat down opposite him. "How did it go?" he asked as the carriage began rolling away.

"Not *nearly* according to plan."

CHAPTER THIRTY-SEVEN

BROTHER

"**A**rturian was there?" I exclaimed, leaning forward in my seat.

"Yes. He was on the balcony just now. He still doesn't know you're involved," Francie said, shifting in her dress.

"Did you tell him anything? Does he know you're in the RCM?"

"No. I distracted him and got away," Francie played with her hair with shaking fingers. Something was bothering her, and I couldn't help but feel like it had something to do with the broadening gulf between us. She'd been keeping something from me for weeks, and it had been wearing away at me.

"What intel did you gather from the meeting?" I asked, shaking off my unease.

"It should wait... until we're with Orin," she answered, leaving me deflated. Her countenance was so distracted that I decided not to press it.

"Where the hell are we?" I asked after opening the carriage door. We'd jerked to a stop beside a glistening pond bordered by a deep forest, along with one other carriage.

Francie leaned out. "Are you sure we got in the right carriage?" she whispered.

"Yes, it's the same one. I stayed with it the whole time." I climbed out of the carriage and took a few steps towards the pond.

"You must be Levick Roale," a voice as smooth as honey sounded from behind our carriage. Francie gasped and clambered out to stand beside me.

A tall, radiant woman stepped out from behind the carriage and stood before us. She wore a plunging silk dress of lavender purple, and her long black hair reflected the moonlight as it fluttered in the breeze. She had an oval-shaped face, and sparkling eyes that shone silver.

"Good to see you again, *Julianna*," the radiant woman said, a smirk gracing her red painted lips.

"Do you know her?" I muttered to Francie, but as I looked over, she was in a low curtsy.

"Your Highness," she said, head bowed in respect.

Oh, no... What fresh hell have we gotten ourselves into?

"Are you going to bow? Or shall you continue trying to catch fireflies in your mouth?" the princess said, crossing her arms primly and eyeing me.

I gathered my wits and dropped to a knee. "My apologies, Your Highness."

"Say nothing of it. You've been quite useful, you know," she said, smiling in satisfaction. The moon reflected against her glossy black hair, adding to her mesmerizing features.

"I don't know what you mean…" I said as I rose, glancing at Francie. Her eyes were distant, and her nostrils flared.

"Orin, you can come out," the princess called, tilting her head a bit. The second carriage's doors opened, and Orin Strickland emerged. My heart dropped, the hope of our movement dissolving in front of me.

Shit. The crown knows about the RCM. We're going to die here.

The same thoughts seemed to go through Francie's head, as she'd paled and taken her throwing stance.

She didn't know, either.

"It's not what you think," Orin said with a relaxed smile. "How did you think we funded our work?"

"I'll be needing my dress back soon," Princess Eadlin said to Francie with a wink. "Although, I'm not sure I want it anymore…" she trailed off, a cringe pulling at her sensual lips.

I was too confused to ask about whatever *that* meant. "Orin, are you telling me the RCM is just a pawn of the Crown?"

"Now, now, Levick. The princess operates independently of her mother," Orin said, splaying his hands in an amicable gesture.

"Silence, I will explain myself." The princess took a few graceful steps closer to the pond, then turned to us. "My mother has made some questionable alliances, which have led to turmoil amongst the common folk of Friese. Meaningless, excessive deaths have plagued our working class for decades. Our wealthy aristocrats may not notice the growing discontent among the population, but I have. No society can function properly when the majority of the population is oppressed to oblivion by the wealthy and powerful." She paused and took a deep breath. "The time has come for a change of leadership in Friese."

The pure political cynicism of it hit me full-force. "I don't believe it—you just want the throne!"

The princess's eyes grew cold as she looked down her nose at me. "My family's star has been falling for years. I'm not even first in line for the throne, Harley is. I've never intended to wear the crown. I've spent the last few years forming a coalition of minor houses who've felt disenfranchised by my mother's reign. The plan was to weaken the major houses through civil war between them, and when my mother was ousted, my coalition would take control and rule by group vote. Each social class would've been represented, and the Skylords would've filled their proper roles as military leaders. However, my original plan has been rendered obsolete by the emergence of a new, more imminent threat."

"Augustus," Francie said, relaxing her posture.

"I take it you accomplished your mission tonight? After I *rescued* you?" Eadlin asked with a smile. I glanced between them, suspicion curling in my mind.

What happened in there?

"Yes," Francie said as she turned to face Eadlin again, obviously embarrassed. "There is a large shipment coming in from Port Harrow in Trenica. The day it arrives is the day they'd *start*. I presume they meant the start of his takeover."

"When is it?" Eadlin pressed, tilting her head forward.

"I'm going to need some assurances first."

The princess scoffed at her. "Is that a joke? I have been silently funding the RCM since before you even knew what it was," Eadlin said, her voice like a knife. She had a way of speaking that commanded respect and compliance. "I have no firm plans of killing anyone you know. That will have to be good enough."

Francie took a deep breath before nodding hesitantly. "October tenth."

For all of her poise, even Princess Eadlin gasped. "Four days? That's all we have?" She placed a hand on her carriage to steady herself.

Four days until a war in Friese.

"Well... I suppose it's good that I brought my guest. We will surely need his help if your report is true," the princess said darkly as a third carriage approached, pulled by a pair of inky black geldings. Their leather bridles were adorned with dark red detailing.

A cold, sinking sensation pulled at me as it came to a stop next to the pond. "Who's in there?" I called out, stepping in front of Francie.

"No one you need to be protecting *her* from," Eadlin said with an amused smile.

Not him. Please, not him.

She opened the carriage and Arturian Exley stepped out, clad in an immaculate black suit with the red Exley crest over his chest. He looked tired, and his hair fell next to his face.

"What am I doing here, Your Highness—" He stopped in his tracks upon seeing the people gathered in front of the pond. His eyes froze on Francie.

What does he know? Is this why Francie was acting aloof in the carriage?

"Before you start asking questions, I'm going to sum things up for you." The princess gestured to Orin. "That is Orin Strickland. He is the leader of the Revolt of the Common Man. He is working with me to stop the atrocities being committed by people like your father." She gestured to me. "That is Levick Roale, but I have a feeling you two know each other. He works with us." Arturian briefly glanced at me, but quickly returned his gaze to Francie.

"Last, but *certainly* not least, is our dear Francesca Hanover." As the princess spoke, Arturian's eyes remained locked on Francie's, searching for something. Fear, maybe? "A selfless volunteer, loving niece, and somehow in possession of one of the most valuable weapons this world has to offer." Eadlin's eyes narrowed on Francie.

She knows about Francie's windblade... and she's exposing it to Arturian.

I was about to cut in, but her next sentence stopped me.

"But you need no introduction to her. You two are *clearly* well acquainted, from what I saw tonight," the princess finished with a chuckle.

My stomach dropped, growing nauseous at the implication. "What is she talking about, Francie?" I glanced at her, but her face was devoid of color, her eyes locked on Arturian's.

"Oh... she hadn't told you," Eadlin said quietly.

"Told me what?" I glared at Arturian, whose face remained a stony mask. "Did you hurt her?" I asked Arturian with a low snarl, stalking towards him.

"Of course not. You should be the one to tell him, Francie," Arturian said coolly. *Always* calm. *Always* composed. I locked my jaw as I stopped in my tracks.

I turned and searched her eyes, and it all made sense. Why she'd kept me at arms-length, how she got quiet whenever Arturian was mentioned...

The truth became glaringly obvious and crashed over me like a tide.

"You love him, don't you?" The words ripped from my throat like a knife. I stared into her eyes, but all I found was guilt. Her face was confirmation enough.

I walked backwards a few steps as it hit me. My stomach turned with betrayal as I looked back and forth between them. How long had they been carrying on? I'd been in love with Francie for *years,* and she fell for my *best friend?* The deception felt like a knife between my shoulders. All of her odd mannerisms and reactions suddenly clicked into place, leaving me reeling.

What a fool I've been. How could I have missed it?
He loves her, too. How could he not?

I asked the question that was eating me from the inside—straining to keep my voice even. "When?"

She hesitated, daring a glance at Arturian. "My birthday."

"Over a *month* ago…" I said, anguish finally overtaking the shock. "Wait." I stopped short. Francie's true lineage flashed through my mind, and my nausea increased. She was Adolpho's daughter. "But Francie, he's your—"

"No!" Francie shouted abruptly, eyeing Orin and the princess, who watched the scene in quiet incredulity. "No, he isn't." She looked at me with an expression that seemed to say, *not here. I'll explain later.*

I shook my head and took a few steps closer to her, running my hands through my hair. "But the other night," I started, thinking of our kiss, "you let me—"

"Don't finish that sentence," Arturian growled as he started to intercept me, but Francie motioned him away.

She just stared at me, guilt and shame written all over her face. She let me kiss her while she was in love with Arturian. Francie *knew* there was no future with him. That's why she'd allowed it.

"Francie… He's getting married."

"I know, that's why I—" she started, but stopped when her eyes shot over to Arturian. His brows were upturned as he worked his jaw, showing more pain on his face than I had ever seen. She turned back to me, holding my gaze with glassy eyes. "I am so *incredibly sorry* for not telling you." She took a shaky breath. "It seems I can't stop lying to either of you."

I glanced over at Arturian, whose eyes held a complex mixture of frustrated emotions as he gazed at Francie.

"We need to get back on track, here…" Orin said, shifting awkwardly.

Arturian ignored him, eyes still on Francie. "Are you alright?" He spoke only to her.

"She could kill all of us in an instant—she's fine," Orin said, rolling his eyes. Arturian didn't seem surprised at all by the comment, confirming my suspicions.

He already knew.

"Yes, I'm fine," Francie replied with a slight nod.

"I'll speak to her alone," Arturian said with all the entitlement of a Friesian Skylord, walking towards Francie.

I fumed, stepping between them. "No, you're the son of our enemy."

"Boys, let's not do this," Eadlin chimed in, clearly uncomfortable.

"Levick, you're one of my oldest friends. In honor of that, I'm warning you—move. I am no threat to her."

"Maybe not physically," I hissed, bitterness burning through me.

Arturian looked down at me, his face cold and detached. "Measure your words carefully, Levick. Words said in anger are of equal permanence as those said with a sober mind."

"It's okay, Levick," Francie said, sliding a gentle hand over my arm. "We'll be right over there, on the other side of the pond."

"Francie..." I shook my head in disbelief.

"Let it go, Levick. I have a feeling he won't hurt her," Orin said, giving me a sympathetic look.

Arturian walked around me, took Francie's hand, and led her away.

"I can't believe I called you my *brother*," I bit out after them. Arturian paused his steps and glanced over his shoulder at me.

For the first time that night, his eyes were soft—brows knit together in inner-conflict. He looked as if he was going to say something, but he looked down, then turned away. The pair of them walked along the pond, Arturian's hand brushing Francie's lower back in a gesture so familiar it made everything heartbreakingly real.

Once they were out of earshot, Orin directed a freshly icy glare at me. "You two knew the Exley heir this entire time, and didn't think to tell me?"

CHAPTER THIRTY-EIGHT
THE CARRIAGE

As we walked, I took a deep breath and attempted to stow away the anxiety that threatened to overtake my good sense. The look of betrayal on Levick's face refused to disappear from my mind, threatening to implode any inroads I might make. Friese's fate could hinge on whether I could convince Arturian to ally with us. The time had come for me to lay all of my cards on the table and trust him to make the right choice for us. For *Friese.*

As soon as we were out of earshot, Arturian turned and leveled an intense stare at me as we walked beside the pond.

"Why did you try to steal that book from my nightstand? Was it for them?" A dangerous edge ran through his even voice, making my pulse jump.

I was still ashamed of what I'd done and wished Orin had never asked me to do it. If I was being honest with myself, I was relieved when I realized he'd taken the book back from me before I escaped the mansion. When I got back to Orin's house the next morning, he gave me an earful for failing on my mission.

"Yes," I whispered, looking anywhere except at his accusatory stare. "He thought the book might have theories on how to... destroy the windblades."

His reaction, though subtle, betrayed the furious storm raging beneath his calm exterior. However, his response was level and measured. As usual.

"Such madness would leave Friese exposed to the hostile nations encircling us. They've waited for centuries for an opportunity to strike. Eliminating the Skylords would give them exactly what they wanted."

I nodded. "Yes, I agree with you. But you have to realize what led to the creation of the RCM... and why they'd be tempted to resort to such drastic measures."

Arturian said nothing, but I could see him flexing his jaw as he stared ahead into the night. Mist curled up along the edges of the shore, swirling and dissipating as we stepped through it.

I cleared my throat. "My intention was to study the book and ensure there was nothing he could use before I handed it over. However..." I bit at my lip, "there's something you need to hear."

I pressed my eyes closed, praying for the strength to be honest. "I know this isn't news to you, but Friese is falling apart from the inside. I've witnessed men die in senseless accidents because of long hours and overworking at the port. Good women whore themselves in the streets because their husbands are gone, and they have to find some way—*any* way—to feed their children. The Skylords have been abusing their power and using the rest of us as tools to increase their wealth." I paused for a moment, taking a deep breath. "I'm not a fool. I know there isn't a tenable future for Friese without the windblades. But I do think there needs to be a change. Someone needs to be advocating for those people. For *my* people."

Arturian listened to me, his eyes still distant. However, after a moment that felt like a lifetime, a small smile tugged at the corner of his lips.

"Francesca Exley, Noble Skylady of Friese and Defender of the Weak."

My heart almost stopped at his words, until I realized he likely referred to me in such a way because of my father, Adolpho Exley.

He turned to me, his eyes soft but resolute. "I fundamentally disapprove of the tactics the RCM employs. I believe that revolts and rebellions are usually bloody, death-filled tributes to self-righteousness." I started to interject my disapproval, but he cut me off. "However, I'm not so completely blind and encased in my privileged bubble to miss what's happening in Friese. I agree with the RCM about one thing: there must be change, or the situation will erupt, and take thousands of innocent lives with it."

I breathed a heavy sigh of relief. "That brings me to our current predicament..." I toyed with a loose strand of hair. "Your father is planning to overthrow the queen in four days, and take the throne for himself."

I didn't bother to pad the statement. I studied his reaction, and to my relief, his disbelief was genuine.

"No, he would've told me if he were planning something like that," Arturian said with infuriating conviction.

"Then maybe *you* can tell me why he has a large influx of weapons coming in at the port." I cut in front of him and stopped. "Or why he met someone from Trenica tonight, discussing a *very important shipment*, and how its arrival would be the *start* of something."

Arturian stared at me, but his eyes were glazed over, deep in thought.

"Trenica... oh," he said, breath rushing from his lungs. "That's why you were at the ball tonight."

I nodded, and some of my hair came loose and fell around my face.

"He told me he was planning on introducing trade from Trenica..." he began, but stopped himself. A cool breeze brushed over me, making me shiver.

"Arturian, I know what you're thinking," I said, hoping he wasn't considering supporting his father's plans.

No. I know him, and he wouldn't. He wouldn't leave Friese in the clutches of a murderous maniac.

"How could you possibly?" he mumbled.

The question wasn't malicious, but honest. I didn't have a title to consider. A duty. A *father*. I imagined that the urge to display undying loyalty to his father was overwhelming. However, there were things more important than family loyalty.

"A war, Arturian," I whispered, getting closer and staring up into his eyes. "He has to be stopped. I know he's your father, but could you imagine the kinds of things he'd do as *king*?" I shuddered at the idea of Augustus on the throne of Friese.

Arturian turned to face the pond. The moon and stars reflected off the water, and I could see the rest of our party watching us from the other side.

Finally he spoke, his words carrying a crushing gravity. "This is what I've been trying to avoid. War, unrest... death. All I've wanted to do was maintain the position of our house, and one day inherit the title and the blade. I would've sacrificed almost anything for that." He paused, knitting his eyebrows together. "However, I know my father. He would transform Friese into a hellscape." He stood silently for a long moment. "Do you realize what you're asking of me?"

"I could do it," I offered, though the idea of more killing made me nauseous.

"No, it has to be me. I'll need his windblade if House Exley is to live on."

"Oh." I tried to hide my disappointment. He spoke as if he planned to carry on the house alone.

"I didn't say there wasn't a place for you, though," he whispered so softly, I almost didn't hear him. He trained his dark eyes on me, swirling with a familiar blue flame.

I held his gaze, confused by the statement. "What do you mean?"

"Another time. We have plans to make," he said, beckoning me to walk back with him along the shore.

Pale moonlight shone down on Arturian's stoic face as he walked beside me. I could tell he wanted to bring something up, but I waited for him to speak. After a moment, he lifted his head and said, "You kissed him." It wasn't a question.

"Come and talk to me when you're not betrothed to some-one else," I said, my tone more bitter than I meant it to be.

He clenched his jaw. "I knew it would happen."

"Why do you say that?"

"He's loved you for years," Arturian said, still looking ahead.

I had suspected it, but hearing it out loud was still shocking.

"It doesn't matter, anyway," I mumbled, lifting my dress up to step over a rock.

Arturian looked over at me. "Why not?"

I raised an eyebrow as I glanced at him. "Why do you think?" I shook my head in frustration. "It seems my mind and my heart are at odds."

Wordlessly, Arturian reached over and laced his fingers with my own. In my frustration, I almost yanked my hand away, but the contact sent a wave of warmth up my arm and through my body. It was good... it was *right*.

"I won't do it," Arturian said, furrowing his brows. "My father's schemes will die with him; my engagement included."

My breath caught in my throat.

He continued, "Despite my recklessness at the ball tonight, Eliandre is a good woman, and I don't wish to hurt her or damage her reputation. I'll have to find a way to do it wisely." He squeezed my hand. "It took me too long to realize it, but I can't marry anyone else, Francie. It would be a lie."

My heart felt like it would beat out of my chest. A lump formed in my throat, rendering me speechless. So, instead of speaking, I stopped in my tracks. Our fingers still intertwined, Arturian turned to face me, a questioning look on his handsome face.

"You're serious?" I asked. I didn't want to get my hopes up—our situation seemed so impossible, and my heart already felt like it had been split a dozen times over.

He brought his free hand up to my face and ran a knuckle over my cheek. "I'm serious," he breathed. He leaned in as if to kiss me, but stopped himself. I tilted my head—disappointed. "Levick hates me enough right now. If we're going to work together, I shouldn't fuel that fire."

I took a quick glance over the pond, only to see the rest of our party—Levick included—watching us like hawks. Arturian was right. We didn't need to create more conflict by twisting the knife. He tugged on my hand, and we continued our walk.

"I'll have to thank the princess for choosing that gown for you," Arturian said, dealing me a subtle smirk as we walked. I would've forgotten I was still wearing it, but for the breeze I felt against my back, making me shiver.

"She has good taste. She scares me a little, though," I finished with a smile.

Arturian chuckled, and I caught a glimpse of his perfect smile in the dim light. He didn't do that enough. "I try to stay on her good side. Although I wasn't thrilled to see her earlier tonight."

I blushed at the memory of our kiss. I wished we were somewhere alone, without a nosy audience.

"Did you do that just to distract me?" he asked, shrugging off his jacket to drape it over my shoulders. I smiled in thanks—the temperature had dropped quickly and I was shaking in the cold.

"Sure. Let's go with that," I said, earning another smile from him.

"Francie." He stopped walking before we got too close to the others, tugging me over to face him. He tilted his head as he leveled an inquisitive but gentle stare at me. "The lies between us... they've been a caustic agent, eating away at any trust we could hope to build. I need to know, are you holding anything else back, or are things finally open between us?"

I stared back at him, admiring the way his hair brushed against his sharp jaw in the breeze. His dark red buttoned shirt contrasted dramatically with his dark hair and blue eyes.

Levick. He still doesn't know Levick is a windwalker.

"There is something..." I began, knowing the lies needed to stop. "But it's not about me."

He cast a suspicious look at me, but noticed me staring at the people who waited for us. Thankfully, he picked up on it.

"You can tell me later," he said as his eyes softened, and he placed a hand over my back.

As we approached the carriages, the princess stood with her arms crossed. "You should know better than to keep a princess waiting, Exley," she said, only teasing a little.

"My deepest apologies, Your Highness," Arturian said, the smallest hint of sarcasm in his words.

Levick stood from a rock he'd been sitting on. "If we're going to work together, we might as well get it over with."

Orin laughed as they gathered near the carriages. "That's the spirit. Now, let's plan a sabotage."

Orin, Eadlin and Levick climbed into the princess's carriage, leaving me and Arturian alone by the pond. As the first carriage rolled away for the short trip to the bell tower, Arturian helped me climb into the Exley carriage. I settled on the red velvet cushions, and he sat down opposite of me before signaling to the driver to get going.

The cabin quickly grew warm from our body heat, and I began brushing strands of hair away from my shoulders. I leaned forward to take off Arturian's jacket and found myself mere inches away from his face. My actions were having their expected effect—he was watching me slip the jacket off of my shoulders, tracking every movement with dark eyes.

We were alone in a moving carriage.

Where nothing could interrupt us.

I met his eyes with a sultry gaze, but leaned back again, resting against the carriage. He seemed disappointed, but the expression was quickly replaced by intrigue as I lifted my hair and began fanning myself, eyes closed and head tilted back. "It's warm in here, isn't it?"

"You know what you're doing," Arturian said in a husky rasp.

"I don't know what you're talking about." I sneaked a peek at him. His expression was one of self-restraint, but it was crumbling. I took a deep breath until my dress was straining against me, and arched my back in a slow stretch. "It's a bit cramped in here... I suppose it's a good thing this is such a brief trip."

His restraint broke. He slid across the cabin and pulled my mouth to his. His other hand slid over my waist, gripping me with desperate fingers. I couldn't help but smile against his lips, and he took advantage of the opportunity to take the kiss deeper. He tilted my head to the side with his hand and began gently nibbling at my neck.

"Don't leave marks," I chuckled in a breathy whisper.

"Next time, my *summer storm...*" he mumbled against my neck.

Next time.

He pulled away, to my distaste, and slid the front window down. "Make an extra loop," he commanded the driver, before pulling the window back up. He took me back into his arms, determined to make the most of our short bit of privacy.

Arturian helped me pull his jacket back over my shoulders before helping me down from our carriage. Eadlin and Orin stood outside of the bell tower, clearly unsure about the place. The faint moonlight shone upon its faded white paint, giving it an eerie look.

Eadlin had sent the third carriage back to the palace, and Levick had refused to ride with me and Arturian in our carriage. While we would've liked to mend the fences with Levick, we certainly didn't mind our short bit of time alone together. I hoped my cheeks weren't still burning as hot as they felt.

"We thought you two were right behind us. Got turned around?" Eadlin asked, looking at me with a sly smile.

Arturian nodded. "It's dark," he said at a volume only Eadlin and I would hear. He knew that excuse would fool no one. My blush burned hotter, and I tried to let the cool breeze calm it.

Eadlin nodded, a cheeky look on her face, and turned back to the bell tower. "Are we sure this is the best place to plan things?" Eadlin asked as she played with a long strand of hair.

"No one will see us here. I've lived here for years and no one's ever caught me," Levick said, peeking out the front doors.

"It's just so... *quaint,*" Eadlin said with poorly hidden disgust.

"It's better than that soulless place you call a palace," Levick mumbled as he swung the doors wide for us. Eadlin blinked, raising her eyebrows in incredulous offense.

"Enough, both of you," Orin said, rolling his eyes as he walked past Eadlin. "If we want to keep that maniacal murderer off the throne, we have to learn to work together."

I cringed at Orin's brashness.

His son is standing right here...

I glanced at Arturian to see that his face was a well-composed mask, and he made no response. I gripped his hand and squeezed it, looking at him in encouragement. His lips turned up a bit at the corners before letting me lead him inside after the others.

After we entered, Levick glanced at me, eyes flashing to the Exley crest emblazoned on the breast of the jacket I still wore. He quickly looked away to gather candles and light them. Orin and Arturian began dragging chairs into a circle around Levick's dusty table as I wiped it off with a rag. Eadlin began dragging a chair of her own with about as much grace and dexterity as someone who's never had to lift anything heavier than a glass of wine. I smiled to myself and moved to help her.

"Thank you," Eadlin said as we carried the chair together. "I apologize, for earlier." I looked up, surprised. "I was unaware of the... *group dynamic* among you three. I never meant to cause any strife between you."

I cringed. We set down the chair, and I pulled Eadlin aside near the staircase.

"I appreciate that, Your Highness, but it was entirely my making. My lies are my responsibility," I said with a polite nod.

I jumped in surprise as Eadlin took my face in her hands. "Dear girl..." she whispered, eyes full of endearing sentiment.

I'm your age...

"I'm so glad we found you." She smiled at me. I smiled back, despite feeling slightly patronized.

I'm glad you found me, too.

Eadlin's countenance shifted, and glanced over at Levick and Arturian, and then looked back to me. "I see you've wrangled the jacket off our favorite bachelor." I blushed, but nodded with an awkward smile. Eadlin leaned in closer, eyebrow raised. "What do you think it would take to get the plucky boy's jacket? I'm icier than the mood at a Yorke soiree."

She said it with such seriousness that I let out a muffled snort of laughter.

"If you're done with your girl-time, ladies, we have some work to do," Orin called over, annoyance heavy in his voice. Levick sat next to him, and Arturian sat on the opposite side, looking confident but markedly out of place.

"Watch your tone, Strickland, or I'll have some other goon lead my resistance," Eadlin said with an easy smile, brushing her silky hair away from her face. He shook his head, rolling his eyes.

She shot me a playful glance, made a subtle gesture as if she was putting on an invisible jacket, and sat down next to Levick. I covered my amused smile as I took my seat next to Arturian.

"Thank you for joining us tonight, Mister Exley," Eadlin said, flashing a charming smile across the table. "I understand how delicate of a situation you're in, but I'm relieved our dear Francie swayed you in our favor."

I glanced over at Arturian and saw his mouth pull up at the corner, but the emotion didn't reach his eyes. They were as cold as the mountain peaks of Trenica, and harder than the steel forged in Grevalst. My stomach dropped.

"How amusing that you profess affection for her," he said, his voice laced with feigned amusement, "especially considering you sent her into my home to steal from me."

I swallowed the lump in my throat—I hadn't expected him to confront them about it... but there was always something brewing under the surface with Arturian.

The room went silent, and I studied their reactions. Eadlin gave a subtle but shocked glance at Orin, who seemed to sink back in his chair.

Levick was the first to speak. "You did *what?*"

"I didn't recognize her, and I almost killed her," Arturian growled, still staring daggers at Eadlin.

Orin scoffed from his chair, and every pair of eyes in the room fell upon him.

"She wouldn't have let you kill her—you wouldn't stand a chance. You wouldn't even be her first." He let out an incredulous laugh. "She has a windblade, for Echna's sake."

I bristled at his words. He was far too presumptive of the lengths I'd go for his sake. I wished I'd never broken into the estate that night. I'd been burying my frustration with Orin for the sake of the mission, but it was reaching a boiling point.

"Enough Orin," I said, surprising myself with my frankness. I could feel my companions' stares settle on me. However, instead of backing off, I leaned into it. "When I agreed to help the RCM, you promised not to use me as an assassin, yet I have the blood of half a dozen men on my hands." I paused, and the weight of my words stilled my companions. "I remember every pierced heart. Every rolling head. Every faint trickle as their blood spilled over the floor." I clenched my jaw, staring daggers at Orin. My heart throbbed as I saw them in my mind... my *victims*. "Don't make the mistake of assuming I am an endless cache of violence. I am *not*," I said, my last words nearly a growl.

Orin's mouth fell ajar, and I couldn't help but notice Levick looking down at his hands, brows furrowed. Eadlin simply stared at me, her eyes wide and her lips pursed. It was a look I never expected to see on the princess's face: *mortification*.

Warmth spread across my thigh as Arturian slid his fingers over it, landing on my hand. He laced his fingers through mine and squeezed, and the pressure seemed to release some of the tension inside me. I took a deep breath and looked over at him. His jaw was clenched as he searched my eyes—his concerned expression a jarring contrast to the glare he'd given the others.

Eadlin's voice shook us out of our shared moment. "I had no knowledge of this mission," she said, going to great lengths to control her voice. "Orin, a word."

Eadlin rose from her seat and stared at Orin with the authority of a queen. He scowled but complied, and followed her through the front doors and into the darkness outside.

Immediately after they'd gone, Levick stood and made his way upstairs with no explanation. I sighed as I watched him leave, but Arturian's thumb brushing over my hand brought my attention back.

"Do you want to talk about it?" Arturian asked in a tentative whisper.

Could I even share such horrors with him? Would he even look at me the same way? Despite my doubts, I nodded. "Not now... but yes." I knew I couldn't bear it alone anymore.

We said nothing for a while—the only sounds were the voices arguing outside.

"I don't trust Orin," Arturian began. "That night he sent you to break in—if I'd hurt you..." he bit at his cheek as he stared down at the table.

"You didn't," I said, cutting him off. I knew better than to let him dwell on it. "We're both here, and working together. That's what matters."

He nodded, but said nothing.

"He wants what's best for Friese," I said, my voice barely above a whisper, "but I'm not sure we agree on what that looks like."

"I guarantee Eadlin doesn't," he said with a glance over at me. "She'd never agree to any plan that involves eliminating the

Skylords. I don't know her very well, but I know she's got more wisdom than that."

I ran a finger over Arturian's knuckle. "I hope this isn't the end of their partnership."

"No matter what happens between them," he began, looking over at me. "We'll stop it. Together."

"Any more surprise confrontations you want to spring on me?" I asked, tilting a coy smile at him.

Arturian's eyes gleamed in the candlelight—the light of a thousand stars reflecting in them. "Nothing you need to worry about."

CHAPTER THIRTY-NINE
THE PLOT

A couple of minutes later, Eadlin and Orin walked in from outside, looking tense but determined. "It's behind us," Eadlin announced, curt and final as she sat back down at the table. Orin wore a scolded look on his face, but took his seat. "Where is the boy?" Eadlin asked, glancing around the room for Levick.

Arturian chuckled. "Upstairs."

Just then, Levick made his way down. A tautness held him rigid as he crept down the spiraling steps, his expression betraying nothing. "Everything in order?" he asked, looking directly at Orin. I couldn't help but notice how he evaded my gaze.

Eadlin straightened in her seat and pushed her shoulders back. The purple gems on her dress gleamed in the candlelight, reflecting around the room in a starry display. "We're united. Let's get to work."

Levick pulled his chair out and sat down beside Eadlin, who still eyed his jacket with jealousy. I bit at my top lip to keep from smiling. We all sat in silence for a long, tense moment before someone spoke.

"I have terms," Arturian said just as Orin was opening his mouth to speak.

"Is that so?" Orin said, ridicule heavy in his voice. He seemed anything but discouraged by the verbal lashing he undoubtedly earned from Eadlin. "By all means. Why don't you lead the RCM as well?"

Eadlin cleared her throat, dusting the arms of her chair. "Orin, dear." She aimed a pointed glare at him. He clenched his jaw and leaned back in his chair.

"I'll kill my father. No one else," Arturian said evenly, ever-composed. His shirt had somehow remained pristine and unwrinkled, complementing his serious demeanor. I looked away before someone caught me staring.

"No. It'll be Francie, obviously," Orin said, shaking his head in exasperation. I noticed Levick glance up at Orin, brows raised in surprise.

"It's my right as the heir to House Exley. This is not negotiable," Arturian said, staring Orin down.

"Honestly? I don't give a damn about your line of succession."

"Orin," I began before anyone else could retort. "The fate of House Exley could be very consequential after the fact. If they lose their blade, they'll be dissolved, leaving a massive power vacuum. Is that what you want when we're on the brink of chaos?" I made sure to lock eyes with everyone at the table. "Or would you rather have House Exley on our side?" I finished, glancing over at Arturian. He watched me with an unreadable expression.

I met eyes with Eadlin, who wore a smile of approval. "Well, I think our blonde blade thrower has made quite a salient point."

I glanced at Levick, but he said nothing.

"I want the biggest threat to Friese eliminated in the most efficient, surefire way possible. That means having *Francie* sneak up on him and slice him seaward and sideways," Orin retorted, not satisfied.

Arturian countered him, "My father has suspicions about her. She can't do anything clandestine—once he saw her, he would pursue her."

"Why the hell would he suspect her?" Orin asked, loud and intense.

"It doesn't matter—"

"It's not important."

Levick and Arturian answered at the same time.

Eadlin raised an eyebrow at me, which I ignored. They were trying to protect my identity, which I appreciated. I wasn't ready to reveal my Exley blood to the leader of the RCM and the Princess of Friese. There was no way to reveal it without either implicating myself and Arturian in a seemingly incestuous relationship, or telling the truth and confessing Arturian was illegitimate and had no Exley blood. Neither option seemed appealing.

Definitely not the time to open that particular can of worms.

"Okay," Orin conceded, but with a suspicious look at them. "Then I'll move on to our next options. Mister Exley, here, is an obvious advantage, as he has trust and nearness to his father. Why not slay him in his sleep and be done with it?"

Eadlin broke into a melodic laughter across the table. She laughed so genuinely and for so long that tears formed in her eyes. She brushed her hair from her face and composed herself. "Oh, dear, dear Orin. You don't understand the Exleys very well if you think murder in the night is a tenable option. I barely kept quiet when you suggested Francie *sneak up* on Augustus Exley." Saying it out loud apparently highlighted the absurdity of it, and she had to stifle another incredulous chuckle.

"Does he have the hearing of a bat, or something?" Orin asked.

"No." Arturian's voice was as serious as a hurricane. "But my father is not the kind of man who will be killed in his sleep. Trust me on this—it would fail."

"He's right," Levick said, and I was relieved to hear him speak.

"Do you have any suggestions, then?" Orin asked in exasperation, to no one in particular.

I steeled myself and spoke up. "He *suspects me*." I got questioning glances from around the room. "I would be the perfect bait. Let me lure him in, weaken him if I have to, and Arturian will finish the job."

"No," Arturian said, his voice as hard and firm as the stone under our feet. I met his eyes for a moment, and despite their cool, dark blue color, they seemed as hot and intense as burning flames. "I won't use you as bait."

I was about to argue my case when Eadlin chimed in. "Oh, sweet Francie. We just finished establishing that Augustus will not go easily, and you've clearly never faced a Skylord. Let alone the strongest one in Friese. There isn't a Skylord in this kingdom who could face Augustus alone."

"Arturian..." I said, turning to him.

"It's true. My father has a mastery of the blade that rivals those of the early days," he finished, and I noticed Levick shift uncomfortably from the corner of my eye.

"I have an idea," Levick interrupted my thoughts. A long silence passed as we waited with bated breath.

"Well? Spit it out!" Eadlin exclaimed, leaning forward on the table before cringing back and wiping her elbows off.

"Arturian has access to his father's study. I'll bet that's where he keeps most of his sensitive information. Arturian should investigate the study and try to discern *how* Augustus plans to execute an overthrow of the queen. Yes, he has weapons, but they alone wouldn't be enough against the Royal Guard. Augustus has been importing more weapons than he has personal guards, and it's not remotely close. There must be something else in the works, or Augustus isn't half as smart as we give him credit for," he finished, leaning back in his chair and folding his hands.

A moment of thoughtful silence passed over the table. "Color me impressed, Mister Roale," Eadlin began, "but that still doesn't address what we should do if Augustus somehow *does* have the soldiers required to take the palace."

"We expose it," Arturian said. "My father may be the strongest Skylord in Friese, but he wouldn't survive a conflict with ten—even twenty Skylords. If it became public that he was trying to overthrow the queen, there would be *at least* that many coming to her defense."

"I have a few Skylords from minor houses who would come to our aid if needed," Eadlin admitted.

"And how many does *he* have in his pocket now? The Yorkes, at least—considering your *betrothal*," Orin said with a doubtful scowl. "That's still a massive war in Friese, killing hundreds, if not thousands, of civilians." He leaned forward, rubbing the bridge of his nose. "We want to stop this thing before it starts."

Images of war-torn streets formed in my mind. So much blood, death, and destruction...

The idea of outright war in Friese horrified me. I wouldn't let it happen. Not while I still wielded Asgora.

"Let me do it." I stood from my chair. "Let me lure him. I know you think I wouldn't survive it, but we'd have the element of surprise."

"Francie, there's no way—" Arturian began, but Levick cut him off.

"I'll go with her," he said, looking at me with a meaningful gleam in his eyes. I smiled at him and nodded.

With a windwalker on my side, I won't fail.

"That's very cute, Levick, but I think your cheers and emotional support won't do her much good when Augustus is throwing his blade at her heart," Eadlin said, unable to contain her exasperation.

"I have... advantages," Levick said awkwardly.

Where are you going with this, Lev?

Orin cocked his head in suspicion. "Like what?"

"Archery. I'm an expert archer," he said with an impressive amount of feigned confidence. Arturian raised an eyebrow, but said nothing.

Not so terrible at lying now, are you?

Eadlin glanced back and forth between us, but let it go. "I suppose we don't have many more options." She took a stray, glossy strand of hair from behind her ear and began braiding it absent-mindedly. "Arturian will gather intelligence on his father as soon as possible, and if necessary, Francie and *Levick*," she said with an incredulous look at him, "will lure Augustus into a trap, and distract him for long enough for our dear Exley prince to put a knife in his heart."

A silent concurrence sat in the room as we all glanced at each other. The responsibility suddenly felt overwhelming. The fates of everyone I knew could be hanging in the balance.

"What of Harley?" Arturian asked, jolting me out of my thoughts.

Eadlin gave Arturian a knowing smile that left me curious. "You know Harley. He knows nothing of this, and is all the better for it." Arturian gave a curt nod in response.

The sun began peeking through a nearby window, reflecting in my eye. The entire night had passed, but the masquerade ball felt like an eternity ago.

"We should get some rest," Levick said, standing and pushing his chair in.

"Is that his polite way of telling us to vacate his beautiful, enchanting home?" Eadlin said, smiling at me.

"If it was polite, it wasn't intentional," Levick said almost playfully. I allowed myself to feel hopeful.

I let the others leave through the front doors, but stayed behind until it was just me and Levick in the room. He blew out candles and put them into cupboards, moving with lethargic care.

"Levick," I began, "about earlier..."

"Don't bother, Francie," he said, looking up at me with a resignation that made my heart sink. "We have to work together for the sake of Friese. But you lied to me. You kissed me while you were in love with *him*." He stared at me, forlorn. "My two closest friends... where does that leave me?"

"Lev, I never meant to—" I started, taking a step towards him.

He held his hand up, stopping me. "A fool. It leaves me a fool, Francie."

My heart broke as I watched him finish gathering things from the table, putting them in a nearby cabinet. "I'll see you soon, yeah?" he said, his words friendlier than his tone. I nodded and made my way out the doors.

It was mid-morning by the time my carriage pulled to a stop in front of the inn. Arturian had walked home, so I'd had it all to myself, leaving me alone with my corrosive guilt. Levick had every right to be angry with me, but I'd hoped it wouldn't be the end of our friendship. Despite everything that had happened, for the next few days, our destinies were intertwined.

After greeting a very confused but relieved Crysta, I went upstairs and slept for almost five hours. It wasn't until the afternoon that I woke up to the sound of my door opening. "I'm up, Crysta," I murmured.

The last thing I saw was a hand coming up from behind, roughly covering my mouth and nose with a foul-smelling rag, sending me back to sleep.

CHAPTER FORTY
THE SEA-CLIFFS

ARTURIAN

*That which a lifetime can build, can be felled in a
single moment.*
- Augustus Exley

It was late afternoon when I woke up, already feeling a sense of foreboding about what I would have to do. The evidence we'd spoken of was irrefutable, and I feared the imported weapons were just a small piece of a larger issue. My father did nothing halfway.

I dressed myself, staring at my reflection. I wore a dark blue buttoned shirt and black riding trousers. A deep sense of unease plagued me as I fastened the last of the buttons on my shirt.

Please, let them be wrong.

The more I thought about what the future of Friese would look like under my father, the more resolved I became. It was time for me to choose a side.

The weight of my responsibilities settled on my shoulders like the weight of the Exley mansion itself. I knew I had to be the one to end my father. Yet, somehow, the weight seemed lighter than the one I carried the day before. I wasn't alone anymore. My heart twinged as I thought of Francie... how she'd kissed me at the masquerade ball. The way she looked at me when I told her I'd dissolve my engagement. I smiled to myself, realizing my inner-conflict was folly. I'd chosen a side long ago. In the Exley port office, next to a burning fireplace. That was where the trajectory of my life changed forever.

I slid a sleek black jacket over my shirt and made my way out of my rooms. I walked down the hall until I found one of our maids pulling a cart piled with linens.

"Trina, have you seen my father today?" I asked, and the maid jumped. She was young and beautiful, with hair the shade of hot flames.

"Oh, sir. I'm sorry, I didn't see you there!" She gave me a toothy grin while straightening the linens on her small cart. "Lord Exley left this morning. Wherever he was going, it must've been important from the way he was acting."

I smiled before thanking her and making my way downstairs.

As I entered my father's study, the grim painting of Adolpho loomed over me. I paused, studying it closely for the first time. I'd been referring to Adolpho as *grandfather* for years, but it was all a lie.

That's not my grandfather... that's Francie's father.

The reality of her parentage was still jarring for me. Exley blood ran through her veins.

I tore my gaze away and poured myself a tall glass of salt rum. I reached the point of no return—I might as well drink an overly-priced glass of rum.

My father's fine imported desk sat against a large window, casting a warm glow of afternoon light on the room. The ceiling in this section of the Exley mansion was as high as the ballroom's ceilings, standing over twenty feet high. Such a room could easily make someone feel small, but I hardly noticed anymore. I walked over to the desk and slid open the top drawer. I nearly stumbled back at what I saw.

A sketch of my mother, Adriana Exley, sat in an ornate frame in the otherwise-empty drawer. She was breathtaking, with long blonde hair and expressive amber eyes. I clenched my jaw, wishing I could remember her image myself. At only three-years-old when she died, I never learned what it was like to have a mother. My mind wandered to Francie and Levick, whose mothers were also dead.

What a group we make.

I shook off the sentiment, closed the drawer, and began searching through the rest. I returned everything to its original location after searching, knowing Father would notice any and every change. It wasn't until I reached the desk's bottom drawer that I began feeling the increasing certainty of my father's guilt. I pried a large, thick file from the drawer and laid it on top of the desk, pausing for a moment.

I didn't know what I wanted to see—a lack of evidence wouldn't exonerate my father. There were too many signs already. However, a small part of me wanted the entire ordeal to be a massive misunderstanding. I nearly laughed at my own sentimentality. My father was a cold, calculating man who would do anything to further his own wealth and power.

I wish you weren't this way, Father. But I won't let you burn the kingdom down for your own ambition.

I flipped open the folder, revealing plans, maps, and detailed architectural schematics. I scanned through them, flipping from page to page.

No. There's no way. These are...

Barracks.

My pulse quickened as I continued my investigation, unable to look away. It wasn't long before I almost wished I had. A thick stack of papers sat before me at the bottom of the folder—all formatted the same way. Every page had sections for height, weight, age, and specialty... but each one of them bore different names.

These are conscription papers... and there are thousands of them.

"No crazy shit today, Hampton," I muttered, patting the antsy horse's neck. "This is important," I said, more to myself. We set off through the field as the sun made its way closer to the horizon. I was struggling to process what I'd discovered—there was no more hope for my father's innocence. There was only preparation.

As I approached a forest trail, I paused and opened the map I'd found in my father's desk drawer.

South...east. There.

I entered the trail and followed it for a few minutes until it seemed to end.

Peculiar...

A faint banging sound echoed through the woods, coming from southeast of me. I dismounted and looped the reins around a branch. "I'll be back soon," I said to Hampton, stroking his nose. The horse didn't seem thrilled to be left behind, but he wouldn't fit through the overgrowth.

As I crept through the woods, the sound grew louder.

What is that?

Finally, the branches cleared enough that I could see the vague outline of a large, rectangular structure in a patch of recently cleared land. Gleaming brightly under the sun, the building clearly hadn't seen many Friesian storms. A single soldier in an unbuttoned uniform chopped wood on a stump nearby. The red lettering on his shoulder was unmistakable. He was an Exley soldier.

I silently cursed my father for his insatiable ambition. However, the longer I stood there, a heavy unease settled upon me. There was only one soldier—the rest of the area seemed empty.

Where are the rest of them?

I stifled the urge to panic as I began making my way back to Hampton. Being discovered was the last thing we needed before our next move.

The sun was setting during the ride back, and clouds were gathering overhead—the rainy season in Friese was year-round.

As I led Hampton back into the stable, I noticed a stiff piece of Exley stationery folded and sitting up on a table, next to a glass with a few drops of salt rum sitting in the bottom. My pulse quickened as I picked it up.

Dearest Son,

I understand now why you've been dragging your feet on your task to find and eliminate the blade-thief in the slums. She's quite beautiful; I see how she could've lured you in with her... charms.

I hope you enjoyed looking at her while you could. She won't be as pleasing to the eye when you see her next. I have her at the northern sea-cliffs. Come kill her and take her blade. If you don't, I'll throw her off the cliff myself, and you will never get a windblade for as long as I live. Even when I die, I'll be sure it is by my own hand. It's time to decide. What would you sacrifice for the sake of Exley?

My greatest nightmare unfolded in front of me. A black cloud descended over my senses, leaving nothing but hate and rage. I grabbed the empty glass and flung it at the stable door, swearing.

Francie... he has Francie.

Sensing my distress, Hampton nudged me with his nose, snapping me into action.

"Levick!" I yelled at the top of my lungs as Hampton slid to a stop in front of the bell tower, followed by Smoke, whom I'd quickly saddled. "Levick, come out!"

I continued to call to Levick as Hampton circled the clearing. After an unbelievably long couple of minutes, Levick emerged looking as if he'd just woken up and gotten dressed. "What's going on?" he asked, his eyes shooting wide as he sensed my urgency.

"He has Francie. He knows who she is!" I yelled, not bothering to provide more context. Thankfully, Levick didn't need it. He slipped his boots on and ran over.

"We have to go *now*," I barked, gesturing over to Smoke.

Levick swung onto the gray horse's back and we rode north, our animosity momentarily forgotten. I felt sympathy for Levick—he knew what it was like to love Francie, and I couldn't imagine the pain of losing her to someone else. I only hoped he could forgive me for long enough to save her life.

"I don't know what kind of secret talents you have that made you so useful to the RCM, but I'm going to need them," I called over my shoulder as Hampton led the pair of horses out of the woods and into the road.

"Will he kill her?" Levick yelled ahead.

Although I'd known the truth, hearing the question aloud injected fresh panic into my veins.

"Yes."

We made our way through the port slums, taking the most direct route north to the cliffs. As soon as we cleared the forest and entered the outskirts of the slums, I could sense something was amiss. Shouting echoed in the distance, and I caught glimpses of people running back and forth across the streets.

"What the hell is going on out here?" Levick shouted.

As we rode next to the docks, wind began ripping past us, blowing the flags off of a couple of trade ships nearby. I had to duck down to avoid getting hit by an Exley flag tumbling through the air. The shouting grew louder, and a crowd came into view.

"Damn it," I yelled. They were blocking the road.

Levick brought Smoke up to ride beside us, squinting at the chaos occurring ahead. "They're... fighting."

He was right. Crowds of dock workers were brandishing makeshift weapons and holding a line against Crown Police officers. As we got closer, the screams and yelling grew more intense, despite the harsh winds carrying the noise away. We stopped five horse-lengths from the gruesome scene and watched a massive man grip a police officer by the throat and throw him to the ground. I clenched my jaw at the senseless uproar.

"Ress!" Levick yelled, looking ahead. The large man turned to look at us, and I instantly recognized him from our fight in the slums. His face was red with anger, and his giant hands were clenched in deadly fists. He gave the officer one last kick to the head and ran towards us.

"Levick," I growled. "This guy hates me."

He glanced at me in confusion, but didn't have time to respond before Ress approached us.

"What the hell are you doing with *him*, Levick?" He glared at me; his posture was hostile and prepared to strike.

"Didn't Orin tell you?" Levick asked.

Ress shook his head. "It's been an absolute shitshow. I haven't seen him in a while."

"We don't have time for this," I said. "*Francie* doesn't have time."

"Francie?" Ress's face twisted in alarm.

"There's no time to talk, we need to get through," I called over to Levick, who seemed suddenly locked in an intense focus as he stared out over the bay. "Levick!" I yelled, trying to break him out of his trance.

However, before I could get Levick's attention, a rogue gust of wind nearly overturned two ships anchored off-shore, ripping across the top of the water. The bay seemed to ripple towards us like a rising tide. The brawling crowds were momentarily distracted as people shouted in panic, noticing a newly formed tidal wave heading their way. I couldn't look away from the nightmarish wall of dark water barreling towards us.

What is that?

"Get out of here, Ress. Arturian! We have to go *now*!" Levick's voice snapped me out of it, and I noticed the crowd had retreated inland, leaving a gap along the port road. Ress gave me one last glare before turning to run west. The wave was getting dangerously close, but we didn't have time to waste.

Without another moment's hesitation, I urged Hampton forward, directly into the path of the wave. My horse's hooves beat against the cobbled road, sounding like a drumbeat before a disastrous scene in a play. Salty water sprayed against my face, clouding my vision. I refused to look, but I could feel the presence of the gargantuan wave as we raced past it. A loud crash and a startled whinny sounded from behind me, and I knew Smoke had almost gotten caught in it.

"We're okay!" Levick called ahead, and I breathed a ragged gasp of relief. "Don't stop!"

Even so, I couldn't resist the urge to witness the chaos, and glanced backwards. A torrential stream of water crashed onto the road behind us, spraying Levick's back with water.

A flash of red and black caught my eye, and my stomach dropped.

Those weren't Crownies.

That's why the barracks were empty. Father's soldiers... they're all out here.

It's happening right now.

We barreled down the road, and I tried to calm my rising panic. We weren't ready. My father had outsmarted us all. I wondered if he'd already killed the queen—if he was the *king*.

"One problem at a time," I said to myself, and tried to focus solely on Francie.

Hampton and Smoke heaved with effort as they carried us up the rocky trail to the top of the cliffs. They looked like stone obelisks jutting into the Broad Sea north of the port. However, today they held an ominous resemblance to headstones.

"Good work, boy. We're almost there," I whispered to the exhausted horse. My voice remained even, but murder had been on my mind the entire ride.

As if I needed another reason to kill him.

"There!" Levick called from behind me, pointing at a gap in the trees up ahead. We were almost at the top. "I'll get off here—I'm more useful if I'm not seen," Levick said urgently, already sliding off of Smoke and looping his reins over a branch. I hastily agreed, and Levick darted off into the woods without another glance.

Before continuing, I did my best to channel my fury without abandoning logic and reason. If I wanted Francie to survive, I couldn't simply ride in and begin throwing knives. I closed my eyes for a moment and let Hampton lead us out of the last bit of forest.

"It's just like you to bring a horse so close to a ledge," a smooth, commanding voice called from afar.

I peered through the looming darkness to see my father standing on the edge of the cliff, the twilight sky behind him. Even from a distance, his eyes blazed with determination. He had his arms wrapped around something.

No... someone.

Upon seeing her, the only sound I heard was my own rapidly beating heart. A red haze threatened to completely take over my vision. Smears of blood covered Francie's beautiful face, and her hands seemed to be tied behind her back. Father held her tight to his chest and glared over her shoulder at me. Strands of his long, unbound hair clung to her bloodied chest.

"Francie!" I called, my voice hoarse.

"They have Crysta!" she screamed.

I dismounted and ran closer, my legs pounding against the stone. As I drew closer, the extent of her injuries became clearer. Her skirt was dirty and tattered, and she wore no shirt except a thin binding covering her breasts. To my dismay, it appeared as if it had once been white, but had been soaked through with crimson blood. A gory laceration bled from the left side of her chest, over her heart. Its markings looked unnervingly detailed. My blood boiled.

"What did you do to her!?" I roared, nearly ten horse lengths away.

"Do you like my handiwork?" Father smiled at me. "I can't tell you how fucking difficult it was to keep from completely piercing her as I did it."

I stopped in my tracks, horrified.

He did it with his windblade. I can't believe she survived that.

"Father... just step away from the edge! Please!" I pleaded, holding my hands out. I was desperate for a way to diffuse the situation before it exploded in front of me, taking the woman I loved down with it.

My father's lips pulled away in a sinister smile. In the dim light, his teeth looked sharp. "You are going to throw a knife through her heart." His smile tipped up a bit more along the corners. "Right here," he purred, dragging his fingers over the carved-up flesh on her chest. Francie's screams of agony shattered and infuriated me as I watched her face twist.

"I made a nice target for you," Father said, smiling knowingly.

I peered at the wound and bit into my cheek. My suspicions were true—it was the Exley crest. I bolted forward, but stopped short when Father brought his hand up to encircle Francie's neck.

"Now, now—don't be rash. I'm going to let her go, but if she moves a muscle from this cliff, I'll have her aunt tossed over the edge." He motioned to his left, and I watched a tall captain approach, dragging an unconscious woman behind him. He wore a type of fine black metal armor I'd never seen before. His light hair had been cropped short, highlighting a ruddy, red complexion.

"Crysta—" Francie called out, but her words turned to airy coughs as my father gripped her throat tighter.

"If you try to take aim at *me,* they're both as good as dead," he said, his voice confident as he leaned in close to her neck. His heavily lidded eyes taunted me.

"Bloodlines can't have two windblades! One always dies!" I yelled.

"No one has tried in centuries. I think it's time to put that theory to the test. If you refuse, I'm sure Captain Stone would be incredibly useful to me with a windblade." He gestured to the uniformed man who held Crysta. "Especially considering the *windwalker* that's been causing trouble."

Windwalker? There hasn't been one in centuries...

I could've sworn recognition flashed over Francie's face as she looked over at the captain. He glared at her with pure hatred in his eyes.

I flexed my fingers before withdrawing a pair of knives from their sheathes under my jacket.

Father nodded, a satisfied smile tugging at his mouth. "Don't miss," he said as he released Francie's neck, letting his fingers run through her bloodied hair as he backed away. Upon losing the support, she stumbled backwards, precariously close to the edge.

"Francie!" I called out in a panic.

My father scoffed. "Tick, tock, son. I won't wait forever."

Francie shook as she stood, and her wide eyes darted between me and Crysta. "My hands are bound," she said through rapid gasps, knowing she was powerless.

"Francie, I'm so sorry," was all I managed to say. My knives felt like lead in my fingers as I tried to calculate a way to resolve the situation that didn't end with one or both of us dead. My eyes kept being drawn to the gory Exley crest carved into Francie's chest.

Father groaned. "That's enough of that," he flicked his hand forward, and the woman held by the captain silently began leaking blood.

Francie shrieked in horror. "Crysta!"

The soldier dropped the body on the ground and charged at Francie.

"Stone!" Father roared after him, but he was ignored. In one split second, I flung one of my knives at the captain, striking him in the shoulder and slowing him down. Out of the corner of my eye, I saw my father swing his arm at me.

"Arturian!" I heard Francie yell, but didn't realize why until a second later. My face erupted with white-hot pain, and I felt blood running down my neck.

Not good.

I thanked Echna I could still see with both eyes and threw my second knife. It impaled my father in the thigh, and he dropped to one knee, groaning in disbelief.

There was no time to waste. Captain Stone was still advancing on Francie, and her hands were still bound, rendering her defenseless. She shuffled backward on unsteady, trembling legs. I fumbled for my spare knives, but I wasn't fast enough.

"Your blade is mine!" Stone roared as he made to close the gap. He stretched his arms towards her as he barreled on—an unstoppable force of kinetic energy dead-set on taking something he had no right to.

"I would rather kill myself," she shouted. Despite her wound, blood loss, and fear, her posture was straight. The determined look in her sky-blue eyes was the most terrifying thing I'd ever seen.

"Francie, no! Please!" I cried out, still running towards her. The fabric of my reality began tearing into pieces, leaving me exposed and helpless.

This isn't happening. It's a nightmare. It has to be.

I was too late.

Stone made his last lunge at Francie, and she met my eyes for an infinite moment. A thousand shared memories echoed through my mind. The way her hair flowed in the wind as she fearlessly walked across the branch of that old oak tree at the edge of the Exley property. How her breath caught in her throat as I held onto her in the bay on my birthday. The chorus of thunder and raindrops against the roof of the port office as we danced along the edges of intimacy.

Please don't take her from me. I'll have nothing left.

"*I love you,*" Francie mouthed before falling backwards off the cliff.

CHAPTER FORTY-ONE
A RACE AGAINST FATE

When the time comes, Echna will bestow a windwalker upon Friese as an act of mercy—as a champion for her survival. Only a Caelator created by Echna herself will be able to stop the bloodshed.

- The Chronicle of the Caelators

Branches and vines beat against my face as I sprinted through the forest. Screams echoed through the trees, bringing a fresh urgency to my steps.

I know that voice.

Francie... please hold on. Please.

I broke from the trees, and horror filled my body. Despite the distance between us, I could see Francie's bloodied body being held against Augustus's chest, shielding himself. Arturian stood at a distance, shouting and holding his hands out.

Don't be a fool, Arturian. You can't negotiate with him. You can't win a game that he's designed himself.

A branch snapped behind me in the forest, and I spun around just in time to dodge a steel sword slicing at my mid-section. An Exley soldier attacked me with precise, trained swings. I brought my hands up to my chest like I practiced, flattened my hands as if I were preparing to push against a wall, and thrust outward with all of my strength. An *explosion* of wind erupted from my hands, and the guard flew backwards three horse-lengths until slamming against a tree. He fell to the ground, motionless.

I stood for a moment, shocked by what I'd done. However, an anguished scream from the cliff-side tore my attention away.

Did she just say... 'Crysta?'

I turned around to see Francie hunched over, standing even closer to the edge than she had been.

Her hands are bound... she's completely helpless.

Overwhelming desperation possessed me as I realized what was about to happen.

I have to get to the bottom of that cliff. Now.

I took off through the woods, using every ounce of energy I had to push myself forward. All of my frustrations and heartbreak dissolved as I contemplated what would happen to Francie if I wasn't fast enough.

I turned through the trees, the winds keeping me upright as I leapt from jagged rock to mossy ground, descending the sloped side of the cliff. The terrain became treacherous as I descended further, but there was no time to turn and take a more level route.

"Stop!" a commanding voice called out from nearby, almost breaking my concentration as I dodged a tree. An athletic Exley guard chased after me from above, and I cursed as I realized my disadvantage.

Please don't be a knife-thrower. Please don't be a knife-thrower.

I repeated the prayer in my mind as I continued down the slope, angling towards the port-side of the cliffs, just under where Francie was standing. I couldn't hear them anymore.

Sharp, hot pain burst from my back.

Damn it... he's hit me.

I could feel the short blade wedged between my back muscles and the warm blood seeping out of it. Every movement of my arm felt like I was dragging my muscles over a razorblade. I gritted my teeth and turned my head, looking up at the Exley guard, who was smiling in satisfaction.

"I said *stop*," he called down, brandishing a new knife.

I threw my arm up at the guard, causing a rippling pain through my shoulder and back. A weak, but still focused gust of wind knocked the guard off-balance, and he stumbled sideways off the rock he was standing on. Thankfully, it was steep enough that he couldn't recover his footing and continued tumbling down the rocky slope.

Continuing my run, I turned the corner to where the cliff met the water. It stood over twenty stories tall, and it was without slope.

Almost there...

My heart dropped as I saw a tangle of blonde and red leaning back over the ledge. "No!" I cried out through exhausted heaving.

I'm not close enough.

Then, in a moment that seemed immortal, Francie fell from the edge of the cliff, her body completely in the air.

"Francie!" I yelled, but it turned into a groan as a knife dug into my leg.

The guard... he survived.

My traitorous leg failed me and I crashed to the ground, landing roughly on a rock. My gaze shot up to see the woman I loved falling through the air, with barely a hope of saving her.

CHAPTER FORTY-TWO
LONG LIVE THE KING

ARTURIAN

"Francie!" I called out, my voice raw and broken. I'd finally gotten my spare knives out and used one of them to impale Stone through the jugular. He bled out next to the edge of the cliff, and I spared him no further thought.

She's not gone. She can't be gone.

As I stumbled to look over the edge, a severed strand of hair fell next to my bloodied face. I turned around to see my father sitting with one hand placed on his injured leg, and the other extended at me. His aim was sloppy from the blood loss—I had never seen him miss.

I approached Stone's dead body and pried the knives from the layers of skin and muscle. As I rose from my grisly task, I turned to my father. He shook as he knelt upon the gray stone, leaking pools of blood over it. My lip curled up in disgust when I saw the look on his face. *Satisfaction.*

Face burning and dripping blood, I stalked over to my father. Taking his hands, I laid them over his lap, and pierced my throwing knives through them and into his thighs. He groaned in pain but didn't shed a single tear. His jaw was set as he glared at me, knowing his own teachings had been used against him.

"It's over, Father," I said, my voice cold and dead. Between the pain from the gash on my face and the pain of losing Francie, I was nearing the edge of oblivion. I forced myself to focus on the moment I was in. The only thing I could achieve was justice.

Father involuntarily shook from blood loss as he leaned against a boulder.

"I used to think about this day with absolute dread," I said, crouching in front of him. "Don't misunderstand—I always wanted the blade. But the idea of killing my own father was unthinkable to me," I said, wishing I could be that innocent, caring boy again. I leaned in closer, slid a hand over the knife buried in my father's left hand, and twisted slowly until he let out a guttural moan.

"However, today... that idea doesn't seem so terrifying after all." I yanked the knife from his hand, which began leaking thick trails of blood.

"Now... you know sacrifice," Father hissed through shaking breaths. The moon emerged from a dense cloud, casting its pale light upon the dying man. In that bitter, revolting moment, I understood the inordinate price of power. Of the *windblade.*

Without hesitating, I drew back and plunged my blade into my father's heart.

A sick smile slowly spread over the edges of his paling lips. Through raspy gasps, he whispered something just before the last bit of life left his broken body.

"Long live... the *king.*"

The next morning, I burst out the doors of the Exley mansion. My guards had just finished briefing me about what had transpired last night, and what was still unfolding in the streets. Early the previous day, my father had his new, elite coterie of guards, the *Red Legion*, capture Queen Lesynna and her husband in stealth. He'd executed them in their own palace, and sat himself upon the throne of Friese for mere hours before he kidnapped Francie. The other Skylords were nowhere near skilled enough to face him themselves, and would never agree to an alliance to face him together. Most of them pledged their fealty shortly after learning of the takeover, and many were unsurprised at the development. My father's power-hungry nature was well known.

After learning the king and queen were dead and the only heirs were missing, the Crown police force declared allegiance to my father as the new king. After I made it down from the cliffs, his new army *and* the Crownies were waiting for him. They swore their loyalty to me immediately upon learning about his death.

"Your Majesty, it isn't safe here. Please let us escort you to the palace," newly promoted Captain Coran Trust said from atop his intimidating chestnut stallion.

Your Majesty.

A pit formed in my stomach at the words.

What use is this title to me? Francie is dead and Levick abandoned us.

I compartmentalized my grief and anger. Friese was in a state of complete unrest—there were entire sections of the slums that were blocked off by RCM rebels, and the police couldn't get in. My force was scouring the city for signs of the prince and princess, but they must have gone into hiding as soon as they'd learned of the coup. I supposed they were lucky my father hadn't gotten to them before he died—he would've ended the Ainsworths for good.

I walked past the black and silver royal carriage they'd brought for me, and took Hampton's reins from a groom.

"Your Majesty, riding in the open is a security risk," Coran said, his voice tense.

"I'll take that risk, Captain," I replied as I mounted my horse. A group of king's guards flanked me on their horses, forming up in well-trained efficiency.

I gazed upon my ancestral home. Vines twisted up the walls, looking bare as the seasons had changed and the weather had grown cooler. My horses grazed and nipped at each other in the distance, but I only saw the ghosts of my friends. Racing across the pastures together, drinking in the stable... making a point to climb every old oak tree in the field.

Visions of children—*my* children—haunted me like phantoms. I could almost see their big blue eyes shining with excitement as they watched the horses chase each other. I could nearly hear their laughter... a tinkling, musical sound. It would have been a good place to raise a family. Before the anguish could emerge from the box I'd forced it into, I urged Hampton north, towards my new destiny.

Four days later, I stood in front of the elaborate marble throne of Friese, cloaked in black velvet. My face remained a gruesome thing to behold—a thick gash ran from below my left eye and down to my jaw. I refused to cover it.

The Ainsworth's things had all been burned, and their wealth reallocated. Hundreds of people had gathered in the grand hall to witness my coronation.

"Do you swear upon your life to protect Friese from war, famine, death, or any threat to her well-being?" the aged priest of Echna asked, projecting his feeble voice as he read from an ancient parchment scroll.

"I swear it," I said, my voice devoid of emotion.

I knelt before a small table, and Eliandre Yorke approached. A flowing gown of gleaming silver trailed behind her, settling over the steps when she stopped. With movements that showed years of formal etiquette training, she lifted the elaborate platinum crown from its pillow, and placed it atop my head.

The priest advanced, his arms shaking as he announced his declaration across the throne room. "I present to you, Arturian Exley, Sovereign Skylord and King of Friese."

"Long Live the King," Eliandre said in her smooth voice.

I stood and faced forward. The gathered crowd chanted her words, filling the grand, silver hall with noise.

Long live the king.

Long live the king.

Long live the king.

My father was dead. The woman I loved was dead. My closest friend had abandoned me.

I was so incredibly alone.

EPILOGUE

I'm *going to die.*

Air ripped past my face, my hair flying up above me as I fell a hundred feet towards water as hard as concrete. I thought of Arturian and prayed that he'd survive the night. As my time ran out, I closed my eyes and hoped to see Crysta and my mother soon.

Pain radiated through my body as I regained consciousness.

I'm not dead.

"Nice catch, Roale. I might have to be nice to you, now," a familiar voice grumbled from nearby. I recognized it, but it felt like it came from a dream.

Ress...

"Can't believe you kept that party trick a secret for as long as you did."

My body bounced back and forth, adding to the aches. I was being carried—at a break-neck pace. Their sense of urgency was palpable.

"Do you think she'll live? She looks pretty pale... he really carved her up," Ress asked through heavy breaths.

"She'll live."

I felt his chest rumble as he spoke. Levick was the one carrying me.

A chilly, unsettled wind brushed over my exposed skin, making me tremble. I instinctively curled in closer to Levick's chest, and I felt his arms tighten around me.

His lips brushed against my hair. "You'll live," he whispered, his tone soft, but commanding.

The world faded around me, and the only thing I was certain of was the warmth pressed against me. I tried to stay awake, but slipped back into the darkness.

I woke again on what felt like a pile of blankets, to sounds of arguments close by. I seemed to be outside, but it was dark. Ship bells rung an ominous tune, accompanying an unnerving, faint chorus of shouting and crying.

When is it? Where am I?

A throbbing, burning pain radiated from the left side of my chest, all the way down my arm. Every breath felt like I was splitting open at a hundred different points.

"They're dead, Eadlin. If you don't get out of here, you will be, too," Levick's voice said from nearby, his tone harsh and firm. It was an unfamiliar sound, coming from him.

A realization hit me like a deluge of ice-cold rain.

The floor is... rocking. *We're on a ship.*

"Harley's not here! I can't leave if there's a chance he's still out there—" Eadlin hissed, but Levick cut her off.

"Exley men are crawling the streets, looking for you. He got the drop on us," Levick said darkly. "The queen is dead. Augustus is the king of Friese, now."

Dear Echna... if that's true, Friese is lost.

The princess's poorly stifled sob interrupted my fatalistic thoughts.

"Tell me again why you aren't coming with us?"

I felt the panic all the way to my bones.

Leaving Friese? Without Levick?

"I'm the only one they don't know about, and someone has to hold the line," Levick said, urgency heavy in his voice. "Orin left me in charge. I can't leave Friese now."

Orin must be missing... or dead. And if Augustus is king... Did Arturian live?

"I'm sending Ress with you. He'll protect you two while Francie recovers."

I groaned as the reality hit me. I was being sent away.

"She's awake," Eadlin said, her voice growing closer.

My eyes opened to see Levick and the princess crouched over me in concern. Eadlin looked uncharacteristically disheveled—her hair was tangled and secured in a loose tie. She wore a long-sleeved dress of mauve silk, but it had multiple tears along the hem. Levick had a tan neck scarf pulled up over his nose and mouth, and his leg was wrapped in a bloody cloth. Above them, royal blue sails fluttered in a foggy night sky.

"I won't leave," I whispered.

"They're swarming the streets, Francie. You're in no state to defend yourself." Levick's green eyes gazed down at me with nothing but concern. I felt unworthy of it.

Ress thundered up to us. His thin gray shirt strained against the thick, corded muscles of his arms as he leaned towards us, holding a rigging line. "The Crownies are working their way down here. We need to pull up the anchors—it's time to go."

Levick nodded in acknowledgement and yanked his scarf down. His expression was serious, as if the weight of countless new responsibilities had matured him in a matter of minutes.

"Is Arturian dead?" I choked out. Simply asking the question almost sent me into an inescapable despair. The image of his bloody face appeared in my mind, as vivid as the moment I saw it.

"I don't know. Things are chaotic out there." He leaned in close and brushed a strand of hair off my forehead. "I have to say goodbye, Francie." His mousy hair hung above his eyes, messy and windswept.

"No..." I tried to sit up, but fresh pain exploded through my chest.

"Stop, please." He cupped my neck and lowered me back down.

I settled against my makeshift bed of blankets and stared up at Levick. His eyes were a deep forest of green—full of life, strength, and promises of new beginnings. My chest tightened at the thought of leaving Friese, and my breathing became shallow and rapid.

"This is my home, Levick. I can't leave now." My voice was a breathy rasp as I reached for his arms, wrapping my fingers around them in a desperate cling to familiarity. I noticed Eadlin backing away a bit, giving us some privacy.

He leaned in close, sliding his hands over the sides of my face and into my hair. "You need to heal, Francie. If you stay here, he'll find you."

"Don't do this. Please, Lev," I whispered as I ran a shaking hand over the back of his neck.

He slid a thumb over my cheekbone, his eyes softening. "Francie, I—" he began, his breath catching a bit, "I love you."

The breath rushed from my bloodied chest. I'd known it already, but for some reason, I never expected to hear it directly from him.

He bit at the inside of his cheek, blinking away the wetness in his eyes. "I know you love him. So please... let this be my last gesture. Getting you the hell out of this war zone."

He said the last words with such conviction that I couldn't form an argument against it. I couldn't speak... I couldn't *breathe.* Tears began welling in my eyes as I gazed at the boy who had been my dearest friend for seven years. Despite everything we'd said, done, and lied about to each other, I trusted him more than I ever had.

Levick leaned down and pressed his forehead to my own, holding it there for a long moment. I squeezed my eyes shut, desperate to cling to that moment—to reach up and seize that bright, full moon, and hold it in its place for a little longer.

"Those two will take care of you," he whispered, speaking of Ress and Eadlin.

He pulled away a bit and placed a tender kiss against my forehead. "*Live,* Francie."

I couldn't contain the broken sob that escaped my chest when he pulled away.

"I'll come back," I said, already feeling him slipping away.

Levick brushed his fingers over my cheek as darkness began creeping along the edges of my vision. His final words imprinted themselves onto my heart in an enduring vow:

"I know you will."

Acknowledgements

First and foremost, I'd like to thank my husband for enduring the late nights, the compulsive writing, and my endless talking about this book. When I first started working on it, my son was one year old and I was pregnant with my daughter. Despite having to shelf it for a couple of years, you always encouraged me to pick it back up, and I'm so glad I did. I never would've had the confidence to finish this book if not for you. You're the best beta reader, editor, and husband a girl could ask for.

I'd like to thank my other beta readers, Indiana, Kira, and Tabitha, for giving me *excellent* constructive criticism and feedback. This book wouldn't be what it is if not for you.

A big thank-you to my kids, who are only three and five right now, but provide me with endless inspiration and laughter when my mind is feeling stagnant.

No one can write a decent book in a vacuum. Sharing my writing with others has been my biggest source of inspiration and motivation. Thank you all for believing in me!

ABOUT THE AUTHOR

Kelly Farina is a fantasy author who enjoys writing stories full of love, magic, and a bit of angst. She is also a wife of an amazing husband, and a mother of two young children who keep her entertained when she isn't reading or writing. When she isn't drafting, editing or brainstorming, she enjoys running and spending time outside with her family.

Connect with Kelly on social media for the latest updates:

Instagram: @kelly.farina.author

www.kellyfarina.com

www.ingramcontent.com/pod-product-compliance
Lightning Source LLC
Chambersburg PA
CBHW051128130726
47988CB00005B/1746